STARS IN THEIR EYES

Lauren Blakely

ALSO BY LAUREN BLAKELY

The Caught Up in Love Series

(Each book in this series follows a different couple so each book can be read separately, or enjoyed as a series since characters crossover)

Caught Up in Her (A short prequel novella to
   Caught Up in Us)
Caught Up In Us
Pretending He's Mine
Trophy Husband
Playing With Her Heart
Far Too Tempting (A spin-off, this book also ties into
   Stars in Their Eyes, since the hero is the brother of
   the *Stars in Their Eyes* hero)

Wrapped Up in Love

(A Caught Up in Love new adult spin-off series)

A Starstruck Kiss (A 150-page novella launching the
   series and the start of William and Jess's love story)
Stars in Their Eyes (A full-length 250-page novel, and
   the sequel to William and Jess' love story)
21 Kisses (A full-length new adult novel about Anaka's
   cousin, Kennedy, releases February 2015)
Stealing Her Love (A full-length novel starring
   Anaka and her love interest Jason, releases in
   summer 2015)
Untitled Novella (December 2015, a new adult novella
   starring *21 Kisses* characters)

The No Regrets Series

(These books should be read in order)

The Thrill of It
The Start of Us
Every Second With You

The Seductive Nights Series

(The first four books follow Julia and Clay and should be read in order)

First Night
Night After Night
After This Night
One More Night
Nights With Him (November 2014 – a standalone
    novel about Michelle Milo and her lover
    Jack Sullivan)
Sweet, Sinful Nights (Brent's book, March 2015)

The Fighting Fire Series

Burn For Me (Smith and Jamie)
Melt for Him (Megan and Becker)

ABOUT

A Starstruck Kiss

A sexy and swoony new adult romance...

There are no two ways about it — William Harrigan is a certified babe. He's sexy, smart, and British, and he wants nothing more than to charm the pants off of fellow college senior Jess Leighton. Well, he does want other things; he just can't tell her about the job he's working on since it kind of, sort of, maybe, possibly involves her. Jess, who moonlights as a celebrity photographer, is laser-focused on earning enough money snapping pics to pay her way through grad school, but when the criminally handsome William starts moving in on her turf, she's got to fend off the competition from him as well as resist her desire to smother him in kisses because William makes her heart race and her skin sizzle.

Too bad this man is not to be trusted.

Right? Except if Jess wants to snag the million-dollar picture she desperately needs, she'll have no choice but to trust Will, and he'll have to come clean about everything he wants from Jess. Including her.

DEDICATION

This book is dedicated to
Violet Duke, who gave me the keys to
unlock the true heart of the story.

WARNING: The hero in this book is not an asshole. He is hot, charming, smart, funny, ripped, gorgeous, respectful and completely panty-melting. Please proceed.

Note: All the celebrities, movies and TV shows in this story are made up, though many are modeled after real celebrities, movies and TV shows. The entertainment references are designed to be a send-up of Hollywood culture. I hope you enjoy the clues. Also, this is a mystery. You will meet many characters, so come along for the ride…

A STARSTRUCK KISS

New York Times and USA Today Bestselling Author
Lauren Blakely

A 150-page novella in the
Wrapped Up in Love series

Book 1

By Lauren Blakely

MONDAY
Weather: 70 degrees, Sunny

CHAPTER ONE

<u>Jess</u>

He would be here any minute.

I was ready for him.

I wore my dark blue skinny jeans, a gray V-neck T-shirt, navy blue lace-up sneakers, and a pair of cheap black plastic sunglasses I'd picked up from the dollar store on Wilshire. My mission was to blend in, so I was mascaraed and lip glossed, but no more than that since I didn't want to draw attention to myself. In short, I was everything a good twenty-one-year-old paparazzo should be, and I was scoping out a playground shot to show that stars are just like us.

This was an easy assignment and the pay would reflect it as well as the company. Plenty of us got the ev-ery-Monday-alert, and the park was teeming with shoot-ers. Nearby was the soul-patched and jaded former wire photographer who moved on to playground and shop-ping shots when news services stopped paying well, and the big, bearded, leather-jacketed guy who worked for the foreign tabloids.

Parked on a bench with my chem homework open, I whipped through formulas, glancing up every few seconds to see if Range Treadman had arrived. He was due any minute. He was clockwork. He was the cog that kept the trains running on time, and every Monday afternoon at three-fifteen he arrived at this playground with his two kids. The pride of Australia, Range was a top-notch, triple-threat, singing, dancing and acting star of stage and screen who'd headlined a big superhero flick a few years back, and aspired to live a life scandal-free and be known only as a family man. Which is why I wasn't the only paparazzo here. I'd high-tailed it straight out of advanced chemistry class the second the bell rang, having scheduled my senior year pre-med classes precisely so I could make my regular star stakeouts.

My bank account was a hungry thing. It needed to be fed regularly, and photos were its primary food source.

Twenty seconds later, Range arrived in his red, fully electric car with tinted windows. The guy who snapped shots for the Australian papers moved quickly, snagging the first picture of the superstar unbuckling his precocious three-year-old son from the car seat. Next came Range's seven-year-old, and she wore a cherry red beret with a pair of dove gray capris. I grabbed a quick picture of the girl, but I didn't need that shot for my boss. I needed it for my best friend and roomie, who could use it for her Burn Book.

Range reached for his daughter's hand, then laughed with his mouth wide open and perfect straight white teeth showing. Give credit where credit's due—that man knew how to work the cameras he pretended he didn't see. I clicked more as Range and his little girl ran the final few feet to the jungle gym in a kind of deliberate slow motion that ensured his well-muscled arms could be seen in any shots of the doting dad and young daughter. No wonder half the female population in the United States over twenty-five had a crush on the hunky actor.

Range's little boy had already gone up and down the slide, and now helped himself to a swing. As if it had been scripted, the megastar put his big hands on the chains of the swing and began to push his young son. Range leaned his head back, straightened up his spine to make sure the full breadth of his gym-sculpted pecs from beneath his sky-blue T-shirt could be made out from even the most distant lenses, and flashed another bright and posed smile.

Another click. Another shot. Another afternoon at the playground.

I placed my top-of-the line Canon inside my backpack, hopped on my black scooter, and snapped on my helmet. I headed to my boss' office to show him the afternoon take. The whole lot of them would net me maybe a hundred bucks. But that was a hundred bucks I didn't have before, and medical school wasn't even close to free.

CHAPTER TWO

Jess

Twenty minutes later, I pulled over to the curb in front of a one-story office building, rolling past a scratched-up silver motorcycle that looked like it had seen its share of years. I bumped my scooter up on the sidewalk, jamming it into bike parking, then slid a thick and heavy lock through the tire and the pole and headed to J.P.'s office at the far end of the building. A trip to his office translated into cash, and cash fed those ravenous bills on my kitchen table.

I stopped near his door when I heard a voice I didn't recognize.

But one I instantly responded to. Delicious and British. The twin combination sent a zing down my spine.

"Right. I should be able to get you something, no problem."

Damn accents. They nearly obliterated all my finely-tuned control. And I was the kind of gal who liked being in control. All. The. Time.

"Get me something good and I'll have more for you," J.P. said to him.

"A challenge. I'll take it," sexy-accent-guy said with a confident tone to my boss.

Please let him be ugly. Let him be a hideous troll.

I walked in as he stood up.

Damn. He wasn't ugly from behind. He had a fantastic ass, and the perfect kind of jeans to show it off. Nice back too, firm shoulders, and hair that clearly needed to be touched.

I took a deep breath to steel myself. I prayed that he had bad teeth. Crooked, yellow, snaggly teeth that would make me run for cover.

But when he turned around I was greeted by one of my favorite, and most frustrating, sights on the planet—a hot guy about my age. He wore jeans that hung nice and low on the hips, scuffed-up black boots, and a blue T-shirt that showed off toned arms. A pair of gold-rimmed aviator sunglasses hung on the neck of his shirt. He had dark hair, a whole mess of it, and eyes like a very angry sky.

Eyes that caught me surveying him from top to bottom.

If I were a blusher, I'd be beet red. Fortunately, the blushing gene skipped me, so no one ever knew when I was embarrassed.

He tipped his forehead to me. "Hey." Then he gave me a quick once-over, and a small grin.

Thank God I wore my best jeans and had a touch of that casual, wind-blown look from my scooter ride over here. Plus, I was thin and trim–something I'd always worked hard at being. Whether through exercise or other means.

Wait.

Why did it matter if I looked good? I definitely didn't care if he was checking me out. I didn't have the time to admire the opposite-sex scenery these days. I had loads of work and school and bills begging for attention, so I issued myself a few firm and sharp instructions: *His accent will not melt you. His eyes will not hook you.*

"I'm William," he offered, and I forced myself to barely acknowledge him, instead silently cursing the universe for dropping a too-fine specimen into my day.

"Hey," I muttered, brushing past him into the office.

"Thanks for the biscuit, J.P.," he said, and I stole a quick look as William held up a half-eaten chocolate-covered biscuit that would ordinarily be served with tea. He took one more bite, and rolled his eyes to indicate it was scrumptious. My mouth watered slightly; it was probably a delicious biscuit indeed. It was also an indignity, as far as I was concerned, that guys could eat treats with such careless abandon. I wanted to eat with that kind of attitude. I longed not to be tempted by food.

He finished, then flashed me an irresistible grin that was one part cocky, one part lopsided and one part devil-may-care insouciance. "You should try the biscuits. They're fantastic," he said to me as he picked up his backpack, and slung it over his shoulder.

"Thanks for the tip," I said dryly, because wouldn't it be nice if I *could* just try the biscuits and eat only one? Alas, that was not my strong suit, so I practiced abstinence with sweets. And other things.

He left, and I turned around to shut the door, hoping that it would shut him out of my head too.

But as I was closing it, he stuck his boot in the door.

"I can recommend cookies too, if you'd like. Chocolate cake. Brownies. Tarts. Pies," he offered, rattling off all sorts of sugary concoctions, each word playing on his lips like a tantalizing treat, as if he were trying to win me over. Or, perhaps, gain the upper hand. But upper hands were my stock in trade, so I turned things around on him.

"When I'm in the mood for a huckleberry pie, I'll track you down," I said, giving him my best red-carpet smile. "Now, if you'll excuse me."

As he walked down the hall, I spotted a strong and sturdy motorcycle helmet strapped to his backpack. He must be the owner of the scratched-up silver motorcycle.

Hot. British. Rides a motorcycle.

If he turned out to be a smart one, he'd be all my weaknesses.

An errant butterfly bounded through my chest. Damn fluttery thing.

But I had no time for weaknesses, or butterflies, in my life. I pulled hard on the door, snapping it shut and leaving him behind.

<u>William</u>

As I elbowed open the door, I tapped the search bar on my mobile phone. Dropping my sunglasses over my eyes, I keyed in the name "Riley Belle," then waited as the beach ball made its rounds. Someday, somewhere–I was convinced of this eventual possibility–we'd live in a world where cell phone searching wouldn't be the equivalent of staring at a watched pot that never boiled. But for now, I heaved a sigh as I mounted my bike and kept my vigil on the screen. The sun blasted high above, a perfect yellow orb that delivered rays of happiness as far as I was concerned. I didn't miss the English weather one bit. Not even a single iota, and hadn't since I flew across the pond for my junior year abroad that turned into staying my senior year too. Some people say they want four seasons; I was not one of those people. I say give me perfect day after perfect day, so I suppose that's why Los Angeles suited me quite well.

Quite well indeed, and so much better than the homeland.

As the phone chugged along, a text message dinged from the name *Hack*.

I thumbed it open and read. *So what's the story with the new gig? Think you can keep this one for longer than a weekend? - Your big brother. (Don't forget–I'll always be older and wiser and better looking)*

I typed a quick reply. *Don't worry. I won't embarrass the family in front of good old Uncle James. (And you will always be older, which means you'll be grayer and fatter).*

After I fired off the note to my brother Matthew in New York–he'd caught American fever too–the Riley

Belle search results appeared, so I clicked back to the browser and scrolled through them on a mad dash for the best image. I had to kick unholy ass on this job for a million reasons, not the least of which was to end Matthew's ribbing. I needed a quick visual of the subject. I tapped a close-up of Riley Belle, then studied her features until I had damn near memorized her face. Right; she was the brunette with the sunshine smile and chocolate eyes. Or so this story said on some entertainment site. Probably a suck-up one. After all, who uses words like *sunshine* and *chocolate* to describe a hot girl?

As I tucked the phone into my back pocket and revved the engine, I ran through better words for hot girls. *Blond, sarcastic, a fan of huckleberry pie.*

I pulled into the westbound traffic, weaving among cars, with my focus on the beach.

Oh, there was one more word. *Competition.*

She was the competition.

Jess

The memory of William's pinchable butt and lickable lips was front and center as I sank down on the worn and cracked vinyl couch kitty corner from J.P.'s desk.

"Jess," he said in his gruff voice. "You might want to pick up your jaw from the floor."

"If my jaw is anywhere near the carpet it's from your handiwork as a baker," I said quickly, pointing to the tray of the chocolate-covered biscuits on his desk. Sure, they looked delicious, but I'd been caught red-handed and I wanted an alibi as I denied that William had me all agog.

He rolled his eyes. "Right. You were salivating over my kitchen skills. Not that hot man in the well-worn jeans."

"You are correct, sir," I said with a straight face because there was some truth to his comment. I stood up, picked up the tray, and carried it to a table in the corner, placing the biscuits far away. There. Now I wouldn't be tempted to gobble them and then throw them up, like I'd done every now and then for many years with other delectable treats. But no longer. I'd been on the wagon for two full years now, one hundred percent in control, and I had to stay that way.

No. Matter. What.

I returned to J.P. "Just thought they'd look better over there," I said with a shrug.

"Right. Sure. You were just rearranging. I also didn't notice you giving sexy, scrumptious Will the old once-over."

Perfect adjectives.

"If my eyes were on him, it was only to size up the potential competition. So which is he? My competition or your next boyfriend?"

"He's either a shooter or a suitor," J.P. said, kicking his feet up on his desk and crossing his ankles. "Which way do you think he swings?"

"You never can tell in this town. Everyone's acting."

"He acts straight then," J.P. said, shaking his head as if he were sad that William liked girls. I was happy. But I couldn't be happy. I reminded myself I didn't care about his preferences.

"Shame for you. He's criminally handsome," I said, admitting begrudgingly what J.P. and I both already knew. William was a certified babe.

J.P. gave me a knowing look. "Shame for you if he can shoot as well as he looks."

"Doubtful. The pretty ones belong in front of the camera. But who has time for boys anyway?"

"You should make more time for boys, Jess. Maybe you wouldn't be so tightly wound."

I scoffed, because boys were on the back burner. "If I wasn't this tightly wound, you wouldn't have any good pictures from me. I'd be a blathering mess of hormones and lust rather than your top shooter. I don't give in to boys because boys scramble brains and I do not function well with a scrambled brain," I said. In fact, I worked hard to avoid the temptation to fling myself bodily at beautiful guys.

Fine. I was guy-crazy. I knew that about myself. I fucking loved them. I loved their chests, and their arms, and their hair, and their eyes, and their guy smell, and their jeans and their abs...and well, you get the point. I loved everything that made a guy a guy, and I was often caught staring at the pretty ones. That's why I stayed away as best as I could. Beautiful guys were trouble, and so I regularly warred with all such impulses to align myself with one horizontally.

Especially considering what happened to my brain the last time I was involved with a guy. His name was Thadd, with two Ds, he was a business major, a movie fan, and one of the best times I'd ever had. In fact, hanging out with him was so much fun that my grades nearly suffered, and when I got my mid-term progress report sophomore year, it might as well have come with a warning—*falling for a guy is known to cause plummeting grades.* Fortunately, Thadd found himself distracted by an art major the same day that I planned to cool it with him, so that alleviated any and all guilt on my part for ending things with him for a little reason like nearly failing, when he was nearly putting his dick in another girl.

I unzipped my backpack, and handed J.P. the contents of the digital card from my camera.

"All yours. But the shot of Velvet Treadman isn't for you," I instructed, referring to Range's seven-year-old daughter in her beret and capris. "So don't take it."

J.P. snapped his fingers. "Damn. I was thinking she'd be about ready for a fake I.D."

"You're not getting any of those shots from me. Maybe Criminally Handsome will get you some of those," I said, since I didn't specifically want to ask what William was angling for, whether for a glimpse of stars behaving just like us or for a mug shot for J.P.'s other business making the best un-bustable fake I.D.s in Hollywood for studio execs' kids, celebrity offspring, or anyone rich enough or thirsty enough to come calling on the former caterer, now photographic impresario. J.P. ran both a legit business as a photo agency, and a not-so-legit one aging up the under-twenty-one crowd. Even though I wasn't J.P.'s only celebrity shooter, I needed to know if William was horning in on my turf or supplying ID shots.

"Or maybe he'll get a shot of Riley and someone else in the cast of *The Weekenders* hooking up," J.P. mused, giving me my answer—William was a paparazzo too.

Then my pulse quickened as J.P.'s tip registered. I nearly forgot about William because very little excited me more than a star stakeout. I raised an eyebrow, curious who the starlet Riley Belle might be seen with from the cast of *The Weekenders*. After years of rewrites, Solomon Pictures had just finished casting the remake of the story of five high schoolers forced to spend a Saturday together in detention. In the new version, a sixth student was added to the story because the studio wanted everyone to couple off at the end. Riley Belle played the cheerleader.

"Is it Riley and Miles? Riley and Nick? Or Riley and Brody?" I asked, peppering J.P. with questions. "I bet it's Riley and Miles."

He pointed at me. "Option #1 it is."

"I knew it," I said, pumping a fist. I'd been tracking Riley Belle's career for years, as a fan, and as a photographer. Riley was a darling of all directors after she earned an Oscar nod for her turn as a runaway in an indie breakout hit a year ago. "Miles has been vocal about having a crush on her since they met at the party for his wolf-turns-into-an-angel movie last year."

"That tanked."

"Obviously," I said, in the off-hand, casual cool of the Hollywood insider that we all thought we were. "Everyone knows angels are so last year."

"But the cheerleader and jock from *The Weekenders* are so this year. Perhaps even this day."

"Where? Now? I want in," I said, my fingers clutching the desk like I was ready to pounce.

Hookup shots were close to gold. In the pantheon of payouts for photos it went like this: playground shots were at the bottom, parking ticket and pedicure shots were located a notch above, then night-on-the-town pics landed a bit higher up. They were followed by hookup shots, which rocketed the shooter to another pay range altogether that could only be topped by the image of a celebrity unraveling by food. The people loved a public pigout more than just about anything. I'd managed to earn enough to cover a handful of college classes with a tidy triumvirate of meltdown-by-food shots about a year ago, including a rather embarrassing one of a former child star downing a key lime pie in his car when he thought no one was looking.

But even though the photographic evidence of the most-shunned Hollywood possession of all—an expanding waistline—had graced my portfolio, I hadn't grabbed the brass ring yet. Because there was one kind of picture that trumped them all. The most priceless and rare.

The wedding shot.

I'd never come close to a wedding shot and probably never would. But a hookup shot of someone from *The Weekenders* could net a whole handful of bills, so I wanted that pic to be mine.

"Venice Beach. Riley and Miles have been seen taking sunset strolls as they walk her dog together," J.P. said, and when I stood to go, he held up his big hands to slow me down. "Let me get the Treadman shots first, Jess."

"Come on, come on," I said, rolling my hands in the *speed-up* gesture. "I'm not about to let Criminally Handsome get the first shot of the cheerleader and the jock," I said, my territorial instincts kicking in. I protected my turf like a mama bear, and that deliciously handsome British boy would not get in my way.

"Treadman's looking good, and such a good guy," J.P. said and licked an approving lip at the photos on his screen. "*The Strip* will run these," he added, referring to one of the online sites he fed his photos to. Then he fed himself, popping a biscuit into his mouth. I dug around in my backpack for my gum. It would distract me from the tantalizing look of that biscuit.

"Treadman's always a good guy. That's why he's only worth one hundred dollars. But *Up Close* will run hook-up shots of Riley and Miles."

"God, I love *Up Close* and its millions of readers," J.P. said.

"It's a deep and meaningful love for me, too," I said, as he slapped a cool bill in my palm. I slipped the Andrew Jackson inside my bra and headed for the door.

"Wait," he said, as I turned the handle. I looked back. "Want to know what else I'm hearing related to the Belle family? And this isn't something I'd share with anyone but you."

My ears pricked, and a smile darted across my lips. In-sider secrets made me tick. "What else are you hearing?"

"I got a little tip on a wedding date," he said, sucking all the letters of the last two words as if they were juicy and delicious, "for the hottest wedding in town, that of Riley's older sister Veronica."

A shiver of excitement raced through me. Veronica Belle and Bradley Bowman were Hollywood's hottest young couple these days. They had gotten engaged six months ago. Guessing where and when the wedding would be was the parlor game of Hollywood.

"What's the date?"

"Supposedly this weekend. Somewhere on the beach."

"The beach? That could be anywhere."

"I know. Better start asking around. I want you to be the one to nab the shot."

"I will be the one. Even though security at the wedding will be insane," I said.

"It will be. Absolutely one hundred percent insane. So insane, that a picture would be worth more than a thousand words. A picture would be worth many, many thousands of dollars."

My heart skipped with a sick kind of longing. That would cover a lot of semesters of med school. I needed that photo desperately, and I needed it before the first bill came due in two more months.

"I'll ask around," I said, like the eager beaver I was.

"That's my bloodhound."

Or maybe that was the better comparison.

CHAPTER THREE

Jess

I popped a piece of spearmint gum into my mouth and chewed ferociously as I knitted my way through the cars. On the route to the beach, I ran through the possibilities for getting into the wedding.

Bradley Bowman and Veronica Belle were the toast of the town, their sweet romance eliciting *oohs and ahhs* from onlookers. The young twentysomething stars had fallen in love last year during the shooting of Griffin Studios' *SurfGhost*, a tale of a come-back-from-the-dead wave rider who falls in love with a girl afraid to swim. It was a megahit, with women of all ages swooning over their star-crossed love story.

Given their high profiles, the wedding details would be under wraps. That meant I'd have to dig. I could ask my mom, a makeup artist, if she'd heard anything. Like a hairdresser, she picked up all sorts of little details as her clients gabbed while having their faces done. Another option was my roomie Anaka. I could ask if her dad, Graham Griffin, who greenlit *SurfGhost,* would be at the nuptials. But if I got in through Anaka, then I'd risk her dad knowing about my job, and the more under-the-radar I flew, the better.

The key to being a good paparazzo was to be surreptitious. You needed to get in someone's face when you had to, and then get out just as quickly. Stealthiness was critical to my operations.

Anaka's cousin Kennedy, in New York, was another option, as her mom was a TV show producer, who was often invited to the fetes of the famous. Her mom had cast Bradley Bowman in a guest spot on her popular Sunday night show *Lords and Ladies.* But that might be too roundabout a way in, though I'd check with Kennedy later just in case.

The smell of the ocean grew stronger, so I shelved the wedding strategy until tonight when I'd have more time to noodle on it. For now, I had another shot to chase. I reached Venice Beach, parked, and began trolling for Riley and Miles.

The boardwalk was teeming with its usual assortment of characters. A man in stilts and a red, white and blue top hat crutched past me, threatening to knock down other passersby, like a hipster kicking a hackey sack and a mustached man in a lime green speedo riding a unicycle.

As I scanned the crowd for Riley, I carefully sidestepped a speed-demoning set of cyclists in matching zebra-striped bike shirts ripping toward me. The ocean waves lazily lapped the shore as street musicians plucked out twangy notes on their acoustic guitars. I kept up my pace, eyes peeled, ears perked, on alert. The usual camera-carrying suspects, such as Soul Patch and Leather Jacket, were nowhere to be seen, nor were the other regulars I'd grown accustomed to running into on red carpets, at coffee shops, outside gyms, and along the clandestine spots in parks, parking lots and nightclubs that the famous thought were secretive.

No one else was scanning so I figured Riley and Miles weren't a widely known tip yet among the paparazzi.

Which meant it was Criminally Handsome and me going fishing for the hookup shot, and it would be a race for first in. I spotted him hanging out by the ice cream shack on the edge of the boardwalk. He sat at one of the wooden picnic benches, his long legs stretched out in front of him, looking so cool and edible. I needed to look away. But knowing the enemy isn't a step one should ever skip.

I snapped mental pictures–of his cheekbones, his thick mess of hair, the faint trace of stubble, then on down to the flatness of his abs, though his stomach was hidden behind that blue T-shirt.

Still, as a physician-in-training, I could tell he had fine obliques, as well as solid rectus abdominus muscles. His arms were toned, and his muscles strong. Being pre-med, I needed to familiarize myself as much as possible with musculature. When I had finished tucking away my virtual shots, I surveyed the rest of him, noting that he had a soda in one hand, and his other arm rested on his waist now, probably covering his camera. He took a drink of his soda, and seemed to be enjoying it and the view.

Hmmm…He had the whole *act casual* routine down, but something didn't add up.

Sitting was never the best way to land a shot. You needed to be on your feet.

Besides, I happened to know there was a new dog water fountain a few hundred yards down the beach. Since Riley was crazy about her chihuahua-mini-pin, Sparky McDoodle, I was betting that would be a better spot to lie in wait. As I neared the water fountain, artfully avoiding a rollerblader in leg warmers bopping out to oversized headphones as she weaved disco-style down the path, I had the precise feeling of being followed. It was a feeling I knew well, a feeling I was used to in my profession.

I turned around, and there was my competition walking toward me.

"Hey. I didn't catch your name earlier. I'm William," he said, his gorgeous gray eyes fixed on me. They shined, they twinkled, they blazed. They did everything a hot guy's eyes could do.

"You already told me your name," I said coolly, doing my best to look away, down the beach, at the sky. Anywhere but the fineness of his face in front of me. Because then I'd melt.

"Last name is Harrigan. See? There. I've given you both my names. All you have to do is give me one of yours," he added, his sexy voice threatening to make my stomach flip. I simply couldn't deny that the words and the way he said them sparkled in that accent of his.

Resistance, Jess.

I kicked myself mentally several times, and the final kick was enough to maintain the stony look on my face, and the straight line of my lips. I would not smile at him. I would not be sucked into his orbit of good-lookingness. Besides, he was probably well-trained to use his kind of extraordinary handsomeness to throw me off the scent of photographic battle. Like he knew his looks were a powerful weapon against the female opposition.

"Did you get the picture already?" I asked, challenging him because I needed to remember he was the competition. *Only* the competition. "Is that why you're talking to me? You sent it off to J.P. and now you're just taunting me?"

He laughed. "No, I didn't get the picture. No, that's not why I'm talking to you. And no, I didn't send it off to J.P. seeing as I didn't get it, pursuant to answer number one." He tucked his thumbs into his jeans pockets, his camera slung around his neck, then shot me a captivating smile. Instantly, my stomach practiced its best handspring.

My god, the man was a charmer, and I tried desperately to look anywhere but at him. "Very cute," I muttered, relenting the slightest bit. "The whole *pursuant to answer one* thing."

The corner of his lips quirked up. "I'll take *very cute* as a good sign. So do you have a name? Or shall I just call you Girl Who Likes Huckleberry Pie?"

I smiled, and looked at the ocean so he couldn't see my face. "I do have a name. And truthfully, I don't really like pie."

"Not any kind?"

"No. Not any kind," I said, lying because I didn't want him to know the truth. That I'd once loved pie too much. That when my carefully controlled world had spun out of control back in high school, I'd turned to pie, or ice cream, or cookies for a once-a-week binge and purge. I'd never been heavy, but only because I never let myself get heavy. I'd been the poster child for secret bulimia—the kind so *manageable and mild* that hardly anyone knew my struggles. Thadd never knew that the shock of my shitty grades when we went out had sent me back to the cake tin. I'd kept it all well-hidden, until I finally managed to kick the habit shortly after him thanks to Anaka and her encouragement. Now, I kept tempting food and tempting men at a distance. Which meant I *had* to walk away from Tempting William. No matter how sexy and adorable he was.

"I should go."

"I'm sorry if I rubbed you the wrong way."

"You didn't rub me any way at all," I said hastily, then instructed my brain to remove all thoughts of rubbing—the right way, of course, because he'd do it the right way. I was sure he'd do everything the absolute, toe-curling, mind-blowing way.

William

Could American accents be any more endearing?

The answer was no, and no, and no.

It was simply impossible, and this whole damn country was rife with them, like a fucking paradise. God, I loved America, and California was a slice of heaven. No, wait. It was manna from heaven, and that's even better, right?

I shook off the queries though, because who cared about matters of divinity when right in front of me the hot girl was doing her absolute Olympic best to rein in a smile. As if she were fighting every instinct that told her to curve up her lips. She pursed them together, then brushed a few loose strands of blond hair from her cheek and glanced away. She wanted to dislike me, which only made her more intriguing. I turned on my best gentle-manly charm.

"Well, it was a pleasure to meet you, and I'll just have to imagine then that you have an equally lovely name," I said, and there it was again. That smile when I said *lovely*. Ah, perhaps she was an Anglophile. Certain words said in an accent simply undid the walls in American women– *lovely* was one of them. I was not above using it. Besides, it had the added benefit of being true.

She was lovely.

And hot.

And feisty.

Translation–everything I liked best.

"Jess," she breathed out in a low voice, as if it cost her something to give me this little nugget.

"Jess," I repeated, liking the way her name sounded. I could tell for her even sharing a small detail was hard. But I loved little details; they told you the things you wanted to know about people; they were clues you could assemble into a whole puzzle. I held up my index finger as if making a pronouncement. "And I bet it's just Jess. I bet it's not even short for Jessica. Because I don't think you'd use a nickname."

She shook her head, as if she were trying to suppress a laugh. "It's just Jess," she said in acknowledgment, and I wanted to pump a fist in victory. I'd read her right. Now the question was how to keep reading her because maybe she wasn't interested in backing off. Sure, I had a job to do, and hell, she was part of it, but jobs were infinitely more fun when they included one hot, blond California girl. American girls were my kryptonite. British chicks had nothing on ladies in the land of the free and the home of the brave.

"Just Jess," I said playfully.

Then, I felt a quick rush of wind, and heard the sound of tires spinning wildly. "Coming by," a voice called out. Jess quickly moved to the left.

The voice turned frantic. "Right! On your right!"

What the bloody hell? Cyclists were supposed to ride on the left but this guy was barreling down the path pedaling like the chain had sprung free. Right at Jess. Instinct took over, as I lunged forward, wrapping my hands around her arm, and yanked her out of the path of the careening cyclist who must have been dead-set on catching up to his pack. I tugged her to the sand to make sure she was safe.

Then, a loud smack rang in my skull, and my forehead throbbed.

Jess

I breathed hard, the wind knocked out of me from surprise. When I looked up, William was the one wincing.

"Are you okay?" I pointed to his forehead, now marked with a scrape. My heart lurched towards him, and my blood pumped faster with worry. I didn't want him to be hurt because of me.

"Don't worry about me. I think that lamppost got in my way," he said, gesturing to the streetlight along the boardwalk.

"You hit the streetlight when you were pulling me out of the way?" I asked, incredulous, but also amazed.

"I didn't want you to get hit," he said, as if there were no other choice but to save me from the bike. "The cyclists around here can be crazy."

I reached for his forehead, gingerly touching near the cut. "You sure you're okay?"

He nodded. "It's totally nothing. I'm sure it'll look cool later when it becomes some rugged scar."

I smiled again. "Scars are rugged."

"See? It was worth it." He flashed a smile at me. The man was so charming I'd need a new word for charming. He was *more than charming.*

"Well, thank you. That was quite gallant of you," I said, pretending to bow grandly.

"Just call me Gallant William," he joked.

"Do you need a Band-Aid, Gallant William? I have some with me."

"You carry Band-Aids?" he asked, sounding as shocked as if I'd said I was packing heat.

"You don't?"

"I'm a guy. I don't carry Band-Aids. I also don't need one for my forehead, but thank you for the offer."

Then I heard an even more beautiful sound. The sweet soprano voice of a rising starlet calling out to her accessory dog. "Sparky, do you want some water?"

William and his bravery slipped into the rearview mirror.

I was the horse at the gates, ready to be the first out. I didn't even need to bring the camera to my eyes. I whipped it out of my backpack, held it in front of me, and snapped picture after picture of Riley and Miles laughing as Miles held down the button that sent streams of water shooting into a green-rimmed silver bowl at dog-eye-level and Sparky McDoodle happily lapped up his H_2O. They didn't even notice me.

"Oh, Sparky McDoodle, you are so adorable. Isn't he cute just drinking water?" Riley said to Miles, her right profile in frame.

"He is adorable at everything he does," Miles said, flashing his cute actor smile at Riley.

William might have snagged some shots too. I stopped caring about him, because I had a higher calling, and I was off and running to the public restroom a hundred feet away. I raced into a stall, slammed the door, unzipped my backpack and yanked out my laptop. I grabbed the card from my camera, slid it into the drive, downloaded, and uploaded, and sent the pictures to J.P.

When I left the stall five minutes later, there was a reply on my phone from J.P.

"Check out *Up Close* in twenty minutes. Pics will be there. Come by tomorrow for $$."

Cash. My favorite four-letter word.

Looked like I was a little closer to the price of admission for next semester's anatomy class, and learning exactly how the knee bone was connected to the leg bone.

CHAPTER FOUR

<u>Jess</u>

"Do you want to get an ice cream?"

The question came from William as I walked down the boardwalk, and I prayed I'd heard him wrong. The last thing I wanted was to get an ice cream with William because that's the first thing I wanted. The ice cream and the time with him. Especially because he wasn't only handsome. He was *gallant*.

"Why would I want to get an ice cream?" I tossed back casually.

"Why wouldn't you want to get an ice cream?"

"I'm not hungry." I didn't make eye contact. The second I re-engaged with him, I'd want to spend more time with him. I kept on a path toward my beat-up black scooter with the well-worn seat. I'd bought this scooter myself because it was the only model I could afford, and even then it was used, and even then I'd haggled at the dealership for a lower price. But it was all mine. I owned that baby outright and I loved it.

"You don't need to be hungry to get an ice cream," he said, in a matter-of-fact tone, as if this were a completely obvious answer. "It's like in that movie with Paulie DeLuca, *Anyone's Dough,* when he offers a doughnut to the lawyer who's trying to take over his firm and he says –"

I couldn't help myself. I knew the movie. I loved the movie. "*–Since when do you have to be hungry to eat a doughnut?*"

We said the line in unison, and William couldn't hide a big, fat smile. "You like the movies, don't you?"

As if he'd learned my naughty little secret. I didn't hide my affection for films, but I didn't wear it on my sleeve either. And William had already figured it out. Like he'd figured out that I wasn't Jessica.

Smart guy.

"Of course I like the movies," I said, rolling my eyes, as if that would work as my Smart Guy Repellent so I could keep him at bay. "Name me someone who doesn't like movies. That's like not liking sunshine. Or puppies."

"Or pie."

I shook my head. "No. It's normal to dislike pie."

"But not ice cream. So why don't you have an ice cream with me even if you're not hungry since that's what Paulie DeLuca's character would have done in *Anyone's Dough,*" he proposed, and this man was getting under my skin in more ways than one. I might have been Scientific Jess, OCD Jess, Driven Jess when it came to school, but movies were my guilty pleasure, and my soft spot.

I wished I'd brushed my teeth in the bathroom a few minutes ago. Not because I had bad breath. But because having minty, fresh toothpaste breath is the one surefire way to make sweets taste bad. Sort of like drinking orange juice after brushing. Ergo, a clean mouth not only was good for the teeth, it was also good for resistance. To sweets and to the hot guys who proffered them.

I pursed my lips, considering if I wanted to give in, and William seized the moment. "Ice cream is like a Band-Aid for me. For my forehead scar." He brushed his fingertips across the small cut, and dropped the corners of his lips into a frown. "Besides, I hear the soft serve is irresistible especially with the shells that harden. I bet you like hard shells," he said, and raised an eyebrow. He was no longer talking about ice cream. He was talking about me. Seeing through me, and my very hard shell.

Since my resistance was already shot, I relented. "Fine. But only because you have that rugged scar and you like *Anyone's Dough.*"

"Two reasons. We're making progress."

William

I did like *Anyone's Dough*. I also didn't want the conversation to end. Plus, I *needed* her. Was it a crime that I would both benefit from talking to her, and that I'd enjoyed it so far?

Of course not. It meant I was a *lucky bastard*, as my brother Matthew would say.

We headed to the ice cream shack, a few feet away now that we'd managed to walk a good length of the boardwalk together. A group of guys were playing volleyball on the sand, yelling loudly in Spanish each time someone served.

"Chocolate or vanilla?" I asked.

"Vanilla with a chocolate shell," she said.

I ordered for us both, opting for chocolate-on-chocolate since I was of the belief that you can never have too much of a good thing, and chocolate was one of those things. The guy behind the counter handed us our cones, and Jess reached into the front pocket of her backpack.

I waved her off. "I've got this."

She shot me a sharp look. Oh, she was an independent little American vixen. What a turn-on. Feistiness was like a good drug to me.

"You don't have to pay for my ice cream," she said firmly as she opened her wallet.

She was not going to win on this front. I grasped her wrist gently and tugged her hand away. "I am aware of that," I said softly, looking into her eyes. Bright blue, like a clear sky. "I certainly don't have to pay for your ice cream. I'm sure given your fantastic photographic skills, that you are more than capable of paying for it yourself. But I asked you, and more than that, I *want* to buy you an ice cream."

"Fine. Thank you," she grumbled, and I placed a hand on the small of her back as I led her over to a nearby table. She shrugged off my hand. I didn't let it bother me. After all, I'd won the first battle—she'd agreed to spend more time with me.

"So," she began, lingering on that word as she took her first lick of the ice cream. I wasn't even sure if it was intentional, or if it simply couldn't be helped, but let's be honest—there's just something about a girl's tongue licking something sweet that makes a guy's mind wander. Mine was taking a quick trip into its dirtier corners, of which there were plenty. Sometimes I wondered how my brain even found its way out of all that terrain to let me function as a normal human being in civilized society. Like right now, as I imagined the taste of her lips. The feel of them. The things she could do with that tongue...

"What's your story? You're obviously not from here."

Like a slingshot, I'd been returned to Planet Clean. "You're direct."

"I am. So..." she said, her tone making it clear she was on a hunt for information and wasn't going to stop 'til she got it. She was relentless. Another trait I admired. It probably also meant she was fiery in bed.

Oops. There my mind went again.

"I'm an open book. I grew up in London, my parents are BBC producers, my older brother is a rock critic," I continued and she raised an eyebrow at the mention.

"That must be a fun profession," she said.

"I'm pretty sure he's madly in love with his job, as well as his fiancée."

"Glad to hear he has strong feelings for both. And you?"

"Am I madly in love with my job? Because I don't actually have a fiancée," I said in a faux whisper as if she'd suggested something terribly scandalous.

"Thank you for clarifying. Because you look like you're about to be married."

"It's the scar, right? The rugged scar?"

That learned me a small laugh, which then turned to a quick intake of breath as she ducked. "Watch out," she said, as a volleyball soared in my direction this time. I reached out a hand and caught it easily in my right palm. A guy in black swim trunks trotted over to me, shouting at his friend in Spanish, "Dude, you need to be more careful. You have the worst serve in the free world."

I tossed him the ball. "I'm not sure it's the worst serve. Maybe the second or third worst?" I offered and the guy cracked up.

"How's your serve?"

"Not too shabby," I said.

"Then come join us later."

"Maybe I will."

"Thanks man," he said and high-fived me before he jogged back to the makeshift court.

I turned my focus back to Jess.

"You speak Spanish?"

"I do?" I asked playfully.

"Well, you just had a whole conversation with him in Spanish," she said, arching an eyebrow.

"I'm pretty sure that was just a couple lines."

"Either way, I'm impressed."

"Wait until you hear my Japanese then."

She smirked. "Oh, I'm *sure* you speak Japanese too. By the way, nice catch."

I shrugged. "I used to be a volleyball star back in the home country. It's huge there on all our beaches, as I'm sure you know."

"Right up there with soccer, I bet," she said, keeping it up.

"But the Japanese thing?" I said, shifting to serious as I took a big bite of the ice cream cone. "All true. I'm studying East Asian languages at the University of Los Angeles."

"That's an unusual major. I go there too. But I'm a bio major. Pre-med."

"I'm allergic to science classes. I have a doctor's note excusing me from taking them."

"And what exactly does this note say?"

"That they induce severe narcolepsy, followed by incurable boredom, and finally metastasizing into absolute numbing of the brain tissue. So, as you can see, it would not be beneficial for me to take them. And I suppose that, combined with the school's 20,000-plus attendees, explains why I've never seen you around campus before."

"Maybe you have seen me," she said, posing it like a challenge. "Maybe you just don't remember."

I shook my head and leaned closer. "No. I've never seen you. Because I'd remember you," I said, and maybe I was laying it on thick, but again, I was speaking the cold hard truth. I had an excellent memory for many things, but especially for pretty girls with sexy lips and trim little waists. Mix in the attitude, chase it with a California accent, and you were pretty much permanently imprinted on ye olde little brain of William.

Jess

He might be studying East Asian languages, but he clearly double majored in the art of flirting. "Yeah, right," I scoffed. "You're a junior? Are you twenty? Twenty-one?"

"Senior actually. And yes, twenty-one. So no need to worry. I'm totally legal. For anything you want," he added, in a far-too-inviting tone that made me want to say yes to anything. My stomach flipped, like a disobedient little witch.

I shifted away from his talk of *anything*. Because, despite all his charms and quick wittery, something was nagging at me. The sheer coincidence of us. I crinkled my brow as I posed the question: "What are the chances that there'd be two seniors at the University of Los Angeles working for J.P. and his coterie of celebrity magazines and sites?"

"College isn't free," he said, keeping his gaze fixed on me the whole time. His dark, stormy-eyed gaze, such a contrast to that sunshine-y personality.

"Hmm. That's usually my line," I said. Though, these days it would be *medical school isn't free and the bill is due in two months for your first semester.*

"Looks like we have something in common, Jess," he said, leaning back in his chair as he took the final bite of his cone. He had the casual, laidback attitude down pat. He looked damn fine too playing that role. That's what worried me–was this whole banter-like-the-best-of-them part of a plan to bamboozle me? Was it all a role? "We're both working stiffs," he added.

"Seems we are," I admitted, and I partially wondered if he was paying his way through college too in the pursuit of the next thing, like I was as I aimed for money to pay down the monster of med school. But if I started asking, as curious as I was, I'd wind up in a longer conversation, and that would be grade A top-choice trouble. Because I already liked talking to him.

Just as I liked the ice cream cone.

My brain warned me: *danger ahead.*

I took one more lick of the cone, a bite of the chocolate shell, then tossed the cone in the nearest trash can.

His eyes widened. "You chucked your ice cream? How can you chuck an ice cream cone?"

"That was all I wanted." Because it was true. Because I'd worked hard to be able to stop at a few bites. I could do the same with his British Hotness. I was damn proud of myself for having mastered restraint in matters of food and hot guys. I stood up. "Thank you for the ice cream."

He rose too. He was taller than me by a good six inches. Which gave me a perfect view of his full lips as we stood face to face. Which made me want to touch them. To run a finger over them. Assess how they felt. Lean in for a kiss. A guy like that, funny, hot, totally at ease–he had to be a great kisser.

Scratch that. I bet he was an excellent kisser.

He tilted his head to the side, pressed those nice lips together, then took a beat as if he were a touch nervous. "Do you want to go out for another bite of an ice cream cone sometime?"

Oh no. Was he asking me out? No way. He was just being friendly. He was scoping out the competition. Nothing more. "So I can have another bite and then toss it?" I asked, because it was so much safer to avoid the possibility.

"How about a chocolate cake? You wouldn't throw that out, would you?"

"I might toss it."

"What about pizza instead?" he suggested, undeterred by my lack of an immediate yes.

I shook my head.

"Fries?"

Another shake.

"Sandwich? Burger? Hot dog?"

Shake. Shake. Shake. Restraint. Restraint. Restraint.

"Don't tell me a salad," he said, and flung his hand dramatically across his forehead. "Now, I know I'm in L.A."

I raised my cheap sunglasses on top of my blond hair. I was going to have to kick the door closed. Whatever he was doing–asking me out, or egging me on–it needed to end. Because if I went along with him then I'd have the whole ice cream. Him. Lick him up and down and all around like the tastiest ice cream there ever was. Kiss him all over. Grab him and pull him against me, and feel how we aligned. He had to go the way of the cone. "Harrigan, this isn't the part in the script where the heroine caves and agrees to go out with the guy."

He lifted an eyebrow. "Oh, so I'm the guy in the script? Does that mean I'm the hero?"

"Well, you're either the hero, the villain or the gay best friend," I said, my lips curving up in a traitorous grin. Damn him for being so easy to talk to, and about my favorite topic.

"Definitely not the gay best friend," he said quickly. "Not that there's anything wrong with that."

"I already have a best friend, and she's a she, so that part isn't being cast for this picture."

"But there are other roles still open? Like, could I be an anti-hero?" he suggested playfully.

This man was trouble. Too much trouble for my secret little predilection–casting the movies that played out in my head. Naturally, I had to keep going. "Possibly."

"Or what about an accomplice?"

"That's another role for sure. So is nemesis."

"I could be a good nemesis. Or maybe even reformed bad boy?"

I suppressed a smile. He looked like a reformed bad boy. He talked like a good guy. He could be a bad-boy-makes-good. Everyone loved that role. "It's really up to the writers. Which role you'll play," I said.

"What do the writers think?"

I didn't answer right away. I narrowed my eyes, and sized him up and down. Which fit the conversation, and also afforded me the extra bonus of checking him out close up, and cataloging his features. Captivating eyes like thunderclouds. Chiseled cheekbones with a hint of stubble. Fantastic dark hair. Gorgeous smile. Toned, tall and strong body. Verdict? Too good to be true. He had to be a mirage. A figment of my imagination. "The writers haven't decided yet."

"Is that a yes to pizza? Because pizza is like sunshine. You can't not like it."

"Pizza as in a pizza date?" I asked, as I furrowed my brow, deliberately wanting to keep him on his toes.

He smiled again. He was unperturbable. "Yes. Like a pizza date."

I stroked my chin, as if considering his request.

I *did* want a date. Very much so. I knew where it would lead though. To trouble. To distractions. To a supreme lack of focus on my goals.

But a kiss? A kiss was just a kiss. I could say yes to a kiss. He hadn't asked for one, but I had a hunch I could take one. Besides, what were the chances I'd see him again? I wasn't going to run into him at school. If I hadn't so far, then it wasn't going to happen now. I'd already proven I was faster on a stakeout than he was, so I'd smoke him as the competition.

He was the ice cream. I was the eater. I didn't need the whole cone. I could take a lick. One tasty decadent lick, and then walk away.

Piece of cake.

I leaned in, brushed my lips against his, and took him by surprise. He was startled momentarily, and didn't respond for about a fraction of a second. Then, he kissed back. It was a tentative kiss at first, his lips soft as he slanted his mouth against mine. A starter kiss on the boardwalk while the sun fell in the sky, its lingering rays warming me. He gently placed a hand on my cheek, exploring my mouth more, running the tip of his tongue across my lips, then deepening the kiss in a way that made me very nearly forget where I was. I shuddered and tingles raced from my stomach to the tips of my fingers, lighting up my insides. The kiss radiated throughout me, dizzying and delicious and a promise of so much more. It was the kind of kiss that took over your brain. That made you believe in possibilities, in perfect chemistry.

This kiss was the sun warming me, it was cool ocean waves lapping at the shore, it was the song you wanted to blast in the car.

As his tongue slid over mine, my heart beat faster, and I gave in to the moment, relinquishing all my fine-tuned control. My mind was hazy, and I kissed him harder, craving more. Because he tasted so freaking good. No, he tasted fantastic. Like chocolate, and a hot, sexy guy all at once. A hot guy who knew how to kiss a girl. Who kissed both tender and insistent, his touch hinting at all the ways he could do other things to me, and wanted to. He looped his hand around my neck, threading his fingers into my hair, tugging me closer. He'd taken the reins on the kiss, exploring my lips, brushing his fingertips along my cheek, dropping his other hand to my waist, our bodies sliding snugly into place. There was something that felt far too right about the way we aligned, his strong, firm chest against mine, his hips near enough to me that I could tell precisely how much he liked kissing me.

A lot.

And as much as I liked kissing him. I ran my hands in his hair, so damn soft and thick, the kind I just wanted to hold onto. All night long.

Come to think of all–all day too. Yeah, I could skip a class or two for more of this.

That was the problem. The last time I'd had a kiss that made me melt, I nearly failed organic chemistry. And that had sent me spinning.

After a few minutes of fantastic kissing on the beach, I had to put a stop to it.

I broke the kiss.

"That would be a *maybe* to a date," I said, then I smoothed my hands over my shirt and walked away.

CHAPTER FIVE

<u>William</u>

The black and white ball sailed over the net. I watched and waited for it to hit paydirt or be slammed back into my face. When it pummeled the sand on the other side, I pumped a fist and my friend John clapped me on the back.

"World's meanest serve," he said.

"You know it," I said as we returned to the back of the line and waited for the other guys to have their shot. It was two against two, and we were playing some of the guys I'd run into with Jess in the late afternoon. The sun rested on the edge of the ocean now; it would drop down below the horizon any minute, and leave behind peach-pink brushstrokes of color against the blue sky.

"I got a number today," I added.

"For what? Pizza delivery? I got that number too. It's called Red Boy's and they make the best pie in Venice Beach."

"They do make extraordinary pizza. Thank God you'll be able to get it whenever you want," I replied, then locked fingers, lunged forward, and returned the incoming serve. Seconds later, it screamed back over the net and John made a run for it, then spiked it cleanly into the opposing team's side. The guy who'd retrieved the ball from me earlier signaled a time-out to talk to his teammate.

"So did you get the number from a bathroom wall, William?"

"Yes. It was your number. It said for a good time, *don't call John.*"

"Ooh," he said, clutching his chest as if I'd wounded him. "What's the story for real?"

"Met this girl on a job today. Got her number from the employer."

He held his hands out wide. "You couldn't even score her digits yourself?"

"She pretty much jumped me on the boardwalk."

"Oh, this gets better and better," he said, chuckling deeply. "What you're telling me is she made out with you, and left you without her number, and you somehow think she wants to hear from you?"

The other guys called out that they were ready. We resumed play, and after a few more fast serves and returns, the ball roared straight at me. I dove for it, returning it quickly over the net as I got acquainted with the sand. I rolled on my back, looked John straight in the eyes, and said, "As you American schmoes say, ab-so-fuck-ing-lutely."

"Cocky English bastard. Here for two years and you think you're God's gift to women."

Hardly. But there was just something about Jess that made my pulse race. Okay, fine. My heart was sprinting anyway from the game. Still, she had a certain way about her that made me want more of her. Maybe it was her boldness; because let's face it—most girls don't just kiss you on the boardwalk and then walk away. The ones that do? Smart guys need to follow them.

I was a smart guy.

Jess

The roasted potatoes with rosemary seasoning were delicious and I told my mother so when I visited my parents that night. I lived in an apartment by the university, but I liked my parents, and I tried to have dinner with them once a week. The mission was made simple by them living a couple blocks away from the hospital where I volunteered a few hours a week, so I stopped by after a quick visit to the children's ward with their dog, Jennifer.

Plus, I needed wedding intel and my mom was often a good source of celebrity whereabouts because of her job.

"This chicken is pretty much the best I've ever had," I said, then speared a piece of broccoli sauteed with lemon. Jennifer, a bull mastiff-great dane mix, lay on the floor several feet away, a hopeful look on her big jowly face as she scanned for anything that might fall. She knew better than to lunge though. I'd trained Jennifer myself after we adopted her from a local shelter four years ago when I was a senior in high school. She was phenomenally obedient because I'd relied on the best, using tips from Wednesday Logan, host of the popular dog training show *I'm a Dog Person* on the cable channel Animal World. Jennifer was also certified as a therapy dog, which meant she was well behaved enough to visit patients in hospitals, rest her snout on their beds and endure lots of petting and loving. We'd just finished visiting some of the kids in the long-term care wing, and the dog had done her job brightening their day.

"Oh, stop," my mother said and pretended to be embarrassed. But she was an excellent cook, and she knew it. Plus, it couldn't hurt buttering her up.

"No, seriously, Diane," my father chimed in. "I read an article today in *Chicken Connoisseur* that said Diane Leighton has officially been declared the best chicken cooker ever."

"What else can I ever want for in life than to be a great chicken cooker? Besides a grandmother and thank the heavens that'll be happening soon," my mom said, beaming.

She hadn't stopped beaming since my brother Bryan had emailed us all an ultrasound picture two weeks ago. His wife Kat was ten weeks pregnant, and expecting twins.

"It's going to be like this for the rest of Kat's pregnancy, right?" I said playfully to my father.

He nodded several times. "Every single day. She's working through combos of twin names."

"Chloe and Cara," my mom offered. "Those are today's picks. If she has two girls."

"Obviously," I added.

"Jess," my father said. "How's the star shooting business? Get any great pics lately?"

"Every day," I said because it was true, and because I didn't want my parents to worry about my job or my ability to pay my own bills. My parents were what you'd call mortgaged to the hilt. It wasn't their fault, but it was their and our reality after my dad's firm—through no fault of his own—had become a poster child for the kind of financial problems that typified the last recession, as in *cooking the books.*

When his firm went belly up while I was in high school, they lost all their savings, and my college fund, so I had to pay all the bills myself. While my brother did well for himself running a successful company in New York that specialized in cufflinks, tie clips and money holders, I'd never once asked him for financial help, nor did I plan to. Besides, Bryan put himself through school with his job; I was expected to do the same. I had a camera, and that paid my way.

I didn't want to stay on this subject for too long, so I moved to another one. "Mom, did you fill in on *The Sandy Show* this week?"

"Yes, the regular gal wanted to extend her maternity leave one more week," my mother said. A freelance makeup artist, she specialized in last-minute avails and fill-ins for TV shows. It was a strange niche, but yet her ability to jump in at a moment's notice put her at the top of most rolodexes, including that of the producers at *The Sandy Show,* one of the top daytime talk shows. The host was friendly with Veronica Belle and Bradley Bowman, and had once joked on-air that she could officiate at their

wedding since she'd been ordained to perform cere-
monies.

But where there was a joke, there was often a kernel of
seriousness. Maybe she was going to the wedding. Maybe
she was going to be at the altar declaring *I now pronounce
you man and wife*. Or maybe someone on her staff knew
something about the wedding. I had nothing, and I had
to get something, if I was going to try to stake out a
money shot.

"I wonder if Sandy is going to the wedding," I said in
my best off-hand voice.

"Oh, I'm sure she is," my mother said, and none of us
needed to say the names of the soon-to-be-betrothed. We
all knew there was only one wedding anyone in this town
was talking about right now.

"Maybe they'll hire you to do the makeup, mom," I
mused as I sliced a final piece of chicken. I estimated
with the chicken and potatoes, not to mention the ice
cream, that I'd hit my calorie limit for the day, so I ate
the last bite, then carefully laid my fork and knife in a
criss-cross on my plate.

"Oh you're funny, Jess. You're so, so funny."

"It would be interesting though, to find out who's doing the makeup, don't you think?"

My mother rolled her eyes. "You are such a gossip
hound," she said, but she was smiling. "You and your father. He's addicted. I'll have to send him to a twelve-step
program soon."

My dad shrugged his sheepish admission as she gave
him a wink.

"I wonder where the wedding will be," I said.

"Malibu," my mom said. "The gals were talking about it at *The Sandy Show*. Supposedly at one of Veronica and Bradley's friend's homes."

Score! Now all I had to do was narrow down the couple's lists of friends. I tossed out names of Veronica's closest actress friends, and my mom shrugged at each name. Her gossip compartment was closing. She started to clear the table.

"Don't give Jennifer the chicken until everything is clear," she said to my father, as she brought plates to the sink.

"I'd never do that, Diane," my dad said, and I shot him a hard stare to second my mom's command.

"Dad," I admonished, as he gave a backhand toss to the dog, his former college athlete quickness coming in handy as he furtively fed Jennifer. She knew the drill; she caught the chicken in her mouth like a frog ensnaring a fly. "What? She's not begging. She's still lying down."

I shook my head, but smiled nevertheless.

My dad leaned closer and whispered, "Speaking of gossip, did you hear that they're close to casting Ren Canton in the remake of *We'll Always Have Paris*? I read it in *Hollywood Breakdown* this afternoon."

"Ren Canton is just a pretty boy who likes to take his shirt off. How can they even consider him to play one of the greatest roles ever? He doesn't even look old enough to own a bar in Morocco."

"If I had a gin joint, I'd never let Ren Canton within a mile of it," my dad said, then blew air through his lips. "To top it off, it's a three-pic deal. If the deal goes through, he'll be in *Queen of the Nile* and the *Sicilian Eagle* too."

"Ugh. I think my dinner just came back up," I said, but then cursed myself for the slip-up.

My dad's face fell. "You're not doing that again, are you?"

"No. And it was only once," I said, and grabbed my plate to help my mom. It wasn't only once, but I wasn't doing it anymore, so it didn't need to be discussed. They'd never known about my problems with food, and they didn't need to know. I had everything under control, the way I liked it.

CHAPTER SIX

William

I parked the bike in the lot at my apartment building later that night. John and I had won the round of beach volleyball. At least, I thought so. We didn't entirely keep score. Games like that were just for fun. I unhooked my helmet, tucked it under my arm, and threaded my way through the other vehicles in the lot. Grabbing my cell from the pocket of my shorts, I scrolled to Matthew's number.

He answered on the first ring. "Better make it quick. I'm about to head into the Knitting Factory with Jane."

"Is she performing tonight?" My brother was engaged to Jane Black, a smoking hot and ridiculously talented rock star who'd won a Grammy for an epic break-up album—one that was inspired by the guy *before* my brother.

"No. We're seeing Matt Nathanson. Jane loves him."

"You're so getting laid tonight. That guy is like catnip for women."

Matthew laughed. "That may be true. About the Matt Nathanson catnip. And that may be true on the other aspect of your comment, though I think it'll be because of my skills, rather than the other Matt."

"Yeah, keep telling yourself that."

"To what do I owe the pleasure, or rather the pain, of this phone call," Matthew asked as I walked into the entryway of my building.

"Just letting you know my new assignment is going quite well. Surprisingly so considering how long it took for him to even give me the time of the day."

"Well, he's always been a bit of a bastard, right? Too bad mum's sister can't quite smell the stench of prick that surrounds him."

"*Uncle* has never been a pleasant word, but he pays in cash, so that's all that matters for now."

"Think it can turn into something more?"

My chest tightened, as it often did when I thought of my highly limited options. "That's the rub, isn't it? Only if there aren't millions of other Americans who can do what I do."

"Well, all you can do is try to be the very best at it."

"I know," I said, in all seriousness. "I just wish I had a *specialized skill set*, like you do covering rock music. I have a few more interviews so we'll see if those pan out as well."

I walked to the mailboxes and slid a key into the slot for mine. Matthew had been in the United States for nearly a decade now, thanks to his work as a music critic for the leading music magazine in the world. It was the kind of *specialized skill set* that allowed for work visas to turn into green cards. Matthew was even marrying an American woman soon too, but he was already a permanent resident before he proposed. Lucky bastard. He didn't even *have* to marry her to stay. Not that he should marry her for *that* reason. Not that anyone should. And not that I was angling to get hitched to keep two feet on American soil. I simply adored this country, and wanted desperately to stay.

Hence, my need for employment. I'd already tried my hand at several jobs since landing here for my junior year abroad, and turning that into a senior year stay too. Matthew had tried to help me find work, but even though he's in high-demand, he's not in charge of any hiring at his magazine, so there wasn't much he could do. Plus, both the music industry and the journalism business are highly competitive in the first place for Americans *without* any specialized knowledge. That meant most of the connections he and Jane have in the business didn't pan out for me. I'd also tried parlaying my language skills into a part-time translation job that could become full-time, but I'd been turned down for having no experience and no degree. *Yet.* I had an interview at a new agency on Wednesday morning specializing in court translators so perhaps something would come of that.

"That's the challenge, isn't it? You do so many things well, but we need to find the one thing you do that no one else can. In the meantime, maybe the State Department will forget your visa is up. Bureaucracy and all," he offered as the mail tumbled out. On top of the stack of bills was an envelope from the State Department.

"Not likely," I said as I ripped it open. It was a re-minder that my student visa expired in two months, and if I didn't find an employer willing to sponsor me to turn that student visa into a work visa I'd need to skedaddle then. I told Matthew about the notice.

"You could do grad school," he suggested, trying to be as chipper as he could.

"That just delays the inevitable. Besides, then I'd go into debt. College is covered. I somehow doubt mum and dad want to pay for more education," I said, as I read the cold, harsh reminder from the United States of Amer-ica that my days were numbered as graduation drew near.

"Hey, I've got to run. Jane says we need to get inside. She also says she adores you and will hire you as a groupie if you'd like," he said, and I could hear the play-ful glint in his tone.

"Tell her she picked the wrong brother. Tell her to marry me."

"I'm sorry. I believe there is a problem with this con-nection. I better hang up now or else I'll fly out to L.A. on the next plane to pummel your dreary ass to the ground."

"Enjoy the show with my future wife."

Once inside my apartment, I flopped down on the fu-ton, grabbed the slip of paper from my wallet with Jess' number, and cycled through my best options. I wanted to see her again. I also needed a job. She was both to me. Was that so wrong?

Jess

I read over Anaka's shoulder later that evening, enjoying the latest entry in Karina's Burn Book.

How is it possible that Velvet Treadman has yet to receive the memo that berets are out of fashion? I mean, they are just soooo last year. In fact, they're so last year they're like the year before last year now. The only acceptable fashion for one's head is a pillbox hat, thanks to the princess. Velvet, dear, do call me before the next time you set your little feet on the tanbark of a playground, and we'll have a refresher course on the basics.

Love, always

Your friend,
Karina Templeton

Anaka had started her uber-popular, completely anonymous blog for fun a year ago, and now it had become a bona fide online hit. In it, she dispensed fashion advice under her *pen name*, posing as the famous offspring of a now-divorced pair of movie stars—the eight-year-old fashionista Karina Templeton.

"Who knew that little Karina would have so many opinions on berets," I said, as I returned to my chair. The kitchen table at our apartment near campus was littered with fashion magazines, celebrity tabloids, and my science textbooks.

"Karina has an opinion on *everything*," Anaka said, as she picked up her glass of wine and swirled it, a faux-haughty look in her eyes, as she spoke in character. "Including the fact that you look beautiful even in your simple T-shirt and jeans," she said, returning to her regular voice. Anaka was always encouraging and I loved that about her.

"And you're beautiful to me because you rock at being a friend," I said, shooting her a quick smile.

"Oh stop, stop. You're embarrassing me," she said as she took a took a sip of her wine. "This is delish. Are you going to have some?" She waggled the bottle of white at me.

I shook my head. "Wine makes me sleepy." I tapped my coffee mug. "I need to be ready at a moment's notice."

She rolled her eyes. "It's not as if you're already working 36-hour shifts as a resident."

"I know. But you have to train early to stay awake for days."

"All I can say is, thank God I'm a creative writing major. And speaking of, why isn't anyone making me an offer to turn Karina's Burn Book into a movie? I had 300,000 visitors last month," she said, then reached for a handful of cherry jelly beans from the glass bowl on the table, popping some into her mouth.

I reminded Anaka of her plight in her quest to snag a movie deal for her blog. "Because no one knows you're the amazing, all-powerful force behind the blog."

"But seriously. Do you think Karina's Burn Book would make a hilarious movie or even a TV show?" she asked, because Anaka dreamed of being a screenwriter, and had even written three original scripts that I personally thought were everything any studio could ever want

—she had humor, mystery, romance, and happy endings in all her scripts. But she didn't want to rely on nepotism, so she wouldn't show her father, Graham Griffin, any of her screenplays, nor her Web site that I was sure could somehow be turned into a movie too—just add plot.

"Yes. Provided you can weave in a story, some peril and an antagonist."

"*An* antagonist?" she said with a snort. "Everyone is an antagonist as far as Karina is concerned. Because nearly everyone commits fashion crimes."

"There you go. Now all you need is a plot."

"Karina fends off a dangerous paparazzo," she said, suggesting a storyline immediately.

I laughed. "Speaking of a dangerous paparazzo, or dangerously attractive ones, I ran into a constitutionally good-looking fellow shooter tonight," I said, as I tapped my pencil against the notebook sheet in front of me that was filled with organic chemistry formulas.

"Constitutionally good-looking? That high up in the ranks?"

"So good-looking, his looks would have to be codified and written into all the law books as a special amendment," I said, then twirled the pencil between my thumb and forefinger, and sighed as I remembered William's handsomeness.

"I trust you procured pictures?"

"For Karina's Burn Book?"

"No, for me." She banged a fist on the table. "Photographic evidence of constitutional hotness must always be shared. It's the democratic way."

"No. But I kissed him by the beach."

Anaka shrieked and nearly spilled her wine. I loved shocking her. "Details, Jess. I want every sordid detail."

I dropped the pencil on the table, spread out my hands wide as if I were a screenwriter pitching a new script in a producer's office. Because this–scripting a life like the movies–was the one thing that took the edge off me. "Imagine if you were casting the perfect romantic comedy with a hot British guy. But not a tortured hero. The completely irresistible, charming hero."

"Why are you talking to me then? Why are you not making out with him right now?"

That was a good question. That kiss was epic, and I could still feel the aftereffects in my body hours later. All I had to do was close my eyes, replay, and I'd be right back on the beach savoring William's lips on mine. Of course, I could also rewind to our conversations, to his relaxed and easy way of chatting, whether about food or about the roles we all played. Or to his quick reflexes in saving me from the cyclist.

I wondered if the scratch on his forehead was hurting him. If he needed me to kiss it and make it better.

As soon as I thought that, I wanted to smack myself. I needed to get him out of my head now.

"You know why," I said, as I pointed to the *tuition due* notice in the middle of our table, scattered on top of our mail, including Jennifer's therapy dog renewal certificate. Anaka knew well and good that romance didn't mesh with me. Just the memory of those out-of-control days sophomore year when I'd become beholden to food made me cringe. I was a control girl, and had every intention of staying one. That's why I took that brief hit of William and nothing more. Okay, more like a long and lingering hit. The kind that could feed a late-night fantasy alone in my bedroom.

"You are so not fun," she said with a huff. "Why did you kiss him if you don't want to go on at least one date?"

"Because all I wanted was a quick fix, nothing more. I need to focus on finishing my senior year and paying for med school next year. There is no time for boys, guys or men. Speaking of love, is there any chance you can find out where in Malibu Belle and Bowman are getting hitched? I hear it's at one of their good friend's homes. And I need that shot to pay for next year."

"Sure," she said. Even though Anaka didn't believe in nepotism for herself, she took advantage of tidbits her dad might drop and fed them to me. We were quite symbiotic.

"Are you going to the wedding?"

She scoffed. "As if. Besides, if I had gotten an invite don't you think I would have told you? My dad's definitely going though so I'll see if I can get some details. Let's get Kennedy on it too," she said, and opened up an email.

"It's like we share a brain sometimes," I said. "I was going to suggest we ask your cousin."

"Then I'll just copy you on this note," she said with a wink as she tapped out a quick email, then closed the browser. "Now tell me more about this kiss with the hot British guy."

I was about to give her all the details, every single one, when my phone buzzed. I pulled it from my pocket and looked at the screen.

There was a text message from a number I didn't recognize.

How do I move that maybe to a yes?

* * *

An hour later, I still hadn't replied. Nor had I deleted his note. Which meant I was still squarely in the *maybe* camp, and definitely not in the *no* camp, but absolutely fighting off the *yes* camp.

Because on the one hand, there was that bill. That bill was my future. But on the other hand, here was my present. The tingles that raced down my spine every time I replayed that moment on the boardwalk reminded me of how much a good kiss could turn a day around.

On the third hand, I *had* been on a nice even keel with food and grades for a few years now. Perfect even. No slip-ups when it came to bulimia, and nothing less than a B when it came to grades. Maybe I *was* stronger. Maybe I knew how to handle change without spiraling. Perhaps I could manage a little flirtation from a distance.

After washing my face, brushing my teeth, and slipping into bed, I chose the third path. I clicked on his text, adding him to my contacts, and listing him as HBG for Hot British Guy. Keeping him nameless would help me keep him at the necessary distance, I reasoned.

I tapped out a reply.

Generally speaking, one relies on moving trucks for such tall tasks.

I hit send, then hit the pillow. Seconds later, the phone vibrated.

HBG: Funny thing. I have a truck. With a very large bed.

A grin tugged at my lips. Damn that William.

Nice try. But I saw your bike.

I switched off the lamp on my nightstand.

HBG: You were checking out my wheels?

He had me on that one.

Maybe I was. And I'm not sure that bike has enough room for a yes.

I held the phone tighter, eager for a reply.

HBG: But it definitely has enough room if you ever want to go for a ride with me.

My eyes floated shut as a spark rushed through my veins. How I would love to get on the back of his bike, wrap my arms around his waist, and hold on tight.

I thought you were asking me out for a pizza. Now you want a ride too? You are demanding.

I tossed the phone to the foot of my bed, as if that would stop me from wanting to hear back.

But in seconds, it lit up again. And in seconds I swiveled around and clicked open the screen.

HBG: That's only because you kissed me. Now I know what I'm missing if you say no. Don't say no, Jess. I want to see you again, and I want to kiss you again.

William

I cracked open a beer, waiting for a reply. I tuned into a new Spotify station on my phone that Matthew had sent me–it was chock full of rising new bands he said I'd love. I leaned back against the counter, took a long pull, enjoying the fizz of the cold drink. I closed my eyes, listening to the music and hoping for a reply.

Everything I'd said to her was true.

After two songs, I checked my phone.

But she never wrote back that night.

TUESDAY
Weather: 70 degrees, Sunny

CHAPTER SEVEN

<u>Jess</u>

Habit is a hard thing to break, and I had no plans of stopping my check-my-phone-the-second-my-eyelids-flutter-open routine. Which meant I'd already protected myself from temptation. With last night's unfinished–deliberately so–text exchange tucked safely into a folder on my mobile phone so I would never touch it again, William was washed clear from my brain.

Safe and sound from his far-too-alluring texts, I opened my email the next morning.

I was greeted by a photo of a trim and slender Nick Ballast, an actor on *The Weekenders*. The picture was courtesy of my father, who'd forwarded an email alert from the home page of *The Strip* before he'd left for work.

Look who's being photographed with his personal trainer! xo Dad

In this photo, Nick was out for an early morning run on the trails with his personal trainer who he'd hired when he slimmed down after a stint at fat camp.

I zoomed in on the photo. Nick seemed to be looking straight ahead and appeared to be chatting with his goateed-companion, but as I studied Nick I could tell he was cheating a bit to the side. He must have know the photog had been there, had probably even tipped off the shooter. Ballast had wanted this shot in the magazines and online. He wanted the world to know he was in fantastic shape. I couldn't fault him. I'd want the same thing too if I were him, and to be honest, I was glad for him.

Ballast was a former child star who'd played an adorable batboy more than a decade ago in a sports movie, but when he hit high school he turned into a chubby teenager who'd lost part after part due to his ever-expanding waistline by a mere age seventeen.

About a year ago, he'd been spotted eating a Twinkie and guzzling a Slurpie in Century City, a bit of flesh poking over his belt. The picture was dubbed *Nick Balloons!* and it made the cover of many tabloids. That wasn't my shot. But I did score a scoop on what happened next. After that very public testament to his largesse, he started hiding his food. I'd gotten a tip that he was a notorious car eater, and I supposed I should have felt sympathy—or better yet, empathy—that he didn't want to eat in public, but I also sniffed opportunity. Besides, someone was going to catch him on camera sooner or later—that's an immutable law of Hollywood—and it might as well have been me.

I staked him out, and snagged a shot of him gobbling up an entire key lime pie inside his black BMW while parked under a tree on the side of the road. Next, he was seen scarfing on tubs of ice cream, a box of cupcakes, and a bag of chocolate chip muffins, all my shots too, before he finally admitted that food had gotten the better of him.

He checked himself into Waterfall Spa, and three months later checked himself out, a tanned, trimmed, toned and revitalized specimen of movie star primed for a comeback. He admitted his problem with food on the talk show circuit and spoke openly about his issues.

"I struggled, Sandy," he said to the talk show host. "It's not easy in this town. I was sixteen years old and having food delivered to me from those calorie-counting services, so I could stay in shape, and it was seriously hard. I couldn't take it anymore, but rather than get a healthy grip on things, I let myself go all the way the other direction. I ballooned up. Those pictures in the tabloids were a wake-up call," he admitted to Sandy. She nodded, patted his knee, and told him he was a talent at any size.

"Thank you. But I feel better now. I feel good about myself. I feel like I can have a healthy relationship with food, and hey, that's not a bad thing, is it?"

As he said those words to Sandy, I'd wondered if I had a healthy relationship with food or if I was one key lime pie away from snapping. But I'd reasoned I was safe since I didn't care for key lime pie. As for Nick, whatever he was doing now was working. He landed the role as the new sixth student in *The Weekenders* and was exercising in advance of the shoot that began in a few weeks. It was a plum role, and he'd vied with many other actors for that sixth slot, including the bleached blond with the broody brown eyes, Jenner Davies, who'd battled aliens in his last picture, then warred with front desk employees in a bout of life imitating art. Earlier this year, he'd punched a front desk clerk while on a press junket for the alien flick, and was caught on video, including the moment when he flexed his biceps in the lobby afterward, preening like a Mixed Martial Arts fighter as the clerk's cracked lip bled.

My dad and I had watched that video together several times. It was one of those things you simply couldn't look away from. The incident unfolded as a grainy shaky cam captured Jenner from across the hotel lobby asking the clerk in a faux-innocent tone, "I'm a little bit confused about something."

"Okay, how can I help you, sir?"

"Is there a reason I don't have a room with a view?"

"I'm so sorry, sir. We're all booked," said the clerk, who didn't seem to recognize the actor.

"So that's the reason? Because that just doesn't make a lot of sense to me on the planet I live on. And that's planet Earth, correct?"

"Um, yes," the clerk answered, clearly confused with the line of questioning.

"And on this planet, I would get a room with a view."

"I understand, and I would love to give you one but we're all out," the clerk replied.

"Perhaps you could rearrange some room assignments."

The clerk then gave a gentle laugh as the cell phone camera holder zoomed in on the pair. "I'm sorry sir, we don't do that."

"Did you see *Planet Patrol*? Because I want to show you what happens on my planet when things don't make sense."

Then Jenner's fist met the clerk's face. Next, Jenner blew air on each bicep as if they were guns. It was a perfect reenactment of his character's reaction after he'd slammed his knuckles into the alien that had slithered out of his co-star's mouth in the climactic scene in *Planet Patrol*.

The cell phone videographer who'd caught the whole hotel lobby encounter would make a good paparazzo, because Jenner had no clue he'd been recorded until "I Want a Room With a View on my Planet" became a viral sensation the next day.

I suspected Jenner's publicist pulled some crisis duty and crisis dollars because the requisite apology from the teen star poured forth less than twenty-four hours later. "I would like to extend my deepest apologies to Mr. Garcia at the front desk. Not only was I suffering from jet lag due to the promotional activities surrounding the film's launch, I also had become so wrapped up in the role that I behaved as the character, rather than as Jenner Davies. I sincerely regret my actions yesterday. I hope to show the world who the real Jenner Davies is, and I have made a donation to a charity of Mr. Garcia's choice."

Ah, the charitable donation route. Hollywood's version of absolution. Do something naughty, cruel, stupid, idiotic, or selfish in front of a lens, and earn forgiveness by becoming a charitable supporter. Many charities relied on the funds that came from this town's sinners trying to wash away their bad deeds. Just recently, I'd seen a photo of Jenner picking up trash on the beach with a coastal cleanup charity—he was clearly trying to rehabilitate his tarnished image.

"Just trying to do my little part for the big world," Jenner said when an entertainment news magazine interviewed him on that same beach as he delivered his canned response. His little part, though, wasn't enough yet to win back the good graces of casting directors and studios–no one would touch him after the hotel lobby incident.

I closed the email, giving Nick Ballast a mental pat on the back. Good for Nick for beating out Hollywood's #1 teenage douchebag for the coveted part, and for working out.

A new email arrived. Anaka's cousin Kennedy had replied so I opened her note.

I have a good friend who was invited. I'm going to see him later today, so I'll ask for more details. When are you coming to NY again? We should see another show.

xoxo

I nearly squealed with excitement. Then I sent a quick reply.

You are a rock star. Hope to see NY and you soon. By the way, is this friend a hot guy?

xoxo

Jess

I showered, dressed, ate an apple and a plain yogurt, and hopped on my scooter to swing by the hospital. I needed to drop off Jennifer's certification renewal with Helen, the bawdy salt-and-pepper-haired woman who ran the volunteer program, as well as the hospital's human resources department. I knocked on her open door, and she quickly waved me in. She was guzzling a latte, and pointing to the computer screen.

"It's Reeve Larkin," she said, waving a hand in front of her face, as if she were fanning herself. "Shirtless. From *Escorted Lives Part III.* I'm dying from the hotness."

My eyebrows shot up to my hairline. "Show me," I said because Reeve was a certified babe. He'd risen to stardom in the first two *Escorted Lives* pictures, based on the mega bestselling erotic romance novels, and while he'd been shirtless in the first two flicks–not to mention pants-free too–his chest was still a sight to behold.

Helen leaned forward and kissed the screen. "Some day he will be mine," she said, leaving red lipstick marks on Reeve's chest.

I laughed. "Good luck tearing him away from Sutton," I said, referring to his wife, well-known in Hollywood circles for her work as a casting director.

"A woman can dream," Helen said in a wistful tone, then gulped more of her latte.

I handed her the papers. "Dream big then. And here is Jennifer's renewal."

"Excellent. Keep bringing that hound by. The kids love her, and I love chatting with my favorite gossip hound," she said.

"The hound and the hound are happy to be here. See you next time."

Several minutes later, I pulled up to the university parking lot for my advanced biology class. After the lecture on gene organization, the professor reminded us about the quiz tomorrow, then tossed out some rapid-fire sample questions. I'd been studying for it for weeks, so my mind wandered briefly to William, and his coursework. He'd been speaking Spanish yesterday at the beach, then said he knew Japanese, and was studying East Asian languages. I wondered how he knew so many languages, why he took pictures, and if he was paying for college himself as well. Most of all, I was curious how he felt about all those things. Did he feel the way I felt? Tense. Poised. The weight of your world on your shoulders.

The professor called on me, and asked me a question about cell structure. I wasn't paying attention, so I plucked an answer out of thin air.

"Very good," he said, and I was pleased that my impromptu guess was correct. Good thing William hadn't worked his hot guy magic yet to distract me from school. I had to stay strong though, and remain impervious to his charms.

CHAPTER EIGHT

<u>William</u>

A quick Google search revealed the initials MT stood for…waiting, waiting, waiting.

Ah, there it was.

Of course.

Monica Tremaine. That was all I needed because everyone knew she had the most distinctive identifying feature in all of celebrity culture.

I raced through the hall in the University of Los Angeles building where I'd just finished my two morning classes in Traditional East Asian Civilization—one for Japan, one for China. J.P. had sent the assignment only three minutes ago. As I picked up the pace, I tapped out a curt reply: *I'm on it. Will have them.*

Rushing to the parking lot, I hopped on my bike and started the engine. Desperately needing to land the shot first this time, I repeated J.P.'s orders as I weaved through late morning traffic. *Get a shot of MT. She'll be ordering an iced latte in an hour* at *the Sbux near those punk crap shoe stores on Melrose.*

After finding the spot, I parked, than grabbed a position, leaning casually against a shoe store that peddled buckle-laden boots and chunky platform shoes. My eyes were shielded with my aviator shades, but I wasn't trying to go incognito as a shooter. Besides, the celeb I was pursuing wanted to be recognized. This celeb preened for all the cameras, and dozens of photographers were lying in wait for the call of the booty. Across the street, I noticed a guy with a soul-patch pacing the sidewalk as he clutched a camera. A couple stores over, a gray-haired and well-weathered guy smoked as he fiddled with his camera lenses. Down the street, a girl with a red braid hunched over her Vespa, waiting to snap a shot. They didn't even pretend with Monica. There was no need to. Monica lived her life in the public eye.

I scanned for Jess, but saw no signs of her. Equal parts disappointment and relief washed over me. I wanted to see her, and I also wanted to beat her this time. But if she wasn't here, she wasn't in the race. Though, it was entirely possible some of the other shooters here were also in JP's arsenal and that he'd pitted me against someone else in his employ.

Fine. That was fine. I didn't have fantastic reflexes for nothing. Jess might have smoked me in the quest for Riley Belle yesterday, but today was a new day, and a Monica Tremaine payday would not elude me.

A minute later, I spotted the most famous ass in the world, and the woman it was attached to stepped out of a black town car. Hell, this ass was the size of Kansas. The caboose on Monica Tremaine could double as a shelf. Maybe hold a few books. Park a frappuccino there while you hunted for change. I zoomed in on the rear end first and snapped a shot of it because J.P. could peddle one of those bad boys to an online site run by a purple-haired pseudo-journalist who liked to draw doodles on his celeb photos. This ass was a hell of a canvas for doodling. I pulled back the focus and captured a few pics of her heading into the coffee shop.

This was a two-part shot, and it was the second one that was most valuable. The swarm of photographers waited like hyenas to pounce on the prey.

Willing prey, mind you.

Soon, she was on her way out, a massive handbag dangling on her arm, and a venti iced drink of some variety in her other hand. Her shades were high on her head.

"What are you drinking, Monica?" someone called out.

"Soy chai latte," she replied when she spotted the questioner–the dude with the soul-patch. She pretended to point at something beyond him, brandishing a huge smile as if to say *Hey, look at that adorable bit of absolutely nothing that I'm pretending to admire for the camera.*

I snapped more pictures of her, capturing the happily staged point, then the lowering of the shades as she continued to smirk, then the first cold taste of soy chai deliciousness on her bee-stung lips.

A driver held open the car door and she slid into the backseat. The show was over as quickly as it had begun. This woman gave new meaning to the phrase wham-bam-thank-you-ma'am with the way she played every move for the gossip rags.

As soon as the car turned into noontime traffic, I dug my phone from my pocket and rang J.P. I wanted to let him know that I'd pulled off today's shoot far better than yesterday's.

"J.P. here," he said gruffly as I raced into the shop.

"Hey, it's William. I got the shot."

"Yeah? Where is it?"

"I'm heading into Starbucks right now to get on the wifi and send to you."

"You do that," he said, and he sounded distracted. Or disinterested. The latter was more concerning.

"It's a great shot," I said, keeping up the conversation as I snagged a chair.

"I'll be the judge of that. Just get moving and send it to me. The first to post is the first to gloat," he said. "And yes, I do know that doesn't rhyme but it's close enough."

"Indeed it is," I said, as I grabbed my iPad and sank into a chair. "Hey, so I was just curious. How did you know Monica Tremaine was going to be here?"

I was greeted by silence. Dead silence, and my heart dropped for a second. Had I pissed off J.P.? I hoped to hell not. I needed this man on my side.

"Seriously?" he finally said, his voice doing a fantastic impression of the adjective *irritated*. I could practically see him rolling his eyes.

"Well, yes," I said. "Seriously."

"Her PR firm puts out an alert for her. She wants to be shot. That's why the photo is only worth a few bucks.

Now, send that bad boy to me, and stop asking questions that make you look like a noob."

Noob.

As he ended the call, I fired up my photo software, downloaded the pics, and sent them off to J.P. I was tempted to add a line to the email that said, "I was just kidding. Of course I knew that."

But then I really would look like the noob I was. And who wants to be a noob?

Besides, I had other masters to answer to, like the name blasting now on my phone. *Uncle James.* Grabbing my iPad, backpack and phone, I scurried out of the Starbucks and back onto the street. A woman in red high heels walking a miniature poodle with a black and white polka dot collar glared at me for nearly knocking into her.

"Sorry," I muttered to her, as I answered the phone. "Hey James."

"Give me the good news," he said, not bothering with hello. The man really took crassness to a new level. "Are you getting the intel?"

"I'm working on it," I said. "I'm getting some good shots."

"Shots? I need more than shots. Shots aren't good enough, kid."

"Yes, of course. That's all part of the plan. More than shots," I added, bristling at the condescending name he used for me. *Kid.* For some reason, it bothered me more than *noob.*

"When will these 'more than shots' be coming? Because you did fine managing the records, but if you expect anything more from me, I'm going to need more from you," he said. "That's the way it goes here."

James, an American, had married my mum's sister many years ago, a pairing that sent her out of merry old England and setting up home here. He'd been running his firm for more than a decade and had built a respectable business in Southern California. But even though I'd been in the States for nearly two years and wasn't just job-hungry–I was job-starving–he'd refused to send me work for the longest time. I didn't want to beg him for help; I wanted to be my own man. But finally, Matthew called our mum, who called her sister, who narrowed her eyes and told James to stop being a prick and help out her nephew. After all, James was in the rare position of being in charge of hiring for an American company, so that made him a prize as far as my American job-hunting connections went. He begrudgingly hired me for a little work here and there doing computer maintenance, then handling the databases, then managing a long list of names for an upcoming project, and I'd been fortunate enough when he moved me into *field work*. I crossed my fingers that the field work would turn full-time, and that he'd sponsor me for a visa. But there were no promises. There never were with James. He'd always been a bit of a dick. But he was family, so he was the family dick. At least he wasn't a Harrigan. Some small solace.

"Soon, very soon. I promise," I said.

"I am a fan of *very soon*. I am not a fan of *soon*. That clear?"

I bit back my annoyance. "Very soon it will be," I said.

He said goodbye and I stood in the middle of the sidewalk, the warm California sun reminding me of all that I loved about this town.

Every day, every second, the clock was winding down on days like this.

I paced down the block, then back again, then once more as I pondered my options.

But it came down to this–Jess was my only in. I ran a hand roughly through my hair, racking my brain for the limited information I had on her. I had to try again to see her, but to do so I'd need to break down those walls she had.

I snapped my fingers when it hit me. Though I barely knew her, she'd already given me the necessary clues.

<u>Jess</u>

When my final class ended for the day, I caught up with Anaka and walked to the scooter parking.

"I have a plan to get some wedding deets for you," Anaka said, brushing her nearly black hair off her shoulders. "My mom emailed earlier to remind me about a charity dinner thing we have tonight that the studio is sponsoring. They want me with them to present the whole perfect family united front –"

"But it's not a front. You are the perfect family," I pointed out.

She nodded. "True. It's kind of ridiculous that I actually like my parents."

"And it's equally ridiculous that I like mine."

"We will remain ridiculous together. Anyway, so I'm going to weave in the wedding questions while we're driving to dinner."

"Brilliant."

"Right? It'll be casual, car chatter, blah blah blah. It won't seem like I'm angling for something."

"Again, why have you not shown your father any of your fabulous screenplays?" I asked, as I turned on my phone to see if J.P. had an assignment for me. I had it powered down during the day so I wouldn't be tempted. If I knew there was an assignment coming through at noon, a chance to snag proof of a clandestine lunch date, or a catch a midday shopping trip, I'd race out of class and chase a picture, and Tuesdays were my busiest days for classes. I had to avoid the tease, and I did that by going dark.

Anaka gave me a quizzical look. "What does planning to talk to my mom about the Bowman and Belle wedding have to do with screenplays?"

"Because this is my point. You plot everything. You plan everything. You're always mapping out the next scene, the next thing, the way to solve the problem. You're like the bald guy who ran mission control in the aborted Mars landing movie," I said.

"But I have better hair."

"You have hair. And it is way better."

My phone dinged like a church bell. A message from J.P. I touched the screen and scrolled: *Up for a pedi patrol late afternoon? Should be some TV beauties from that LGO hooker show getting toes done in the usual spot.*

J.P. must have gotten a tip from one of his very many assistant sources. That was where most of his out-and-about assignments originated. The assistants got a little thank you from J.P. in the form of extra cash.

"Hey, I gotta go," I said, and strapped on my helmet.

"Ooh, what's the assignment today?"

I told her and her eyes lit up. "I need a mani-pedi. Can I come?"

"What? And cramp my style? Love you. I'll see you later. Besides, you have your dinner thing."

"Get me a good shot."

"Always."

As she walked off, I double checked the message from J.P. Then I spotted a new one. From HBG.

HBG: Did you know that Sullivan West will be out-running Nazis tomorrow evening at the Silver Screen Theater on Wilshire? First time in more than a year that Bandits of the Forgotten Crown is being shown on a big screen in L.A. I'd love to take you.

Damn. My heart started tap dancing on my brain.

Then I read a second text from him.

HBG: P.S. Did you know the Silver Screen Theater has….wait for it…air-popped popcorn? You probably knew that but I have a hunch you might be a fan of air-popped popcorn. You are, aren't you?

As I re-read the note, the tap-dancing sped up, my damn heart beating out a staccato rhythm so quickly that all logical brain cells were quashed. The rational lobes shut down, and I was left with only the emotional, hormonal ones that took control of my fingers and made me reply with a *You've got your yes.*

Because movies, air-popped popcorn and the Silver Screen Theater on Wilshire formed my trifecta.

As I headed for the strip of street with the best mani-pedi salons in town, I found myself looking forward to seeing the movie with him.

But when I arrived at manicure row, I wasn't happy to spot William Harrigan parking his motorcycle down the street too.

That fact that he was here could only mean one thing.

CHAPTER NINE

<u>Jess</u>

"Tell me I'm not paranoid. Tell me you're not phasing me out."

"You're not paranoid," J.P. said. "I'm not phasing you out."

I ducked into the doorway of a juice cleanse store, pressing my back flat against the brick wall so the pair of mommies pushing strollers could exit. "Tell me why he's on the same stakeout two days in a row then. You used to send me solo."

"Competition is good for the soul, Jess. Either that or I'll just tell you now I'm secretly practicing for the match-making business I'm going to open soon and you and Criminally Handsome are my first test," he said, and I could hear the tease in his tone, like a cat playing with a mouse. He was toying with me, and he was having a damn fine time.

"Well, you're failing because I don't like him," I said, patently lying, as I stepped out of the doorway, and paced down the block, far away from the hot guy who I'd stupidly agreed to a date with. Next up on my to-do list? Cancel the date.

"Ah, that's just how you feel now. He'll grow on you."

"Doubtful. But seriously. Why are you doing this? Why are you sending him out on the same jobs?" I asked, and there was the slightest quiver in the way the words came out of my throat. I crossed the street, putting distance between William and me. I thought I'd beaten him yesterday, but he was back for more. There was no way I was letting him win this little turf battle no matter how sexy his accent was or how charming his texts were.

"Jess, you're not my only shooter," he said, in his no-nonsense voice. "You think I close operations when you're in class? Ha. The stars of the world are out and about 24/7, and so are my shooters. Besides, it's his second job of the day. He already got a picture of Monica Tremaine drinking an iced latte down on Melrose. Two pics actually. One I sold to my purple-haired friend, the other to *Star Sightings*. Cha-ching," he added, making a sound like a slot machine.

"Monica Tremaine," I said, smacking my free hand on my forehead. "Everyone takes pictures every day of Monica Tremaine drinking iced soy chai lattes on Melrose. She's a reality show star! She sends out press alerts when she goes to the grocery store!"

"Sometimes, a man's gotta go for the low-hanging fruit."

"Just don't phase me out, please. I need this job," I said in a desperate voice as I pictured the *tuition due* notice perfectly on my table. Taunting me. Mocking me. "Please, J.P."

"Jess, we're all good," he said gently. "Go get me some pedi shots, and I'll pretend I never heard that little hitch in your voice when you sounded like you were about to cry."

"*There's no crying in baseball,*" I said, quoting a famous sports movie line, as I recovered to my usual, hardened self.

"That's what I like to hear. Now, go take your pissed-off-at-the-world attitude and let it fuel a little photo shoot."

I ended the call, slid the phone into my back pocket, and marched back to the three-block stretch full of bou-tiques and cafés and yoga studios and yoga-clothes-selling studios and pilates places and places selling pilates things, each one bookended by a nail salon. It was like shooting fish in a barrel sometimes on this street if you showed up at the right time. At other times, it was a ghost town when it came to famous faces. Today, I assumed my best casual afternoon stroll demeanor as I ambled past the stores, perused the entryways, and scanned the pedi chairs as if I were simply looking for a good leather seat complete with massage roller and remote control. I didn't see Evangeline Harris or anyone else from the LGO show J.P. was talking about—*Stacked,* a series about hookers that left all the viewers hot and bothered every Sunday night.

As I conducted my recon, I did my best to avoid William. I pretended I didn't see him on the other side of the street. I acted as if I didn't notice that he was doing the same thing I was doing. I made believe he wasn't mirroring me, and that I didn't agree to a date with him either. I certainly hadn't engaged in any flirty texting with him.

But I couldn't fake it any longer, because a few minutes later, he was crossing the street and walking towards me, all six feet and then some sexiness of him. He had the look, all right. The jeans, the loose and sexy tee that hinted at his abs, but didn't reveal too much, the nicely toned arms on display, those eyes like a stormy sky, and that lopsided grin that I wanted to lick and kiss and smack the hell off his too-fine face.

"Fancy meeting you here," he said, and then flashed a smile. I wanted to arrest him for the smile. It was the sort of grin that should be outlawed for being impossible to not adore.

"Yes, I'm so surprised to see you here that I'm about to faint of not surprise," I said as I stepped onto the next block.

"How was your day?" he asked, as he helped himself to walking next to me.

"It was great," I said, emphasizing the past tense.

"And it no longer is, I take it?"

"No, actually it just got eons worse," I said, hoping the lie I'd just spun would shoo him away because I'd spied Evangeline, the biggest-breasted of the big-breasted stars of *Stacked*, and she was suckling an iced coffee, and talking on her phone while wearing short shorts and a red T-shirt and having her toenails polished a shade of purple. One of her co-stars, the pushing-forty veteran lady of the night, sat next to her.

I didn't want William to see the pirate's booty I'd discovered, and I knew how to get him out of the way. He was a gentleman, and I would use that in my favor.

I smacked my palm against my forehead. "Crap. I think I forgot to lock my scooter. I better go check it." I swiveled in the other direction, and then very deliberately stepped on my right foot with my left, as if my feet had gotten tangled up, and I proceeded to trip on the sidewalk. I braced myself with my palms. Even though I knew what was coming it still hurt when my hands met concrete. But I didn't care about a scrape if this ruse worked out.

"Ouch," I said and winced. The wince wasn't fake.

He knelt down next to me. "Are you okay? Can I help?"

I shook my head bravely, putting on my best game face. "I'm fine," I said, and pursed my lips together. I tried to stand, but moaned as if it hurt too much. "My scooter," I muttered. "Someone's going to steal it. I have to go lock it."

"Let me go check for you, Jess," he said, and then trotted down the block, his back to me, on his way to my scooter. I jumped up, unzipped my backpack, grabbed my camera, and popped into the doorway of the salon to snap several zoom-in shots of the actress with the larger-than-life breasts, then a few more of her companion.

A short woman with a white lab coat ran to the door and held her palm up, the official sign for *get your damn camera out of my store/face/life.*

"Get away," she said, in a thick voice and motioned down the street.

With a quick smile and a nod, since I'd gotten what I came for, I turned away from the shop. Off in the distance was William, checking out my scooter, tugging on the lock as if to verify that my ride was indeed safe. It was. It was as safe as the second I'd left it. Which gave me another minute or two to send in the shot. I grabbed my laptop, downloaded the photos and hit send as he walked back to me with a curious, but knowing look on his face.

He pointed to my laptop, then to my knee, then my scraped hands.

"Quick recovery?"

"Seems I made one."

"Your scooter's safe."

"So's my job. For today at least."

"You played me," he said, but he didn't sound mad. He sounded impressed.

"It worked," I said, pride suffusing my tone. "But the scrapes are real."

"Yeah, I feel terrible. Shall I go hunt down a Band-Aid for you now? Oh wait. You carry them with you. You're always prepared."

"You never know when you might have to take a fall to be first," I said, and rooted around in the front pocket of my backpack for a Band-Aid. I found one, peeled off the wrapping and started to press it onto my palm.

"Let me help," he said in a soft voice, laying the ends of the Band-Aid onto my skin. He stepped closer, his body now officially in the zone of supreme nearness–the zone that would allow for hands to explore chests, and arms to be wrapped around necks, and lips to lock again.

I held my breath. My hands tingled under his touch. "This is the part in the script where the reformed bad boy touches the heroine for the second time," he whispered.

I wanted to close my eyes and linger in the moment. But I had to be stoic. I couldn't say what I wanted to say. That this was the moment when the heroine's skin raced from the barest touch. So I lied. "This is the part where the heroine doesn't even notice."

He raised an eyebrow. He held my gaze. I didn't look away in enough time. My breath caught, and my lips were parted. "Hi," he whispered in a voice that was getting under my skin.

"Hi," I said against my better judgment, against my brain.

"Are we still on for the movie tomorrow?"

"You're just asking me out because I'm the competition, right? *Keep your friends close and your enemies closer?*"

"I'm asking because I want to go out with you. Not because you're the enemy."

I scoffed. "At least you admitted I'm the enemy. That's why you're asking me."

He raised his hand, reaching gently for a strand of my hair. My feet felt wobbly with him so near to me. The earth was suddenly operating at a bizarre angle. I pressed my palm against the brick wall behind me to steady myself as he ran a finger along my hair. So softly. "I swear," he whispered, pinning me with his gaze. "I truly want to see the movie with you. Say you're still going with me."

Wanting to believe him, but knowing better, I grabbed

onto that kernel of self-restraint, and slipped away from him. "I don't know. I need to stay focused on school and work," I admitted.

"What about now? Do you want to hang out? Get a bite to eat? Are you done with classes for the day?"

I nodded. "Yes, but I have a quiz tomorrow morning in my advanced bio class."

"A quiz?"

"Yeah. A *quiz*."

"I bet you've been studying for days, right? Weeks, even? You're probably way ahead?"

I begrudgingly nodded. "Yes," I admitted. I knew the material cold. This morning's question in my advanced bio class reaffirmed how ready I was.

"Okay, so the quiz isn't really an issue. Since I know you don't like food, do you want to go get a pedicure, Jess?"

"I do my own nails. So unless you're the one getting a pedicure…" I said, letting my voice trail off, figuring that would keep him at bay. Guys didn't get pedicures. The ones that did usually didn't like girls. I started to walk away.

"I'll get a pedicure if you come with me," he offered, and I stopped in my tracks because William was going toe-to-toe with me without blinking an eye. "Think of it as work."

"As long as I can pick your color," I said, because I could play this game of brinksmanship too.

"Have at it."

Oh.

He was calling me on my bluff. I didn't intend to get called on, so we walked into a shop called Daisy Nails that was painted a bright shade of yellow, and I headed straight for the bottles to choose the one best for him.

CHAPTER TEN

William

She surveyed the colors in the rack on the wall, a smirk on her face. "Hmm, I could see you as an orange."

"Orange? Really? I thought for sure you'd say pink," I said.

"Is that a hint? You want me to pick pink?"

"No. I just figured you'd choose what you thought would be the most embarrassing color for a guy to wear."

"I'm not that easy to read, Harrigan. I'm not necessarily going to make the obvious choice," she said, and truer words were never spoken. She was a tough one, which made her all the more alluring.

So damn alluring with her feistiness, combined with her accent, mixed with her prettiness. She had it all–brains, beauty and a prickly, take-no-prisoners attitude that drove me crazy. *Crazy for her.*

Then, James's words flashed like a neon sign. *Very soon.*

A pang of guilt touched down inside me with the reminder that I needed to move faster; I wanted to tell Jess
the full truth about my job, but I also wanted to get to
know her better without an agenda. If I'd met her under
other conditions, I'd still want to get to know her. Besides, once I did, then I could let down my guard about
my twin motives. There. *Bye, bye guilt.*

"Okay then. Which color?"

"Red," she declared as she plucked a bottle from the
plexiglass shelf. "Fire engine, cherry, apple red and you
must wear it for at least a day."

"This is going to be great when I go for a swim tomorrow," I muttered, shaking my head. I could already hear
John's voice when he saw my toes. *Note to self–wear socks
for next twenty-four hours. Even in the ocean.*

We turned around and walked to the counter.

"One pedicure, please," Jess said to the woman seated
behind the high white desk with a daisy drawn on it. She
glanced up at us, an eager look on her face quickly replaced by a bored one when she realized we were plebes,
not celebs. "Go take the chair by the dryers," she said,
gesturing vaguely.

Jess scanned the shop, then leaned closer, her shoulder
brushing mine. "So typical," she mumbled.

My ears pricked. Perhaps this was a clue. "Right," I
said, then rolled my eyes and flubbed my lips.

"They always do this. Seat us regular people up front
so they can keep the leather chairs by the back open in
case a celeb comes in."

Ah. Now that made perfect sense. "Well, they need to keep them away from riffraff like us," I said, picking up the conversational thread quickly.

"Totally," she added.

Another manicurist filled up the water in the foot tub at the base of a brown leather pedicure chair. "Did you pick a color?" she asked Jess because she probably thought she was the one getting the pedicure.

"Yes. For my friend," Jess said with a devious twinkle in her blue eyes.

I plopped down in the seat of the chair and began untying my laced-up boots. I dropped my boots and socks on the floor, swung my feet over the water, then let them hover as I rolled up the cuffs of my jeans. I dunked my feet into the water, and leaned back into the chair. "Ah, I'm relaxed now," I said, making a show out of enjoying myself as the manicurist began. "So Jess. I'm your friend now?"

She furrowed her brow. "Hmm?"

"You called me your friend. You said *For my friend*."

She shrugged a shoulder, and looked away as her lips dared to curl up in a smile. "It's just an expression." She eyed me up and down. "All ready for the spa treatment?"

"Almost. There's one more thing." I handed her the remote control for the massager portion of the chair. "I'm going out on a limb here, Jess, but I have this feeling you might like to be in control."

She hit the button for knead and did not bother to hide a wicked grin as the machine rollers pushed hard against my back, moving me forward like a crash test dummy with each roll.

"Ah, doesn't that feel relaxing." I was going to hold my own and then some with her.

"Let me give you an even more relaxing one then," she said, clicking on the remote to boost the speed to a level that simulated bakers whacking rolling pins on my back. I bumped against the industrial-strength massage chair without letting on that it was the most annoying piece of furniture ever created.

She relented, turning off the controls. "You're relaxed now," she said with a wink.

"I'm cool and calm and zen," I said as the manicurist scrubbed the heel of my right foot. It tickled, so I cracked up and pulled my foot away.

That made Jess laugh. "You're ticklish."

"I guess we aren't all as tough as you," I teased, as she glanced at the door, shifting from side to side as she peered through the glass.

"You looking for someone?"

She returned her focus to me, crinkling her brow. "Aren't you?"

"Um..." I began, but didn't know how to continue because I was thoroughly flummoxed. I held out my arms in question. "Who would I be looking for?"

"Someone famous," she said as if the answer were obvious.

"Right," I said quickly, as if I were doing the same thing. I *should* be doing the same thing. "Of course. I'm scoping for the stars. I've got stars in my eyes."

"My brother says that about me."

"Brother. Now we're getting somewhere. Tell me about this brother since I told you about mine."

She gave me a look as if to say I was lucky to get any information. "He's in New York. He runs a company. He's going to have a baby soon."

"He is? That's impressive. Some new advancement in science like that movie *Inconceivable* with the former governor of Texas who used to be the Swiss bodybuilder?"

"No! He and his wife. My god, everything that comes out of your mouth is a twisted joke," she said, but she said it admiringly, so I was pleased.

"Why thank you. When is this baby due?"

"Several more months. They're having twins. My sister-in-law is awesome. She loves movies too, but she doesn't work in Hollywood. She's a jewelry designer, and they're madly in love. Even though it took my brother five years to figure out he needed to win her back after he broke up with her when she was eighteen," she said then told me more about Kat and Bryan, then about Bryan's cufflink company, Kat's necklaces, and her own parents' jobs. She lit up when she talked about them—she was a family girl, and that was so cool. No issues, no trouble, no bitching about her parents or how she was raised. She simply liked them; I was the same way about my family, and it warmed my heart to know we shared that.

I told her as much. "Have I mentioned how cool it is that you get on well with your family?"

"Thank you," she said with a sweet smile. "Sounds like you do as well."

"I do. Very much so. Tell me more about you. So far, I know you're crazy about your family, movies, and photos, you're going to be a doctor, and you do your own nails." I wasn't angling for information; I was simply enjoying talking to her. I lowered my voice as I asked the next thing, sensing she was a private person. "Do you do your own nails because you don't want people seeing you do the things the people in your photos do?"

She was instantly tense.

CHAPTER ELEVEN

Jess

I straightened my spine. He was spot on. He'd read me like an open book left on the coffee table just for him.

Not wanting to admit he was right, I shook my head. "No. I do it myself to save money," I said, because I'd rather play the money card than the uptight-in-public card. Besides, I was the observer. I wasn't the observed. Even though I didn't warrant being the subject of any shot, I didn't want to even take the chance that someone might see me with my shoes off, or with my mouth open, or with my guard down. Avoiding a potential *Nick Balloons* moment of any sort was an abiding goal in my life.

"Ah, gotcha," William said, and nodded. He seemed as if he understood. "Let me see those hands then."

"My hands?" I asked, as the manicurist patted the white towel on the edge of the foot tub, a sign for William to place his foot there for drying. He did as instructed, reining in a laugh and she patted his foot down, then began filing his toenails.

"Yes, your hands, Jess. We're in a nail salon. It's totally acceptable."

I held out my right hand, and he moved my fingers so they touched his palm, sending tingles down my spine. He pretended to inspect my nails closely. I pretended I didn't care that his hands were on me. My body said otherwise though, as a shiver of want rolled through me. I made a note to smack some sense into myself tonight, because right now sense had vacated. It had a way of doing that when William got close to me.

"Navy blue," he said, in his low and sexy voice that left an imprint of longing inside me.

"Navy blue what?"

"If I'd have picked out a color for you, I'd have picked navy blue. To go with your eyes. They're dark blue," he said, looking at me.

If I were in a movie, if I were that kind of a girl who was soft and sweet and eager, I'd gasp and say *you noticed.* Then, he'd nod once, and whisper "*I notice everything about you.*"

Instead, I swallowed the dry knot in my throat.

"Dark blue is my favorite color," he said softly, then started to slide his fingers through mine. I never knew holding hands could be such a turn-on. But as he laced his fingers though mine, flesh against flesh, my skin sizzled with the first sparks of a darker, deeper desire.

My eyes floated closed for the briefest of seconds. This had to stop. I was dangerously close to soaring away on a cloud of borderline lust. I was in a nail salon of all places.

I opened my eyes, desperate to grab hold of some kind of witty comeback. But anything and everything fell through my fingers with the way his dark eyes were hooked on me. I didn't trust William as far as I could throw him, and seeing as I wasn't terribly good at throwing guys, that wasn't very much or very far.

Yet he was so hard to resist.

He made me feel so many things. From the way he talked with me, as if he truly wanted to know me, to his carefree ways, to these sexy little moments when he shifted from talking to touching, it was as if we existed in this private little bubble of connection. I didn't want to leave this island of burgeoning heat either.

"Right now, gray is my favorite," I said in a voice I barely recognized.

His lips curved up slowly as he grasped my hand. I didn't even notice the manicurist anymore, and I doubt he did either, as we seemed to inch closer, to crave contact and meet in another kiss.

But the moment caved in on itself when my phone bleated loudly. Once. Twice. Three times. I let go of his hand to swipe my phone from my back pocket. My mother had texted, and her note popped up on the screen.

Just finished up with Sandy. Her assistant happened to mention while I was doing Sandy's eyes that the bridesmaids are picking up their dresses late afternoon tomorrow in Manhattan Beach, and that the officiant should be there too to pick up the matching bowtie and cummerbund for her tux.

Forget kissing William. I wanted to kiss the screen. I wanted to kiss Sandy's assistant. Maybe even my mom.

I tapped out a quick reply. *Nice work. Happen to know where? What place? Did you get details?*

As I sent the message, I spotted Lolanna Winnifred, the sixteen-year-old daughter of a six-packed and strapping action star who'd been a fingerless mitten model before he made it big on the silver screen. Immediately, I went into stealth mode. I scrolled through my phone, acting casual, but keeping my eyes on Lolanna as she walked into Daisy's Nails too. I checked out William, happily enjoying his pedicure. He didn't so much as look up when Lolanna, who was designing a collection of mittens now too, walked past him, heading straight for one of the reserved chairs in the back. Lolanna scooted up on a chair, wriggled off her teal blue flip flops with a cloth flower on the toe strap, and settled into the chair, over-sized sunglasses still on.

I typed more on my phone, as if I were answering a message, then laughed at the screen, positioned it higher, tapped it twice to zoom, and snapped a shot of Lolanna soaking her feet. Anaka would make good use of the photo.

William tipped his forehead to his feet. The manicurist was starting to polish his toenails red. "Didn't want you to miss the main attraction, Jess."

"Of course not," I said, tucking my phone into my pocket.

The lady next to William started looking at Lolanna, and then a woman across from us peered over the top of her home design magazine at the girl. All the while, he didn't seem to notice a thing.

I cocked my head to the side, considering the constitutionally good-looking British guy in front of me. Was he acting clueless or did he truly not recognize the teen daughter of one of America's most bankable male action stars? How could he miss her? Every night I studied my flash cards. I had a whole stack of index cards with celebrity faces pasted on them. The ones with children had their kids' pictures on the back side. Thanks to my daily regimen of review, I could spot a face in seconds— from the A-list down to the D-list, their offspring, their significant others, and sometimes even their agents and managers too, but usually only if they were dating or doing said agent or manager.

"What?" he asked, when he realized I'd been staring at him. "Do I have something on my nose?"

"You don't recognize her," I said, as if I'd caught him rooting around for money in his mommy's purse.

"Sorry?"

"You don't recognize her," I repeated in a low voice, and nodded slightly in Lolanna's direction. He followed my move, and I watched his eyes survey the sun-glassed-girl quickly, then he returned to me.

"Sure I do."

I put my hands on my hips. "Who is she then?"

"You know, she's *that* girl," he said, and waved a hand dismissively.

I laughed and shook my head. "That is hilarious."

He held up his hands sheepishly. "Fine. You caught me. I am not one hundred percent up to speed on American celebs. Which movie did she star in?"

I laughed again, then leaned closer to him to whisper Lolanna's pedigree.

"Oh yes! Exactly. I was going to say her next."

I shook my head. "And I thought J.P. was trying to give me a real run for my money."

"You don't think I'm worthy competition?"

I pointed from my naked nails to my blue eyes. "Let's just say I'm more impressed with your color matching skills than with your facial recognition abilities. You obviously don't practice the latter, do you?"

"The latter?"

"You know, flash cards. Web site studying. Photos of famous faces. Don't you practice?"

"Of course, of course. I could spot the BBC stars like that," he said, and snapped his fingers. "But, like I said, I need to get up to speed with this side of the pond. Do you? Practice a lot?"

"Of course. How else would I be able to do my job? You never know when, where or who you might run into. Always be prepared."

"Right."

"Why aren't you taking her picture now that you know who she is?"

"Well, didn't you? I mean, we're working for the same guy. He always takes the first to file."

"This picture isn't for him. The shot I got is for my best friend only."

"Does she run a photo agency?"

I shook my head. "She uses them in this really spoofy, funny sort of way. Here. I'll show you," I said, then I tapped on my phone to call up Karina's Burn Book. But I stopped before the page loaded. Something about this moment felt too close, too intimate. I might want to press my body against his, but I wasn't ready to show him my best friend's tongue-in-cheek, anonymous Web site. Whether he recognized Lolanna Winnifred or not, he was still the competition. Besides, he might very well be asking me for ice cream and pedicures for the very same reason I was saying yes to his requests—to glean information.

"Darn. Page not loading," I said, and stuffed the phone in my back pocket.

"Bloody phones," he said with a nod, as the manicurist put the finishing touches on his toes. "Mine was slow as hell while I was looking up the movie times earlier. Speaking of, are we back on?"

"You think now that we've shared a pedicure–or rather that I've watched you have your toes done–that a movie is happening?"

He shrugged sheepishly. "I was hoping so."

Then it hit me. *Keep your friends close and your enemies closer.* I wanted to know what he was up to. I wanted to know why he didn't recognize Lolanna. "You know, William, I believe if we finish up soon, we can even see that film this evening. Let's not wait 'til tomorrow."

<u>William</u>

We rode separately to the theater. It was only a few miles away, and we both knew the back roads, so she followed me as we sped away from traffic and to the Silver Screen Cinema. Once we arrived at the theater, I was no longer thinking of my slip-up at the salon over Lolanna, nor was I thinking about James's *very soon* directive. I was thinking about taking a girl I was interested in out on date.

I paid for the tickets, held open the door, snagged the popcorn, and then sat down next to her in a mostly-empty theater after she picked two seats by the side. As the lights dimmed, she dipped her fingers into the air-popped popcorn tub.

She flashed me her smile, and her dark blue eyes seemed to twinkle. "I only said yes because of the popcorn," she said, but I knew she was teasing; I knew it especially because she leaned in closer to me, brushed her lips across my cheek, and breathed softly, "Thank you for the popcorn."

"Feel free to say yes again because of the popcorn then," I whispered, feeling like I was buzzed on her.

"*Yes*," she said as the opening credits began.

CHAPTER TWELVE

William

Somewhere around the big crawl-under-a-truck-to-es-cape chase scene, I reached for her hand. She didn't resist. She let me slide my fingers through hers like I'd done at the nail salon. Slowly, then more quickly, our fingers were laced together and she squeezed my hand. My mind was a haze, swirling with nearness to her, even from *this* kind of contact, which was the simplest, most basic kind. Hand in hand, fingers entwined. But then, there's some-thing to holding a girl's hand, to the way she responds, to the suggestion of how bodies might come together. Be-cause holding hands can be the prelude to so much more.

While I might have asked her to the movies to ferret out more details about her job, any ulterior motives had been banished well before the curtain fell. They were so far in the rear view mirror now, as we touched, that I could no longer see them. She brushed her shoulder against mine, and when she shifted closer, the sexy honey scent of her hair drifted into my senses. All I had to do would be to inch closer and press my lips against the sweet skin of her absolutely kissable neck.

Truth be told, that was all I wanted to do.

Screw the movie, screw the job, screw everything else but continuing what we'd started. I bent my head closer to her, speaking softly near her ear. "Jess, were you going to kiss me again in the nail salon?"

"Maybe," she whispered. "Are you going to kiss me now?"

"If I do, you'll miss the scene when he rides across the desert on a white horse."

"That's my favorite scene."

"Then you don't want to miss it."

"No. I don't want to miss it. So make it worth my while," she said, her tone an invitation.

She didn't look away. Her blue eyes were wilder than usual as I brushed her hair off her neck, savoring every second of her response to the anticipation, from the way her breath visibly caught, to the delicious moment when her lips parted the tiniest bit, her body making it clear what she wanted.

The same thing I did. To be closer.

I started slowly, dusting my lips against hers, the barest whisper of a kiss. It was the first sip of champagne, a promise of what's to come, of sweet, tantalizing touches that make you intoxicated soon on the whole damn bubbly glass.

She made the sexiest little sound, a tiny murmur as I pressed my lips to hers once more.

I moved in for another kiss, sweeping my tongue against the curve of her lower lip, kissing away her gasp. Then we went deeper, tongues meeting, swirling, tasting. The heat inside me rose as the kiss evolved, turning into a long, slow, deep wet kiss. My favorite kind. I could kiss her all day, all night, I could kiss her all over, and I desperately wanted to. Because the way she responded, tugging me close and spearing my hair with her fingers as she practically grabbed my skull, sent my blood racing.

All her hard edges melted when we kissed. The barbs, the snark, the teasing disappeared. We were not the same people who doubted each other; all our cards were on the table as we touched.

After several hungry minutes having each other's mouths for an early dinner, she dropped a hand to my arm. She ran her palm along my bicep, then my forearm, as if she were tracing me. Her touch sent a bolt of pure lust through my body, and I wished we were anywhere but here. The theater might be mostly empty, but it wasn't private, and I wanted to do so many private things to her. Touch her breasts. Slide a hand under her shirt. Unbutton her jeans. *Feel her.*

I settled for traveling to her neck, layering soft kisses on a path up to her ear. I nibbled on her earlobe and whispered, "Worth your while?"

"So worth it," she said, her voice some kind of combination of purr and moan.

I'd take that combo. Hell, I'd take it again. I returned to her lips that were like a magnet for mine. Jess intrigued me, fascinated me, and turned me on. She was a model of restraint most of the time, but the second we connected physically, all bets were off. Because then, we were only chemistry, atoms and electrons smashing into each other, seeking each other out. Her mouth was sweet, sinful and demanding at the same time because she kissed me back so passionately and with so much untamed heat that my mind–or maybe it was my body–leapfrogged ten steps ahead to the movie ending, taking her back to my place, and exploring the rest of her trim, slim, lush figure.

But when the credits rolled, she untangled herself from me, smoothed her hair, ran her hands down her shirt, and thanked me for the movie.

"I have to go study."

Minutes later, she was driving off on her scooter into the Los Angeles night.

She was fucking masterful at walking away, and leaving me far too turned on.

CHAPTER THIRTEEN

<u>Jess</u>

Ice in the freezer.

Water in the faucet.

A big fat plastic bowl somewhere in the cabinet under the stove.

With my teeth gritted and my jaw clenched, I mixed the three ingredients, then dunked my head in the ice water.

Surprise, surprise. It was freezing, and I nearly yelped under water.

But stoicism ruled me now that I was home. I needed to clear my head, and I needed to clear it fast.

Ten seconds.

I'd failed at my mission. I'd gotten nothing but hot and bothered at the movies. I'd gained nada when it came to understanding the man that J.P. was pitting against me. Instead, I'd let my lust-fueled body do all the talking and let him kiss me through my favorite scene.

Twenty seconds. My teeth would start chattering soon.

Fine, I'd seen the movie eighteen times already and I could watch the final minutes on YouTube if I wanted. But still, being near sexy, charming, fun and flirty William had a way of turning my brain to mush.

A big, blob of useless, formless mush. If I kept going, I'd fall back into so many bad habits. I couldn't chance it.

Thirty seconds. I had frozen him out.

I flipped my wet, cold head out of the water and took a deep breath. There. My hair was soaked, my face was wet, but my sanity had been restored.

Time to focus. I brushed the wet strands off my face, pulled my hair into a ponytail, and opened my books on the table. I finished my last biology assignment, studied for my French class and reviewed chemistry formulas for fun. Satisfied with my schoolwork, I spent the next thirty minutes researching bridesmaid shops in Manhattan Beach. I found two and read all the online reviews, as well as magazine write-ups of the shops, but neither one felt like the kind of place Veronica Belle would rely on for her bridesmaids' sartorial needs. I called up a map of the fanciest shopping section in the area, and zoomed in on the stores, hunting for a boutique that might not scream bridal store, but might in fact, be precisely the type of place where a star, her girlfriends, and her younger sister would go for a final fitting. I located two possibilities and opened another tab to research them more when my phone alerted me to a text message from Anaka.

Future Oscar-Winning Screenwriter: Stop the presses. Ceremony's not in Malibu AT ALL. That was a decoy!

Excitement rattled through my veins. I wrote back in seconds.

Well???? Where is it? I am on my knees praying you know.

Her reply was swift.

Future Oscar-Winning Screenwriter: At a ranch in Ojai owned by a famous Oscar winner!

"And the answer is Chelsea Knox," I said out loud, pretending to slam a game show buzzer with my victorious answer.

I grinned, big and wide and pleased because we'd cracked the code. Veronica Belle and Bradley Bowman were quite clever indeed to have planted the fake nugget about a Malibu beach wedding. They wouldn't be the first Hollywood couple to sow the decoy seeds, but it was a time-honored trick for a reason. It worked. Paparazzi and the public would be hunting for a whiff of them off the cliffs in Malibu when they'd actually be walking down the backyard aisle of the twenty-acre ranch owned by Veronica's close friend Chelsea Knox, a poster child for the vegan movement and the winner of an Academy Award a few years back for her portrayal of a paraplegic governor in *State Business*, a film she'd also directed. Chelsea Knox used her Ojai Ranch home as a haven for rescued llamas, ostriches and pot-bellied pigs. She called it Knox Ranch.

I replied to Anaka: *Have I told you lately that I love you?*
Future Oscar-Winning Screenwriter: Tell me again.

I wrote back. *So much that I have a photo of Lolanna Winnifred getting a pedicure.*

Future Oscar-Winning Screenwriter: Cannot wait to see it when I walk through the door in 30 min.

With the gem of the wedding location tucked safely in my head, bridesmaid research was even more rewarding. I returned to the open tabs and mapped the distance between the two most likely dress shops. Fortunately, they were only three blocks apart, so I stood a good chance of being able to stake out both at the same time tomorrow from a yogurt store across from the two boutiques. Maybe I'd even get lucky and not only snare a shot of the bridesmaids—that would likely score me a cool one thousand dollars—but also learn a little more about the Ojai Ranch wedding plans.

Because that's where matters grew complicated. Quite simply, Knox Ranch was a fortress.

Chelsea had bought the seven-bedroom, five-bath property with a ten-stall stable and a kidney-shaped pool three years ago. The address of the ranch home was a matter of public record, so technically, I could hop on my scooter and ride past the ranch's front gates right now. The problem was the graveled driveway itself was one mile long, and the entire property was fenced in with steel gating designed to look like weathered wood.

Anyone could ogle the front gates. Hardly anyone could get past them.

Finding my way in would take more digging. But with the bridesmaid plan of photographic attack in place for tomorrow, I clicked over to my email. Scanning my inbox quickly, I spotted a note from my brother and opened it first. He'd sent me a dog meme, as we often did for each other, this one featuring a picture of a Husky staring into the camera asking "What do you call a dog magician?"

Then, I read Bryan's words: *Wait for it, Jess. Wait for it.*

He made me scroll down further and further still in the email for the punch line. A photo of the same dog, as if he were laughing, with the punchline: *A labracadabrador.*

Snickering out loud, I read the rest of Bryan's note:

It's totally cheesy. But admit it—you laughed, right?

Anyway, how's everything? I can't wait for your graduation. Kat and I are excited to see you with your mortar board in June. Top of the class, I'm sure. Did you hear mom is sending cute twin names to us? I replied to her latest with my suggestion—Spock and Kirk for boys. It's possible she might not be speaking to me.

Love ya,

B

I tapped out a reply: *As always, I am thrilled that you have succumbed to the joy of silly meme humor. Perhaps next time you really want to freak out mom, suggest Abercombie & Fitch for boys and Laverne & Shirley for girls. I'll let you know if I can hear her screams of mortification from my apartment.*

Love ya too,

J

I answered a few more emails, including one from Kennedy, in which she'd responded to my hot guy question with—*yes, very much so. Hot, and beautiful, and sweet.*

But the situation is very complicated. As I contemplated such romantic entanglements, my phone rang. I didn't recognize the number and for a brief moment I hoped it was William but then I remembered he was listed as HBG.

"Hello?"

"Hi, I'm looking for Jess Leighton." The caller was confident, young, and accent-free. Bummer.

"This is Jess."

"I'm Keats Wharton. I just recently started up a photo agency and I am suitably impressed with your work."

"*Suitably* impressed. Not a bad adverb to throw around. But, how do you know my work, Keats?" I didn't try to hide and I'd been solicited for freelance gigs before, but I liked to know how the purveyors of said freelance work found me.

"It's my job to know who the best shooters in town are, and you've gotten some impressive shots. Those pictures of Nick Ballast when he turned a bit portly were epic." There it was again—the series that had earned me nearly half of the money in my medical school fund. Even so, the totality of the balance wouldn't even cover one semester. "I also appreciated your series on Shelley Mari wearing tight shirts and yoga pants a day after her baby bump rumor. You were the first to debunk the possibility that she was pregnant," he said, referring to a picture I'd snagged of the blues-y singer heading to The Getty while wearing the slinkiest of slinky outfits a few weeks ago.

"I enjoy a good photographic debunking as much as the next person," I said and then waited for Keats to get down to details, though I was delighted that he was familiar with my oeuvre beyond my best known work.

"I have a special assignment for you."

"What is it?"

"I don't really want to talk about it over the phone. I'd rather get together in person and give you the details. But it's a relatively easy shoot," he said.

"Relatively easy is never actually easy. But then again, this job isn't easy."

"Would you be able to meet tomorrow?"

"I don't know," I said, and kicked my feet up on the table. He couldn't see me, but it was a power pose, and I felt I needed power. Besides, this was how a titan in business and world affairs would position himself during a pivotal phone call scene in a movie. I tilted the chair legs back slightly.

"I'll pay you half up front. It's a $10,000 job if you can get the picture."

The chair wobbled with my enthusiasm. I grabbed the edge of the table and righted myself before I cracked my head on the floor. "What type of shot? Don't tell me it's a wedding shot because those go for more. A lot more."

"It's a hook-up shot. And I'll have a location for you. Can we meet tomorrow morning to discuss?"

"Yes. But what's the name of your agency?"

"A Thousand Words," he said and I typed it into my browser and called up his web site. He had several decent shots of celebrities on there.

"Fine. I can meet you at seven-thirty at the Coffee Bean," I said, and I gave him the location nearest my apartment.

"You're an early bird," Keats said admiringly.

"And since I can catch worms, I assume that's why you're hiring me."

When he hung up, I pictured $10,000 dancing in front of me. Then I pictured eating a few bites of chocolate cake and actually enjoying it. Keeping up the reel of happy images, I pictured William kissing me. Then I pictured him kissing my belly. Then I pictured him kissing my...

I stopped my reverie when the phone buzzed again. I clicked it open.

HBG: Just in case you were wondering, I still have red toes tonight, and I'll still have them tomorrow.

There it was again. The zoom. The spark. The shivers. My body lit up as I thought about seeing him. My stomach somersaulted with the possibility of another kiss.

Evidently, the ice water trick had no lasting effects. Because I quickly replied: *Will need verification then.*

Which was a terribly dangerous thing to say since it meant I wanted to see him tomorrow. But I did, oh how I did.

Another buzz.

HBG: I'm still replaying that kiss.

My skin was hot again, and before I could dunk my head once more I replied.

Me too.

WEDNESDAY
Weather: 70 degrees, Sunny

CHAPTER FOURTEEN

<u>Jess</u>

At seven twenty-five, I ordered a plain coffee from a rather peppy coffee purveyor at the counter who asked me twice if my name was Jess or Jeff.

"Not that you look like a Jeff," he said hastily. "But I thought it would be a fake name. Right? Because people use fake names for coffee all the time."

"Actually, my coffee shop name is Fred," I said in a deadpan voice.

He wrote *Fred* in Sharpie on the cup.

I added sugar to Fred's coffee and headed outside to keep my eyes peeled for Keats. I had no idea what he looked like, but I had a hunch he'd be able to find me, especially since there was only one other person at the outside tables, and she was doing a series of sun salutations in her maroon yoga pants while playing tic tac toe on her smartphone.

At seven-thirty on the dot, an egg-shaped, mint green electric car pulled up, the driver parking by the curb. A red-haired guy with ruddy cheeks and a small, pert nose got out and walked towards me. He carried a silver coffee thermos in one hand, and a tablet computer in a faux black bamboo case in the other. He wore a pink button-down shirt, crisp and untucked, but a size too large. I was willing to bet he'd borrowed it from an older brother. He had on shades. His were small and mirrored. He whipped them off as if he practiced the move in the mirror each morning, then flashed a whitened and brightened grin at me. He placed his tablet on the table.

"Jess Leighton, I'm Keats Wharton," he said and extended a hand.

"Pleasure to meet you. Do you want to get a coffee?"

Keats tapped the side of his silver thermos. "I went on a caffeine-free diet a year ago, and have literally never had more energy. I have my chia seeds mixed with unsweetened cherry juice right here."

I stifled a gag. I might be all about healthy eating, but there is just something patently wrong about the juxtaposition of *unsweetened* next to *cherry juice.* He settled into the empty chair, flicked open the tablet case, and plucked out a business card.

"A Thousands Words is a good name. What's your story?"

"I graduated from UCLA last fall. I started my agency a few months ago and we've done well so far. Let me show you some of our placements."

He tapped on the browser and showed me an image that I'd seen run yesterday in *In The Stars.* It was a shot of the bleached blond Jenner Davies serving meals at a soup kitchen, part of the actor's efforts to rehabilitate his image after the whacking he'd bestowed on the front desk clerk at the hotel during his *Planet Patrol* tirade.

"One of my photogs landed this shot last week of Jenner."

"Nice," I said because it wasn't a bad photo. It was probably planned; I suspected Jenner's publicist had arranged and ensured that photographers were on hand to capture the young, embattled actor's suddenly selfless ways. "And necessary," I added.

"Totally," Keats said, then scrolled to a few other shots —images of TV stars posed on red carpets, and unposed on Melrose as they shopped. When Keats stopped his show-and-tell, he took a long swallow of his chia-seed-festooned-beverage, and gave a satisfied smack of the lips. "But as for the job for you, I came to you because of the shot you took on Monday on Venice Beach. Of a certain starlet, her cherished dog, and her supposed new beau."

"*Supposed*? Miles is a 'supposed' for Riley?"

"Or simply one in an assembly line of beaus. I have it on good authority that the little Miss Riley Belle is not only dillying with Miles Sterling, but she's also dallying with the director of the film."

I didn't act shocked. I didn't let on that I was surprised. But I was. Riley didn't seem the type to get a little something going on with a director. She was talented, successful, and—well—smart. A smart girl wouldn't get involved with a notorious ladies' man who was also twice her age. Of course, being twice Riley's age only meant that Avery Brock, the English-born director of *The Weekenders*, was thirty-six.

The real issue though was that Avery Brock was taken. Married to a leggy Brazilian supermodel, he'd reportedly strayed from her before. There had never been photographic evidence of his past dalliances but it was Hollywood's worst-kept secret that he liked his ladies of the spring chicken variety, and had been rumored to have romped with a few other young stars. Would his wife take him back after yet another fling? He had a boyish face and the sort of moppish hair and sweet brown eyes that could make you want to forgive him if he gave you his best puppy dog look and a self-deprecating line.

The technique certainly worked on the entertainment press—I'd seen a video of him a few weeks ago being interviewed on a British entertainment show about *The Weekenders*. The interviewer asked why the script had languished so long in rewrites, and he'd simply remarked, "Eh, it's probably my own fault, right? I had to get in there and muck it all up. But I'm doing my best to *unmuck* my own mess."

Then he flashed his innocent grin, and the interviewer chuckled, won over by Avery's wit at his own expense.

"Their affair literally just started up, and they're meeting tonight after a script read-through," Keats said.

I wanted to add that they weren't just meeting after a script read-through; Riley was likely meeting her director *after* a read-through that came *after* a final dress fitting for her sister's wedding. But I kept my own secrets. Keats didn't need to know I was chasing a wedding shot of Riley's equally in-demand sister. "Do you know what time for the tryst?"

He shifted his right hand back and forth like a see-saw. "Anytime between nine and eleven. I can call you if I'm able to get more details. But for now, I know they're planning to meet over in this warehouse-y area in Burbank, not far from a UPS facility and some car detailing shops. It's very quiet, and there's a cul-de-sac at the end of the road, with a little trail that runs behind the businesses."

"Sounds sketchy," I said. All things being equal I'd have preferred a nice well-lit daytime location on the beach.

"It's all businesses. Busy during the day. Quiet at night. It's where you'd never expect a randy director to take the next ingénue he's trying to bang."

Keats gave me more details, and I wrote them down. Then, he paused and gave me a hard, expectant look. "Do you accept?"

"You have the money?"

He re-opened his tablet case, reached into an inside pocket, and pulled out a white envelope. I peeked inside, eyeing several crisp bills. I tried not to suck in a deep breath of enjoyment, but boy were they beauties. *And this little one goes to human anatomy. And this little one is for biochemistry.*

I'd wanted to be a doctor for as long as I'd ever wanted to be anything, and even the hospital dramas on TV with their multiple impalements and catastrophic accidents couldn't turn me off medicine. Medicine and me were a perfect match—logical, but intuitive too.

"So you'll get the shots?"

"Of course," I said, and dropped the envelope into my backpack, as if I were regularly accustomed to clients handing over such big and delicious unmarked bills.

"Will you email me the shots tonight?"

"No. I'll meet you tomorrow and give them to you in person. I'm sure you're an upstanding guy and all, but cash talks better than people."

He pointed his index finger at me and snapped. "Don't you know it. Girl after my own heart." He leaned back in his chair, a pleased look on his face that he'd initiated a new business transaction. Keats had more than Monopoly money to throw around, and if I were him I'd be satisfied too.

"I can meet you at twelve-thirty tomorrow to give you the pictures. Somewhere on the promenade?" I said, because I had my volunteer visit slated with Jennifer at the nearby hospital tomorrow afternoon.

"Perfect. Rosanna's Hideout?"

"I'll be there," I said, then thanked him and said goodbye.

When I was safely out of view, I swung my backpack around front, dropped my hand inside, and clasped the bills all the way home on my scooter as I marinated on the Riley and Avery connection. Maybe they were simply meeting about her production company. Maybe she was going to tap him to direct a project, rather than to direct his lips onto hers. A part of me hoped that was the case. I liked Riley; I didn't want her to be the type to canoodle with a married man. But if she was going to, I'd gladly take the money from a shot.

When I reached my apartment, Anaka was still sleep-ing. I gathered eggs from the fridge and sprayed a light dusting of olive oil on the skillet. As I cooked just the whites, I spied a pile of mail on the nearby table, includ-ing information from my bank about obtaining low-in-terest loans for medical school. I scoffed silently. I was allergic to loans, and determined to find the cash to pay for school, just as I'd done for the first four years.

My parents had planned to help pay for college, but they'd been blindsided. One day when I was a sophomore in high school, my dad came home from work, his jaw tensed, his eyes deadened. He held on tight to the door-frame that led into the kitchen. My mom was making dinner, and I was doing homework. "My company is be-ing investigated for fraud," he said in a monotone. He was a vice president at his firm.

The next several weeks spiraled into a dizzying domino-like rush of hushed conversations, tense mo-ments, and the kind of pathetic hope you harbor that the worst—well, financially, the worst—*isn't* about to hap-pen. My dad had always been an upbeat, happy man. At the time all this went down, he was anything but, and his moods rubbed off on my mom. They snapped at me for every little thing. Bed not made. Yelled at. Dishes not cleaned. Scolded. They were both tightly wound, knobs turned well past high for many months. His firm and its pension fund cratered, taking every employee's financial future in the rubble of the wrecking ball. The only good part was that my dad stayed out of the line of fire because he'd never been the one skimming off shareholders. Leaving with his reputation intact was all he could hope for as he looked for a new job.

Eventually, their moods unsoured when it set in that there was literally nothing to be done about the lost savings, except to start over. I resolved then to keep far away from loans. I vowed to stay in charge of my own fate, from school to money to what I ate to how I exercised.

But how could I take charge of my own future? Photography fit since I'd always had a steady hand, and a good eye, and had been taking pictures of anything from caterpillars to cakes to friends at the pool since I was in kindergarten. Sunsets were a favorite subject of mine too, and a peach-violet sky hanging over the Pacific adorned my bedroom wall. As I'd grown older, and had fallen in love with the world of celebrity around me, I captured photos of stars I saw on the streets, or the beach, or in stores.

They were everywhere in LA, and so paparazzohood was a natural career choice for a gal in need of a new nest egg. At first blush, my life appeared complicated, from balancing classes, chasing photos, planning for medical school, and managing my volunteer work. But in reality, my world was simple. I had one motivation–pay for school to become a doctor, and photos were my means.

Everyone had a motivation. Any decent screenwriting book will teach you that.

After I ate breakfast, I headed to the science building, considering what Riley's motivation with Avery might be. Was it a career move to land a role? Was it love? Or was it simply to scratch a naughty itch?

Later, when I finished my advanced bio quiz, I returned to that topic. If everyone had one, what was William's in taking pictures? Was he simply trying to pay for school? Or was there more? And were those kisses in the movie theater part of his goals, or were those kisses obstacles in the way of reaching his goal?

Whether he was the good guy or the bad guy was still up in the air.

CHAPTER FIFTEEN

<u>William</u>

As I walked into the kitchen buttoning my shirt, John peered at my feet from over the open the fridge door. "Something you want to tell me, Will?"

John took a swig from my milk carton, guzzling the beverage.

"Yes, as a matter of fact I do have something to tell you. And that is this—there is a store called the grocery store. You go there. You buy milk. You put it in your fridge. Across the hall. In your apartment," I said, pointing to the door.

John shrugged in a way that said he had no plans to do that. "By the way, you're out of milk, and so am I," he said. "That's why I stopped by. Plus, your door was unlocked. Dude, how many times do I have to tell you— you're living in L.A. now. Lock your door," he said as he thrust the carton into the shelf on the door. "Americans like myself are freeloaders."

I shook my head. "No kidding, and by the way, do not put the milk carton back in the fridge, especially since it's empty."

He yanked open the fridge door, plucked the milk-free carton from its spot, and slapped it on the counter. As the door fell shut, he eyed my bare feet again. "You moonlighting as a drag queen? C'mon, admit it. You were out last night with the whole full face on, right?" He mimed drawing a circle around his face. "Mascara. Eyeliner. Lipstick, right?"

"Yes. I was. I had my feather boa and even my fake eyelashes. Please don't borrow them without asking like you did the last time," I said as I finished buttoning the shirt, then began knotting a tie.

"Okay, seriously. Why are your toenails red, why don't you lock your door, and why in the hell are you wearing a tie?"

"One, my toenails are red because a hot girl dared me to do it. Two, sometimes I forget when I come home from a morning swim that the guy who lives across the hall from me has no sense of boundaries—my bad—and three, I have a job interview in thirty minutes."

John crooked out his elbow and stared at a nonexistent watch on his wrist, then at me. "You better get going. There is nowhere in this city you can get to in thirty minutes."

"It's one mile away at an agency for court translators."

"Like I said, there is nowhere in this city you can get to in thirty minutes."

"I'm on my way. I just need socks and shoes."

"No, go barefoot. That's how all the translators dress here," he said as he headed to the door. He stopped to glance back approvingly at my feet as I tugged on socks. "By the way, excellent answer to number one. Hot girl dares rock."

"That they do, man. That they do."

* * *

John was right about traffic, so I did that thing that Los Angelenos rarely do. I put one foot in front of the other and I walked. Along the way, I called James and gave him what little details I'd been able to glean so far.

"Decent start," he said begrudgingly after my report. "Now I need more. Oh, and I have a few more hours to throw your way on the other project we've been working on. Things are gearing up on that one, and now we just need to get the names in place," he said, and then shared more details.

"Great. I'm on it," I said, as I stopped at a light, waiting for traffic. "Maybe I can come on board full time when the school year is up," I suggested, and hoped to hell he didn't hear the twinge of desperation I felt.

He laughed. "We'll see, kid. You need to get me more info for my client from the field before I can even think about *that* request."

"I will," I said, feeling like the dog chasing the rabbit at the races. I wasn't sure if I'd ever catch up. I had little tempting teasers of opportunities all around me. But none were paying off yet.

"Oh, one more thing," James said before hanging up.

"Yes?"

"For the little project I just told you about. You're going to need a date. Think you can convince anyone to go with you?"

I gritted my teeth. James had such a fine way with words.

Then he explained why, and I instantly knew there was only one person I wanted to be my date. How to convince her would take some finesse though, especially since she'd taken off with barely a goodbye last night.

* * *

The no-nonsense woman with her brown hair pulled tightly in a bun peered at me over gold-rimmed glasses. Her office was a testament to bare-bones decorating. There was a pencil holder on her wooden desk, a black framed photo of her degree on the brown plywood walls, and a beige carpet. She tapped my résumé once more. "Impressive coursework. Impressive language skills. Excellent fluency. There's only one problem."

"Yes?"

"You don't have your degree."

"But I will in two months," I said, doing my best to keep the worry out of my tone. We were seated in her office at the employment agency that handled court translators.

"You should return then, Mr. Harrigan," she said, and slid my résumé across the desk back to me.

"Thank you very much," I said, flashing her my best *I appreciate your time* smile.

As I hit the sidewalk outside her office, I crumpled up the résumé and tossed it into the nearest trash can. In two months, I'd be back in England unless I found an employer who'd sponsor me to stay.

I ran a hand through my hair, frustration rooting deeper in my chest.

I grabbed my phone and looked at the time. I had a class in an hour. Jess had a class this morning too–advanced bio, she'd told me. Sighing heavily, I gave in once again. I searched for the location of the advanced biology class at the University of Los Angeles, and hoped to hell she wouldn't see me tailing her.

Especially since I'd need to ask her on a date for this weekend.

CHAPTER SIXTEEN

<u>Jess</u>

I could understand why detectives might have big butts. Stakeouts involved a lot of sitting. A lot of waiting. A lot of time to expand one's rear. That's why I stood instead, leaning back against the brick façade next to the Top-It-Yourself Yogurt Gallery across from the pair of potential dress boutiques.

I'd been here for more than an hour, and had already finished my chemistry work, as well as several more pages in my French translations. My camera strap was looped over my arm, and the camera itself was tucked neatly underneath my light jacket. The warm weather didn't call for a jacket, but I needed it to hide the obviousness of a camera with a lens on it. I had yet to spot the bride or any of her bridesmaids. All I'd seen was a large orange tomcat sunbathing in the window of a bauble and bead costume jewelry shop across the tree-lined street. I was going to have to call it a day soon, and figure the tip my mom had picked up had been a flimsy one, through no fault of her own.

After waiting twenty more minutes, I decided the bridesmaid final fitting was clearly a bust. I started to pack up, tucking away my coursework, and checking the zippers on my backpack. I walked down the block towards my scooter, when my finely-tuned celebrity-radar sensed a shift in the air. There was a sudden hushed energy near me, a low hum as shoppers and other passersby started to turn their heads, to tap their companions, to start the sentence *Is that…*

It was a question asked all day long all across Los Angeles where anyone at any minute might spot a celebrity.

In this case, they were asking the question I wanted to hear.

"Is that Riley Belle?" a girl in green leggings whispered.

"Is that Riley Belle?" a young mom pushing a stroller asked.

"Is that Riley Belle?" a guy in gym shorts said.

I swiveled around, scanned the sidewalk, then the one across the street, then I saw her. She'd just stepped out of a black town car. Her brown hair was windswept and luxurious and she wore huge red sunglasses, an orange fitted tee, and a jean mini-skirt. She was tall, and thin, and she didn't look like the rest of us. She looked like a star. Even as she tried to hide behind her glasses, there was just something special about her, as there always was with a silver screen beauty. They didn't look like civilians. They looked as if they'd descended from planets in the oh-so-far-above-average galaxy. She clutched her brown-and-tan chihuahua-mini pin dog against her chest, then carefully placed Sparky McDoodle on the sidewalk, his petite paws touching the concrete, his leather leash firmly in her hand. She started to walk in the direction of one of the boutiques I'd pinpointed, a focused look on her face. Her blinders were on; her eyes were only on her dog and her destination down the block.

As I reached for my camera, a lazy but loud meow boomeranged from across the two-lane street. The orange cat had caught sight of a squirrel in a tree and was waggling his furry cat butt, poised to chase. The second the tabby bolted for the squirrel, I heard the sound of nails scrabbling against sidewalk, and a loud, high-pitched bark that could only belong to a very small dog. Sparky McDoodle yanked hard on his leash, so hard that Riley Belle tripped, fell on one knee, and lost her grip on the leash. Her darling was off like a shot, racing to cross the street as a blue Prius turned the corner heading straight for the pint-sized pup.

Instinct took over. I stopped analyzing and ran into the street. The skidding sound of tires hit my ears as I stepped hard on Sparky McDoodle's leash. I lunged for the dog before he met the black rubber of a car's wheel.

My heart sped up and my focus narrowed, as my hands wrapped around his tan and brown belly. I scooped him up as the Prius jolted to a worried stop. Sparky McDoodle's ears were pinned against his head, and his heart galloped at a rabbit's pace. Expelling a deep breath I hadn't realized I was holding, I oriented myself. Still on high alert, I found myself standing in the street, next to a parked car. The driver of the Prius was opening his door, his hand on his heart, relief etched on his face, and several people stood and stared. Then someone clapped, and I walked back to the sidewalk, stepping onto the curb as Riley flung herself at me, wrapping her arms around me, and her dog.

"Oh my god. You saved Sparky McDoodle. You saved Sparky McDoodle. You saved Sparky McDoodle."

She was on repeat, and she couldn't stop saying those words. I handed Riley her dog, and he snuggled into her neck, as if he could escape into the safety of the familiar.

"He's so scared. His heart is beating so fast. But he's okay. He's okay. He's okay," she said, all the words tumbling out of her lipsticked mouth in a rush. Tears streaked down her cheeks. "You saved him. You saved my dog."

Riley pulled herself out of the hug, but kept a hand on my arm. Her voice started to break. "You have no idea how much this means to me."

I kind of did by then, but I figured it was best not to point that out. "He's really a sweet dog. And he loves you so much," I said, gesturing at Sparky McDoodle as he tried to burrow into Riley's arms.

"He was going after that cat, wasn't he?"

"I'm pretty sure he wanted to be on a first name basis with the orange tabby."

"I have been working so hard to train him to stop chasing cats. But he just can't resist them," Riley said.

"Well, it's kind of fun to chase something that's running from you," I said.

Riley smiled that winning smile she had that won over fans, and audiences, and evidently, a hard-edged paparazzo, because I was smiling too. She was infectious. Damn her.

"That's funny," she said and laughed. She gripped my arm. "What is your name?"

"Jess."

"Jess, I *have* to take you out to thank you. Would you let me buy you lunch or brunch or coffee or dinner or something sometime?"

"Sure," I said, putting absolutely no stock in the possibility that she'd follow through on her invite. It was an invite of the moment, born of adrenaline and gratitude, of a narrow escape, not of any real prospect of friendship. But she was glad her dog was safe, and so was I. The fact was, I'd have done the same for anyone's dog.

Riley reached into her electric blue purse made out of a quilted vinyl material. She found a pen and a piece of paper, wrote down her phone number, and handed it to me.

"That's my direct number. Call me anytime."

I folded it up and stuffed it into the front pocket of my jeans. I supposed I could call her and ask if she'd let me into her sister's wedding, but I had a wild hunch she'd say no. She looked at me with her big brown eyes. They had flecks of gold in them. "Now, give me yours."

I wrote down my digits and handed her the paper.

She tucked it into an inside pocket in her purse, beaming at me. "I'm totally calling you, and Sparky McDoodle and I are going to take you out. You have no idea. This dog is my soulmate. He is the love of my life."

Then her eyes shifted, and she seemed to notice something or someone down the street. She tipped her forehead to the end of the next block. "Say cheese," she whispered to me, and then she wrapped an arm around me. "That girl always gets my picture. Can you cheat to the right?"

I angled myself slightly as a girl in the distance with long red hair fastened in a tight braid snapped several shots from a long-lensed camera. It was Flash, or so I called her. Another young paparazzo, she must have been staking out Riley too, and I was about to become the subject of a celebrity photo spread, something I dreaded. My only hope was I would be identified merely as the "good samaritan" and not as a celebrity photographer.

In two seconds, Flash bolted, probably on her way to file the photo, and Riley turned back to me. "Thank you. My right side is so much better than my left side."

I nodded. "Totally understand. I don't like my left side for what it's worth. Even though no one takes my pic."

Riley nodded. "See? You understand. Everyone else also tries to placate me and blow nonsense out their mouths and say 'Oh, Riley, you look good from every side' but that's crap. Everyone has one side that's better than the other."

Riley said goodbye, and I figured it was the last time we'd exchange words, so I didn't waste one ounce of emotion on the guilt that slithered into me over the fact that I'd be taking her pictures tonight. I shed that feeling, as I slinked off, trying to make myself unnoticeable, even as a few people stopped to say I was brave, that I was awesome, that I was fast as hell to save a dog like that. I just nodded and smiled without showing my teeth, wishing I could pull out my camera and grab a shot of Riley walking into the boutique. But I didn't want to show my hand. I couldn't chance it. I didn't want anyone to snap a picture of me taking a picture of Riley. Besides, now I'd have to be extra careful tonight because she knew who I was. As she walked into the boutique, I ached to take just one shot of her entering the shop with Sparky McDoodle safely in her arms.

But I resisted.

I looked away, focusing on tonight and earning the other half of the $10,000, not the missed opportunity of a bridesmaid fitting. I pushed my bangs off my forehead, and shook my head, as if I could shake off the whole bizarre encounter. Then I saw a too-familiar face across the street. Decked out in jeans, and a blue faded T-shirt, William was reading a paper while sitting on a green slat-ted bench. His camera was slung around his neck, resting against his stomach. He wasn't even trying to hide his camera. He waved to me, and grinned broadly, and I wanted to smack him.

Because he wasn't here for Riley this time.

The bastard had followed me. Red smoke billowed out of my eyes. Flames of anger licked my chest. I marched across the street and right up to him. "Fancy meeting you here," I said through pursed lips.

"Seems J.P. keeps sending us on the same stakeouts. Riley this time."

I narrowed my eyes and shook my head. "Wrong an-swer," I hissed.

His eyes widened, and he gulped. "What do you mean?"

"I wasn't actually here on a Riley stakeout. I was here for another reason. J.P. didn't send me on this assignment. I sent myself, based on a tip I got myself. Ergo, you weren't sent here by JP. Ergo, you're following me."

"Or, I'm working for another agency now?" he offered up meekly.

I shook my head. "What's your story? What's your real story? Because you're not really a paparazzo."

CHAPTER SEVENTEEN

<u>William</u>

I could have spun a new lie. I could have concocted some sort of fable, pretended I didn't see her, or stalked off to my bike.

But she'd busted me, and it was time to man up.

Her arms were crossed and I swore I could see smoke pouring forth from her nostrils. She was going to walk away when she heard. But she deserved the truth. She didn't deserve, though, to have everyone nearby witness our conversation. A throng of onlookers across the street watched Jess. Some even had their cell phones poised, ready to capture her.

"Can we go somewhere and talk?" I said quietly.

She looked around, glancing up and down the sidewalk. "The street is fine with me."

"Right, and me too. But you still have crowds of people checking you out." I pointed to the other side of the street as surreptitiously as I could. She stole a look. "You're the girl who saved the star's dog."

She huffed, grabbed me by the camera strap and dragged me around the corner to a quieter block, then pulled me into a long entryway that led into a store selling polka-dotted dresses for toddlers that would become stained with organic ketchup or fair-trade-harvested chocolate syrup the first day they were worn.

"You're not a paparazzo," she repeated. "You didn't recognize Lolanna, you didn't go for the shot of the LGO ladies at the salon, you barely even tried to get Riley's and Miles' picture at Venice Beach, and on top of that, I *know* J.P. didn't send you here because J.P. didn't send me here. Who are you?"

I swallowed, then took a deep breath. I didn't try to curl up my lips or sling a zingy comeback. Instead, I answered her without sarcasm or a smirk. "You're right. I'm not here on assignment. J.P. told me earlier today he won't have any more work for me because I only got one shot—Monica. I don't recognize celebrities, Jess," I said, and it felt like a confessional, and I was glad I no longer had to lie about my terrible inability to spot famous faces. Telling her I'd lied wasn't going to win her over, but I still had to come clean. "I've been moonlighting for a private detective agency in the hopes of finding a permanent job so I can stay in the States after I graduate."

Her jaw dropped. "You're a private detective?"

I shifted my hand back and forth as a see-saw. "Sort of."

"Sort of? What the hell?"

"I'm doing some work for one. Well, a security firm."

"And that work involved following me? Me?" She tapped her chest, as if she could make it extra clear precisely who I was hunting.

"I'm not following *you,* per se."

"Me per se? What the hell is *me per se*?"

I scrubbed a hand across my chin, wishing this didn't sound so clandestine. But there was no true way to finesse saying *I was following you but I really dig you too, so can we still go out?*

"My Uncle James runs a security firm. He has a private investigation division. I have to go back to England in two months when my student visa expires, unless I can score a job with a company here willing to sponsor me for a work visa, so I've been doing everything I can to find work because I'm dying to stay. I'd done a little bit of work here and there for a private investigator in London my first two years at university. I took photos of cheating wives, cheating husbands, suspicious business partners, that sort of thing people hire private detectives for."

"Hate to break it to you, but I'm not married, not cheating, not in business with anyone, and not doing a single fucking thing wrong," she said and emphasized her indignance by poking me hard in the sternum.

"Ouch," I said because it actually hurt.

"Oh, I'm so sorry. Are you wounded?"

"I'll manage," I muttered, thinking asking her to be my date this weekend might not pan out. Call me crazy, but I had a wild hunch Jess wasn't so fond of me right now.

"Who are you working for? Who is your uncle's client?"

"I can't tell you everything."

She raised her hands, giving me a clear brushoff. "Whatever. I'm done. See you later. I have work to do."

I reached for her arm, clasping my hand around her wrist. She flinched, but turned back to me.

"I can't tell you everything," I said. "But I can tell you everything I know to be true. James's firm was hired by a publicity shop. They rep a bunch of actors, talent, writers, whatnot. They wanted to know how the paparazzi were getting so many shots of their clients. That's the assignment I was on."

"How?" she asked with a scoff. "Because that's what paparazzi do."

"They wanted details. Specific details. How the tips work, how a stakeout works. To better help clients who are always getting captured on camera when they don't want to be."

"And they assigned you to follow me? Why me? And don't say it's because I'm the best, because I'm not."

"They didn't assign me to follow anyone in particular. They just want general intel to share with their client. James won't even tell me who the client is who wants the info. I swear, I have no idea. I went to J.P. and I pretended I was a photog so I could get a sense of how it worked, what he heard, how the assignments came in, how a stakeout went. I'm just supposed to get intel for James to share with his client."

"And what have you learned, private dick?"

I spoke softly. "That when you're pissed —"

She cut me off again. "Don't. Don't make one of those cutesy little comments that guys make in the movies. *Like when you're pissed, you have this vein in your forehead that pops out and it looks so adorable,*" she said in a sing-song voice.

"Do people think veins in foreheads are adorable? Maybe it's an American thing, but that's not really what does it for me when it comes to a hot girl like you."

"I'm not even going to ask what does it for you when it comes to a hot girl because that is so not the conversation we're having right now."

"Can I tell you what I've learned, Jess? Since you asked."

"Fine."

"That when you're pissed, I don't like it. And I don't want you to be pissed. Because I like you. I like spending time with you. Because I'm completely attracted to you, I love kissing you, I want to go out with you–that is all real."

She rolled her eyes. It was a champion-level eye roll. "How does that have to do with anything? You wanted intel. You used me. You kissed me and used me, and followed me. Whatever happened between us is over."

I couldn't let that happen. I had to lay it out for her as best I could, regardless of whether asking her to be my date this weekend was even still a remote possibility. The truth mattered more than the job James had for me. The truth mattered because I wasn't the kind of guy who lied to a girl about liking her. I liked Jess, and if the State Department booted me out of this country in two months or not, I wanted her to know the truth.

"The kisses weren't lies," I said, and nearly reached for her hand, wanting to reassure her through touch. But words would have to suffice, since her arms were crossed over her chest. "The conversations weren't lies. I love talking to you and hanging out with you and taking you to the movies. And for the first two days, I didn't follow you. We were on the same shoots, and yes, I was trying to learn what I needed for James simply by taking the pictures too. But you were so good at the job, and so good at getting pictures, and I'm dying to stay in America. I love it here. You're lucky enough to be from here and to get to stay," I said, my voice now a desperate plea for her to understand me. I didn't know that she, or anyone frankly would, but I needed to try. "I want to stay in the same way that you want to go to medical school. It's my future, it's my dream. My student visa ends soon and I've been looking for work everywhere and I keep hoping I'll get this job or that job, but I've been getting turned down for everything, which sucks royally. Here was this chance with James and I'm trying desperately to keep up, so I followed you here to see what you were up to next," I said, and it pained me to admit it, but the truth was all I had to stand on. "I'm sorry. I'm really sorry."

"You should be sorry. That's crappy," she said, her features tight and angry. "Following people is shitty."

"But don't you kind of follow people for your job too?"

"Are you calling me out on being the pot calling the kettle black?"

"Kind of, yeah. But it's true. I follow people. You follow people. What's the difference? Neither of the people we follow wants to be followed."

"Nobody wants to be followed, William! But the people I follow are celebrities. So it's fair game. You played me, so I'll see you later," she said, holding up her hand like a stop sign, then turning her back to me as she began to walk off.

As if it were happening at a rapid-fire pace, I saw my future crater as the distance between us grew with each step she took. The letter from the State Department loomed in front of me, like a red countdown clock blaring out the remaining days, hours, minutes. I had one job prospect and I had to do whatever I could to keep it afloat. Jess was my way in. She was the *only* lead in my grasp for the field work James had me chasing. Without her, I'd have nothing for James on how the paparazzi worked, and I needed that for his client. I couldn't lose Jess or I'd be leaving on a jet plane for the homeland in two months, and the prospect of dreary old England was a lead weight in my stomach. I desperately needed Jess; but I also had something tantalizing to offer her.

"Wait," I shouted as she reached the curb. "Jess, please wait."

"Why?" she asked, barely acknowledging me.

I raced to her and placed my palms together, a plaintive plea for her to forgive me for lying.

"What I'm trying to say is I truly am sorry, and I want to make it up to you. And I have a way to make it up to you."

She scoffed, and started to walk off. "Right. Sure."

"I just told you my uncle runs a security firm. His firm is handling the Bowman-Belle wedding. I can get you into the wedding." I gulped, but moved on quickly, because she'd say yes, she'd surely say yes, right? "If you'll be my date."

CHAPTER EIGHTEEN

<u>Jess</u>

My jaw dropped. It likely clanged on the sidewalk with a loud crashing din because that's how shocked I was.

There was no way he'd just said the most beautiful, wondrous words. Not the *be my date* part. But the *get you into the wedding* words. Because those were magical. Those were the keys to the medical school kingdom.

I stared at him, studying his face for clues. Was he tricking me? Playing me again? Were his eyes lying to me? Those gorgeous gray storm clouds seemed honest and true. I didn't try to be tough or cool. Instead, I let down my guard. I wanted this. I needed this. "You can? For real?"

"Yeah," he said and nodded a few times. "James is having me handle some of the desk work, records and stuff, so I'll be at the wedding. I can sneak you in."

"You'll be at the wedding?" I asked again because this felt too good to be true.

Which meant there was no way it could be true.

"Yes. I'm helping him to keep track of the list because we're using a new app that matches pictures of faces to the guest list, and I set it up for him. I'll get your name on the list as a wedding guest. I'll be there and he asked a few of us to make sure we blend in by having dates. Once all the guests have checked in, he wants us to appear as if we're guests as well, so the other guests feel more comfortable."

I'd heard about that app. It was being tested by a few event planners who had raved about it, but it wasn't well-known or widely used yet. "Right, they don't want to feel like their every move is being watched by security. But what's the name of the app?" I asked, jutting out my chin as I tested him.

He rattled off the name, and as he said it, a layer of doubt peeled away from me. Underneath it, the shimmering possibility of no longer crashing, but feasibly attending, the wedding of the century bubbled up. Still, I wanted to be certain. "You're not playing me? You can really can sneak me in?"

"I'm not. I swear I'm not and we have to be super careful, but I can definitely get you in, under the radar."

I lifted my chin. "Where's the wedding?" I was tense all over as I waited for him to answer. If he said Malibu, I was gone.

"Ojai Ranch. Chelsea Knox's home. Saturday. Two p.m. In her backyard. In between the pools."

Excitement roared through my veins as he said all the right words. His answers matched Anaka's info. This changed everything. If William was willing to help me get into the wedding, then I didn't care that he'd played me. Because he wasn't truly a player; he was the reformed bad boy, and boy did I like that archetype. "I think I'm in love with you," I said, then impulse took over and I leaned forward, placed a palm on his cheek, which was the tiniest bit stubbly, which was the biggest bit sexy, and planted a kiss on his other cheek.

He blushed. "Well, I think I'm in love with you, too."

"Okay, so what's next?"

"There's only one condition to this."

My heart sank. I did not want a condition. I wanted access. I wanted it handed to me on a silver platter. But nothing was free. "What's the condition? Does it involve chocolate cake or huckleberry pie? Please say no."

"Someday, you are going to want a chocolate cake. For now, here's the deal–I help you. You help me. You help show me the inner workings of how you get the pics. I'll never share your name with my client. I'll never let on where I learned it all. But you'll show me around. Bring me with you for the next few days so I have enough to report back to James and by extension to his client. That way I can keep my job for now, and that job helps you get into the wedding without anyone knowing you're a photographer."

Fine, so he wasn't Captain Altruism. But then I wasn't either. Besides, given what he was offering me, there was very little William could have asked in return that I'd have turned down. I didn't want him to know I was putty though. I breathed out hard, as if the request bothered me. The truth was, I'd be grateful for his company tonight in the deserted warehouse section of Burbank. I wasn't keen on a solo trip, and William was six feet tall and then some, and his chest had a nice breadth to it, and his arms were well-muscled, and he could be my bodyguard without even knowing it.

I held out a hand. "Partners."

He shook. "Partners."

To be continued...William and Jess' love story and Hollywood wedding-crashing adventure continues in the novel STARS IN THEIR EYES.

STARS IN THEIR EYES

A 250-page novel in the
Wrapped Up in Love Series

Book 2

By Lauren Blakely

ABOUT

Stars in Their Eyes

A sexy and swoony new adult romance...

Celebrity photographer and college senior Jess Leighton desperately needs to crash the wedding of the year. Snapping just one pic of the A-list Hollywood couple tying the knot will pay her way through grad school. But with security tighter than the bride-to-be's corset, she'll need more than her camera and smarts, she'll need help from her biggest rival--hot, British, motorcycle-riding William Harrigan, whose sexy accent can melt the panties off any woman. He's the last person Jess should trust, but he's her only ticket in.

William Harrigan wants one thing – to stay in L.A. past college graduation. With a student visa set to expire, the clock is ticking. When he lands a gig that pairs him with the beautiful blond spitfire Jess, he's scored his best shot at living out the American dream. Winning her trust would be a whole lot easier, however, if he didn't have ulterior motives...

But there's no faking the intense attraction between them. Try as they might to resist each other, soon sparks are flying, as they devise a plan to sneak into the ceremony. But when Jess' new celebrity client raises the stakes, she starts to smell blackmail, and soon she and Will are chasing down cheating directors, staking out clandestine trysts, and making fake IDs, all while sneaking scene-stealing kisses and hot nights together.

The audience loves a happy ending, but in a town where everyone's acting and no one's playing by the rules, can Jess and William find their own ever after in time?

CHAPTER ONE

<u>Jess</u>

"Do you realize your shirt has been touched by the blessed? That you have Sparky McDoodle scent on you? We could auction this off." Anaka pointed to my black V-neck that I'd picked up from Target a few weeks ago.

"Who on earth would buy this shirt?"

"Are you kidding me? This is the shirt that the girl who saved Sparky McDoodle was wearing. You're all over the gossip sites." Anaka clicked to one of our regular online haunts.

The photo of Riley Belle and me was on the home page with the words in big, blazing font "Save the cat? Save the dog!" It was a takeoff on a popular screenwriting book, *Save the Cat*, that suggested writers should always find a way to have the hero or heroine do something noble, like save a cat, to win the audience's sympathy.

I pulled off my T-shirt and tossed it into the hamper in my room. "I need to jump in the shower. Don't you dare steal my Sparky McDoodle-marked T-shirt while I'm in there," I said, and wagged a finger at her. I headed into the bathroom and closed the door most of the way.

A minute later Anaka called out. "Oh my god. We have our first bidder, Jess."

"A good auctioneer would drive the price way up. But, while you're working the bids, can you please pick out a new shirt for me to wear?"

As I shampooed my hair, Anaka tossed out another question. "Why are you showering again? Supposedly to get dog scent off you?"

"If I go to the Riley stakeout tonight smelling like her dog, and if she brings him along, then he might run over to me again," I shouted, so she could hear me above the water.

"Hmm," she said loudly. "I think there's a logical fallacy in that."

"What is the logical fallacy you've uncovered?"

"Dogs don't sniff out their own scent. They sniff out the scent of other animals or of people."

"Either way, I don't want to take a chance."

"Funny. But I don't believe you."

I rinsed the conditioner out of my hair, turned off the shower and grabbed a towel. I wrapped it around me, then poked my head out the open door. "Why don't you believe me?"

"I think you might be showering for the hot British guy."

"Please," I said, rolling my eyes to show how little I cared about William.

"It's true. You can admit it now, or admit it later, but admit it you will."

"We are only a means to an end for each other."

"I don't believe you for one iota of a second," Anaka said, falling back on her red-and-pink bedspread. "Why else would you team up with him?"

"Um. Hello. He's getting me into the wedding."

"If he were just getting you into the wedding, you'd just go to the wedding with him. But you're not. You're going out with him at night."

"On a stakeout, Anaka!"

"That's what you call it, and maybe it is one, but the best friend always knows when love is in the air," she said, as she tossed me a dove gray shirt with glittery stars embedded in the sleeves.

"Seriously?" I held up the shirt. "This is your shirt. And do you even own anything without bling?"

"You know I don't believe in wearing plain clothes. That's the simplest thing I own," Anaka said, and gestured to her own outfit. She wore a purple scoop-neck shirt, a jean skirt, thigh-high striped gray and lavender socks, and heeled lace-up boots with a Victorian flare to them. Her black hair was swept into a twist on top of her head.

I marched into my bedroom, grabbed a blue T-shirt from a drawer and pulled it on, along with underwear and jeans. I returned to her room, and held out my arms for her appraisal.

"Perfect. You skinny bitch."

"You're exactly the same size."

She grabbed at her belly. "Don't make me show you my love handles. Because I will."

I poked her stomach with a finger. It was flat. "You're beautiful."

"And so are you," she said emphatically. "Whether you're a skinny bitch or not."

"Now you're just practicing all your *help the friend who used to have an eating disorder* tactics," I said.

"Is it working?"

"Like a charm." Then I snapped my fingers when I remembered I needed something from my brother for the wedding. "Hold on. I need to send Bryan a note," I said, grabbing my phone and firing off a quick email request to him. I dropped the phone on my bed, then returned to the altar of the bathroom mirror where I applied a light dusting of blush to my cheeks, then blow-dried my hair, as Anaka and I chatted. "And now," I said, turning off the hairdryer, "I'd like to become a pixie-cut redhead."

Anaka rubbed her hands together, made a beeline for her closet, and pulled out a hot pink box. She flipped it open, and extracted one of her many wigs.

"Voila." She gave me the stocking cap to hide and flatten my own hair, and I tucked my hair into it, then pulled on the auburn-ish wig and considered my reflection.

"He's going to think you're so hot as a redhead," she said.

"I'm wearing it so Riley doesn't recognize me."

"If William can't keep his hands off you, don't say I didn't warn you. But wait...don't forget the golden rule of a good romantic comedy film," she said in a teacherly tone as she wagged a finger at me.

"What's that?"

"Think of all the good ones. *Late Nights in San Francisco, When My Best Friends Met, You've Got Me.*"

"Love those," I said, pining momentarily for the golden days of romantic comedy, and not just the times of black and white, but a few decades ago, when stories were fresh, when the leads held out, when the writing wasn't predictable.

"They don't make movies like that anymore. I'll tell you the big flaw with rom-coms today."

"Please tell me."

"They let the leads hook up too early. A good romantic comedy needs to be full of simmering *will they-won't they* tension until well into the third act. Then the first kiss can come. Then the misunderstanding. Then the final scene when they make up and live happily ever after."

"Delayed gratification," I said with a nod. "Then it's too bad I already kissed William twice."

"We're just talking about the movies, Jess. In real life, you can and should kiss him three times tonight."

Like that was going to happen.

CHAPTER TWO

William

I spread the blueprints against the wooden gate outside a branch of the Burbank Public Library as we began our wedding planning in a well-lit spot before the stakeout. It was ten minutes after eight, the sun had set, and Jess scanned the map from the light of an old-fashioned streetlamp nudged into a corner nook in the reading garden.

I'd brought three pages of the layout of Chelsea Knox's spacious property that James had shared with me when I was working on the computer maintenance for him. To develop a full picture of the venue, I'd compared his blueprints to the publicly available photos from real estate listing services, flyover photos, and a Google image search.

"Veronica's going to get ready here, right inside the east wing of the house. We've all been instructed that absolutely no one is allowed in the east wing under any circumstances," I said, tapping a bedroom layout on the second floor that overlooked the ostrich and llama pool. "The ceremony itself will be under the bamboo veranda, which is right next to the pond full of mechanical koi."

"Mechanical koi?"

"Chelsea Knox thinks it's inhumane to raise fish in any form," I said as if the answer were obvious.

"I trust there won't be salmon on the menu?"

"There are three menus. Dairy vegetarian, vegan and raw."

"Will you be guarding the crudités then?"

I laughed. "I'm sure there will be a mad rush for the carrot sticks. We're going to have plainclothes security officers all throughout the grounds, around the perimeter, but also along the driveway, inside the house, and by the pools."

"What are they doing about the possibility of helicopter shots?" she asked, thoroughly running through her questions, looking all the more alluring in her redheaded wig tonight. Though, in all honestly, she'd be hot to me if she had purple hair. Blue hair. Green hair. Didn't matter. It was her attitude that had hooked me from the start.

"They're renting a tent."

"Smart plan."

"And James also has a helicopter for security in the sky. To watch over and make sure everything is safe. So even though you're going to be on the guest list and James told me to bring a date, we have to be incredibly careful to keep you under the radar. I don't want you to get caught, and I don't want to screw over James either. My thinking is we need a fake name for you and a fake ID. We don't want anything traced back to you or me or him when the pictures leak out. Enough people know you're a shooter. This way, neither James nor the wedding planners would be able to put two and two together that the shots came from you."

Her eyes met mine. For one of the first times, she seemed nervous, worried even. "You're not going to get in trouble for this, are you? I don't want your uncle to get hurt either."

Her concern was sweet, and worked its way around my heart. "Don't worry. You're good at your job. I've been watching you," I said with a wink, and she rolled her eyes.

"Seriously though?"

"I'm serious. Look, you know how this goes. We can do everything we can to keep the wedding private, but someone is going to get a shot somehow. I know I'm taking a risk, but I'd just as soon it be you who gets the inevitable shot, so let's make sure of that."

"You're risking a lot to get me in there," she said softly.

I didn't say anything at first. Just kept my eyes on her. "I know."

"Thank you," she said.

"Hey, as long as you are as sneaky as I know you can be, the picture won't be traced to you or James or me. It will just seem like it came from some random guest. Hence, why we need to make sure there is no Jess Leighton at the wedding."

She swiped her hand through the air as if she were wiping away her identity. "Jess Leighton won't exist on Saturday."

"You can get a fake ID then?" I asked, and I liked that Jess and I were a team now. We both needed each other. We'd come to a truce, and we each could help the other.

"I can get a fake ID, but my fake name is Fred. Is that going to be a problem?" she asked in mock seriousness.

"Maybe a little. Any chance you could be a Fredericka?" I suggested.

"I can totally pass for a Fredericka," she said in some sort of random indistinct accent.

I laughed. "What the hell kind of attempt at an accent was that?"

She shrugged sheepishly. "Italian?"

I placed a hand on her shoulder, gripping her lightly and shaking my head. "No, that was not an Italian accent whatsoever," I said to her in Italian, and she furrowed her brow. "But you are so fucking hot even when you try to put on a ridiculous accent that I still want to fuck you. Especially since you look even sexier with that red wig on."

She tilted her head curiously, her fake hair moving perfectly in synch with her face. "You speak Italian too?"

I nodded. "I do."

"What did you just say?"

"That I'm glad you're not mad at me anymore."

"Who said I'm not mad at you?" she asked, shooting me a narrow stare.

"You're here with me and we're plotting to rappel *Espionage Style* into a wedding this weekend," I said, naming the famous spy movie franchise. "I'm giving you something you need and you're giving me something I need."

She sliced a hand through the air. "And that's all."

I grabbed her hand, and kissed her palm. Cheesy, I know. I wasn't above a cheesy move. "I'm sorry," I said, again in Italian.

"How do you know so many languages?"

"My parents know Spanish. They both studied it in school. They spoke it at home so we could know another language early on. I was good at it. Picked it up quickly. Matthew knows it too, so we all talked to each other in Spanish. When I was in secondary school, I spent a summer in Italy and learned Italian."

"You picked it up in one summer?"

I nodded, proud of my accomplishments in this area. "You know how some people are crazy good at math? They just know how to do complex math from an early age or play piano really well from when they were younger?"

"Yes."

"I'm like that with languages. Maybe it makes me a freak. But it's just something I can do. I started teaching myself Asian languages when I was teenager and I refined that here in college."

"That's amazing," she said, shaking her head. "I guess you're more than just the Hot British Guy."

I stroked my chin. "Tell me more about this Hot British Guy."

She reached into her back pocket for her cell phone, swiped her thumb across the screen and showed me a text message from me. Labelled *HBG*.

"My text message name?"

She nodded. "Yes."

I grinned wildly. "I need you to know that I completely approve of that name. And now I need to give you a nickname. How about Hot American Girl?" I suggested but we both cringed at the same time.

"HAG," she said, crinkling her nose.

"Sexy American Girl," I offered, but then nixed it quickly too.

"SAG is bad."

I snapped my fingers. "We have the same problem with Beautiful American Girl. Damn you hot American girl with the AG initials."

She laughed and her lips curved up in the sexiest smile. I brushed the pad of my index finger against her lips. "Jess," I said softly. "I'm so sorry I deceived you about the job, but all this?" I gestured from her to me and back as I looked in her eyes. They were big and round and looked so damn vulnerable as she nodded for me to keep going. "It's all real. I think you're hot and beautiful and sexy and funny and smart and it drives me absolutely crazy how you try so hard to dislike me."

She rolled her eyes. "What if I'm not trying? What if I really do dislike you?" she tossed back, her eyes sparkling now, saying otherwise.

"Then stop me before I kiss you again," I said bending my head to her neck to layer a soft kiss on her skin. But just as I was about to map her with my lips, she pressed her hands against my chest.

"William," she said, her voice a warning. "I don't want to be used."

"How is it using you if I kiss you?"

"Weren't you kind of using me before?"

"And we're using each other now. But we're also not using each other because we're being open about it. Yes, I needed to understand how you did your job, and now you're telling me and that's helping me with the most important thing to me–potentially staying here. And now you're using me and I'm helping you with information so you can possibly get the most important thing to you–money for med school. So we're using each other to help the other person get what they most want."

I glanced down. Her hand was still on my chest, but instead of pushing me away, she fisted a handful of fabric. "Use me," she said in a purr and tugged me in for a kiss. A quick, searing, hot kiss that fogged my head. The taste of her was intoxicating, like summertime and honey. Within seconds, I'd forgotten where we were, what we were doing, and who we were staking out. All I wanted was more of her.

She broke the kiss. "What did you really say to me in Italian?"

I brushed her hair from her ear, buzzed my lips along her neck and nibbled on her earlobe. Then I whispered, "How much I want you."

She gasped as if I'd just said the most scandalous thing. "*William.*"

I pulled back. "That's the truth, Fredericka."

She looked away, as if she were trying to avoid the prospect of an *us*. Jess was back and forth tonight. Hot and cold. She was kissing me, and pushing me away. Maybe she was warring with herself over whether she was truly mad at me or not.

"Moving on to my secret identity for the wedding," she said, back to brisk, business-like Jess. "Can I just pick a simpler name? Like Claire?"

"Claire with the red hair," I said, shifting gears too. "What's your alibi?"

"I'm a celebrity dog trainer, of course," she said, with a glint in her eye. I recognized that look—it was the one she had when she was excited about a plan or a strategy.

"Naturally."

"I can have J.P. make that ID for me by Friday. Claire Tinsley sounds like a perfect name for a celeb wedding guest-slash-celebrity dog trainer."

"Great. You'll be a solo guest, so you'll come to the gates one hour before the wedding starts, and Sal—he's with us and he'll be doing the check-in—will have your name on the list as Claire Tinsley."

"And then I just walk inside and blend in with the other guests?"

"Not that simple. They'll be checking for cameras. They're asking guests to leave their cell phones at the check-in."

"Ouch. But that's standard procedure at these events," she said quickly.

"I don't really know how you'll get a camera in, Jess. I mean, I can get you in, but that's as much as I can do. It's not as if I can smuggle in a camera and disassemble it, and leave it in parts in the kitchen cabinets and then have you reassemble it, like in some heist movie."

"Let me think on the camera issue and whether any heist flicks are actually realistic and useful research for me when it comes to reassembly. But I'll come up with something. I definitely don't want you to get caught smuggling, and I promise you won't get in trouble at all."

"Aww. I think that might be the nicest thing you've said to me, Jess. Will you be wearing a wig on Saturday too? Because you look hot in this red wig."

"Maybe I'll be a brunette with long wavy hair and a flouncy white floral party dress. No one would ever suspect it was me."

"Good. And that's the key to pulling this off. You're just a wedding guest, you'll take surreptitious pictures during the ceremony, and you get the hell out. Try not to talk to anyone. Even if we have you on the list, I don't want anyone to know you or to be able to remember you. James is kind of a prick, but I don't want to screw him over."

"I totally understand," she said, then her phone beeped. She checked it and read a message out loud. "*Source says they'll be finishing up the read-through within an hour, then heading to Burbank. All systems go.*" She tapped out a reply, then turned to me. "And now for my part of the information exchange. That was a message from my client, letting me know that his source says the targets will be heading to the rendezvous point shortly."

"So that's how it works? Random tips?"

"I don't know who his source is and I don't ask, but it's probably some assistant on the *The Weekenders*. Generally speaking, the sources are either assistants, hotel doormen, maitre d's, or publicists."

"And are they all on the take?"

"Some of them. When the tips come from assistants, it's either because they're power hungry and this is their way of feeling in control, or they're getting paid off by the photo agencies to call in locations. Then there are tips that come from assistants because the stars want their photos taken. It's this weirdly symbiotic relationship. Stars supposedly hate us, right?" she said, referring to the paparazzi.

"Sure," I said, agreeing with her.

"But yet they need publicity. They need to maintain their fame. There are only a handful of stars so big and so secure in their careers that they don't need to court the press and the paparazzi at all. Everyone else, they kind of want and need to be seen. Then, there are stars who make sure to have very specific photos taken. You know Range Treadman?"

"The Australian actor," I said, feeling like I'd answered a game show question correctly. Given my lack of interest in celebrities, the fact that I'd known the name of even one felt like a huge accomplishment.

"He takes his kids to the same playground every Monday at three-fifteen. He's always there, always happy, always involved with his kids. And every photog shows up because his press people put out an alert to let all the agencies know where he'll be. Because he *wants* to have the image of the family guy out there. So he goes to the playground, acts like he doesn't see us, but smiles the whole time. It's his way of controlling his image. He makes it seem as if we just happened to catch a shot of him on the playground."

"What about all the shots of stars leaving their gyms or going to yoga? Is that the same thing? They want to be seen being fit and healthy?" I asked, rattling through some of the questions James had said he wanted answered for his PR client.

"A lot of photogs and their agencies just keep a running list of who goes to which gym," she said, then named the locations of the most popular gyms for the famous. "Then photogs just camp out and wait. Some of the regular guys who shoot all day—they just have these spots they go to and kind of lie in wait for stars to come by. A lot of personal trainers tip us off too. Trainers are the biggest gossips in the world. They also know their stock rises if they're *outed* as the trainer of someone famous."

"This is great," I said, mentally filing away the juicy info.

"And then there are some trainers who might not be tipsters yet, but you still see them in so many pictures with so many different stars that you start to recognize them as well. Like Nick Ballast's trainer," she said, and I arched an eyebrow in question. The name felt vaguely familiar, and it tripped on the edge of my tongue as a name J.P. had mentioned once.

"He's on *The Weekenders*. With Riley. Former child star, had a weight problem for a bit, now works out like crazy. His trainer has this goatee," she said, stroking her chin. "They're always together now because Nick is Mr. Exercise and Healthy Eating these days."

"Gotcha."

"And I suspect Nick *wants* to make sure those pictures get out," she said, and her voice sounded slightly strained when she talked about Nick.

"What about the pictures someone doesn't want out? The meltdown shot, the yelling at the front desk clerk shot, like Jenner Davies? Because you couldn't miss that video. It was everywhere."

"Sometimes, those are just dumb sheer luck. Or a series of tips and you keep whittling them down, and following someone 'til you finally get the money shot."

"Speaking of the money shot, I'm guessing we should get going?"

"Yes, but you know how you said they're going to be checking everyone for cameras at the wedding?"

"Right."

"I think I'm going to need to check you right now."

"What? You still don't believe I am who I say I am?"

"I believe you, but that could be because you're an incredible actor. Fool me once, shame on you. Fool me twice, shame on me. I need to be the only one getting pictures right now of Riley and her director."

"You're going to pat me down?" I raised an eyebrow and grinned, then held my hands up high and spread my feet wide. "Have at it, Doctor Leighton. Have at it."

She looked at her feet. "I'm just being careful."

"Please be very careful when you touch my stomach then. As you know, I'm highly ticklish."

Jess

I started by placing my hands on his shoulders. They were strong and firm. Running my hands quickly down his arms, I felt his biceps and triceps next, and they were so sculpted and toned to perfection, that I did everything

I could to catalog the proper names of the muscles so that I would only think about him scientifically, and not about the way he felt under my hands.

Because he felt fantastic. He had the kind of body I could hold onto all night long. The kind I wanted to explore with hands, lips and tongue.

Moving quickly over his chest, then down to his flat belly, I pressed my lips tightly together, so I wouldn't make a sound, or release a breath, or even utter a word because his abs were so trim, defined, and neatly lined. If I wanted to, I could have traced the edge of each one, lined the contours of his smooth body. I closed my eyes for a second, inhaled sharply through my nose, and patted his hips, outer thighs, and down to his calves.

"There, done. You're good," I said as if I were a TSA agent finishing a pat-down.

"You didn't get my inner thighs, Jess," he said in a totally serious voice, egging me on.

"I trust you."

"Are you sure? You don't want to check my thighs? Just to be safe. I could be hiding something," he said, raising an eyebrow.

"Are you? Hiding something?"

"Honestly, right now, it's not very hidden."

I bit my lip, and tried so hard to resist. But I couldn't help myself. I cast my eyes downward and caught a glimpse of the bulge in his pants. Restraint flew out the window. "You liked the pat down?"

"I did," he said, his eyes darker, wilder. His voice was huskier. "Is this all clear now?" he gestured to his crotch. "I'm not using you. I meant everything I said in Italian, and everything I said in English too about you being sexy, funny and smart."

Sharp, hot tingles took my body hostage. They demanded squatter's rights in my heart. My brain was commandeered by a heightened desire that flooded every damn cell in my entire system. I wanted to climb on top of him and kiss him. Then strip him down to nothing and touch him all over. I wanted to lick him up and down. Hell, right about now I simply wanted to feel him against my body, clothed or unclothed. I craved contact, connection, and the purity of the chemical reaction we had. We were science, we were two substances in a lab that mixed perfectly, whether it was the banter or flirting or the way we seemed to want to pounce on each other.

Whatever it was, I found myself letting go of my worries over control, balance, habits. Gripping them less tightly the more time I spent with him.

I didn't want to admit that I liked him, but I couldn't keep it hidden any longer. "I feel the same about you," I said. Giving voice to those words made me feel as if a superhero of vulnerability had bestowed me with her powers momentarily. "You make me crazy, but I like that you make me crazy, and I think you're great too. But we also really need to go. We should take one vehicle as we head to the stakeout spot."

"Right. Two would be more suspicious."

We strapped on helmets, then I hopped on his bike and wrapped my arms around the abs I'd felt a few minutes ago. As I pressed my chest against his back, I was close enough to sniff his neck and the ends of his hair, and the clean, freshly showered, hot guy scent of him.

He'd taken a shower too.

For some reason, I trusted that shower, and what it meant, so I let go of another small kernel of doubt that I'd been holding onto. With it gone, I brushed my lips against his neck, and he groaned in response, grabbing my hand and holding it tight against his trim waist. Then he said something to me in Italian that sounded very close to what he'd said before.

"I want the same," I whispered in his ear as he revved the engine and took off.

CHAPTER THREE

<u>Jess</u>

I definitely didn't have to do squats tonight. My thighs were going to be rock hard. I'd been crouched down for thirty minutes, behind a low stone wall around the edge of a parking lot that a car detailer shared with a body shop. On the other side of the street was a smog testing facility and a tire dealer. At my feet lay a crushed Big Gulp cup, a sandwich wrapper, and several empty bags of chips. This must have been a prime lunchtime picnic spot for litterbugs.

Keats was right—the warehouse section was the perfect location for sneaking around since no one was around. This stretch of street was deserted at night.

With my camera strap around my neck, I was ready for whenever I saw the star and her director show up. I wasn't sure how far away they were, but timing in L.A. has a way of stretching and unfolding many times. They could just as easily arrive in seconds or in hours.

"So yeah. I've got a lot of intel right about now on how the paparazzi work," William said in a dry voice.

"Okay, what have you learned, my protégé?"

"Well, my mentor, I have learned that it is, in fact, almost identical to how being a private detective works."

I laughed. "Yeah, pretty much. Lots of waiting, and watching, and hoping, and then just a few seconds or so to take a picture."

"Sounds like my job."

"And the tips aren't that different either," I said, as I ran my fingers absently up and down the camera strap. "So really, what does your client think he or she will learn? That the most intrepid photogs are invisible? Or that we hang out in trees like lemurs ready to spring?"

"As you swing around the city wearing super-spy goggles with bionic vision, right?" he asked, miming putting on a pair of glasses.

"I left those at home tonight, but yes. I do usually wear my bionic glasses."

He shrugged. "I guess that is the sort of stuff the PR shop wants to know. But honestly, it probably won't make a difference. I have a hunch this is one of those cases where the publicity firm's client is probably doing something shady, and isn't owning up to it. Like this guy, the director Avery Brock. He's a dick," William said with a sharp edge to his tone.

I turned to him. "Yeah. He is."

"He's giving my countrymen a bad name. This'll be, what, his third affair with an actress he's directed?"

I counted off his alleged priors in my head. First, there were the tales of his tryst with the just-turned-twenty-one lovely Plum Lange who played the best friend of the head cheerleader in tge high school football flick *The Rivalry* and whose name was a source of endless puns in the tabloid headlines—she was a plum Plum. Next came the stories of his escapades on the set with Andromeda Blue, who starred as a teen drifter living on the road in *Lonely Nights Without Me*. Andromeda, who went by Andy everywhere except in the title credits for her films, had appeared quite heartbroken in the photos I'd seen of her after the film's press tour and their time together had ended. She'd gone sunglasses and sad eyes all the way, since she'd reportedly been in mad love with him. Avery probably batted his big brown eyes and told many a self-deprecating joke to win back his wife's favor after that one.

But now, he was at it again with Riley Belle.

"Yep, third. If you believe what the press says," I said.

William shook his head. "His wife should leave him. She deserves so much better. Anyone deserves better than that."

"Probably," I said, but who knew what their story was? Maybe they had an arrangement. Stranger things had happened. I cocked my head to the side when I heard the faint stirring of a hybrid car engine nearby, followed by a second vehicle, also with the same barely-there swoosh to its motor. There was hardly a celebrity in this town who didn't drive a hybrid or an electric, so my ears had been trained to pick out the softer hum, even the distinctions between models.

I peered over the low stone wall as a silver Nissan idled briefly, then cut the engine. Right behind it, a dark green Toyota parked.

I was quick to the draw, a gunslinger in the Old West.

Snap. Snap. Snap.

I grabbed shots of Riley and Avery exiting their respective cars. I snagged images of them walking hand in hand to a metal bench outside the smog facility. I recorded their every move for digital posterity, thanks to my sturdy and dependable top-of-the-line camera that I didn't even need a flash for, so they had no way of knowing I was lurking nearby as they settled in on the bench.

I zoomed in, as they chatted, as she smiled and looked in his eyes, as he tucked a strand of her brown hair behind her ear, as he ran a hand down her bare arm, then as he leaned in for a soft kiss on the lips. The tabloid readers would go wild. They loved a tawdry tryst. The entire time I made sure to capture her right side. That would be my gift to her, since Hollywood itself was the gift that kept on giving—there was always something to photograph.

Soon, they stood up and walked back to his car. She slipped into the passenger side, and they drove a few hundred feet down the street.

"Are you going to shoot more?"

I scrolled through the window on the back of my camera, checking out the night's take. I had easily snapped more than one hundred pictures of them.

"I believe my work here is done." I rose, grateful to be free of the crouch. William stretched too as he stood, then handed me my helmet. I hopped onto the back of his bike and we rumbled off to the library.

"What's next?" he asked, as I unlocked my own scooter.

"I hand these over tomorrow in the early afternoon."

"Do you have another stakeout?"

I shrugged. "Who knows what shenanigans tomorrow will bring? I see the client for lunch, then volunteer at the hospital. But do you want to meet up in the afternoon? The hospital is close to campus."

"What do you do at the hospital? Distribute Band-Aids from your ever-present stash?"

I rolled my eyes. "Aren't you just a funny guy?"

"Why, thank you," he said, adopting a deliberately smarmy grin. "Seriously though. Do you do medical stuff? Like a shot clinic?"

I reined in a grin that threatened to spread across my face. I found it adorable that William had no clue about medicine or hospitals, just like he was amused at my lack of language skills. I shook my head. "I don't even have a bachelor's degree, William. No one is going to let me give shots. I bring my parents' dog to visit the kids. Jennifer's trained as a therapy dog."

He reached for my arm and trailed his fingertips down my bare skin. Goosebumps rose as I shivered from his touch. "The fact that you do that is completely cool. Which also means it makes you even hotter," he said.

"Thank you. So you want to meet me and you can go with me on whatever shoots I'm on in the afternoon, and we can fine-tune wedding plans?"

"All work and no play," he said with a mock sad face.

"Of course. We are *only* business partners."

"All business. Unless…"

Neither one of us said anything for a few seconds, and I thought about how angry I'd been a few hours earlier when he'd been following me, and here I was now, paired up with him, getting high on that fine line of tension between the two of us.

I could take another hit. Inhale him.

But that would only mess with my plans. Make me lose focus. I couldn't risk that. "I have to concentrate on school and work," I said softly, but it was barely a protest.

"Seems to me, Jess, you're pretty damn good at both school and work," he said, and reached for one of the loops on the belt buckle of my jeans. Gently, he tugged me closer, and I let him pull me into his orbit.

"We're in the parking lot of the library," I pointed out, but it was hardly a *no*. More like an observation. He wrapped his hands around my waist, lifted me and sat me on his bike.

"Now you're on my bike," he said playfully, his hands never leaving me. His hands made it harder for me to remember why I had to keep him at arm's length. Because when he was that close to me, I didn't want any distance. I knew I had to concentrate on school and work, but at the moment I could only concentrate on him.

"Now what?"

"Now this," he said, pressing his strong thigh on the inside of mine, gently nudging open my legs. He moved closer, wedging himself into the space between my legs. Heat flared inside my body as my belly executed a series of backflips that would do an Olympian proud.

His stormy gray eyes remained fixed on me, blazing more intensely as he stroked my thigh with his thumb. I wore jeans, and I wished terribly that they would simply go poof, that the fabric would disappear and I could feel his touch against my skin. But then I'd be naked from the waist down on a bike in a parking lot and if that's not a recipe for awkward I don't know what is.

There was nothing awkward though about the way my body responded to him. He knocked down all the walls inside me, all my control, all my precision-balanced need to have my world spinning at a perfect pace I set and controlled like an engineer. Letting go scared the hell out of me; it stomped on all that I held dear. My life was a ladder, each step leading to the one above, and I wasn't anywhere near the top. I had so many plans. Big plans. I didn't want to risk a single one of them with a distraction like a guy. Nor did I want to risk tumbling off the food wagon once more if I fell for someone. I hated feeling out of control with food, and I didn't want to relapse like I had the last time.

But even as I feared what would happen if I gave in, the truth was, William and I worked well together, and we laughed well together, and we kissed well together, and I'd just landed shots that would pay me more than a pretty penny. Maybe he wasn't as big a distraction as I feared. Maybe I could balance.

Or maybe I was running on lust. Because the slightest contact sent me sky-high, as those delicious tingles un-leashed themselves all throughout my chest with each touch. He swept his thumb along my thigh, up to my hip, and then he hooked it into the waistband of my jeans.

He hadn't even kissed me yet, and my bones were humming a happy tune.

He inched his hands under my T-shirt and, reflexively, I arched my back.

"Mmm," he groaned lightly, then pressed further between my legs, his hard-on hitting me exactly where I wanted him. My mind spiraled, as I imagined more, so much more. I pictured him unzipping my jeans, tugging them down, sliding into me, and sending me into that zone of bliss I so rarely entered, that forbidden world where lust ruled the day. I could have that with him, and I let myself enjoy a taste as I wrapped my legs around him, hooking my ankles behind his thighs.

"You trapped me," he teased.

"Good. I like where you are."

"Me too, Jess. Me too," he said, as he gripped me tighter and gently rocked his hips against me. A slow, purposeful grind that made me moan, and then rope my arms around his neck. I was operating on desire, pure physical desire, but it's not as if I was out of control. I was in control, because I wanted him badly. He was a choice I was making in this moment. I didn't know if we were coming or going, if we were a blip on the radar screen of my life. But it didn't matter. I wasn't thinking about my future or how to make us happen beyond the here and now. I was living in my present, and in this span of time–this seemingly meaningless moment on this planet of a billion moments–this was the only one I wanted to live in. William Harrigan might have stepped into my life on a ruse, but there was no doubt that this thing between us was fully real.

I raised my chin, tilting my face to him. "I'm so turned on," I breathed out, eyes on him, speaking only the truth.

"I hope it's patently obvious that I am too."

That elicited a wicked smile as I rocked against him, feeling his erection pressing into me. "Yes. It's obvious and I like that you're wearing a billboard."

He cracked up. "Yep. That's me. I've got a billboard in my pocket."

Then, feeling daring, I grabbed his hand, and pressed his palm between my thighs, so he could feel–through my clothes–how hot I was for him.

"So do I," I whispered, and his eyes darkened as he felt me. I returned his hand to my waist as I said, "Now kiss me hard, and make me forget I ever pretended to dislike you because that's all it ever was–pretending."

He pumped a fist. "I knew you were checking out my ass from the first time I met you, right?"

I nodded, and I'm sure there was a wicked glint in my eyes. "Now, I'm going to check it out for real," I said, and he moved in to kiss me, gently touching my cheek with the back of his fingers before he slanted his mouth to mine, his lips brushing lightly against mine at first, then more insistently, as he kissed me harder. I looped my arms around his waist and cupped his fabulously firm ass.

A moan rumbled up through his chest as I touched him, but he never let go. He kept kissing me, the kind of kiss that couldn't be stopped, that was like a comet tearing across the sky, hellbent on having its way. The kiss was its own lifeforce, powerful and potent, and left nothing but pure heat in its wake. As he kissed deeper and harder, I tap danced my fingers to the top of his jeans, and dipped them into his pants, under the waistband of his underwear, and there, his gorgeous butt was in my hands, his naked skin all mine.

He pressed harder against me, rocking into me, his movements telling me he liked the way I touched him. Then he dropped his hands from my face, and seconds later, they'd found their way up my shirt, and under my bra.

He broke the kiss momentarily. "When you grope me like that, I hope you understand that it leaves no choice but to feel your breasts," he said, and maybe it was the scientist in me, but I loved that he didn't say boobs or tits or girls or jugs or anything a thousand times worse or cringe-worthy. They were breasts; plain and simple. But then there was nothing plain or simple about how he touched them, kneading in slow motion with an appreciative groan.

"Damn, I love your breasts," he said. He pushed up my shirt to my neck and buried his head between them, kissing one, then the other, lavishing a delicious amount of attention on each as he took turns with his mouth, lips, tongue and hands, like he would never deprive one breast of attention for the other. What a gentleman, treating them both with lusty reverence. I let go of my hold on his firm ass to grab the back of his head and keep him buried against my chest. Everything he did to me felt so incredibly good, as if fireworks were having a fiesta inside my body. I wanted to do everything with him right now, but I also wanted to do precisely what we were do-ing. Devouring each other, and yet holding back too.

Soon, he lifted his head, and his hair was messy and his eyes were hazy.

"You look really hot right now," I whispered.

"You look really hot all the time."

I ran the tip of my index finger lightly across the scrape on his forehead. "Your cut is fading," I said, then pressed my lips gently to the mark on his skin. "I wanted to do that the day I met you," I whispered.

"I wanted that too."

We kissed more, and it was the kind of kiss that marked the other side of the mad frenzy. It was the wind-ing down, the after kiss, the I-can't-stop-kiss-ing-you-even-as-I-adjust-your-shirt-and-you-snap-your-bra-and-we-both-start-to-say-goodbye-to-the-other.

"I know what to enter you as in my phone," he said, taking out his mobile, tapping something in the screen, then showing it to me.

"*Claire Tinsley,*" I read with a smile. "So you know this celebrity dog trainer?"

"I do. And I'm quite fond of her. But wait. Is she a friend of the bride or groom?"

I flashed him a smile. "Neither. She happens to know a private detective."

"What a helpful private eye," he added.

"He's very helpful. And very handsome. He's crimi-nally handsome."

He raised an eyebrow. "And she's dangerously pretty, and I can't wait to see her tomorrow."

THURSDAY
Weather: 70 degrees, Sunny

CHAPTER FOUR

<u>Jess</u>

Early the next morning, I printed copies of the photographic evidence, then saved all the files on my hard drive and my online backup. With that done, it was time for my morning ritual of Hollywood brain exercises. I clicked over to my favorite entertainment news site and read a piece about who might be playing the Gretchen Lindstrom role in the remake of *We'll Always Have Paris*. I scoffed at all the suggestions of too-young starlets. It was an affront that the classic movie–a true example of silver screen perfection–was being redone at all. But yet, I had to be conversant in the parlor talk of who should play the landmark role of the female lead. I jumped over to a story about *The Weekenders*, noting that Avery Brock–*philandering toad*, I mouthed as I read–was doing one more rewrite. That script must have been a hell of a trainwreck for him to make changes this close to shooting.

I stared at the photos I'd shot one more time. The guy was a cheating scum and I hoped the real lesson learned would be to stop messing around. But then again, if people like Brock cleaned up their acts I might not have a job. We were all bottom feeders, needing each other in our sycophantic, symbiotic way.

I made a living off scum like him. His toad-like ways made my job possible.

My phone beeped, and a smile lit through me when I saw a note from HBG.

Just in case you were wondering, I'm glad it's tomorrow right now.

I quickly replied: *Me too.*

But then, a sliver of worry touched down in my belly. I didn't know what I was doing with William, or why I was risking getting closer to him. I knew the dangers, I knew the stakes. The more time I spent with him, the more control I relinquished, like it was slipping through my fingers. If I kept letting go, would I spiral into a zone I'd clawed my way out of?

Maybe I could resist him romantically, I told myself. Maybe I could spend time with him planning for the wedding without liking him more and more.

But I was too logical to believe that line. I *did* like him more and more. So much more that my heart was dancing as we made plans to meet outside the hospital when my shift ended.

My mind was no longer occupied with the director. Good guys like William had a way of making bad guys like Brock fall from my head.

* * *

Keats had secured a table on the deck at Rosanna's Hideout. I spotted him as I walked down the promenade, his mirrored shades covering his eyes. He seemed to relish playing the role of young businessman about to close a deal at lunch, like the rest of this whole town. At the entryway of the restaurant, a large potted fern had been conveniently placed. The owner of Rosanna's Hideout must have known that the restaurant would benefit if paparazzi had an easy hideout from which to snap photos of the stars seated at the tables.

I told the high-cheek-boned maitre d' presiding at the podium that I was joining Keats Wharton.

"Right this way," the handsome and sure-to-be-aspiring-something man said, and led me to Keats' table. Keats stood up, beamed knowingly, and held out a hand. An eager fellow, he gave me a big, gregarious shake. I'd texted him last night with a report on the success of the mission.

I sat down and Keats gestured to a menu.

"Oh, I'm fine," I said.

"I was going to order a pear-and-walnut salad, hold the walnuts. Are you sure you don't want something?"

"I ate on campus," I said, lying, but not caring. I had an energy bar in my backpack, but I was also skilled in holding out when it came to food. I could easily wait until I returned to my apartment that evening. Besides, you never knew who was watching, and I didn't want to wind up like any of my subjects.

No eating on camera. No tables turned here, thank you very much.

When the waiter came by, Keats ordered his nut-free bed of lettuce and a glass of seltzer water, and I asked for an iced tea.

"Lunch of champions," Keats remarked after the waiter left. We chatted about the restaurant and L.A., then he rubbed his hands together and grinned again. "But enough of that. I'm dying to see what you have."

"I believe you'll be pleased." I unzipped my backpack, and reached for the manila envelope with the printouts of the photos I'd taken. "Just a little sampler for you. I also have a draft saved in my email of the file transfer link. I'll send it to you as soon as we're all set."

He undid the clasp on the envelope and gingerly pulled out the photos, looking around to make sure no one else was copping a peek at his $10,000 investment. As he surveyed the images, his eyes widened and his lips curved up. His reddish cheeks grew even brighter. "Nice," he said as if he were salivating on the word. He emitted a brief laugh, the sort of satisfied chuckle you hear in a movie when a hit's been carried out properly and to completion.

"I believe we are all set, Jess."

It was my turn to smile. A satisfied client was the only kind I wanted to have. "Great. I'm glad you're happy."

He tucked the prints back in their home as the waiter brought my iced tea and his seltzer water. He opened his tablet case, removed an envelope, and handed me the rest of the bills. I said a quick thanks out loud, then a silent hallelujah in my head, before I tucked the money into my backpack. I emailed him the link to the rest of the photos.

"Any idea where I'll see them later?" I asked. "I'm always curious where the photos wind up."

Keats' mouth hung open for a few seconds, and when he finally spoke, he talked slowly, like he'd been caught off guard. "Um. Yeah. No. I don't know yet. But I'll let you know for sure." Then he sped up. "Definitely tonight. I'm gonna get these babies out soon. Actually, scratch that. This afternoon."

"I'll just keep my eyes open. And keep me in mind for other assignments," I said, because I'd happily work for Keats Wharton again. Turned out, he hadn't been lying when he'd said the job was relatively easy. Almost too easy, but it paid easy money too and that was my favorite kind.

"You are at the top of my rolodex at A Thousand Words, Jess."

His salad arrived shortly, and we made painful small talk for the next thirty minutes. I feigned interest in the health benefits of chia seeds and the fine details of his workout regimen. When the check arrived, I offered to pay, but he waved me off. I excused myself for the ladies' room. Grabbing a toothbrush from the front pocket of my backpack and a small travel size tube of toothpaste, I proceeded to brush my teeth for the third time that day. When I finished I pressed my teeth together, and considered my pearly whites in the mirror. Nice and straight and clean, just the way a set of teeth should be. Everything was good in the world of dental care. At least one thing was under control and in order.

Plus, it wouldn't hurt to have minty breath when I met William after my volunteer hour.

I left the ladies' room, and Keats was still seated, though the bill had been paid. "I'm just going to stay here, get a coffee, make some calls, get these pictures out. But thanks for coming by, and don't feel like you have to stay."

After I said goodbye, I walked a few blocks past the midday promenade crowds and the gold robot guy who never said a word as he moved his body in jerky, mechanical motions, then the movie theater full of posters for the latest new releases including *Just Another Night*, about a magazine assistant who falls for an advertising executive and sleeps with him on the first date. It had released two weeks ago, sputtering to a fourth-place showing at the box office, because, as Anaka and I had discussed, the love interests should never hook up in the first act of a romantic comedy.

I pushed open the door to the bank, deposited my $10,000 in cash, and left. On the way to unlock my scooter, I remembered I'd forgotten my toothpaste and toothbrush in the bathroom at Rosanna's Hideout. I doubled back two blocks to the restaurant, then froze before I reached the entryway. Keats wasn't alone. He'd been joined by two other guys. One looked a lot like Keats and was probably his older brother.

But the other guy was the one who caught my attention. Because the other guy I definitely recognized. The other guy was on my flash cards.

The embattled teen actor who'd decked a hotel clerk. The bleached blond with the broody brown eyes. Jenner - "I Want a Room With a View on my Planet" - Davies.

The three of them were all laughing and toasting.

CHAPTER FIVE

<u>William</u>

The noise from the Cessna rattled the sky as the dark blue jet hit air at the far end of the runway. Being a guy, it was nearly impossible for me to tear my eyes away from the plane as it began soaring. When I was younger, I had once imagined I'd be a fighter pilot because that is one of the most badass professions a guy can be. For now, I had to focus on turning my under-the-table part-time private eye gig into a full-time-working-visa job.

I forced myself to look away from the plane as it stole through the crystal blue sky.

"This baby looks good to go," James said, patting the side of the silver helicopter on the tarmac of the Santa Monica airport.

"Yes sir. I'll be all ready for Saturday," the chopper pilot said, giving James a crisp salute. "And I will be sure to keep a good distance so as not to disturb the festivities."

"Excellent," James said, and I noticed he was personable with the pilot. Maybe it was just family he saved his douche-y side for. He clapped the pilot he'd hired on the back. The helicopter was part of the security plans for Saturday, circling above Ojai Ranch as the eye in the sky. The pilot's job was also to blend in, which meant make very little noise while somehow circling above the grounds for the whole event. A fine line to toe, and since James was a thorough fellow, he'd wanted to stop by the Santa Monica airport for a triple-check.

"Your turn. I've got three minutes, kid," he said, crooking his finger at me to follow him across the tarmac, his bald spot gleaming in the sun like a bullseye. "Tell me everything you've learned so far." Too busy for even a phone call, he'd told me to meet him here to give him the update on the case he'd assigned me–I called it *Days of Our Lenses, An Inside Tale of the Paparazzo Secrets.* Well, that's what I called it in my head. When speaking to my uncle, I simply gave him the specific details his client had asked for, and made a mental note to procure a fabulous thank you gift for Jess, since her insider information was the reason I still had this part-time job.

"And hook-ups?" he asked. "Those are usually just a tip from someone in the know?"

I nodded as the cool air of the terminal whooshed past us. James walked purposefully, taking long strides across the industrial carpet on his way to his car in the parking lot.

"Yes. That seems to be the case," I said, careful not to reveal details of who we'd staked out last night. Besides,

James had never asked for those particulars–he just needed to know the how and why.

"What about gym shots?"

"I'll get more info on those," I said as he reached the gate to the lot.

"Yeah, you do that. Because I need more," he said, tapping his finger against my shoulder in a patronizing manner.

I drew a deep fueling breath. "Thank you, James. I'd love to keep doing this if this is helpful to you. Do you think you'd be able to bring me on for a full-time position and sponsor my visa?"

God, I sounded like a fucking beggar and I hated it. But I had no choice. I'd been moonlighting for him for three months now and I was dying to know if he was seriously considering me for a job or was dangling me along.

He lowered his shades and peered at me over the top of the tinted frames, only half his eyes visible. "Get me more details and we'll see then and only then. I've got this wedding on my mind and I can't think beyond that to your little employment situation."

He opened his car door and took off.

I flipped him the bird once his car was out of sight.

As I tracked down my bike, a small round of guilt went rat-a-tat-tat against my chest, like a mobster's gun in an old-school crime flick. Yes, Jess was on the guest list, and sure, James had never expressly forbade photographers. But even though he was a dick, I was sneaking her into the wedding.

Except, sneaking her in was the price I had to pay to get the goods that he wanted.

The goods that just might keep me in the country.

As I gunned the engine and drove to see Jess, I wondered if staying in the United States was worth all this effort.

Jess

As I ducked behind the fern, a tumble of questions scurried through my head. Why would Jenner Davies meet with the owner of a photo agency? J.P. never ran around with stars and the people his photogs snapped pictures of. It would be the equivalent of a dog actively courting fleas. The fleas did their work quietly and in the distance, but never letting on they were setting up camp on the canines. Yes, I'd just compared J.P. to a flea, but I knew he'd be okay with the metaphor because he understood the roles, the system, the way things were supposed to work. Stars did not consort with photographers.

And why was Keats' older brother there? The other guy had the same ruddy cheeks, and the same tiny little nose, as if they'd both procured rhinoplasty from an identical mold.

Even as these questions flooded my brain, I didn't let them paralyze me. My shooter's instincts had kicked in, as I crouched by the plant, grabbed my camera and began snapping pictures of Jenner. My main employer would happily take an unposed picture of Jenner Davies. J.P. would prefer it to the plethora of staged shots of Jenner gladhanding with recipients of his pre-planned charitable work. Plus, a random star sighting like this would earn me a few more bucks than a playground shot.

They didn't notice me, and the maitre d' didn't either, or else his palm had already been greased by many a photo agency to look the other way. After I'd snapped enough shots, I tucked my camera in my backpack and retraced my steps to the bathroom, this time on a dual mission. I retrieved my toothbrush and toothpaste, then ducked into a stall and quickly downloaded the shots, sending them off to J.P. from my laptop along with a note that said *Special Delivery: Just a little surprise for you. I know how you like them unposed.*

A few dollar signs flashed before my eyes. The money would be good, and so would his reaction. I couldn't wait to hear about J.P's sure-to-be-gleeful delight when he discovered the unexpected photos. Forty-five seconds later I was rewarded with a reply: *Bring that digital baby to papa. Selling these now!*

Pride from a job well done suffused me as I left the restaurant unnoticed, yet again. I'd need to research Keats Wharton in more detail later this afternoon, but I reminded myself that whatever Keats was doing with Jenner Davies didn't impact me. It couldn't impact me, right? Because the check, so to speak, had already cleared.

A few feet away from the restaurant, I spotted a light blue Vespa, idling on the Promenade. On that blue Vespa was Flash herself, shooting away, snapping the same photos of Jenner.

Satisfaction curled through me as I watched her.

She was good, that girl, but this time I'd been first to shoot. That also meant I was hair's breadth lucky. Had

Flash been a minute earlier, she might have spotted me, and figured out The Dog Savior was really a paparazzo. I'd need to be as incognito as possible before the wedding. For my sake, and William's.

His name alone sent a rush of sweet tingles across my chest, as I remembered last night, and the words he'd said in Italian that I didn't understand. But they had sounded undeniably sexy falling from his lips. My skin turned hot as I recalled his kisses, the way he touched me, the connection between our bodies.

I swung by my parents' house to leash up Jennifer, and as I worked through my volunteer shift at the hospital, I didn't push aside the memories of last night. Instead, I let them skip happily through my brain, warming my body, keeping me company, until the clock ticked closer to William time. When my shift ended, I headed for the exit, the dog in a neat heel by my side, wagging her tail when she spotted Helen, who ran the program, rounding the corner.

"Hey. Did you hear there's going to be an *It's Raining Men, Part II?*"

"Thankfully, Hollywood is finally learning that male strippers are a big draw at the box office."

"I'll be at the theater on opening night with my one-dollar bills ready to toss at the screen," Helen said, patting the dog and chatting more as she walked towards the lobby with me. William was waiting by the door, his jeans and T-shirt hugging him in all the right places, showing off his toned arms without making him look like a show-off. He *was* casual and cool; he didn't try to appear that way. He simply was that way, from how he dressed to his laidback grin. He flashed a smile when he saw me, and my belly flipped, then flopped, then flipped again with butterflies. He was so handsome, and so delectable, and he was here for me. As soon as Helen noticed him, the clipboard she was holding slipped from her hands to the floor with a loud clang. William bent down to retrieve it, quickly handing it back to her.

Gallant William.

"Helen, this is my friend William," I said, and William extended his hand.

"It's a pleasure to meet you, Helen," he said, sounding so proper, and it occurred to me how that was yet another side to him. Funny, smart, and polite. Manners ruled.

"I assure you, the pleasure is all mine," she said with a wink, then said in a loud stage whisper. "He's hot. Have double the fun for me, please."

"Helen!"

"Get out of here, Jess. You're only young once," she said, then tra-la-la-ed down the hall and away from me.

"I like your dog," William said, as he petted Jennifer on the head, then turned his attention to the Great Dane-Bull Mastiff mix who was a gentle giant. "Well, hello Jennifer. Aren't you gorgeous?"

Her tail thumped against the floor.

"Don't think you can work your little British magic on the dog too," I said. "She is immune to accents."

"But you're not," he said, wiggling an eyebrow.

"Evidently not."

As we left, I shrugged an apology for Helen. "Sorry about Helen's sauciness. She kind of has a thing for hot young guys."

Once outside, he grabbed my waist, and pulled me in close, his dark gray eyes fixed on me. The way he stared at me like he wanted me made me molten. My knees felt wobbly from his heady gaze. Those tingles racing through my body an hour ago? They had nothing on the hand-springs my stomach was executing now. "What about your friend, Claire Tinsley? Does she have a thing for hot young guys? Especially the ones who speak many languages and catch volleyballs in their bare hands?"

"I thought we already made that clear," I said, threading my free hand through his hair and planting a quick, hot kiss on his lips that soon became a deep, slow, intense kiss...the kind that melted me from the inside out, and turned everything it touched into gold. His kisses made my head so hazy and my body so warm that I swore they could convince me of anything–the sky is purple, the sun rises in the west, and chocolate is calorie-free. All of that felt true in the way he kissed, turning my world inside out and upside down. All my ambitions, all my plans slinked away in the glide of his lips, the insistent explorations of his tongue, because all I wanted now was to spend the day in this cocoon of his sweet, sultry kisses under the sun.

I broke apart because my leg was wet. Jennifer was licking my calf, her way of saying *time's up, lady.* She batted her big brown eyes at me and nudged my leg once more.

"I need to walk her back to my parents' house before we head out," I said, glancing at her jowly face.

"I'll walk with you." He reached for my hand. "I hope you know I adore kissing you."

Kisses with him were spectacular. Add in his flirty, swoony words, chase them with a touch of naughtiness, and I was quickly sliding down the path to a frazzled brain. Like a marble rattling down a chute, he was poised to knock my carefully controlled life out of orbit.

The only saving grace was that his future was uncertain. He'd be leaving the country in two months if he didn't land a job with a company that would sponsor his work visa. I held onto the possibility that we would never become more than a brief interlude our senior year of college. Neither one of us had the bandwidth for a relationship, or even for more regular dating. There were built-in barriers to protect me from falling.

I could erect more though, just to keep my untamed heart and mind safe as safe could be.

"We should go," I mumbled even though I wanted to sing, to shout, to tell everyone that I adored kissing him, too.

So. Very. Much.

CHAPTER SIX

<u>Jess</u>

William parked himself in a chair at the corner café next to J.P.'s office. "Back in five. I'll tell your former short-lived employer you said hi," I said as I opened the door to the building. I needed to get paid, and get the afternoon assignments.

"Yes. Please do that," he said as he pulled out his iPad to work on homework while waiting for me.

"You liked my surprise pic?" I asked J.P. as I entered his dark and dimly lit confines.

"You made my day with it," he said, swiveling the screen around to show me where the shot of Jenner at lunch had landed–the Web site of *On the Surface*.

"Good. Now make my day, J.P. Why was Jenner Davies having lunch with a guy who runs a photo agency?"

"Huh?"

"The guy in the photo," I said, pointing to Keats on the computer screen on his desk. "The guy he's having lunch with."

J.P. stabbed his meaty finger against the other guy in the picture, the one who looked like a carbon copy of Keats.

"That guy," J.P. said, gesturing to the older of the small-nosed brothers, "is Jenner Davies' publicist."

My eyebrows knit together as I tried to process what he'd just said. "What?"

"Name is Wordsworth Wharton," J.P. said and laughed loudly, then rolled his eyes. "Can you believe it? What am I going to learn next? That his brother is named Keats?"

It was a rhetorical question. Even so I whispered *yes*. But I still didn't move a muscle; I sat in the rickety wooden chair by his desk, with some kind of strange un- expected shock on my features. Keats' older brother was Jenner's publicist, and the trio of them had seemed im- mensely pleased. A sense of unease rolled through me, as if the joke was on me, only I had no clue what it was.

J.P. stared hard at me as if I were two puzzle pieces he couldn't quite align. "Jess, what's the big deal? Actors have lunch with their publicists all the time."

Right. I couldn't let on that Jenner wasn't *just* having lunch with his publicist. Jenner Davies was having lunch with his publicist and also his publicist's younger brother who *happened* to run a rival photo agency that had *hap- pened* to contract for shots of a secret tryst between a young actress and a married director. I had inside infor- mation, but the information didn't add up, so I plastered on my best game face as I tried to mentally connect the dots between Jenner, and the poetically named pair of brothers. Maybe they were all buddies. Maybe Wordsworth was helping Keats grow his business. Maybe their get-together was simply the next item on Keats' agenda for the day.

But that moment of laughter when they all seemed to be in on the same joke weighed on me.

Not wanting to be surprised again, I made a mental note to add faces of publicists to my flash cards because I hadn't recognized Jenner's publicist.

I shifted gears. "I've got a lead on the wedding. Looks like I might be able to get in," I told him. I didn't want to promise too much too soon.

"Tell me more." J.P. licked his lips in that way he did when he was getting excited for a shot, and the green-backs it would bring. "Because I heard from someone at WAM that the ceremony starts at two on Saturday," he said, referring to the biggest talent agency in town that happened to rep Chelsea Knox, Bradley Bowman and both Veronica and Riley Belle.

His source at WAM had gotten the time right. That was good corroboration. Inadvertent, but good. The fact that his source knew the correct time also meant that de-tails on the wedding were starting to leak out so I'd need to keep the ones I knew close to the vest. I didn't tell J.P. where the ceremony was really going to be. J.P. had un-leashed what he had presumed was the competition on me earlier in the week in the form of William; I wasn't going to disclose the most precious detail I possessed, even though J.P. was good to me.

"I know someone on security detail," I said, once again keeping my cards to myself. "Says he can get me in. All I need is a fake ID. Got any idea where in this town I can get one of those bad boys on short notice?" I asked with a wink.

He held his arms in the air, the sign of victory. "I knew eventually you'd cave, Jess! Damn, I impress myself."

"Yeah, preen later. Anyway, I need it tomorrow."

He raised an eyebrow. "Fast turnaround? That'll cost you double."

"You're not honestly going to charge me for a fake ID so I can get into a wedding and deliver *you* exclusively a shot of the most sought-after photo Hollywood has seen in years?"

"Just kidding." He rose and walked over to the one plywood wall in his office that didn't have posters or frames of his greatest photographic hits on it, then yanked down a rolling white blind.

I handed him my camera, stood in front of the blind, and gave a scowl.

"C'mon. Say cheese for the fake DMV."

"Cheese," I said as he snapped a picture. Then I remembered a key detail that rendered this photo shoot moot. "Crap. I'm going to wear a wig on Saturday. I can't use this shot."

"What color wig?"

"Brunette probably. Why? Got extra in your drawer?"

"Yeah. I make fake IDs," he said, as if it were obvious to anyone that he'd keep a stash of wigs close at hand. "Course I have extra."

I contemplated putting on a wig that someone else had worn. I pictured getting lice. I knew better than to wear someone else's headgear.

"If I send you a picture later of me in the wig I'm going to wear, can you just Photoshop it in front of the background? I mean, you were just going to Photoshop me anyway in front of the California license background, right?"

"Get it to me by eight. I've got a hot date, and I'm going off the clock tonight."

"I'll send it to you by then."

"All right. Now do you think you can get your pretty little butt out of here and take some pictures for me over on Melrose?" he said, rattling off the names of several TV stars whose assistants planned to take them shopping today.

"I'm on it," I said. Besides, there was a wig shop on Melrose where I could grab Claire Tinsley's 'do. After all, I had a wedding to crash in less than forty-eight hours.

I found William at the table outside, looking cool and casual and completely kissable. My stomach twisted in knots with wanting him, and then once more with wishing I didn't want him so much.

I tried to tell myself he wasn't the guy I was falling for. He was only my partner-in-crime, and nothing more.

But the rush of heat in my veins, and the fluttering in my chest said otherwise.

I proceeded to share with him all that I'd learned about Keats and Wordsworth, hoping the focus on work would distract me from matters of the heart.

CHAPTER SEVEN

William

A font of celebrity insight, Jess knew everything about every star, from their relationship status, to their list of credits, to their shooting schedules. She also knew about gene structure, and biology, and cells—not that we discussed science—but I found it insanely hot that she was so smart. While I still possessed a supreme lack of knowledge about celebrities, I knew a tad more from spending the time by her side, taking notes on how she documented shopping habits of the stars in a pocket-size black and white notebook.

First, she hustled bracelet-shopping photos of Emily Hannigan, who had a regular role on a hospital show as a one-legged doctor, Jess informed me.

"She's on *Trauma Tonight*. And is in consideration for the Gretchen Lindstrom role on *We'll Always Have Paris,* I read earlier today. You really don't recognize her?" she asked.

"Nope," I'd said, shaking my head. "Though it could be that the pair of limbs are throwing me off."

Next, she nabbed a shot of two mustached young actors who held hands while perusing polo shirts in a nearby shop. "How about those guys? They're all over the magazines."

I shook my head.

"They're Jim and Jack Turner-Grace. They play rival detectives on a set-in-the-70s-cable show. They fell in love on set," she explained. "I thought for sure you'd recognize them. The press loves them and so do their fans. They're about to adopt two little girls from Vietnam."

"How many times do I have to tell you, Jess? It's like you're speaking Russian."

"Because that's the only language you don't speak."

"In addition to *celebrity*."

"I'm going to pretend you didn't say that," she'd said, bumping my shoulder playfully as we left the shop. "I don't understand how you can live in this town and not be addicted to gossip."

"You're such a junkie."

"Card-carrying member."

Then, through the window of a sneaker store, she spotted the fifteen-year-old rising pop sensation Rain Storm—yes, he claimed that was his given name, a Google search on my phone revealed—who'd become a hit after several Ivy League water polo teams had performed lip synchs of his latest tune on YouTube. She snared a picture of him wearing a red plaid vest as he purchased a pair of matching red high top sneakers.

"That's for Anaka, but I'll give it to J.P. too because they both find Rain amusing," she said, then snapped a few more shots of other celebrities along Melrose, including one of the stars of LGO's *Lords and Ladies*, when Anaka's cousin texted her with a tip she'd just landed on their whereabouts.

"Her mom produces the show. But evidently that tip came from some hot guy. Which means, Anaka and I are going to have to get the full story on her cousin's romantic situation," Jess told me as she sent the final set of shots to J.P.

Not a bad take for her for an afternoon's worth of trolling, plus I'd gleaned plenty of intel on a day in the life of a paparazzo. We were both getting something out of this partnership, and I wanted it to continue in all ways. When we were finished, I suggested we stop at the Busy Bee Eatery for a bite to eat, so we snagged a table at a diner decked out in black and yellow decor, matching the name.

"Now it's my turn to help you," I said, and after we ordered, I did some digging online on my iPad, quickly finding a photo of the poet brothers. They wore white linen shorts and blue button-down shirts, and smiled for the camera from the deck of a big boat floating on the water. God bless Facebook, and the ease of finding someone's life story on the site.

"I seriously cannot believe their parents really named them Wordsworth and Keats. It's so affected," I said, as I showed her the picture of the two brothers.

As she studied it closely, I studied her. The gray T-shirt she wore fit her snugly, making her breasts look even more enticing. My eyes drifted to her curves for the thousandth time today, and my mind meandered back to last night and the memory of how soft and wonderful they'd felt in my hands. How she'd grabbed my head and pulled me in close. How her skin smelled so enticing. I shifted in the booth, grateful we were sitting down. Then I returned to the matter at hand because if I lingered on last night I wouldn't be able to form coherent sentences.

Fortunately, any discussion of Keats and Wordsworth was a huge boner killer, so I closed the Facebook shot, and returned to the unposed images Jess had captured at Rosanna's Hideout of the three guys toasting.

"Let's figure this out," I said.

"Do you think they were all toasting to the photos I took? The Riley and Avery shots that I had just handed over? Your client is a publicity shop. You must know something about how publicists operate. Do you think Jenner's publicist wanted those shots? The pictures of Riley and Avery haven't shown up on any of the gossip sites, and it's been more than four hours since he's had the pictures."

She tapped her watch to make her point. It was now five o'clock.

"They're really not anywhere?"

"I've checked everywhere. All the usual suspects," she said, then rattled off the names of several celebrity sites. "The pictures aren't anywhere. And they don't show up on a Google search either, nor on a Twitter search, so they must not have been posted anywhere. It makes no sense. Why would you spend that kind of jack for photos and not get them out immediately? Those kind of pictures drive an insane amount of traffic to a Web site."

"It's weird," I said, contemplating the scenarios.

"It's weird?"

"Yeah. It's weird."

"That's it? It's *weird*? That's your assessment as a private detective?"

"Yeah," I said firmly. "It is weird. Weird meaning fishy. Suspicious. Not quite what it seems."

She nodded with enthusiasm. "Exactly! That's my point. So what do we do?"

"What do you want me to do? Follow Keats? Follow Wordsworth? Follow Jenner?" I asked, offering it as a joke at first, but as soon as the suggestion left my mouth, it seemed Jess and I felt the same way.

Her eyes lit up. "Actually, that's a brilliant idea."

"It is, isn't it?"

"Yes," she said, barely able to contain a grin.

"I'm like your personal PI now, right Jess?"

"*Personal PI*," she said in a deep, TV show announcer voice. "*Premiere episode tonight at nine p.m. When our red-hot hero tries to nab a pair of poet brothers.*"

I raised an eyebrow. "Red hot?"

Her tongue darted out to lick her lips.

"You do that as if it's playful, but you look red hot too."

The waitress arrived with my chicken sandwich and French fries, and Jess's coffee and fruit cup. "Need anything else?"

"Yes, please. Some actual *food* for my friend," I said, eyeing Jess' plate of rabbit food.

"I'm fine. This is completely fine," Jess said to the waitress, who turned on her heels and walked away.

I narrowed my eyes at her plate. "I will follow the Chia Brothers with the Tiny Noses and matching Oxford shirts under one condition."

"What is that condition?"

"I want you to have one of these French fries," I said, leaning back against the light blue vinyl of the '50s-style booth. There was a jukebox at the edge of the table, and soda shop music played overhead.

She shook her head, and bit the corner of her lip.

"I can't," she whispered and pushed her fork through the melons and pineapple pieces. "You don't have to follow them."

This wasn't the strong, confident woman I'd gotten to know. This was another side of Jess. I sensed it was a side she didn't show anyone. It was what lurked beneath all that tough girl armor.

I stripped all teasing from my tone, wanting to reassure her. "Hey. It's okay. You don't have to eat any fries. I'll still check out those guys for you. But you know, Jess, I have to say this. You look fantastic, and you'd look fantastic if you were this big," I said and held my hands out wide, then brought them closer together. "Or this small. What I mean is, I don't have a clue about sizes, but you look amazing now, and you'd look amazing if you ate French fries and more ice cream. And you're just cool, too. And smart. And funny. Even though you totally ride me, and hate me, and think I'm clueless for not knowing celebs. I still think you're funny and fun to hang out with, so I guess I'm a masochist."

That earned me a big grin. "I don't hate you, William. Not at all. Not in the least," she said, her pretty blue eyes locked straight on mine as she spoke.

I knew she meant it earnestly, but I couldn't resist teasing her. I steepled my fingers together. "Thank you so much for not hating me."

"You know it's not just *not* hate." Her voice was gentle, sweet even.

"All the double negatives are confusing me. Why don't you just spell it out?"

"You're fun to hang out with," she muttered, as if she were pretending it cost her something.

"I knew I could wear you down," I said, and picked up a French fry, dragged it through some ketchup, and happily ate it. She looked at the French fry with longing, blinking her eyes once then tearing her gaze away. In that moment, I understood her. Throwing away the ice cream on the beach, turning down my offer for pizza, eating only air-popped popcorn—they weren't part of her hard edge. They were real struggles. Food wasn't a struggle I knew personally, but being in Southern California for even a short while had taught me that body image was a battle for many men and women, guys and girls.

"Jess," I asked carefully. "You know you're beautiful, don't you?"

"Thank you, but that's not it."

"What is it?"

She shook her head, as if voicing her concerns would pain her. She took a deep breath then spoke. "French fries are my downfall. They're more dangerous than you. I haven't thrown up food I've eaten in more than two years, so I'm just trying to stay on the healthy eating wagon."

"I didn't realize it was hard for you," I said, reaching across the table and lacing my fingers through hers.

She let me, her fingers curling around mine. "I don't usually talk about it. It was a while ago anyway."

"You don't talk about it because you try so hard to be so tough. But that's a tough thing, dealing with an eating disorder. And that's a huge thing to be able to move beyond it."

"The last time I did it," she said in a small voice, "it was over French fries." Then she stopped talking, dropped her face into her hands. "Ugh. I can't believe I'm talking about barfing while you're eating." For one of the first times, Jess was fragile. All that armor she wore cracked with a small fissure, and in those tiny breaks she was letting parts of herself be shown.

I joined her on the other side of the booth, wrapping an arm around her. "Hey, it's totally okay. I swear you can't gross me out about food or anything. I didn't mean to make you feel bad by suggesting you eat a fry," I said, squeezing her shoulder gently.

"You didn't make me feel bad," she whispered in a barren voice, her face still covered with her fingers. She wasn't crying. Rather, she was embarrassed and I hated that she felt that way.

"I never should have said anything about the French fry," I said, rubbing her shoulder now with my palm.

She snorted, and it was a self-deprecating sound. Lifting her fingers from her face and raising her head, she composed herself. "You know what? It's fine. It's just a

French fry. I can handle it. I'm not going to be a big baby about a French fry," she said and reached across the table to my plate to grab a fry. She bit into it as if to prove she could do it. Then she finished it, and held her arms out wide.

"There. Did it," she said, clearly mocking the momentousness of eating something that had once been far too tempting.

"And it didn't even bite back," I said, and she laughed, then looked at me.

"Thank you," she said softly. "For not mocking me."

"For being human? Never," I said, then turned serious again. "How long were you bulimic?"

"Through most of high school. I never told anyone, but Anaka figured it out, and was pretty supportive. She even took me to a support group, and that helped me to really deal with it. It was never about food. It was always about control, and I felt so out of control starting in high school when my dad's company went under and my college fund went kaput. So, controlling food felt like the only thing I could manage. But then I stopped, and I was pretty good until I relapsed my second year of college."

"What happened that made you relapse?"

She squeezed her eyes shut momentarily and her face flushed for the first time. I'd never seen her ashamed before, and it made me want to hold her close.

"I was going out with this guy, and the whole relationship was so distracting that my grades suffered. When I saw my progress report, I wanted to die. We broke up pretty quickly, but it just felt like everything was unraveling and I fell off the wagon for a week or so. Anaka, once again, was the one who helped me. I wouldn't have been able to change without her," she said softly. She stared at the jukebox, and her jaw twitched, then seemed to harden as she turned her focus back to me. "But then I got it all sorted out, and I've been fine ever since."

The last words came out too quickly, too crisply. I knew there was something more to it. Something she was afraid of sharing, but Jess wasn't prone to oversharing, and I sensed she'd somehow reached her limit for the afternoon. I took her cue and shifted gears too.

"You know, Jess, I'm a pretty good cook. I can make salads, and pasta with vegetables, and eggs without the yolk," I said, since I was starting to figure out she wanted someone to understand and respect her food choices, not push pizza and ice cream on her if she didn't want it.

She arched an eyebrow. "Now you're just talking dirty to me when you use words like *eggs, hold the yolk*."

There we were, back to the jokes, our familiar territory. "I knew the way to your heart was through healthy food. You're so California."

She held up a hand and shook her head. "Did I say it was the way to my heart? I believe I said *talking dirty*, which means it's the way to my–" she dropped her voice lower "–pants."

A small groan escaped my lips. I bent my head to her neck, pressing a light kiss near her earlobe, then whispered, "Lettuce. Grapefruit. Whole wheat bread."

She inhaled and moaned quietly, as if I were turning her on with my food talk. Naturally, I had to continue. Even if she was playing pretend, she was so damn sexy when her eyes floated closed and her lips parted.

"Broccoli. Carrot sticks," I said in a low, growly tone. She ran a hand across her thigh as if I were driving her wild. "Yogurt."

She turned to me, grabbed a fistful of my T-shirt and tugged me close. "Now, you're just turning me on way too much."

She might have been teasing, but I wasn't. Not one bit and I had the hard-on to prove it. This was getting to be the usual state around her. "Jess, believe me when I say there's nothing I'd rather do than turn you on," I said.

This time, when her breath caught, it seemed for real. No more pretending. "You do," she said quietly, but she quickly returned to safer ground. "Will you tail Keats and Wordsworth as well as you tailed me?"

"No. I'll do a much better job."

"You didn't do a good job tailing me?" she asked as she speared a pineapple chunk.

"I wanted to talk to you. I wanted to get to know you. I noticed you the second you walked into J.P.'s office that first day."

She held her fork in the air. She didn't bring it to her mouth. She didn't put it down. It just hovered in her hand. "From the first day?"

"Of course. You were coming through the same door."

"That's the only reason I noticed you, too. It had nothing to do with your fantastic ass," she said, then wiggled the fork with the pineapple chunk in my direction. "You know you want this pineapple, don't you?"

"Oh, I'm dying for it. Bring it here," I said, and held my mouth open. She fed me the pineapple, and I smacked my lips, declaring it delicious. I was no shrink, but I had a hunch she needed to return to her way of controlling her world, and if that was by giving me a piece of fruit, I'd let her do that. "Now, tell me more about how much you wanted me the second you laid eyes on me."

She threw her head back and laughed and it felt good to both comfort her and to make her laugh. Hell, it felt good to spend time with her. So good, in fact, that it occurred to me how much I'd miss her if the State Department sent me packing in less than two months. In a few short days, she'd somehow become one more thing I found immensely appealing about America. The thought should have scared me that I liked her this much already. But it didn't. Instead, it made me even more certain that I needed to find a way to stay.

She nodded. "So did J.P. He likes boys, too. He called you Criminally Handsome," she blurted out as if making a confession.

"I'm flattered that you checked out my ass *and* that your boss thought I was hot," I said, as I pulled my plate to her side of the table and took another bite of my sandwich.

When I finished chewing, she placed her hand on my arm, wrapping her fingers around me in a way that felt almost possessive, and I liked that from her. "Wait. Turns out, I transposed the order of events. I was the one who called you Criminally Handsome. I was the one who thought you were hot first. And I'm the one who's inviting you to come over tonight after I run some errands. You can make me a salad."

I wasn't sure if she was asking literally or if it was some new code word for dirty talk. Didn't matter. There was only one answer.

But before I could give her my yes, she continued, her eyes truthful as she caught my gaze. "And you can talk to me about salad too."

Another groan escaped me and all I could manage was a one-word answer.

"*Yes.*"

CHAPTER EIGHT

Jess

This would be the scene in the movie with the shopping montage, if I were indecisive and liked to try on and model wigs. But I was decisive.

I selected a brunette model quickly from the dozen or so the sales clerk with yellowed teeth showed me. There was the long, shampoo model look. Then the slightly wavy style. Then the housewife shoulder length bob. Then the crazy curls. Then the boyish wig, which I vetoed because I didn't want to look like a boy at all. Finally, there was the just-long-enough-to-tuck-behind-the-ears-but-just-short-enough-to-show-off-my-neck one.

"That one," William said.

"No," I said, shaking my head.

"Why not?" he said with affront in his voice.

"It's cute, but it's just too obviously a wig. I think I have to go with slightly wavy. It's the most," I paused, noodling on the right words. "It's the most normal. And, to be honest, the most boring. I don't want to stand out."

"Right, right," he said, refocusing on the vital mission —not getting caught on Saturday.

"May I try this on?" I asked the clerk.

"Of course. Here's a cover for your hair," the clerk said, and I took the stocking cap, and the wig.

I turned to William. "You are so not seeing this part. Look the other way."

He swiveled around so he was facing the door. His back was to me. The store was tiny, with wigs on styro-foam heads stacked on shelves from floor to ceiling.

"Now, put your hands on your eyes too."

He did as told. "Do you want to blindfold me as well?"

"I have a scarf if you want," the clerk offered. "It's be-hind the counter."

"Oh, please, bring it on."

"I think we'll be fine without. I'm fast." I tugged the cover over my hair, tucking my blond ponytail beneath the edge of the pantyhose-like material, then pulled on the wig. I adjusted the fake hair, centering the bang-less-look, and tucking a strand behind my ear, to look as natural as possible.

"This one is it," I said, as I checked it out in the mir-ror.

"Can I look now?" he asked.

"Yes, but I'm getting this one."

I didn't wait for his reaction. I simply paid for the wig, chalking up the fifty-six dollar cost as a necessary expense for what would likely be a $100,000 payoff.

"Can you take a picture of me in my wig?" I gestured to the white door that must have led to the back of the store. It would make a good background for a fake ID. "Is it okay to take a picture?" I asked the clerk.

"Go ahead."

I gave William my camera, and I stood against the door.

"Look mad," he teased.

I furrowed my brow.

"Perfect."

"No! Don't use that. Let's do a half-smile," I said, and I knew I looked awkward because I didn't have a very good smile, but awkward would probably be appropriate for this purpose.

He took a few more shots, then showed them to me. "You approve?"

"You are a good photographer. Even though the subject is ornery."

"Didn't I tell you? My specialty is ornery subjects."

"No wonder we get along so fine," I said and put my camera away, dropping the wig in the zippered compartment too. I slung my backpack on my shoulder, and walked out to Melrose. The sun was strong in the sky even in the early evening, and the rays felt good on my bare arms.

"We do get along fine, don't we?" he said, picking up the thread of the conversation.

"Yeah, it's weird but it's true."

Then I spotted a flash of blond hair up ahead, and the fresh-faced smile of an actress I loved. A Broadway in-génue, and my brother's wife's—Kat's—best friend.

"That's Jill McCormick," I whispered reverently to William.

"Who's she?"

"She won a Tony last year for her first ever Broadway show *Crash the Moon*. I saw her in it. My brother flew me out to New York one weekend because Jill is best friends with Kat; she was the maid-of-honor at my brother's wedding. We all went out after the show. Oh my god, she has the voice of an angel. And that's her husband. He was her director and they fell in love during rehearsals."

"A proper love story for that business," William said.

As Jill and Davis neared us, Jill raised her hand to wave. "Jess, is that you?"

I stopped in my tracks, as something like shock and utter delight flowed through me. "I can't believe she re-members me," I said to William.

"You're hard to forget."

Then Jill closed the gap between us and wrapped her arms around me. "How are you? So good to see you again. How's everything? Are you almost done with school?"

"Soon. I graduate in a few months," I said with a huge grin. She was so genuine. "What brings you to Los Ange-les?"

She pointed her thumb at her husband, the dreamy, broody, blue-eyed Davis Milo, a legend on the Great White Way and in Hollywood too. He'd already won an Oscar for a film he directed, along with three Tonys. "We're shooting the movie adaptation of *Crash the Moon*. Davis is directing me again."

"It seems we enjoy working together," he said, chiming in, then he extended a hand and officially introduced himself to me, and to William.

We chatted more, and as we were about to say good-bye, Jill glanced down at my camera. "Are you working right now?"

"I was this afternoon," I said, because she knew I was a photographer, but I didn't want her to feel like I'd been angling for a shot.

"Want to take our picture?"

I beamed. I'd never turn down a shot. "Sure."

"Candid is better, right?" Jill asked with a wink.

"Usually, but you don't have to stage something. I can just snap a picture of the two of you."

"Oh, this won't be staged," she said, then turned to her husband, cupped his cheeks in her hands, and brushed her lips against his in a gorgeously unstaged kiss in the afternoon. They lingered on each other, and his hand skated down to her hips, as if he couldn't resist tugging her closer.

When they separated, I showed it to them on the back of the camera. "I love it," Jill said, then hugged me once more and said to keep in touch before they headed in the other direction.

"This will be great. J.P. loves a great kissing shot. Especially when they're so in love."

"They did seem to be on somewhat decent terms," William said in a dry voice.

"Yeah, just a little."

"Jess," he said as we started to walk towards our respective sets of wheels.

"Yeah?"

"I had fun with you today."

"I had fun with you too, William."

"But I have something really important to ask about tonight."

I tensed momentarily. I had no idea what he'd want to ask or talk about. Or if he was assuming things were going in a particular direction, when I honestly wasn't sure of a thing. "What is it?"

He dropped a hand to the small of my back, then dipped his thumb under the hem of my shirt, tracing the skin on my back. "Is your roommate going to be home tonight?"

I reined in a naughty grin. "No. She has screenwriting class tonight. But that doesn't mean we're going to..." I couldn't finish.

"I know," he said, and stopped walking, pulling me against him on the sidewalk. "But even if I'm only kissing you, I'd really like to be alone with you," he said, and my stomach cartwheeled. "Would you like that?"

It was my turn now to breathe out a barely audible *yes*. A single syllable constructed from hope and hormones and the wish for more with him. Then other words tumbled free. Words I'd wanted to say earlier. Words I could only say now as I started to relinquish another sliver of my carefully-constructed control. "I adore kissing you."

* * *

Too bad I wasn't a makeup hound. I could have cleaned up in my mom's bathroom cabinets. Inside the white cupboard underneath the double sink was a makeup archaeologist's field day. There were eyeshadows in sky blue, electric blue, and sea green; eyeliners in black, cobalt, and chocolate brown; lipsticks in coral, rose, and scarlet; not to mention endless tubs of foundation and powder in every possible shade of skin. To top it off, the makeup here wasn't even in rotation. In her makeup suitcase—three cases tall with its own set of wheels—were the colors and cover-ups she brought with her on her jobs. I grabbed several tubs of foundation, as well as a handful of powder puffs, then left her room.

The scent of couscous emanating from the kitchen was strong and tasty. "Smells good, Mom," I called out.

"Tastes even better," she shouted in return. "You should stay."

"Can't. I have a date."

"Ooh. Tell me more."

"Ha. As if I'm going to share details of the Hot British Guy with you."

"Fine. Then just make sure you don't fall behind on homework," she said as I popped into the kitchen to give her a peck on the cheek.

"Mom, I'm ahead on homework. By the way, I told Bryan your new favorite names for twins are Bert & Ernie for boys," I said.

She narrowed her eyes and pretended to swat me with a kitchen towel.

Shrugging playfully, I egged her on. "But Kat loves those names. I'll tell her you don't and that you prefer Cagney & Lacey. That work?"

"Did you say you needed my Hollywood insider intel? Hmmm. I'll have to reconsider feeding you the bits and pieces of juicy gossip I pick up," my mom said as she stirred the dish, a clever lilt in her voice.

I dropped down to my knees, ready to beg. "I'll tell them I love Chloe & Cara too."

She nodded sagely. "You do that."

"I will. Love ya. Gotta go. Thanks for the makeup cases."

"Have fun playing spy," she said.

I crouched down to pet Jennifer on the snout before I left.

Several minutes later, as I walked up the steps to my apartment, I scrolled through my email, laughing out loud at my brother's latest picture of a dog lawyer making a joke about leashing the witness. Bryan went on to mention that the package I needed for the wedding would arrive tomorrow. I sent off a quick thanks, then clicked open the alert I'd set up for the Bowman-Belle wedding. There was a short item in *On the Surface.*

As the two-day countdown until the fabled Bowman-Belle wedding begins, a well-placed source at a party rental store confirms to On the Surface that an order for a tent large enough for 200 guests, along with folding white chairs, and a white runner is being prepared for a Saturday morning delivery to a well-known Hollywood residence in Malibu.

I smiled as I read the item. Flash worked for *On the Surface.* She'd probably be scouting this well-known residence in Malibu all day Saturday, along with the rest of my paparazzi brethren. But they didn't know where the wedding really was. Let them all run around Malibu empty-handed.

Inside the apartment, Anaka was gathering her materials for class, scooping up papers from the table. They'd been tucked under a makeshift paperweight–her coconut hand lotion.

She stopped to say hi. "Hey! I have the purse you asked for for the wedding. Hold on."

She scurried to her room and returned with a light beige purse. I inspected the inside of the tan shoulder bag.

"Perfect. Let's see how it looks," she said.

I draped it on my shoulder. It fell to my ribs, which was the perfect length. I didn't want a purse that dangled against my hip. I needed one that I could keep a tight grip on.

"Looks awesome," she said, darting into the kitchen to grab a pair of long-handled scissors. She handed them to me, then shielded her eyes. "Just don't deface it 'til I leave."

"Your purse had a good life," I said solemnly.

She pretended to sob as she zipped up her messenger bag for class. "The purse is willing to lay down its life in the service of duty. Besides, you fed Karina the Rain photo and I've been watching my blog traffic go way up tonight. Karina's people love pictures of Rain and his silly little vests."

"Speaking of photos, I still haven't seen one turn up yet of the pictures I took of Riley the night before."

"I bet they're waiting to run them in the morning or something. The best time for a site is always in the morning. The only reason I post my entries at night is I lack something known as patience."

My phone rang, and I looked at the screen on my phone. "Says *private*."

Anaka squealed. "That means it's Riley. Answer it and tell me everything later. I need to run."

"Doubtful," I said, as she walked out the door, and I answered the call.

"Hello?"

"Hi, I'm looking for Jess, and I can't believe I never got your last name."

Anaka's radar was 100 percent accurate. I'd recognize Riley Belle's voice anywhere. I'd seen all her movies.

"Hey. This is Jess. Jess Leighton," I added.

"It's Riley Belle. And you can't see him, but little Mister Sparky McDoodle is here with me in my lap. He says hello. He says thank you again. He says *I love you*," she said, and then laughed, her laughter sounding like the tinkle of a pretty church bell.

"How is Mister Sparky McDoodle? All good, I assume?"

"He's perfect. I bought him a new sweater last night after the incident. He was so rattled, and he always settles down when he has new clothes," she said, then laughed. "I'm just kidding. He's not that kind of dog. He doesn't care about clothes."

I laughed too, though I felt uneven. I wasn't sure how to behave with her. She wasn't what I had pictured. She liked to poke fun at herself. It was strangely refreshing, even as it was unexpected.

"So Jess. I totally want to take you out, like I promised. I have to tell you that I can't stop thinking about what you did for my dog yesterday, and I am so grateful. There's this amazing place along the beach," she said, and then named the hottest new eatery in town, and I didn't bother to ask how we'd get in when it was well-known the waiting list was months-long after being declared the best brunch on the west coast in a fancy food magazine. We'd get in because she was Riley Belle.

"It sounds awesome." Obviously, I wasn't going to say no. "When?"

"Let's see. Tomorrow's Friday, and my lawyer's in town from New York, so we're meeting in the morning to review possible projects for my production company. You have no idea how hard it is to find a good script these days," she said, and she reminded me of my chat with Anaka, kvetching about the same problem last night. "And speaking of problems with scripts, then I'm going to be at the studio in the afternoon for a final read-through of *The Weekenders* because the director made *another* last minute change to the script after last night's run-through." I cringed a bit inside when she mentioned last night, because twenty-four hours ago I was snapping her face lip-locked with Avery Brock and figuring she'd never call, so I'd never have to feel guilty. Now, she'd called, and now I felt mighty guilty. "But that's neither here nor there, so Friday's a no-go. And Saturday is out because I have this wedding thing to be at on Saturday and it's going to last all night."

"Right. Your sister's getting married. You must be so excited," I said, then wanted to kick myself. I sounded like a starstruck sycophant.

"I'm so excited for her too. I'm going to be a brides-maid, and it's going to be amazing. I guess we should make it a Sunday brunch, since I have a thing on Sunday night."

A thing probably meant a second tryst with Avery Brock.

"Let me just check my calendar and see if I'm free on Sunday," I said in a playful voice, pretending to thumb through a calendar. I needed to recover and return to the funny girl Riley thought I was yesterday. Because that's the girl I wanted to be, not a yes woman. "Okay, turns out I'm available."

She laughed briefly. "Perfect. Can we do eleven? Is that too late? I'm just worried about getting to the restaurant on time after Saturday's festivities."

"Not a problem. I'll see you and Sparky McDoodle at eleven on Sunday."

"Yay. Can't wait, Jess."

The call ended, and I studied the phone as if it would emit a report verifying that I really did have a phone conversation with Riley Belle. Was I becoming friends with an actress? It was an odd notion, but then, I was becoming friends too with a private detective who'd been following me, and now was my partner-in-sort-of-crime as well as my oh-so-hot-date in an hour, so odd notions were not unfamiliar this week.

I flopped down on my bed, resting my head on my pillow, flashing back to today in the diner, and in the wig shop, and on the street with William. We'd had fun, I'd felt carefree with him, as if I didn't have the weight of the world on my shoulders. I'd even confessed something I rarely told anyone. But I wanted him to know the real me, not just the me I presented.

Why did I want him to know me?

Because I liked him. I more than liked him. I also liked who I could be with him. With him I wasn't merely the Jess who wanted to be a doctor, who earned top grades, who kept all her emotions in check. That Jess was restrained. She always had the proper handle on any situation.

But there was another Jess, the one who planned disguises, the one who was daring enough to chase down pictures, the one who let insults and invectives from stars who didn't want their photos taken slide off her.

The one I was with him.

CHAPTER NINE

<u>William</u>

I had an address for tomorrow, some Web research for tonight, and a shopping bag full of the ingredients for chicken stir-fry.

The one item I didn't have? Time to tail the boy poets. I had yet to bend the time-space continuum of Los Angeles traffic far enough to track the brothers in the three hours I had free in between saying goodbye to Jess and knocking on the door of her apartment. But I was armed with *other* information, and intel was yet another way to her heart, so I'd take that route for now. I wanted to win her over.

More of her.

When she opened the door, my eyes nearly popped out of my head. Words rattled around in my brain but I could barely gather them in a coherent fashion.

"Skirt," I mumbled, as proper construction of sentences and little details like verbs fled my mind. I was unable to take my eyes off her legs. Her strong, toned, bare legs were on display for the first time. I'd only ever seen her in jeans, and now she was wearing a jean skirt that hit her mid-thigh–god bless short skirts–and a light blue tank top. Her blond hair was swept up in a ponytail that showed off her neck and shoulders. But the skirt…that was all I could think of…well, all I could think of was what was underneath the skirt. How her thighs would feel in my hands. How soft her skin might be.

"Skirt," she said, making a rolling gesture with her hands, as if she were supplying me with the missing word.

I shook my head, like a dog shaking off water. "You're wearing a skirt," I said. My jaw was possibly still scraping the floor.

"Very good, William. You have excellent sartorial iden-tification skills." She gestured to me. "You're wearing jeans and a T-shirt," she said, as if speaking to a young child. "Now, can you try naming this?" She tugged on the fabric of her tank top.

Recovering the power of speech and the use of brain cells, I stepped inside, shut the door, and set my bag down on the floor. I reached for the shirt, taking the fab-ric in my hand as I pulled her in close, brushed my lips along her neck, and whispered in her ear. "Something I want to take off."

She breathed in sharply, and shivered against me. "Ta-bles turned," she said in a low, sexy purr.

I nibbled on her earlobe then dropped my mouth to her lips, covering her in a kiss that I had no choice but to give. Kissing her was not optional. It was mandatory, and as necessary as air or breath. She tilted her face to me, and I deepened the kiss, my tongue meeting hers, tasting, licking, and touching her with the kind of recklessness that some kisses demand. That's how I felt–beholden to this kiss as her apartment faded away, as the music from her iPod drifted out the window, because all my senses narrowed to the press of her lips against mine.

Eventually, we came up for air.

"So, I brought bell peppers, chicken and the most fantastic dessert," I said quickly, segueing playfully into dinner as if that kiss hadn't just nailed me right in the heart.

She ran a hand through her bangs, as if she were clearing her head. "Sounds perfect."

She showed me to the kitchen and I told her I had good news.

"You already started tailing the brothers?" she asked, her eyes lighting up.

I laughed, and roped my arms around her waist, kissing her hair as I moved behind her to start emptying the shopping bag. "I know the way to your heart. Rabbit food and clues."

"I'm easy like that. So tell me stuff," she said, handing me a skillet, spray oil, a knife and a cutting board.

"I did some prelim research online. I found where Keats and Wordsworth live, so I'm going to scope them out tomorrow. I also tracked down one vital piece of information already. You know that Web site for Keats' agency?"

"Yes."

"He registered the domain name about three days ago. The site just went up this week, Jess."

She shivered as if a chill ran through her. "So…"

"I don't know what to make of it yet, but I think it's safe to say he's probably not a legit agency," I said, as I began chopping peppers.

"Crap," she said, blowing a frustrated stream of air through her lips. "I should have looked into that. I never thought to look into it."

"Of course not. It all seemed real. He seemed real," I said, as I pushed the orange bell peppers to the side of the cutting board, moving on to the yellow ones. "The money was real, and he paid you in cash. You're not the one he's setting up. As much as it might seem like he's setting you up, I don't think you're who he's trying to frame."

"Who are Keats and Wordsworth setting up then? Riley? That would make me feel so guilty," she said, dropping her forehead into her palm. "Riley was sweet, and she was happy, and she seemed genuinely eager to have brunch."

"I don't know. But listen, I only have one class tomorrow, so I'll be out bright and early and I'll follow them and see if I can figure out something."

As I set aside the chopped peppers and began working on carrots and broccoli, she nodded. "Okay. But I think you should follow Jenner. If they were both having lunch with Jenner, he's probably the one setting her up."

"That's what I was thinking too. See, great minds think alike," I said, then scooped up the peppers, carrots, and broccoli onto a separate plate before I tackled sautéing the pre-cut cubes of diced chicken.

We chatted for a bit more about the threesome of sneaky Hollywood players as I cooked.

She lifted her nose in the air and sniffed. "Smells yummy."

"Why thank you. I hope you love it," I said, choosing for once not to make a joke. I truly did want her to be happy with what I served. Not only because food was challenging for her, but because I wanted to impress her. I wanted to impress her in the kitchen, with my conversation, and with my hands, lips and tongue. As well as other instruments.

"What were you doing before I came over?" I asked, as I finished the dish, and turned down the heat on the stove. "Doing curls or crunches or studying for your first bio exam next fall, right? Wait, you were making a spreadsheet of celebrity sightings and likelihood of whereabouts."

She smiled brightly at me. "You think I'm hyper prepared?" she asked, but she wasn't bothered that I'd figured out that she was.

"Well, you do have flash cards, don't you?"

"That reminds me—I need to add publicist faces to my cards."

"Oh, well, don't let me keep you," I said, as I began plating the food.

"It's okay. I can do it when you leave," she said with a sexy little wink, as if it were some naughty secret that she was a workaholic.

"What if I keep you busy all night though?" I asked as I ran a hand along the waistband of her skirt on my way to the table.

"You've got a lot of stamina then," she replied.

"I do, Jess. I absolutely do."

"Maybe I'll find out how much some day," she said, lowering her voice to a flirty whisper, the words heating me up.

"Maybe you will. For now, this is your one and only chance to eat this fantastic dinner because after that I'm going to have a hard time keeping my hands off of you."

She opened her fridge, waggled a beer bottle at me in offering, raising her eyebrows to ask if I wanted it.

"Of course."

Then she took one for herself, which surprised me, but made me happy too because it meant she wasn't depriving herself of something worth having due to calories. Even though she only drank one-quarter of it while we ate dinner.

CHAPTER TEN

<u>Jess</u>

The pans were washed, the dishes were dried, and the meal was officially delicious. The conversation was great too. William and I had talked the whole time at dinner— I'd told him more about my favorite movies, and how I got into photography, and I even told him about the pictures I still felt guilty about. The ones I took of Nick Ballast.

He shook his head. "Don't feel guilty, Jess. It shows you're a good person that you feel that way, but truly, everyone is responsible for what they do and their own choices. Just like you. You've taken control of things, and you live your life the way you want now, and Nick is doing the same."

"Thank you for saying that," I'd said, and hearing that from him made another small layer of guilt shear off.

Then it was his turn to share, and he'd told me about the summer he spent in Italy learning the language, and about how frustrated he felt at times for not having a job yet.

"It's like I keep trying with James, and in all these other places too, and it's not happening yet. It makes me feel like I'm not good enough," he admitted in a quiet voice as we put the final dishes away.

William was usually so confident, so sure of himself. But the frustration in his tone was tangible and I would have felt it too in his situation.

"You are good enough," I said firmly. "You just haven't met the right job yet."

That made him laugh. "Like when you say to your unmarried spinster aunt, *you haven't met the right guy yet?*"

"Exactly. But I believe it. There's a job for you. You just have to keep looking. And besides, it seems like you're good at everything. Let me get this straight. You speak twenty languages, ride a bike, have a six-pack, a hot accent, *and* you can cook?" I arched an eyebrow.

"Oh please. You're embarrassing me," he said, holding up his hands in mock humility, as we settled down on the couch. He lowered his voice to a stage whisper. "I only speak five languages."

"Somewhere, there are a bunch of guys who got the short end of the stick. They're sitting around at some sorry dudes meeting, moping about how there was a completely uneven distribution of assets when you were born," I said, and William simply smiled at the compliment.

"See? That's another thing. Great smile. It's like you took everything and left the rest of the guys with nothing," I said, as I reached for the dessert bowl on the table that was filled with blueberries. I popped one into my mouth.

"My, my. Haven't you taken a 180," he said, scooping a handful of blueberries for himself.

"Or maybe I'm just being nice to you because you're following those guys for me," I said, returning to our familiar way of teasing. In a flash, he dropped the blueberries from his hand into the bowl, grabbed my wrists and pinned me. Flat on my back on the couch, my breath came fast as he hovered over me.

"Take it back," he said, his dark gray eyes locked on mine. "Take it back or I'll have no choice but to show you why you like having me around," he said darkly, pressing his groin against me in demonstration.

My skin heated in an instant. I was sure I was burning up all over. "Show me," I whispered, daring him on. He wedged a strong leg between my thighs, spreading my legs open. He lowered himself to me, grinding his pelvis against me in the most excruciatingly slow tease. My brain cells decamped, and rational thought fled the building. Here, on my couch, with music playing faintly in the background, the sounds of Los Angeles evening traffic from the nearby avenue filtering through the open windows, all I wanted was him. He hadn't even kissed me, and I was desperate for more.

"Take it back," he said again, his voice a hot whisper on my neck. My eyes fluttered closed with the scratch of his stubble against me, and the slow grind of his hard-on against the fabric of my jean skirt. I willed him to push it up, to gather my skirt at my waist, and tug down my panties, but that was the hormones talking. I knew I wasn't ready to be naked with him.

Yet.

But even as lust clouded my brain, I managed to speak. "I'm just teasing. I like you, William," I said, laying out the truth. I opened my eyes and looked into his and they were filled with satisfaction, but happiness too. "You know that, right?"

"I know. I just like hearing it," he admitted.

"And I'm really glad you're following them. Not only because I want to know what they're up to but because I like that we're working together," I said, looking up at him. I was still pinned, my arms above my head, my wrists in his hands, and I loved every second of this position.

"Me too," he said softly.

"I feel like we're partners, and it means a lot to me that you're doing this and helping. I know you're trying to get a job with your uncle's firm, so the fact that you're doing all this for me means so much."

"I want to help, Jess. I want to help *you*," he said, his voice sweet as he spoke in a bare whisper. Gone were our usual playful barbs and snark; in their place was only honesty and vulnerability. Those twin emotions scared the hell out of me, but they also felt good. I wasn't accustomed to being vulnerable and letting down my guard, but I'd come to trust William. And I was starting to see—or to *feel*—the benefits of letting him in. This afternoon at the diner, he'd been so caring. Like he was now too.

Which made me realize that was yet another trait he had in the positive column.

"I like it when you help me," I whispered and he let go of my wrists, to bury his hands in my hair and kiss me. It was a tender kiss, one that made me tremble as he swept his tongue across my lips, taking his time before he deepened the kiss, all while running the pad of his thumb along my jawline. There was something so gentle, but possessive too about the way he touched my face as he kissed me. My heart leapt in my chest, like it was trying to get closer to him.

As soon as that thought touched down in my head, I tensed. Because I was falling for him. Big time. I had no clue what liking him this much would do to me. To my control. To my studies. To my quest to stay healthy. To my future. Especially when his future was so uncertain. I stopped the kiss. He pulled back.

"Are you okay?" he asked, brushing my hair away from my cheek.

"Yes," I said, then swallowed. I pressed my lips together so I wouldn't speak, wouldn't reveal all that I was starting to feel.

"Are you sure?"

I nodded.

"You don't look okay," he said, moving off me to lie next to me. "What happened? I think you kind of checked out. I'm a terrible kisser, right?" he said, flashing me that trademark grin that melted me all the way to the ends of my hair and the tips of toes. That feeling–like happiness flooding through my veins–was enough to make me talk. I didn't want to lose this sensation, even for the moment. It was a feeling that wasn't borne from doing well in school or nabbing a photo or checking off another item on my to-do list. It was from falling.

"You know I love kissing you. I was just thinking about what happens when…" I let my voice trail off.

He picked up the thread easily. "When I might have to go back to England?"

"Yes."

"Me too," he said, in a soft voice, as if the question weighed on him.

"I mean, I like you. But what can this even be? It's so hard to find a job."

"I know," he sighed heavily. "Trust me. I know."

"Do you even think you'll stay?"

"I want to. So much. And I like you. So much," he said, and stopped to look at me, his eyes hooking into me. "And maybe now you're yet another reason I really want to stay."

My eyes widened, and I felt the breath knocked out of me. "I am?"

He bent his head to my neck, pressing a soft kiss against my skin before he looked back into my eyes. "Yes. Does that scare you?"

I shrugged. "A little. I mean we only met three days ago."

"I know," he said, running his hand along my hip. "And I have no clue what's going to happen. All I know is I enjoy hanging out with you immensely, and I want more of you."

A ribbon of worry cut through me. *More of me.* Did I have any more to give? I was stretched thin with work, and school, and volunteering, let alone going to medical school next fall. How on earth could I ever give any more of myself? But yet, I couldn't deny that being with William was the one pure spot of pleasure in my life. He was chocolate, he was cake, he was ice cream, and I wanted to gobble him up. The moments with him were the times when I wasn't wound tight. I could let go with him. I wouldn't be able to let go at all next year, or for the next four years once medical school started. Maybe more of him was exactly what I needed right now. A finite amount of more. Not a commitment. Not a promise. Just a smidgeon. He gently took hold of my hand, threading his fingers through mine.

"I want that too, but getting close worries me," I admit. "I don't want to relapse or anything."

"I completely respect that. I truly do, but you're stronger than you think, Jess. I know you worry that you have to have the world rotating at the perfect pace, and everything going a certain way. But if anyone has it together, Jess, it's you."

I didn't answer right away. Instead, I soaked up his words, and the way he seemed to know me so well already. Maybe I could have it all. Maybe I was stronger than I thought when it came to guys and food. Maybe I was on the other side of my eating disorder.

"And look," he continued. "I don't know if I'm staying or going. I have no clue what happens. All I know is the last few days with you have been fantastic and I would love to keep seeing you while I'm here. I would love it if you'd be my girlfriend."

Girlfriend. It was as if all the sound zipped out of the apartment at once, turning the air silent. I hadn't been anyone's girlfriend in a long time, and my body froze at the prospect. But then I thawed because being with him was safe. I wouldn't let myself get too close with him possibly leaving, and with me starting school next fall. Maybe I could truly have my cake and eat it too.

Him.

"You're kind of like cake," I murmured.

He raised an eyebrow in question.

"You're like cake to me and I want cake," I added.

He laughed, a deep rumbly belly laugh that seemed to echo in the room, filling it back up with noise and the sweetness of laughter. "Knowing how you feel about food, I will happily be your cake."

"Then come back on top of me because that felt pretty good what you were doing earlier," I said, and in a heartbeat he was over me again, his hard body aligning with mine.

"Hi," he whispered.

"Hi," I said back, and something about this moment felt like we had stepped over a line and onto the other side.

He rocked against me, his erection pressed hard into my thigh. I shivered as a wave of goosebumps rushed over my skin. I closed my eyes and leaned my head back, giving in to the letting go.

"I love touching you, Jess. For so many reasons," he said as he rubbed against me. "But especially because I like watching you let go of your grip on the world."

"You do?"

"Yes," he said, thrusting against me. "I do. I love it. I love how it's the one time when you let yourself feel good. I love that you do that with me."

"You make me feel good," I said, my breath feathering against his cheek.

"I would love to make you feel even better," he said, and a flurry of white-hot sparks ignited in my belly with the suggestion. Heat pooled between my legs, and I was dying for him to touch me.

"How?" I asked as I looped my hands around to his ass, dipping them back into his jeans once more.

"However you'll let me," he said, his voice turning low and husky, and so full of need. He wanted me to feel good, wanted me to let go beneath him, and that sounded pretty damn appealing to me too. Better than cake, better than chocolate. Touching him was like having all the things I kept at a distance.

"What you're doing right now feels pretty fantastic," I said, as we rocked together, my hips arching into his erection. "But maybe just take off my skirt," I whispered.

In seconds, he'd unbuttoned, unzipped and tugged off my skirt. I lay before him on the couch, wearing only my tank top and a simple pair of cotton boy shorts in dark blue that hugged me low on my hips.

"Fuck," he hissed out as he looked at me, and I couldn't help but thrill at his reaction. His raw, unedited reaction to seeing my panties. Such a simple moment, but such an intimate one too. "My favorite color on you," he rasped out as he ran his fingers against the cotton panel of my panties, feeling where I was wet for him. "You're so hot," he said. "I love that I did this to you."

"You did. Now, do more," I instructed as I grabbed him by the hips and yanked him down against me. I wasn't ready for his hands in my pants, or his mouth. But the feel of him against me? That I could manage, and that's what he gave me, as he began grinding against me.

I moaned with every move he made, arching my back, and gripping his butt hard as he rocked perfectly into me. So damn perfectly that I could feel that delicious start of something. The slow, sweet spread of pleasure all throughout my body. The sensation that a decadent release was within my reach.

"*William,*" I moaned, rocking into him, as waves began to crest inside me.

He said something in Italian. I had no clue what he was saying, but it sounded dirty, and I loved the possibility of the words. He rained kisses on my bare skin, brushing his lips against my throat, my neck, my ear as he moved his body against mine in a dizzying pace, his hard length doing wonders to me even through the layers between us. It didn't matter that our clothes were on, it didn't matter that his skin wasn't touching mine. I was close, so close, and nothing was going to stop this orgasm that hovered on the edge of my evening with him.

"Oh god," I gasped, opening my legs wider and wrapping them around his hips. "It feels so good," I moaned.

"I want you to feel amazing."

And I did feel amazing. Absolutely out of this world incredible as I started seeing stars, bright and beautiful, like the way I felt when I was with him. I wrapped my arms tighter around him, pulled him as close as he could possibly be, and my mouth fell open into an O as my body went there too.

<u>William</u>

So. Yeah. That was hot. Like, crazy hot. I was dying to slide my hand inside her panties, to feel how wet she was, to have her rock against my fingers. But all I really wanted was for Jess to feel good, and for me to be the one to make her feel that way. For her to come just from the friction of our bodies made me want to pound my chest.

But I wasn't that type of guy. Instead, I kissed her more because I couldn't resist. Her lips were delicious, her skin was divine, and her body melted whenever I touched her. Nothing was a bigger turn on than when the girl you like loses control as you touch her. Jess was like that with me, and the way we connected in the bedroom—okay, living room—was yet another reason I wanted more and more of her.

"That was so fucking hot," I said after I broke the kiss.

A faint smile curved her lips, and she still wore the afterglow of an orgasm on her face—flushed cheeks, plump red lips and eyes hazy with desire fulfilled. "It was so fucking hot," she repeated, and I loved that she wasn't embarrassed or shy from coming while I—let's call a spade a spade, shall we?—dry humped her.

She roped her arms around my neck and pulled me back in for more kisses, looping her legs tight around me again. Maybe she was ready for another, and hell, I was up to the task. Very, very up to it.

"You liked my legs, didn't you?" she asked.

"Hmmm?" Her question didn't compute.

Then in seconds, she gripped me with her thighs and flipped me with those strong legs. I was on my back, and she was wedged along the couch by my side. Her hands were fast, and she moved quickly, unzipping my jeans, and grasping my hard-on through my boxer briefs.

I groaned loudly, my eyes floating closed as she touched me. She felt so incredibly good, her quick hand rubbing me. I was reduced to nothing but the desire for her to touch me more. Fortunately, she didn't need me to tell her that. She knew, because she tugged at my jeans, then my boxers, pulling them down far enough to take me in her hand.

Holy fuck. Her soft fingers wrapped around me, and all the air escaped my lungs as she stroked me. "Your hands are like magic," I rasped out as I rocked into her palm.

"They'll feel even better like this," she said, breaking the contact for a second. I opened my eyes to watch her lean across me and grab a bottle of lotion from the coffee table, and pump some into her hand.

"Always thinking," I said, wiggling my eyebrows.

"Lubrication works wonders," she said, returning to my erection and gripping me harder.

"That it does, Jess. That it –" I stopped talking when she started using both hands, stroking and tugging in ways that made my whole body vibrate. I sank down into the couch, giving into the moment with her, to the way her talented hands worked me over.

"God, I want to fuck you so badly," I said to her in Italian.

"I have no clue what you're saying, but I bet it's dirty," she said, laughing as she grasped me in such perfect harmony, using both hands. Sheer pleasure ricocheted throughout my bones and blood as she pumped her hands over me, on me, against me.

"So fucking dirty. I am dying to be inside you, to feel you come on me, to have you under me," I said in that language too, another groan working its way up my throat as her hands flew faster, the lotion doing its job of turning friction into wonderful abandon.

"I love that you talk in Italian when you get turned on," she said, and this time it was her voice, her hands, the fresh memory of the sexy way she'd arched against me, that set me off into a fantastic climax.

I bit off a string of endless curse words, as I thrust hard into her hand.

Minutes later, when we'd both cleaned up, I wrapped an arm around her and pulled her in close. "See, and that's another reason why I hope I can stay in America. All that cake."

She tensed for the briefest of seconds, then relaxed into me.

I had no idea if she wanted the same things I did— more—but for now I had her, so I'd take what I could get it.

FRIDAY
Weather: 70 degrees, Sunny

CHAPTER ELEVEN

Jess

I stretched out my hamstrings at the foot of the trail as I listened to my most upbeat pre-running playlist. There was nothing quite like a jog on the trails as the sun rose. Plus, I was even more energetic than usual. Having a fantastic orgasm last night delivered by a hot guy I was crazy for *might* have had something to do with the good mood that fueled my morning. He'd already texted me at the crack of dawn. His message had sent flurries down my spine–*HBG: Hi. I think I'm still high this morning on you. Can we have a repeat tonight?*

I'd said yes, of course. That man had worked his way into my heart, and somehow he had the secret key to unlock my body. Because the simplest touch from him turned me all the way on. Even his notes unleashed goosebumps in me.

Another note arrived as I moved on to calf stretches.

HBG: Will start the tail soon. Uncle James has demanded I appear at his office this morning. Says he needs to review wedding plans, so at least my delay is for a good cause.

I wrote back: *A very good cause.*

While bouncing on my toes, my phone rattled in my hand once more. Sliding my finger over the screen, I expected another text from William but instead opened a message from my dad.

Guess who's history from The Weekenders?? Nick Ballast. Otherwise known as Nick Balloons!

My Hollywood-gossip-loving eyes widened to full saucer size as I read his note, and the way he'd used the tabloid moniker my shots had inspired for the once tubby Nick. I tapped out a quick reply.

Nick's been cut from The Weekenders? Did the studio boot him?

Ever the early bird, my Dad replied quickly.

The director nixed him. Your mom heard about it this morning from a friend who's an agent at WAM, since a WAM client has been recast in Nick's role.

I gulped, a new fear swooping through me as I dialed my dad–the possibility that I was to blame. "Already? The studio already recast the part?" I asked, quickly segueing from text to talking.

"Crazy, isn't it? That movie's a mess. The script languishes in rewrite hell for the better part of the decade, then more rewrites before shooting, then a cast member axed a week or so before it starts production."

"But who replaced him, Dad?" I asked, as a cold dread seeped through me. I feared I knew who he'd say.

"Jenner Davies. Of all people, Jenner Davies."

I stumbled back, and grabbed hold of a fencepost at the head of the trail.

"You okay?"

"Yeah. I guess his charitable makeover campaign worked even better than he planned," I said, heavily. But it wasn't his makeover campaign that had won him a part. It was blackmail.

* * *

"That's why the photos of Riley and Avery never ran," I said to Anaka, frustration laced through my voice as the sun began its trek up the sky, casting early morning light across the hills. "They were never designed to run. They were taken for leverage, and Jenner used that leverage to blackmail Avery Brock into dumping Nick and stealing the role of the sixth student in weekend detention. Avery didn't want his indiscretions to get out."

All because of me. Because I was seduced by money. Because I hadn't thought to do the simplest of background checks on Keats Wharton. I'd believed he was who he said he was.

"Don't berate yourself, sweetie." Anaka said, after I told her everything as I hiked. I was too upset to jog, so I was power walking, and talking.

"But it's my fault he lost the part, Anaka."

"How would you have possibly known this would happen?" she said, then yawned deeply. I'd woken her up. She liked to sleep in on Fridays, but I wasn't ready to call William this morning and discuss it with him. I needed to talk this out with my closest friend.

"I don't know. But I should have been smarter. I mean, how many one-year-out-college-graduates run photo agencies?"

"How many college students earn a part-time living as a paparazzo? Only one," she countered. "You."

"Two actually. There's another girl, but I think she's nineteen," I said, thinking of Flash.

"Fine. One, two, whatever. It's practically the same, and my point is he seemed totally plausible, and he paid you in cash."

I stopped walking, and pressed my thumb and forefinger hard against the bridge of my nose. "I just feel so stupid," I said in a low voice, as I moved to the side of the trail to let a headphone-wearing guy run past me.

"But Jess. There's no way you could have known Jenner was behind it."

"If I had studied up on publicists in Hollywood, I might have."

"Beat yourself up some more. It's so good for you. But even if you studied the faces of every publicist in LA, you wouldn't necessarily have been able to pick out the younger brother of Jenner Davies' publicist. That's why Jenner and the other dude sent the younger brother. To fool you. They planned it all out. They plotted it. And you have to admit, they did a damn good job."

I resumed my walk, and breathed out hard. "Yeah, they did," I said. From the Web site, to the other photo placements, to the business cards, the plan was beyond solid, and I might never have even known about the ruse if I hadn't stumbled upon the three of them toasting at Rosanna's Hideout when I went to retrieve my toothpaste. Keats had played me all right, but I was merely an unimportant pawn. The real chess piece was Jenner Davies checkmating Avery Brock.

The teen actor with the angry attitude had found his way back on screen with a bribe. And, Avery Brock was exactly the type of person who was susceptible to blackmail, because blackmail only works when you have something to hide. Avery had a lot to cover up. It was ironic how I'd thought Riley was being set up by the poet brothers, when Avery turned out to be the real target. But where there was a target, there was a victim. That victim was Nick, and he was the innocent bystander with the wound from the bullet he didn't see coming. I couldn't just let him take the hit, and lose a job. I had to make good for him.

"I'm going to call Keats and confront him," I announced to Anaka, feeling like I was taking charge of the situation.

"What good will that do?"

"I don't know. But I feel bad for what happened to Nick. Given our, you know…"

"Your history," she said, finishing the sentence. "As photographer and subject, Jess."

"Yeah, and now my photos of someone else have hurt him again," I said, guilt pinging through my chest.

"Look, I hate to say this, but you're one of the winners here."

I scoffed. "Winners? How do you figure?"

"You got paid. You got paid well. You made out okay," Anaka said, talking coolly and calmly through the situation. "Look, Jenner had something on Avery Brock. He knew Avery was up to something, and so he sensed an opportunity and he took advantage of it. That's what Hollywood is. That's what Hollywood does. You should know as well as anyone. You document this stuff all the time, and the only reason it *seems* different now is you feel like you know the people. But this affair was going to happen. And someone was going to get the shots. And someone was going to use them to his advantage, whether or not you were involved."

She was right. There was an inevitability to the whole ruse. If Keats hadn't found me, he would have tracked down another photographer. Still, this was one of those times when I felt about myself the way a lot of other people did about the paparazzi.

That we were scum.

I hung up with Anaka, blocked my number, and called Keats, hoping I'd catch him off guard. There was just something about a call from a private number that made Los Angelenos pick up their phones.

"Keats here," he said, and I wanted to smack him. He was playing the part, and talking like a businessman, even though he was an actor like everyone else.

"I wanted to commend you for your performance," I said, as I climbed up a series of switchbacks on the trail.

"Excuse me? Who's this?"

"Just the *girl after your own heart*, remember?" I said, quoting himself back to him.

"Oh, Jess. Good morning."

"Not such a good morning for Nick Ballast though, is it? I know what you and your brother did. I know who your brother is. Jenner's publicist. I know you guys have something on Avery, and so your brother and Jenner blackmailed Avery to get on the movie."

"Whoa. You're making a lot of assumptions."

"But none of them are wrong. So they're not really assumptions. It's kind of scummy, don't you think?"

He laughed so hard it was as if he were barking through the phone line. "You take pictures of actors and directors cheating with each other and I'm scum?"

When he said that, I smiled, because I remembered I had a trump card. The person who takes the pictures almost always does. I wasn't going to play it yet, but play it I would. "But the point is someone got hurt here. Nick Ballast had nothing to do with any of this. With you, with Jenner, or with Avery. And now he lost his job because of what you guys did. That's just wrong."

"Nick Ballast is a big boy. I have a feeling he'll be just fine."

"You can't know that. Besides, Jenner's plan won't work if everyone knows what's going on, right?" I asked, showing the corner of that trump card. Let him squirm.

I could hear Keats rustling around, maybe getting out of bed, standing up, starting to worry. "What do you mean?"

"Jenner's leverage was that he'd keep Avery's affair a secret in exchange for the role in *The Weekenders*, right? If everyone knew Avery was fooling around with Riley, Jenner would have no leverage to get the part in the first place," I said, even as I wondered how Jenner had known that Avery and Riley were hooking up. How would Jenner have been privy to that info? "But if the pictures got out..."

"You're not going to share the pictures, Jess," Keats said, but his voice wavered. He didn't know what I'd do. He didn't know me.

"I have the copies. I have the files. I could get them to any photo agency and onto any site in seconds."

"But you won't," Keats said, and now his voice was firm, and commanding. I slowed my pace. "Because I anticipated this might happen. And that's why my brother and I picked you. Not because of your shots of Riley and Miles. Because you're putting yourself through college, and then medical school by taking pictures. We researched you, Jess. We did our homework," he said, and a chill ran down my spine. "Call me crazy, but I don't think J.P. and whatever agencies you work for would be happy when they hear you backstab your clients. Because I'm your client, Jess. Whether you like it or not. You deposited the money. You were paid. You want all the photo agencies in town to know you take their money and then turn around and threaten them?"

Silence gripped my throat, like a hand clamping down. I seared inside from the hot shame of his threat. And from the harsh truth of his statement. I wanted to punch him. Not only because he was hitting below the belt, but because he'd found my weak spot, and was using it against me. My Achilles heel. My dreams, my hope, my future of medical school and the way I paid for it–the way I *had* to pay for it. I felt like Avery Brock. I felt like that dick of a director because Keats had leverage on me now.

He was right. I couldn't turn on him because then I'd be known for doing just that. I'd never work in this town again.

"You go ahead and run those pictures and I'll make sure every photo agency knows how you do business."

"You're an ass," I said through gritted teeth.

"Yeah. Probably. That's why I'll be good in this business. It's cutthroat."

"And what are you going to do when other photogs take pictures of Avery? You know someone else will catch him on camera with Riley. It's the inevitable law of Hollywood hooking up," I said, scrambling to regain some kind of foothold.

"The deal will be done by then. The movie will have started shooting with Jenner in the role. We moved first, and we moved fast, and that's what matters. Avery won't replace another actor."

"You don't know that," I pointed out.

"I'll take my chances. But look, it was nice doing business with you. And hey, my hat's off to you. You played it well. You thought you had me. But in the end, Jess, we both get to walk away having gotten what we wanted. I guess you are a girl after my own black and twisted heart. We're just a couple of players in Hollywood after all. Here's to dealmaking."

He hung up first, and I stared at the phone, my head pounding with the anger of having been played. I pushed my hair out of my face, blowing a frustrated sigh across my lips.

"Heads up."

I turned around in time to press myself against a tree to let a group of pink shorts-wearing middle-aged women run past me. They must be a running group, training for a breast cancer run together, because they were led by a younger woman, who was cheering them on, and shouting motivational phrases.

A personal trainer.

As I let them pass, I flashed back on the image of Nick Ballast and his trainer from earlier in the week, recalling that they ran not far from here. Excitement flared in me; the daring possibility that I could make things right. That I could fix my mistake by telling the one person who could do something about this whole mess I'd made.

Nick.

Because this was my real trump card—not photos, but encyclopedic knowledge of celebrities' whereabouts. I knew where stars hung out. I had studied them, memorized their routines, and committed their every habit to memory.

Turning around, I ran as fast as I could back to my scooter. I yanked on my helmet and sped off to the parking lot at the trailhead where Nick had been seen running the other day. Nick Ballast was an early morning exercise junkie, and I hoped against hope that I'd catch him. I'd screwed him over and I couldn't just let that lie. Especially since the news had probably broken by now. When I parked at the trails, a quick check of my email revealed a *Hollywood Breakdown* news alert. I read the item and it was like a hard kick in the stomach with the heel of a sharp boot: *Nick Ballast Booted from The Weekenders; Replaced by Jenner Davies.*

The news my dad had first heard from my makeup artist mom's friend had made it into print a mere hour later. That's how it worked in Tinsel Town. That's why you had to move quickly if you wanted to make a living reporting, shooting, or following the famous faces that speckled the canvas of Southern California.

The lot was empty, so I stretched and waited. After thirty minutes, Nick pulled up and emerged from the passenger side of a brown Mercedes, sunglasses on. His goateed trainer got out of the driver's side, a Bluetooth tucked on his ear. Nick was laughing, and smiling, as if he didn't have a care in the world. He and his trainer headed for the path.

I called out. "Hey Nick."

The look on his face had turned veiled, unreadable. "Hey," he said. He probably thought I was a fan but couldn't be sure.

"I'm a photographer," I said quickly, and with those words the trainer grabbed the sleeve of Nick's T-shirt and nodded to the path. Because photographers were the bad guys. Nick and his trainer began to jog, but I kept pace as I began my confessional. "I don't have a camera with me now. I'm not here to take a picture. I'm here because I know that Jenner bribed Avery Brock to get your role on *The Weekenders*. He bribed him using photos I took. But I had no idea they were going to be used that way. And if I had I wouldn't have taken them."

He stopped running. He didn't seem surprised that I'd mentioned the photos of Avery. He seemed intrigued. "But what did you think they were going to be used for?"

His response threw me off. I'd figured he'd want to know more about the pictures and that he could use my information to get his job back. But instead, his question was inquisitive; it was lawyerly, and it cut me to the core.

"I just thought they'd be used —" I started, but then I stopped. I thought they'd be used on a Web site, or a magazine. I thought they'd be used to titillate the public who craved sordid stories just like I did.

"You thought they'd be used on some gossip site, right?" he fired back. "Whatever these pictures were. You thought they'd just go up online? Just like the pictures of me eating in my car. Did you take those pictures too?"

I might as well be in the witness box because I was getting a grilling before the jury and I was sure that no twelve people would sympathize with a paparazzo.

"Yes," I said in a small voice. But then I spoke up, because I might be a bottom feeder on the lowest rung in Hollywood, but I understood Nick. I had the same issues. I wanted him to know I wasn't that different from him. That stars are just like us. Just like me. "I'm sorry. I feel bad for taking those pictures. I know what it's like to battle with food. I've been there myself."

Nick pushed his sunglasses on top of his hair, giving me full view of his green eyes and boyish face. He raised both his hands towards his left shoulder, took out an imaginary bow, and began to play a make-believe violin.

"Too bad you don't have your camera now to get this shot," he said with a full-on sneer of a smile as his violin-playing hand stopped thrumming in time to flip me the bird.

Then he and his trainer left me in the dust.

I turned back the way I came, anger coursing through me as I cursed under my breath like a sailor. I wasn't swearing at Nick though. Nick had been screwed over, and it had been my fault. Instead, I cursed Jenner, but most of all I cursed myself.

As I reached the parking lot, I forced myself to cordon off the encounter with Nick. I could wallow in it, or I could keep moving like the other sharks in this town, and there wasn't a choice between the two options. I had to stay strong. I had to stay hungry. I had to keep taking pictures whether the subjects liked it or not. I reminded myself of what J.P. had taught me when I started working for him: "*There's a dividing line between celebrities and the rest of us. You stay on your side, Jess, and you never ever apologize for a photo. We're all just trying to make a living in this town.*"

I replayed his words, nodding as if he were here giving me a pep talk. I needed a pep talk because I'd started to go soft. But I could put my hard shell back on. I had to live and die in L.A.

CHAPTER TWELVE

<u>William</u>

After a full morning of being Uncle James' errand boy, a task that entailed picking up his dry cleaning and fetching coffee, I was tired of his run-around. I supposed I shouldn't complain–a job was a job was a job. But yet, he'd shown zero indication that he would sponsor a visa, and sending me out on Girl Friday tasks was unlikely to prove my worth.

As I headed to the printer to retrieve a back-up of the guest list, I heard James' loud voice from his nearby office.

"Your credentials are great. I'd love to have you come in and we can talk more about the details of working here. We're looking to expand and hire more full-timers and I've been the most impressed with you of all the interviewees," he said, and I nearly stopped in my tracks. I continued very slowly to the printer, so I could hear the rest of his chat.

"Absolutely. Come in Monday and we'll nail down the details."

He hung up as I grabbed the pages. What the hell? I'd been practically begging the bastard for a job, and he'd gone and offered a gig to someone else. Annoyance coursed through me. I couldn't catch a break with him, and he was constantly stringing me along. If he was going to keep teasing me, I'd just as soon cut bait with him.

I popped my head into his office, knocking twice. "Knock, knock."

"Come in, William," he said gruffly, barely glancing up from his computer. "You think you could get me a sandwich soon? My stomach is growling."

Deep breath. Take a deep, calm breath. "Of course. Just let me know what kind. And by the way, I couldn't help but overhear as I was walking down the hall that you're hiring someone. I think that's fantastic, and I'm hoping you might have room here for me too," I said, gripping the printouts tightly to channel my nerves.

James sighed deeply and looked up at me, scrubbing a hand across his jaw. "Look, kid. I know you're an eager beaver, but here's the thing in the United States. We build ourselves up. We grab our own bootstraps," he said, bending low in his chair and miming yanking on a pair of boots. "That's what I did. I didn't ask for a handout. And I certainly didn't ask my mommy's sister's husband for a job. I built my own damn business, and those are the type of employees I like to hire." I felt my cheeks redden as he cut me down. "You do a fine job installing software, and doing records, and hell, I even liked the intel you got me on how the paps work. I'm happy to keep throwing you little jobs here and there. A bit of cash for a couple hours' work. But I just can't get you a full-time job. It's against my moral code."

I nodded crisply, as if I understood the depths of the lesson he thought he was teaching me. Inside, I was burning with frustration. Turning crisp with irritation. This was information he could have shared months ago. Instead, he'd been leading me on the whole time, knowing he was never going to put me on payroll. I opened my mouth to speak, and was about to say *thanks for nothing* when I thought of Jess, and the wedding tomorrow. Now was not the time to take a stand. I gulped, rose, and handed him the wedding list. "I completely understand, James. And I respect your morals so much. Now, what kind of sandwich can I get for you?"

"Roast beef with mayo," he said, then returned to his computer without a word.

* * *

"Are you bloody fucking kidding me?"

I shook my head, as I clutched the phone to my ear on my walk back from the sandwich shop. Traffic chugged along at a usual sluggish pace, even on this side street near James' office. "Wish I were. But nope. The bastard made it patently clear he was never going to hire my sorry, pathetic ass. Have I mentioned again how happy I am that we're not blood relatives to him?"

Matthew laughed lightly, then sighed. "I'm sorry, Will. That totally sucks. I really wish I was in a position to hire you," he said, and I wished that too. But the harsh reality was that as connected as Matthew and Jane were in the music business, that didn't equate to finding a job only I could do.

"I know. It's okay. I know you've done everything you can," I said, wistfully. Hell, Jane had even tried to make me her personal tech assistant, but the visa-pow-ers-that-be had said that was absolutely a job for an American.

"We won't stop trying. I promise. And listen, I just heard from my editors at *Beat* that I'm flying out tomorrow to L.A. for an interview with this rising pop band. Let's get together on Sunday morning and we'll brainstorm options for you. We'll see if there are some stones unturned."

A flicker of hope touched down in my chest. I liked my brother, and I always enjoyed seeing him. "That sounds awesome. And maybe you can meet Jess too."

"Wait," Matthew said, curiosity strewn in his voice. "You did not tell me you were seeing someone."

"Well, I'm telling you now. And she's fantastic."

"Then we really need to find a way for you to stay in the States."

"Exactly," I said, as I neared James' office. I could tolerate two more days working for him for her sake, especially since she was calling me now. "I need to go. That's her on the other line."

"Whipped already," Matthew said, and I could hear the satisfied grin all the way from the other side of the country as he hung up and I answered her call.

"Hey Jess," I said.

"There's no need to tail Jenner any more," she said, her voice lacking its usual spark as she proceeded to give me all the details of her morning. My jaw nearly dropped with her story, but my mind was quickly turning.

"Here's the thing. I don't think this story ends here," I said.

"Why not?"

"Because what we know is only the outcome—that Jenner's the newest cast member of *The Weekenders* and that Nick's been booted. We don't know how it started. It's as if we have a script with only the second and third acts. Since I know you like to think of everything like a movie script," I said, speaking her favorite language.

"So what happened in the first act?"

"That's what I don't know. But I want to find out, because it could change the ending."

"How?"

"Because we don't know how Jenner could have learned in the first place about Avery hooking up with Riley. How did Jenner, and by extension, the scheming pair of publicist brothers, know that there was something on Avery Brock? Something to blackmail him with. That's the missing link. How Jenner got the tip in the first place," I said, as I pushed open the door to James' office. "I need to go, but I'm going to go track this down. And then I'm going to take you out tonight."

"I would like that," she said.

We both would. I might not have had a job, but every day there was more of a reason to stay.

CHAPTER THIRTEEN

<u>Jess</u>

Celebrity dog trainer Claire Tinsley was ready. She was twenty-three and had been born on November 2. She was an organ donor, which was quite thoughtful of her. After an early class, Claire's alter ego had spent the rest of the day outside the most star-studded Starbucks in the city, snapping latte runs, coffee breaks, and the no-fat frappuccino fixes of the famous. J.P. happily took my work, handed me two hundred dollars, and then gave me the fake ID.

"You look good as a brunette," he said, then gestured to the plate of miniature Meyer lemon cupcakes on his desk. "Take one."

I wrapped a napkin around a cupcake, and J.P. pretended to tip over in his chair and faint from shock.

"What are you doing?"

"I've never seen you take food before. I thought you survived on the blood of celebrities."

"Don't worry. It's not for me."

"For a boyfriend? You holding out on me?"

"Hardly," I lied, but I looked down so he wouldn't see my eyes as I tucked the wrapped-up cupcake into the front pocket of my backpack.

"You all set for tomorrow? Need anything else?"

I mentally ticked off the pieces I'd need for my wedding costume and the plan to bring my camera inside the event. I'd picked up some wrapping paper at the drug store earlier, along with a pretty white bow, so I even had a gift for the bride and groom. I was good to go, and the twenty-four-hour countdown had started. "I'm ready."

"When do you think I'll see the shots?"

"They're checking cellphones at the gates, so I probably won't be able to get to any sort of device to email you pictures for a couple hours. But by four, for sure."

He rubbed his hands together. "Oh man, I'm like a kid at Christmas. Can. Not. Wait."

"Neither can I," I said, and left J.P.'s office. I stopped at a nearby mall, set up camp on a quiet bench in the courtyard to finish up my bio homework that was due on Monday, and only checked my phone every five minutes for a text from William, so I reasoned that my self-restraint was still strong. I crossed my fingers, hoping he was uncovering the missing scenes—what had happened in the first act.

William

Things I never want to see on my laptop again—this many photos of Jenner Davies. He dominated my computer screen as I studied image after image of the bleached blond teen star. There was a shot of him at the soup kitchen on his whole helping-the-less-fortunate quest, then a picture of him visiting sick children, and finally a photo of him cleaning up the beach. But before he became so philanthropic, he was photographed working out quite a bit.

The paparazzi had captured many images of Jenner pumping iron, running on trails, and doing crunches at a gym with his trainer.

I zeroed in on the gym shot because something about it felt eerily familiar, so I stared hard at Jenner as if I could put the pieces together like that. When I glanced away from Jenner's face to take in the rest of the picture, that's when the clue blared loudly at me. His trainer had a goatee. I flashed back to the stakeout with Jess when she'd told me about gym shots, trainers and Nick Ballast.

His trainer has this goatee, she'd said.

Fine, a lot of guys had goatees. But a lot of guys also *didn't* have goatees. Opening another browser window, I searched for shots of Nick Ballast with his trainer. They showed up immediately, and lo and fucking behold.

Nick Ballast and Jenner Davies had the same personal trainer.

A spark of excitement raced through me.

There it was. The first act. The pieces were coming together.

But then, I told myself to settle down. This didn't prove anything. Lots of trainers had more than one celebrity client. The only way to know if there was anything more to this than mere coincidence was to go to the source.

Since Jess had mentioned the names of some of the most popular gyms in Los Angeles, I looked them up, scrolled through the photos and bios of all the personal trainers, and found him quickly.

His name was Pelly Howland.

I plugged him into Google so I could learn everything about him.

His Web site popped up. Not an over-the-top one, but it advertised his credentials both as a trainer and in entertainment law. He wasn't a lawyer, but evidently he thought it important to mention in his bio that he'd earned his associates degree in entertainment law, and was studying now for his bachelor's in the same subject.

Interesting.

Very interesting.

Those details told me *a lot* about him.

As did the fact that his cell phone number was on his page, along with his email. This guy was hungry. He wanted business. Hunger for work was something I knew well. Now, I needed to know more about what made Pelly tick, so I turned to Facebook where I discovered that he was quite fond of posting photos of himself while wearing a crisp shirt and tie and sharing status updates from *Hollywood Breakdown*, rather than dispensing tips about drinking protein shakes after a workout.

I nodded as the picture of Pelly Howland crystallized. He was a trainer who wanted to be a player. That's how I would hook him.

Grabbing my phone, I dialed his mobile, but it went straight to voicemail. "Hi, this is William Oliver," I began, opting to use my first and middle name rather than last. "Heard great things about you from some of the guys at WAM," I said, tossing out the name of the biggest talent agency. I didn't say I worked there. I simply said I'd heard of him from there, and hoped that would be enough of a lure, that Pelly would feel as if he'd made inroads in the big beast of Hollywood. "Would love to book a session."

Then, I left my number. Next, I tried the gym he worked at and requested a session with him today.

"He's fully booked. How about next Friday at 9:30?"

"No thanks," I said, and hung up.

I heaved a frustrated sigh, but remained undeterred. There had to be something to the Pelly-Jenner-Nick connection, and I needed to figure it out. I'd already discovered that Pelly was social, and active on Facebook. Maybe he was a Twitter fiend too. Quickly, I tracked him down on Twitter, scouring his feed for any clues. His first update of the day boasted about working out on the trails. His next claimed he was booked with sessions all day and *so pumped* for them. Fine, that was the gist of what I'd learned from the gym. Then, he linked to an article about the potential casting of *We'll Always Have Paris*. One more click of the mouse down his feed, and there it was —an update from twenty minutes ago saying his two p.m. session cancelled but he'd make the most of his free hour with some treadmill time.

Or with me, I reasoned, and hoped Pelly checked his messages in between sessions.

After James' runaround this morning, I refused to let this piece of intel elude me. Determined to snag some face time with the man, I was going to have to try to find him at his gym. I pulled on workout shorts and a T-shirt and hunted around for a Bluetooth headset that had come with my phone but I never wore, seeing as I didn't want to ever look like a douche who wore a Bluetooth except for now when I needed to harness that look. As I opened the door, my phone rang.

"William Oliver," I said.

"Hey! Pelly Howland. I just had a cancellation. You still up for a session? Because I would love to fit you in. I'm all about client service," he said.

"How fortuitous. I'll be there in twenty minutes."

I made my way to Pelly's gym, stopping only at a magazine stand along the way.

I parked a block away from the gym, tucked the headset over my ear, slipped the *Hollywood Breakdown* under my arm, and walked inside, looking the part of a young and hungry Hollywood player too.

The trainer was waiting for me by the front desk, a smile on his goateed face. "Pelly Howland, pleasure to meet you."

"William Oliver. And I assure you, the pleasure is all mine," I said, and his eyes stayed on mine at first, then he noticed the *Hollywood Breakdown* in my hand, the Bluetooth in my ear, and the English accent I'd come equipped with. Not that an accent proved anything in this town, but for some reason, it worked like a fucking charm when you needed someone to think you were trustworthy.

Because thirty minutes and a few carefully dropped hints that made me seem like a WAM insider too, my abs were quite sore, and my ears were getting a workout too.

Pelly the Goateed Trainer was like a windup doll. Crank him up and watch him go. All I had to do was feed him bits and pieces of Hollywood insider intel, and his mouth moved. I dropped names left and right that Jess had mentioned over the last few days.

"You think Emily Hannigan would make a good Gretchen Lindstrom in the *We'll Always Have Paris* remake?" I asked as he made me work my obliques.

"She'd be fantastic, but not opposite Ren Canton."

"Who then? Someone like Nick Ballast?" I offered in my best casual offhand tone as we moved onto crunches.

He scoffed, but it was marked with a laugh. "No. Nick is too young for that role."

"He's one of your clients, right?"

Pelly nodded proudly as he held down my ankles. "He is. Damn proud of that kid. He was just cast as a college freshman on a TV show that starts shooting in Vancouver in twelve days."

I mentally pumped a fist, but outwardly kept my cool. "That so? I heard Jenner Davies got Nick's role on *The Weekenders.*"

"He's my client too," Pelly said, and damn, all I had to do was drop a name, and he picked it right up and bragged about it.

"Nick must have been bummed."

Pelly shook his head, and mouthed *no.*

"No?" I whispered in question.

"Nope," Pelly said quietly in a conspiratorial tone. "Nick booked the TV show last week. He wouldn't have been able to do both. The movie shoots here. And the TV show shoots in Canada."

The lights went off. The buzzer beeped. The slot machine played its jackpot tune.

"Ironic that Jenner got the part then," I mused, going fishing for more. Pelly, it seemed, took the easy bait. So far, I'd pegged him right. He fancied himself a player, some sort of rising power broker.

"Ironic," Pelly said, a note of pride in his voice as he tapped the side of his head, "Or just smart thinking."

"Matchmaking, eh? That's what makes this world go round."

"Yes it does," Pelly said, and then offered me his hand. "Time for squats."

I counted down until the hour was up. Not because the workout was hard. But because I was dying to tell Jess that our Goateed Trainer Boy was the missing link.

Jess

After a few hours of homework and rampant phone checking, a message came through that William was at a gym and to meet him two blocks away from it by the Santa Monica Pier. The gym was one I'd told him about as a prime paparazzo hangout. I was proud of him for learning the tricks of my trade so quickly.

I packed up my books, popped into the bathroom for a speedy brushing of the teeth—this time I wanted fresh breath for kissing not for food resistance— and hopped on my scooter to zip west. Twenty minutes later, I found a fast parking spot and locked up my ride. I waved to William as I walked toward him, even though I wanted to launch myself at him since he looked insanely hot leaning against a nearby parking meter, wearing workout clothes—a gray T-shirt and blue nylon shorts. They fit him well, and showed off his strong arms, and strong legs, and made my mind trip back to last night because I knew what was inside those shorts. I'd be lying if I said I didn't want to dip my hands beneath the waistband again. I did want to touch him again. He'd felt amazing, and looked so sexy on my couch with his pants down. Actually, I wanted to do more than touch him again. I wanted to know what he tasted like. And there went a hot spark through my body.

Like a shooting star burning me up.

"Hey," I said, trying to sound neutral, as if that would tamp down the lust clouding my brain.

"Hey to you. How was your day?"

"Um. Fine. Yours?"

"It was shitty this morning because my uncle is an ass and there's no chance he's going to hire me," he said.

My heart fell for him. I knew how much he wanted that job. "I'm sorry. That really sucks."

"I know. Trust me, I know."

"But I'm sure you can get something else," I said, trying to sound hopeful because as much as I considered us short term, there was a part of me that wanted him to stay.

"We'll deal with that another time. Because it's not shitty anymore, since I have good news for you."

Then he told me about his afternoon, every last detail, and I bounced on my toes from the excitement racing through me as I assembled the remaining puzzle pieces. "Are you saying Nick wanted out of the movie to do the show? And Jenner wanted in on anything since he needed a job? And since he and Jenner have the same trainer, the trainer hooked them up with each other and they planned to blackmail Avery Brock together the whole time? That Nick never got the screw? That he actually wanted off the film because he had a better role?" I asked, my brain whirring wildly with the details.

"I'm saying that's an entirely plausible scenario. It answers a lot of questions, doesn't it? Nick and Jenner go to the same gym, they have the same trainer, the trainer is like a good hairdresser and he knows everything about his clients' hopes and dreams, so he sees an opportunity to make a deal. He connects the boys, and there you go. You've got your guy on the inside—Nick. He must have been the one on *The Weekenders* who overheard that Avery was making the moves on Riley, so he and Jenner set up the plan to get the photos with Jenner's publicist. They get the shots, they blackmail Avery, and they get what they want—Nick gets off the movie. Jenner gets on. Nick goes to Canada for a bigger part. Jenner is happy just to have a part. At least that's what I put together with my esteemed private detective skills. Amazing the lengths an actor will go to get or not get a part, isn't it?"

"Amazing too how everyone has an agenda," I said, and I didn't have to feel guilty anymore. Nick was a jerk, Jenner was a jerk, Avery was a jerk, and everyone was angling for something. All I had to do was profit from it and shoot it, like J.P. had said. I wasn't going to let myself suffer any emotion any more for any actor. They were all jobs to me, and jobs I knew how to do. "Do you know what this means?"

"What does it mean?"

I grinned wildly, and pumped a fist. "It means I don't have to beat myself up about Nick Ballast any more since he engineered the whole damn thing. I didn't screw him over. I didn't make him lose the job. He wanted this to happen, so I don't have to feel guilty about anything any more. Oh, but speaking of guilt, I almost forgot. I have something for you," I said and reached into the front pocket of my backpack. I offered him the cupcake. "I brought this for you. J.P. made it. I hope it didn't get crushed."

"I'd eat it even if it got crushed, and I also won't feel guilty about it at all." He bit into the cupcake. "Damn, that bloke can bake. By the way, I said that for you."

"And it sounded heavenly. *Bloke*," I repeated, in a British accent.

"And, my stomach thanks you. I've barely had any-thing to eat today."

"How's that possible? I thought you and food were like this," I said, twisting my index finger around my middle finger.

"This girl I'm working with had me on an all-day stakeout."

"This girl is very impressed with what you learned. And this girl wants to thank you for all that you did."

"Good. Because I want to impress this girl. And I want her to go to the wedding tomorrow, get the pictures, and not feel bad about a damn thing because she shouldn't."

"She's definitely not feeling bad about anything at all right now. In fact, she's thinking about how much she's looking forward to this evening with you."

"Good," he said in an approving voice, pointing to the nearby Santa Monica Pier, with its Ferris Wheel and Roller Coaster. "Do you like roller coasters, by the way?"

"Do I like roller coasters?" I tossed back as if he were crazy for asking. "Do you think there's a chance I don't like roller coasters?"

"I bet you love them," he said, draping an arm around me as we walked. My stomach flipped from the slightest contact. Or maybe it was from the realization that I'd agreed to be his girlfriend last night. That I found myself liking being his girlfriend. We turned onto the pier, strolled along the midway, then past the ring toss and Whack-A-Mole games.

"You know how everyone has an agenda?" he asked.

"Yeah?"

"I have an agenda too, Doctor Leighton," he said, dropping his arm to my waist and trailing his hand along the small of my back, sending shivers through me. I was putty under his hands. Everything he did melted me from the inside out.

"What's that?"

"To see if you scream on roller coasters or raise your arms in the air."

"Wouldn't you like to know," I answered, returning to our familiar teasing, as we slid into line for the roller coaster. A few minutes later as the car chugged up the tracks and we rose higher above the Pacific Ocean, I asked William a question. Because I also had an agenda, and now that my life was about to hit smooth sailing, I could go for it.

"Do you remember when I said I wanted to thank you for what you did for me today?"

"Yes. I remember."

"Do you want to know how I want to thank you?" I glanced at him briefly and his eyes said he was damn curious indeed as the car reached the top of the first hill. The sound of wheels cranking along tracks stopped.

There was silence for the briefest of seconds, and in that silence William answered. "I do want to know."

I whispered the answer in his ear.

Then I raised my arms and I screamed.

CHAPTER FOURTEEN

<u>Jess</u>

It didn't take long to make it to William's apartment. I'm pretty sure he set a land speed record on his bike, and I matched his pace. He held my hand as we walked up the stairs, then as he unlocked the door and flicked on the light.

"Here it is, my humble abode," he said, gesturing to his living room. I barely noticed the couch, the table, the kitchen. I had one thing on my mind, and one need in my body.

Him.

"I'll look later," I said, and grabbed his waist and pushed him against the wall.

"Mmm," he moaned appreciatively as I dipped my hands inside his shorts.

"I'm so glad you have workout shorts on. It makes it so easy to do this," I said, quickly tugging them down to his ankles. His erection sprang free, thick and hard. I wanted to taste him, to touch him, to feel his hands in my hair as he brought me close.

"I aim for easy undressing in moments like this."

I reached for his hard-on, and he drew a sharp breath as my fingers wrapped around him. He rocked into my palm, his breath already speeding up and I hadn't even taken him in my mouth yet as I planned to. But I was about to.

"William," I whispered.

He opened his stormy gray eyes. They were hazy with desire.

"You know how I said this was a thank you?"

"Yes."

I shook my head. "It's not a thank you. I'd never do this to say thank you. I'm doing it because I want to."

Then he grabbed my hair and tugged me in close for a searingly hot kiss, exploring my mouth and devouring my lips, all while he grew even harder in my hand. I broke the kiss and dropped down to my knees.

"Incidentally, that was the hottest thing you've ever said," he said, and then we both stopped talking when I kissed him, then inch by delicious inch I took him in further. He made the sexiest sounds, groaning as he speared his fingers through my hair. He grew harder and thicker in my mouth. At first he watched me, his heated gaze focused on my lips, but soon his eyes floated closed and his moans turned louder. They drove me on.

With my lips wrapped around him, and my tongue trailing up and down, I enjoyed every single second of his pleasure.

Thank you very much.

William

"I lied."

"What do you mean?" I asked Jess a few minutes later as we sank down onto my couch.

"I do have a thank you present for you."

I raised my eyebrows in question, as she stretched across me to reach into her backpack for a small white box.

As she held it in her lap, she fiddled with the corners. My heart beat faster knowing she was nervous. It was adorable and intoxicating all at once, and it made me want to kiss away her nerves. But then, most things she did made me want to kiss her. Come to think of it, I pretty much wanted to touch her all the time. Twenty-four-seven. With breaks only for pizza.

"I thought you could wear this to the wedding. Since it's a pretty fancy date for us," she said, and I swore the tiniest bit of red spread across her cheeks. I'd never seen Jess blush before. She wasn't the blushing kind.

She handed me the box.

"My first gift from you. I will treasure it, whatever it is," I said, and pressed a soft kiss to her forehead that seemed to ease her nerves. I opened the box to find a pair of cufflinks inside. They were some kind of brushed metal and looked like miniature padlocks. "They're lovely."

"I asked my brother to send them. His company makes them from recycled materials, and these are created from the padlocks that people put on the bridges in Paris. He has a deal with the city of Paris, which has far too many locks on the bridges now. He takes the used padlocks and makes them into these beautiful cufflinks. And I thought if you're going to a wedding, you might as well have cufflinks. So, thank you so very much for allowing me to be your wedding date," she said, and her lips curved up into a pretty smile, one that said she was happy not only to be crashing the wedding, but to be doing so with me.

I ran my finger over the cufflinks, then set the box aside. "They're gorgeous, and it will be an honor to wear them tomorrow. And an even bigger honor that you are my date."

"You know, William," she said as she trailed her hands along my arm. "We should watch *Anyone's Dough* sometime. Since that was the first movie we bonded over."

"We should. But it's going to be a long, long time before we get to it because I'm much more interested in doing other things with you."

"Me too," she said with a sly wink.

Then I kissed her for a long, long time.

SATURDAY
Weather: 70 degrees, Sunny

CHAPTER FIFTEEN

Jess

I would miss my cell phone. I kissed the screen good-bye, powered it off and tucked it away in my desk drawer. A phone with all your contacts and access to your email is not something you want to chance losing, even if you have a secret storage area under the seat of your scooter. Besides, I'd picked up a dumb phone at the convenience store for twenty dollars. William and Anaka were the only ones with the direct number. He was already at the event; he'd had an early morning arrival time at the grounds, he'd told me.

I slung my heavy backpack, filled with my dress, my wig, my shoes, the purse and the wedding gift onto my shoulders, and popped into Anaka's room to say goodbye. Lying on her belly, decked out in a bright orange top, a mini skirt, and gray and orange striped knee-high socks, she was tapping away on her laptop.

"Jess! I'm working on my screenplay," she said, beaming at me.

"Good. I figured that would be the only reason you'd be up this early on a Saturday."

"It's coming along. I'm right at the part where there's a big misunderstanding."

"And does everything fall to pieces and the audience thinks there's no chance in hell for the leads to ever work out their problems?"

She nodded, a pleased look on her face. "Of course. I want to devastate the audience."

"Perfect, because they want to be devastated."

"Have you got the dress I left you for the wedding?" she asked. Anaka had loaned me one of the dresses she wore to charity functions with her parents since I didn't have the type of attire a guest would usually wear to a celebrity wedding.

I nodded. "It's folded carefully in my bag. I'm going to change into it when I get closer."

"If you see my dad, look away," she teased, since her father was on the guest list.

"Here's hoping he doesn't recognize me in my wig. But I will do my best to steer clear of him. Text me if you need anything."

"Same for you. I'm heading to my parents' house to do my laundry since they won't be there the rest of the day," she said. Saturday was laundry day for Anaka, and since she was particular about her wardrobe, she preferred to use her mother's washer and dryer, with all the fancy settings and special cycles.

"Be sure the neighbors don't spot you air-drying your lacy underthings on the deck," I said with a wink, and she laughed. "By the way, did you ever get the details from your cousin on her romantic entanglements?"

Anaka rolled her eyes. "She's being super evasive. She just keeps saying *it's complicated*. I'm going to have stop texting and resort to calling."

"Such an old-fashioned way of communicating," I said.

Then I was off, flying down the highway, weaving in and out of cars, on my way to the wedding that would change my life. I didn't feel guilty any more either. I only felt a twinge of early victory. My heart beat faster, and I was bursting with anticipation and the kind of jumpy, happy jitters that precede a Christmas morning. This was it. This was my moment. My big shot. Everything had been planned perfectly.

I signaled, turned off the highway at the Ojai Ranch exit, and drove down the main drag in pursuit of a branch of the local public library near Chelsea Knox's estate. I'd looked it up online, but I'd also seen plenty of photos of Chelsea reading picture books to her young children from the comfort of the bean bags in the kids' reading room.

Pulling into the parking lot, I locked my scooter and headed inside. Libraries happened to have much nicer public restrooms than Starbucks did.

Inside the stall, I changed from my jeans, Converse sneakers and T-shirt into the classy navy blue dress from Anaka, along with beige pumps and the matching beige purse. I brushed out my blond hair, looped it into a low ponytail, then pulled it into a stocking cap. The wig went on next, and I adjusted the edges near my ears, so I'd look like a natural brunette. I folded my clothes, stuffed them in my backpack, and left the stall. At the mirror, I touched up my makeup, kicking it up a notch from my usual look, making my lashes longer, and my lips a shade of light pink, outlined in a darker pink with lipliner. I was ready for a wedding. More important, I was ready to go earn my medical school bills for the next year or so. At precisely two o'clock when Veronica Belle walked down the aisle to the theme music from *SurfGhost* and pledged to honor, cherish and adore Bradley Bowman for the rest of her life, I'd have everything I needed for my future.

I left the library, zoomed 1.7 miles to the road that led to Chelsea's home, and cut the engine, parking my scooter near the cars of the other wedding guests. A twenty-something woman in a pale yellow dress stepped out of the car next to me, and said hello.

"Hi," I replied. I didn't recognize her, but not everyone attending was famous. Claire Tinsley certainly wasn't. I stuffed my backpack under the seat of my scooter, locked the seat, slid my purse on my arm, and held the box with the wedding gift inside it, wrapped neatly in white paper with raised white bells, and a bow that would never come undone. My wallet with my fake ID was inside the purse. I checked my dumb phone one last time as I walked to the line of guests at the gate.

There was a new text from William.

Change of plans.

I froze when I saw those three words. I pressed hard on the middle button on the phone to call up the rest of the message. These dumb phones were slow.

I breathed easily again when I read the rest of the message. *Just wanted to let you know no one's checking IDs any more for the app. All you have to do is give your name. They'll check the list. Claire's on it. James is running me around like crazy so I'll try to find you when I can.*

That was a relief. But yet it was strange. After all the security precautions, the leaks planted about the false locations, as well as the plainclothes security all over the grounds, why would Veronica no longer want the guest list verified?

The girl in the yellow dress gave the security guy her name, and handed over her cell phone.

I closed William's message, and saw one from Anaka had just arrived. Only the first few words appeared on the screen. *Um, my dad's not —*

But the message cut off, and as I stabbed the middle button to open the note, the security guard had already nodded to the woman in the yellow dress and motioned for her to head to the nearby golf cart, waiting to ferry guests from the gate to the house.

I closed the phone before I could read Anaka's message.

"Hi. I'm Claire Tinsley," I said, and my voice sounded scratchy and gravelly. I was trying to sound different, to throw them off the scent. But that was silly, I reminded myself. I needed to not stand out.

The security guard—Sal, I remembered, since William had told me his name—ran his index finger down the paper. My lungs threatened to leap out of my body as he scanned. I didn't see Claire's name on the list. My heart was planning a mutiny as he turned to the next page. My name was always near the middle of any list. Where could it be? Then my insides settled and I remembered why. Because my last name usually started with an L. But today it started with a T.

The security guard found Claire Tinsley's name, then asked for my cell phone. I handed it to him, and he wrote my name on masking tape, then pressed the tape onto the phone. He looked through my purse, patting my wallet and my makeup case. He waved me in. "There's a table for presents right inside the front door."

"Thank you," I squeaked out, as I took a seat next to Yellow Dress in the golf cart. I held on tight to the gift.

That was it. It was so easy, it was beyond easy. I was inside the premises, and now all I had to do was assemble the camera when I reached the house.

"Friend of the bride? Or friend of the groom?"

Yellow Dress was making small talk as the cart bumped over the driveway.

"Bride," I said in my normal voice this time. "You?"

"Same. We went to college together," she said, a cheery smile on her face.

"Oh, that's nice. What did you study?"

"English literature," she said. "What about you? How do you know Veronica?"

Yellow Dress seemed to be studying me closely, and I worried she might recognize me from the photos with Riley and Sparky McDoodle from earlier in the week. But my dog alibi fit that too.

"I'm a dog trainer. I've worked with the family's chihuahua-mini pins."

"Oh my god. That is such a coincidence. I have to ask you a dog question. My yorkie won't stop getting into the cat's food and I feed the cat in the laundry room. I'm so worried he's going to get fat."

I nodded several times, playing the part of the cool, confident dog trainer who'd dealt with this situation before. I flicked back to the episodes I'd watched of *I'm a Dog Person* while training Jennifer. "What you need to do in those situations is set a trap for the dog. You have to leave the door to the laundry room open, set the food there for him, and just wait. When he makes a move for it, then you correct him."

"Interesting," she said with wide and curious eyes. "Do I just give him a sharp *no*?"

I nodded with authority. "Yes. Or else you get a training collar."

She shook her head, her eyes showing fear. "A training collar? Like the kind that pinches them? I don't want to hurt him."

"Of course you don't. But you certainly don't want him to get fat either, do you?"

"That's true. I definitely don't want a fat dog," she said with such supreme worry in her voice that it had to be genuine. We arrived at the house. "You were so helpful. Thank you."

I let her go ahead of me, and when I walked through the door a minute later, I took mental photos of Chelsea Knox's palatial *and* eco-friendly entryway, noting the solar panels high above in the arched roof, and the furni-

ture made from renewable materials in the living room.
Next to the door was a table stacked with gifts. I turned
sharply to my left, and into the first bathroom in the
hallway. I closed the door quickly, locked it, and opened
the wedding gift. I'd wrapped it TV-style, which meant I
didn't have to unwrap it. I simply lifted the wrapped top
off the box.

Inside the box was my gorgeous camera. After setting
it on the counter next to the sink, I put the cover to the
gift back on. Next, I unzipped my purse, and retrieved
the big makeup tub that had once held copious amounts
of powder. Now, the makeup tin held the lens to my
camera. I removed the lens and nested it on the camera.
Then, I reached into the bag and yanked off the masking
tape that had kept a circular section of fabric in place. As
planned, there was now a hole in the side of the bag precisely the size and shape of the end of a lens of a camera.
Carefully placing the camera inside the purse, I positioned it so the lens lined up with the hole. Then, I took
scotch tape from a zippered compartment and used it to
retape the circle of fabric back onto the lens from the
outside, so the bag wouldn't look suspicious. Returning
the scotch tape to the compartment, I double- and triple-
checked the placement of the camera, then shut the
purse, and pulled it onto my shoulder, keeping the side
with the circular, taped-on cutout against my body.

As I checked my reflection in the mirror, I noticed I
was shaking. I took a deep breath, my shoulders rising up
and down. The air filled my lungs, calming me. After
several more breaths, I felt settled again and ready. I

looked at my watch–1:39. Showtime was in twenty-one minutes.

Tucking the empty gift under my arm, I unlocked the bathroom door and nearly jumped when I opened it. William was waiting on the other side.

"You scared me," I whispered, my heart pounding fast in my chest.

"Would you like me to take the gift for Ms. Belle and Mr. Bowman?" he said with an easy smile, one that suggested we were co-conspirators. "I can bring it to the table if you'd like."

"I would like that very much." I handed him the wrapped and empty box.

Then he scanned the hallway. Guests were still entering the house, so he leaned in close to my ear, so only I could hear. "I need to run. James has me doing a ton of stuff all over. But I can't wait to see you later."

"Me too," I said, then he turned away.

I walked to the backyard, wishing I could snap photos of everything along the way, from the back deck that wrapped around the house, to the yoga sanctuary beyond the deck, to the garden full of organic vegetables and fruit that Chelsea claimed to tend and harvest herself.

Instead, I was a good girl, and I headed to the folding white chairs set up underneath the tent and beside the mechanical koi pond. Standing vases of daisies and sunflowers, Veronica's two favorite varieties of flowers, lined the aisles. A long white runner led from the back steps of the house all the way to the makeshift altar under the bamboo veranda where Sandy, the talk show host, would soon officiate. An usher led me to a chair about two-thirds of the way from the altar. I sat next to a woman in a red slinky dress, and a man in khaki pants. I didn't know them.

A string quartet by the altar played classical music.

I held my purse tightly and checked my watch. The ceremony would start in thirteen minutes. I looked around, trying to spot faces as the chairs filled up. Everyone looked vaguely familiar. Everyone looked vaguely pretty and reasonably attractive in a random sort of way. But no face stood out. No features brought instant recognition.

Perhaps the famous guests were waiting until the last minute. Perhaps they'd swoop in and fill the empty seats mere seconds before the bride walked down the aisle. But I flashed back to the half-read text message from Anaka —*Um, my dad's not*—and figured she must have been trying to tell me her dad wasn't coming. Why wouldn't he be here? Why would he have a last minute change of plans and miss the wedding?

I tried to dismiss the flight of nerves that circled me.

Soon, the officiant walked out of the house. She had the same cropped blond hair as the TV talk show host, but she definitely wasn't Sandy. That was odd. Next came the groom, slipping around the chairs so he wouldn't disturb the runner for his bride. I watched him, and something seemed off about his stride, but I could only see him from the back. Several groomsmen followed and they assumed their posts in front of the guests, and I could have sworn from where I sat that Bradley Bowman had more chiseled cheekbones. Even so, I opened my bag, rooted around as if I were looking for a tissue, and kept my right hand inside the bag to operate the camera. With my left hand, I removed the fabric cutout for the lens, freeing the camera to capture the event. I lifted the purse higher, holding it against my chest. I pushed the silver button on the camera several times to capture Bradley as he waited for his bride.

Then Pachelbel's Canon began, and everyone turned their heads to watch the bride. Clutching my purse for dear life, I shifted too, and kept snapping surreptitiously as the bridesmaids walked down the aisle.

The only trouble was, the bridesmaids weren't Chelsea, or Veronica's best friend, or Riley Belle.

Nor was the bride Veronica Belle. My heart sank and my skin burned the furious red of self-loathing when I realized why I hadn't spotted a single familiar face among the guests. Everyone here was an actor. Everyone was a stand-in. Everyone was faking it. That's why no one needed to check IDs after all.

Veronica Belle had staged a decoy wedding, and I'd fallen hard for it. I had the worthless photos to prove it.

CHAPTER SIXTEEN

Jess

I cried stupid tears all the way to the library, wiping the streaky lines of mascara roughly from my cheeks. But more leaked out, a cocktail of anger and self-loathing. I'd been greedy, and I'd been foolish, and that was a dangerous combination. I pulled into the library lot, almost toppling my scooter through my blurry, rage-y haze. When I jumped off, I caught a corner of the navy blue dress on the metal covering of the wheel. I yanked until the fabric came free, tearing the skirt in a slash up the thigh.

Curses flew from my mouth. Enough to send truckers covering their ears.

Frustration poured through every cell in my body. Nothing was going right today, and now I'd owe Anaka a new dress. Hastily, I grabbed my backpack from under the seat, and marched inside to my changing room.

I tugged the dress over my head in one clunky motion, stopping only to wipe more wetness from my eyes. The dress was useless now, so I pressed the fabric against my face, as if I could stopper all the sadness. But I had no right to cry, no decent reason to feel so indignant. This was a job, and the job hadn't come through as advertised. It was only money. I should know better than to cry over money.

There.

Sucking in the last of the tears, I stuffed my wig into my backpack and returned to my regular clothes. When I left the stall, I turned on the cold water in the sink and splashed some on my face. I peered into the mirror and administered a dose of much-needed self-medication: "Get yourself together, Jess. Big girls don't cry."

I let the bathroom door fall behind me, and was about to put Ojai Ranch as far in the rearview mirror as I could, when I heard two librarians at the front counter whispering to each other.

"You have to see these pictures. They just showed up on *On the Surface* a minute ago."

My spine tingled. I stopped at the closest shelf of books, and pretended to look through the new releases as I listened.

"Oh. My. God," the younger of the two women said, stopping at each high-pitched word to catch a breath. "They eloped!"

The floor gave out. My vision went fuzzy. Reaching for the gray metal shelf of books, I steadied myself. I'd never felt faint before, but I gripped the metal tight 'til the moment passed. Then I stopped pretending to listen in, and walked straight over to the counter.

"Sorry to interrupt, but I couldn't help but overhear that someone had eloped," I started, quickly recovering as I did my best to appear calm.

The woman smiled, and her hazel eyes lit up. This was a moment not to be missed—the delicious moment when celebrity news that surprised everyone began spreading across the Internet. She swiveled her computer monitor around to show me the site.

"Veronica Belle and Bradley Bowman eloped to Las Vegas!" She squealed. "They tied the knot literally thirty minutes ago. Can you believe it? They went to an Elvis-themed wedding chapel with just their family members."

The floor tilted once more and the sickening feeling hit my stomach. I stared hard at the pictures on the screen of Veronica in a sassy white mini-dress and Bradley in shorts and a short-sleeve button-down. They were laughing as they left the chapel, two sets of parents, and a few pairs of siblings behind them. Everyone was dressed in casual wear, including the sister of the bride in a cute mini skirt, clutching Sparkly McDoodle in her arms as she smiled brightly. The next shot showed Veronica tossing a tiny bouquet of daisies behind her. Then, there was a picture of the newlyweds and their families hopping into a black stretch limo.

Flash.

The pictures had to have been taken by Flash. She was always one step ahead of me. Now, she was three hundred miles ahead of me in Las Vegas, and probably laughing and smiling as she counted to one hundred thousand.

I swallowed thickly, trying to push down this terrible taste of failure in my mouth.

"That is just so clever," the librarian said, and I realized she'd been speaking the whole time. "We were just talking about how something must have been happening down at Chelsea's home today. I saw the party rental trucks, and then there were florist vans, and a big red car that had some caterer's name on it. What was that all about?" she asked with a kind of awestruck curiosity.

Her friend answered. "It must have been a decoy wedding."

The redhead laughed, as if such a stunt was the most clever thing she'd ever heard.

"Yeah, it was," I said in in a dead voice. "They hired actors. Extra types to show up. Pretend to be guests. Fill the seats. They even had stand-ins for Veronica and Bradley and Chelsea and Riley. They had security too. To make it all seem real."

"That is amazing to go to that effort. To spend all that money to just throw paparazzi off the scent," the redhead said in admiration.

Her friend chimed in. "Well, nobody likes the paparazzi."

Truer words were never spoken, and on that note, I left, and drove all the way home without looking back.

CHAPTER SEVENTEEN

<u>William</u>

Stuck on the other side of the property manning the front door of the estate, I barely even caught a glimpse of her leaving; just a flurry of color–her navy dress, her brown wig, her beige purse, and then, like a mirage in the desert, she was gone.

Minutes later, I was momentarily freed, so I tried calling several times, but her phone rang and rang. I swore under my breath, then with my focus on the gates, I picked up the pace, eager to search for her phone. She'd probably left it behind.

But James corralled me on the way and cut me off. "Change of plans," he barked. "I need you over there in the receiving line. Congratulate the bride and groom."

I tilted my head, as if I could better decipher his request from an angle. "But –" I started. "What's the point?"

"No buts," he hissed. "It's part of the job."

"Did you know it was a fake wedding?" I asked in a harsh clip, because he'd screwed over Jess. Big time.

He gave me a look like he thought I was stupid. "Kid, they're my clients. Of course I knew."

"And you didn't mention it?" I asked, as if I were a lawyer in a courtroom, quizzing a belligerent witness. I reminded myself that whether he was in on it or not, he never knew I was the man on the inside, sneaking in a paparazzo to take clandestine shots. Truth be told, I hadn't a leg to stand on when it came to this moral battle. Still, I was pissed as hell, and keeping me in the dark *felt* wrong.

"Don't get your panties all bunched up because you missed the chance to meet Veronica and Bradley. You'll get used to it in Hollywood," James said, clapping me on the back.

Fighting the urge to roll my eyes and bite out a sarcastic comment, I drew a quick, deep breath, plastered on a smile and said, "I assure you, that's not the case."

He stared down at me with wide and annoyed eyes. "Then get back out there and mingle. That's the job, kid. We've got to keep up the appearance. That's what the client wants. Eat some kale, look like a guest, then be on your merry way. Look, I know you're hunting for a job, and I'm sorry as hell I can't give you one, but do me a solid here and finish this up today, then tomorrow we'll meet with the publicity shop about the paparazzi intel you got for me, and if you do those things, I'll be sure to give you a good recommendation as you look for work, maybe even refer you to a few friends. How about that?"

He looked me square in the eyes, knowing he had something I wanted. Maybe it wasn't a job; but it was something I'd need for another one. A positive recommendation could make the difference in landing a gig in the next two months.

"Fine," I muttered.

Shoving me on the shoulder, James whispered, "Go."

I headed to the line of wedding guests, who were clearly actors, along with the stand-ins for Veronica and Bradley. Taking my turn behind a sea of players, I waited under the hot sun by the back deck, willing the line to move faster so I could escape and track down Jess.

When I reached the wedding party, the fake Bradley extended his hand. "Thank you so much for attending," he said.

"We're so glad you're here," fake Veronica echoed.

"Pleasure to be here. What a lovely ceremony, and such beautiful grounds," I said, and the moment was beyond false, even by Hollywood standards.

"I'm thrilled you enjoyed it," fake Bradley said, never once breaking character. It was like being at an interactive dinner theater. "Please, have some appetizers," he added, gesturing to the nearby waiters circling with trays of small food.

As I walked away, a waiter offered me kale-wrapped asparagus spears, but I shook my head. I spent the next hour logging every detail of the fake wedding. At least I'd have that info to share with Jess. Not that it amounted to much, but it was the only thing I had to offer her. She'd done her part and given me the intel I needed for James. That he hadn't hired me wasn't her fault. But I'd come up

short for her. A heavy stone settled in my stomach knowing I'd failed to deliver my half of the deal.

Jess

Anaka waggled the two pints in front of me. "Are you
sure you don't want gelato? My mom has Talenti's Carib-
bean Dream and Caramel Salt Crunch."

I waved her off. "I will eat all of them," I said, as I lay
on the cool tiled kitchen floor at Anaka's parents' house.

"That's the point. I think you need a pigout session
right now."

"Then I will yak up every last ounce. Maybe even eat
the container too and I'll barf that as well, and then your
mom's cat would eat that."

"Then I'm glad you warned me. I won't waste the good
gelato on comforting you," she said and closed the sub-
zero freezer. She sat down on the floor, cross-legged next
to me. When Anaka had arrived at her parents' house earlier in the day with her laundry in tow, she'd been expecting an empty home. Instead, she was greeted by her mom
still in her tennis skirt when they were supposed to have
been getting ready for a wedding. "I'm heading out for a
tennis lesson and your father booked a last-minute afternoon tee time," Anaka's mother told her, then clued her
in on the whole ruse. That's when Anaka had rushed to
her phone to text me, but I hadn't been able to get to the
message in time. Not that it would have mattered. I'd already been fooled. I was a fool.

Her dad received the alert from the Bowman-Belle
camp a few days ago that the Ojai Ranch set-up was just

that. That the couple was eloping, and he could return his tux to his closet. Everyone who was on the real guest list received the alert too. The couple waited until only a few days before to tell their friends because they wanted the elopement to be as secret as it could possibly be. They wanted their wedding on their terms.

I couldn't fault them, especially given how they'd outsmarted everyone but Flash. Deep pockets made for easy outsmarting. They had the resources to stage a fake wedding all for the simple pleasure of enjoying a real one. A quiet one.

A wedding for their eyes only.

"How do you think the pictures of their real wedding showed up on the tabloids?" I asked.

Anaka furrowed her brow for a few seconds, then snapped her fingers. "You said that other photographer was at the bridesmaid fitting? Taking pictures there?"

I nodded.

"I bet she overheard something then," Anaka suggested, and I nodded. That seemed plausible enough. Clearly, Flash had heard about the wedding somehow. Flash was at the top of her game. She had her ear to the ground, she was fast, and she had good sources, judging from all the times I ran into her on the job.

"What am I going to do now?" I moaned.

"Same thing you've always done."

"What's that? Be a pain in the butt? Be annoying and tightly wound and take stupid pictures of celebrities who are smarter than me?"

"You got outsmarted once. Big deal. You just keep on going," she said in the most matter-of-fact tone possible.

"How am I going to pay for medical school?" I whined.

"You do have $10,000 from Keats, as well as the money you've been earning from your job, right?"

"Yes," I grumbled, because I wasn't facing a zero balance. I wasn't rolling in it, but I had a few bucks to start with.

"It's something, Jess. It's something," she said, punching me lightly on the shoulder in an encouraging gesture.

I breathed out hard. "Yeah, but I need more to pay the first year's tuition bill. What am I supposed to do?" I held my hands out wide, probably looking like I was making snow angels on the floor.

"You'll just have to do what everyone else does. You keep working, you get some loans, and you deal."

If she were anyone else, I'd say *easy for you to say*. Her college was all paid for and then some. But I'd never fault Anaka for coming from means, just as she'd never mock me for not. We understood each other. We understood where we were different, and where we were the same.

"Besides, if all else fails you can just be a plastic surgeon. You'll repay the loans like that," she said, and snapped her fingers.

I rolled my eyes. "Because there's no competition in L.A. at all for plastic surgeons."

"Just look on the bright side. At least you have a date tonight with a hot guy."

I propped myself up on my elbow. "Speaking of, do you think William was in on it? Do you think he knew about it and set me up?"

Her jaw dropped as she rolled her eyes. "Are you auditioning for the role of world's leading conspiracy theorist?"

"No! But come on," I asked, furrowing my brow. "Are you telling me the caterers, the party rental people, the security firm didn't know it was a hoax?"

"Jess, my love, think about this like a screenplay. If you were trying to pull off a big super secret con, would you tell as many people or as few people as possible?"

I shrugged. "He could have known. I mean, he hasn't called. He was probably using me all along."

"Pretty sure he hasn't called because you don't have your phone. Do you want to bet you have a dozen missed calls on your phone when you get home?"

"Sure. I'll bet you a hundred thousand dollars," I said, and managed a small laugh.

"Oh, I'm going to collect because I know he's calling."

We stayed like that for a few more minutes, chatting about everything and nothing, as we always did, and Anaka made me laugh once more when she tracked down her mom's Siamese cat Suede and showed me how she'd taught him to fetch a ball of crumpled-up tin foil, return it, then fetch it again. Soon, her phone rang. She reached for it, checked out the number, and said to me, "I have no idea who this is." Then into the phone, "Hello?"

Silence filled the air, as a knowing smile spread across her face. As her eyes sparkled. As she adopted a look that said she was going to collect on our one-hundred-thousand dollar bet.

"Hi, William," she said loudly. "She's right here."

She handed me the phone.

"Jess, are you okay?" he asked, and his voice was like a massage. Instantly, it relaxed me and somehow made me feel as if the world wasn't upside down.

"Yeah," I said heavily.

"I tried calling you but it just rang and rang and rang. And you didn't have your regular phone, and you didn't take your other phone when you left. I had literally no idea it was a fake wedding. You have to know that. James never told me until after the ceremony. Remember when I told you that we weren't allowed to go near the room Veronica was getting ready in?"

I flashed back to our stakeout of Riley and Avery, when he'd shared the blueprints. "Yes."

"That was why, evidently. They staged it all. And I'm so sorry you didn't get the pictures you wanted. I feel terrible," he said in a soft and sweet voice that very nearly melted me into a puddle on Anaka's kitchen floor. That damn accent was still working its charms.

"Me too. How did you get Anaka's number?"

"After James had me running this way and that, I was finally able to get away, so I went to the security table at the gate, and I went through the whole box of phones and found the one you'd been using. There were only two numbers on it. Mine, and Anaka's. I called hers. Since I knew you weren't at my number," he said, and I could practically see the knowing grin curve up on his lips. He always knew how to make me laugh, and make me smile. "Where are you right now?"

"I'm at Anaka's house."

"Can I come see you?"

I turned to Anaka. "Can William come over?"

She swatted me. "Are we four years old? Of course."

She grabbed the phone, and gave him directions. "I've been dying to meet you all week since she told me you were constitutionally good-looking. *Her words.*"

Then when she hung up, I shrugged. "It's true. You're going to wish he were yours," I said, as my lips twitched in a smile. At least, there was that. He was mine. For now.

CHAPTER EIGHTEEN

<u>Jess</u>

"They still served cake?" Anaka asked, shocked, as she tucked her feet underneath her.

William sat in a cushiony chair across from us, still decked out in his wedding attire, but with a few buttons undone on his white dress shirt. Anaka and I were stationed on the pale blue couch in the living room, and she demanded a chapter and verse rundown on what had gone down after the exchange of the *I dos*, which marked precisely the moment I had taken off.

"Yes. But it was gluten-free cake. And they served all the food too–kale, carrots, and quinoa salad. Chelsea Knox is this big environmentalist so she probably didn't want to waste anything. They'd ordered all the food already."

"God forbid they waste gluten-free cake. Talk about yakking up food," Anaka said, and mimed gagging. "That shit is nasty."

"Stop. This whole conversation is giving me a headache," I said and pressed a hand to my forehead.

Anaka was not deterred. "Were there other paparazzi there?"

William nodded. "At the end, word got out that it was faked so there were a few photogs out on the street near her driveway. Someone tried to climb the fence apparently."

After a few more questions, Anaka brushed one palm against the other. "Well, I have a load of delicates that need tending to, and then I just had this strange notion—maybe it landed out of the blue—that I've been missing Suede so much I'm going to sleep at my parents' house and cuddle with the family cat tonight," she said, then squeezed my shoulder, and winked.

I pulled her in for a hug. "Suede is going to be so happy," I said, teasing her.

"Get out of here, and go enjoy this very good thing you have, rather than thinking about what you don't have," she whispered in my ear.

After she said goodbye at her parents' front door, we walked along her circular driveway to where our respective rides were parked—his motorcycle and my scooter.

I rested my hand on the handlebars, and William stood next to me.

"So," he said, waiting for me to say what happens next.

"So."

"Jess, I'm really sorry about the wedding."

Jutting up my shoulders, I shot him a rueful smile. "Me too. But what about you? Do you still need intel from me? For that publicist client?"

"James wants me to come to one last meeting with the client tomorrow and then I'm done with him. Though he is giving me a nice rec so I couldn't tell him off with a grand *I quit* like they'd do in the movies."

"That's absolutely how they'd do it in the movies," I said, cracking a small smile. "I hate it when life doesn't work like the movies. Sorry things with James aren't panning out."

"Truth be told, he's such a dick that I suppose it's all for the best, and I'll simply have to look elsewhere for a job."

"I'll help you. However I can," I offered.

He took a step closer. "You would?" he said as he touched my cheek with his thumb, tracing the outline of my jaw.

"Of course. I don't know how, but we'll figure something out. Because I really want you to —" I let my voice trail off. Vulnerability was far too uncomfortable a coat to wear. But even so, I had to find the guts to say what I wanted. I had to, every now and then, let go of the way I kept people at a distance. The more I tried to control things, the less I was able to.

"To?" he prompted.

I swallowed down my fear, letting my chest fill only with the strange certainty I felt for him. For us. We were both so disappointed today, so let down in our quests. But at least we had *this*. Each other. We didn't find what we were looking for, but we had somehow found something else other than work or money. "To stay," I said, keeping my gaze locked on his the whole time, watching his eyes light up with my words.

"Me too. So much," he said, lacing his hands through my hair and pressing his forehead to mine.

I didn't know what to say with his hands in my hair. It felt too good for words.

"What now?" he asked softly. "No one to follow. No elaborate spy acrobatics to plan."

"No agenda," I said, continuing.

"Nothing but the present," he said. "What should we do?"

I didn't answer that question. Instead, I pulled back to look into those stormy gray eyes. My lips parted, and my chest rose and fell, and I tried to find a way to restore speech. I hoped he could read my mind, or my body language, as I angled closer to him, but I was sure we were on the same page. I went for it.

"I think this is the moment in the script where the heroine invites the hero to spend the night," I said.

He hitched in a breath. "It's only afternoon," he said, his voice hot against my skin.

"Late afternoon," I amended.

He ran the pad of his thumb across my top lip, and I shivered. "Then this is the moment where the hero says yes."

He lifted my chin and dropped his mouth to mine. We kissed for many minutes that folded into themselves, and in the span of the kiss, I didn't think about money or medical school or pictures. I didn't linger on a single thing except his lips, and his hair, and his hands, and the astonishing closeness of his body.

He pulled away for a second. "Let's go now. I want the rest of the night to start immediately."

We put on helmets and he rode behind me all the way to my apartment.

* * *

We started on the couch. For the simplest of reasons. The bedroom was too far away. As soon as we tumbled through the door, his hands were on my waist and slinking under my shirt, and my breath was already coming fast. I tugged him down on me on the couch, thrilling at the way his long, strong body felt on top of mine. Of course, I already knew how he felt on top of me, but now I was going to know the feel of him in a whole new way, and goosebumps rose on my skin with the anticipation.

His lips found mine once more and he kissed me hungrily, making the sexiest groans as he nibbled on my lips and then explored my mouth. When we pulled apart for air, I pressed my hands to his chest, and looked at him. "I think you're addicted to kissing me," I said playfully.

"So unbelievably addicted to kissing you," he said, a wicked glint in his eyes, as he bent his head to my neck, blazing a trail of kisses up to my ear. "I want to kiss you in other places," he said, his ravenous words making my stomach flip.

"Where?" I asked, knowing the answer, but dying to hear it from him.

"Between your legs. I'm dying to taste you," he said with a heady groan as he lowered his hand to my jeans and palmed me where I was hot for him. In an instant, I responded, his touch heating me up more. I rocked into his hand.

"I want that, William. I want that so much," I said, my breathing already speeding up to a wild pace.

"Let me take your clothes off," he said, his voice barren against the silence of the apartment. That's when it hit me—a little mood music would be nice.

"Hold on," I said as he unzipped my jeans, and I twisted to reach for my phone on the table.

"Shall I smile for the camera? Are you going to take a shot of me undressing you?"

I cracked up as I scrolled through the music. "Count that as a never," I said, finding Matt Nathanson quickly and firing up a playlist. As the poppy, sexy music played, William grinned that devilish grin of his as he skimmed off my jeans.

"What?"

"Matt Nathanson," he said, shaking his head. "He's catnip for women."

"He is. But I'm going to let you in on a secret. You were getting lucky before I even turned him on."

"Excellent. Now, I will continue turning you on," he said, and reached for my shirt, pulling it off me, then un-hooked my bra, whistling low under his breath as my breasts tumbled free.

"I can't resist," he whispered, cupping my breasts and burying his face between them. Gasping loudly under his touch, my back bowed and I threaded my hands in his hair. I arched into him as he took his time lavishing at-tention, each sweet lick from his tongue sending a new round of desire crashing through my body. I closed my eyes, giving in to the moment, to the pleasure, to the in-tensity of his touch. He *was* catnip to me, and I was under some kind of spell, buzzed from the way he kissed and caressed, both tender and hungry. William made me feel wanted, and he made me want to let go for him, which was no easy feat for this control freak. I pulled him closer, as he explored my flesh, sending hot sparks all through me. Soon he began inching his way down my body, trailing his tongue underneath the swell of my breasts to my belly. Then he licked an agonizingly sweet trail down my skin, past my belly button, and right to the top of my panties, where he flicked his tongue along the waistband and murmured, "These need to come off."

"They do," I moaned, tilting my hips to him. Gently, slowly, as if he were memorizing every single second of the undressing, he lowered my panties down my legs, moaning appreciatively when he saw me revealed to him for the first time. "Fuck, you're gorgeous, Jess," he said, and then tore them off the rest of the way. "I can't wait."

And then his lips were on me and I nearly screamed in pleasure. That first touch, that first moment when a guy kisses you there is the finest line in the sand–it's such a moment of sheer vulnerability. It's trusting him with your body, with yourself, with the chance to touch you in one of the most intimate ways. With him, I was bursting with longing, consumed by desire for him. And yet, lingering nerves nagged at the back of my mind, pricking me with the worry, the fear, and most of all, the hope that he wanted me the same way.

Not just my body, but my heart.

Because I wasn't just falling for him. I'd fallen. I was there on the other side, and I sure hoped he'd gone along for the ride too.

Then, I stopped worrying. Because the way he touched me, his lips savoring me like I was the most wonderful thing he'd ever tasted, not only settled all those nerves, but banished them far, far away. Nothing else mattered now, nothing but the here and now, the present with him, as he cupped my butt, angling me closer, flicking his tongue and pressing his lips against me. *Kissing me.* I gasped and moaned. Hell, I thrashed and cried out. Then I grabbed his hair, gripped his skull and held on tight as he drove me to such a wondrous place that I was seeing stars. The whole world around me was silver and gold and pure epic pleasure as I shouted his name, and exploded into thousands of brilliant pieces.

Minutes later, when the waves of pleasure started to ebb, and some semblance of logic returned to my brain, all I could think was I never knew anything could feel so good. I never knew anything could feel that intense. Now I knew, because what he'd done to me was beauty and bliss all at once.

He climbed on top of me, still fully clothed, and kissed my cheek, then my neck, and then he started to speak, but I cut him off.

"You know I have no clue what you're saying, right? I haven't had a magical Italian translation machine inserted in my brain to understand you in the bedroom."

He laughed, then pushed back on his arms to meet my eyes. The look in his eyes was one of satisfaction, but also something else entirely. Something I could almost pinpoint, but was afraid to.

"I wasn't going to speak in Italian. I was going to speak in English to tell you how much I loved doing that to you."

I couldn't help but smile. "I loved it too."

"And now I have to be inside you. I want you so fucking much, Jess," he said, his eyes even darker than usual.

I shivered from the intensity of his words, and he wrapped his arms around me. "Are you cold?"

I shook my head. "No. I'm happy."

A smile curved his lips. The biggest smile I'd ever seen. He stood up, offered me his hand, and led me to my bedroom. He'd never been there before, but it wasn't hard to find in my small apartment.

"No movie posters?" he asked, arching an eyebrow as he scanned my walls.

"I'm a simple girl when it comes to decor."

The only picture on my wall was a framed shot of the sun descending over the Pacific Ocean, rays of peach and dark pink streaking across the twilit sky.

He pointed to the image. "Did you take that?" he asked, as I roamed my hands over his chest, feeling the outline of his muscles through his button-down shirt.

"Yes," I said, working my way down to his pants. "I do more than just celebrity shots. But those are the pictures I take just for fun."

"I never knew," he said. "It's beautiful."

"So are you in these wedding clothes, but I'd kind of like to get them off."

He returned his focus to me. "I can't think of anything I'd rather do than be naked with you," he said, and together we unbuttoned his shirt, and I pushed it off. Trailing my hands down his chest, I watched him as his eyes floated closed and he breathed out hard.

"*Jess.*"

"Yes?"

"I love the way you touch me," he said, and his voice was huskier than usual. It was his sex voice, I was learning. It was the way he sounded when we were alone, and I loved it.

"Good. Because it's one of my favorite things to do," I said, moving to the waistband of his pants. He kicked off his dress shoes as I unzipped his pants, and pulled them down.

Clad only in boxer briefs that revealed exactly how turned on he was, he opened his eyes, and pointed to his pants on the floor. "I should probably get a condom from those pants."

I laughed. "Yes. You absolutely should."

As he bent down to retrieve it from a pocket, I moved to my bed, stretching across the dark blue covers. He joined me, and I glanced down at his briefs, then my naked body. "There's an uneven distribution of clothing between us."

"Take them off," he said, and I could hear the desire in his voice.

I moved my hands to his waist, but then he stopped me, clasping his hand over mine. "Jess," he said, and this time the sexiness was gone; his voice was plain and full of need.

I pushed up on my elbows. "Are you okay?"

"Yes. So okay. So much more than okay. There's something I have to tell you."

And just like that, fear swooped through my body, expecting the worst, even though I had no clue what the worst would be. Except that somehow he'd used me.

CHAPTER NINETEEN

<u>William</u>

The look in her eyes stunned me. They said she doubted me, and that only made me want to reassure her more. To tell her that everything between us was completely true.

Gripping her fingers tighter, I brought our clasped hands to my mouth and pressed a soft kiss to her knuckles. "I swear it's not bad. It's good. At least, I think it is," I said, then ran my other hand through her hair.

"Okay," she said, softly, a tentativeness to her tone. She was waiting for me to go next, and that was perfectly understandable. I gulped, but that was only instinct telling me this was going to be hard to say. It wasn't hard to say. It was easy, like everything I felt for her.

"I just want to say this before we go any further," I began, keeping my gaze fixed on her. "And it's that I'm falling for you so much. It's way more than like. So much more. I'm falling in love with you, Jess."

She didn't say anything for a second, just exhaled. Then her lips parted, and she roped her arms around my neck. "I'm falling in love with you too, William," she whispered, and my heart thumped hard against my chest, flooding with such happiness and hope. Knowing the girl you're crazy for is mad about you too is quite possibly the greatest feeling ever.

Well, there's only one other thing that comes close, and that was about to happen too, since her fingers had found their way to my hand, and she was taking the condom from me.

"Please put this on now, and please make love to me," she said.

I pushed off my briefs, and obliged her request with a speed only race car drivers could rival. She opened her legs for me, and a bolt of heat tore through me. *Take it slow, Will,* I told myself. But fuck, I wanted her so badly that I didn't know if I'd be able to slow down. Settling between her legs, I entered her, stilling when I was all the way inside her. She felt so fucking good that my brain shut down, and my body took over.

So did hers as she wrapped her legs around me, and moved with me, our bodies in perfect synch as if we were meant to fit together. Pleasure pulsed through me from the feel of her, so wet, so hot, and so fucking beautiful as she opened herself to me, her back bowing as I thrust deeper into her.

The sounds she made drove me on, not that I needed any help, mind you. But my focus was on her, and bringing her more pleasure, because the only thing that trumped how intense it felt being inside her for the first time was hearing her moans and noises, and the way they grew more frantic and fevered as I sank into her. I *loved* how much she let go when I touched her, how she gave herself to me with a kind of reckless abandon. Grabbing my hair, she pulled me close and whispered in my ear. "I love this. So much," she said, her breathing erratic, signaling that she was close.

"It's fucking fantastic being inside you, Jess. You feel so good to me," I told her, brushing an errant strand of hair away from her face. Keeping my eyes on her, I pushed deeper, reading her cues, giving her what her body was telling me she wanted. Her face contorted with pleasure, her eyes squeezing shut, her gorgeous lips falling open into a perfect O. Then a silent cry came first. She chased it with the loudest shout I'd ever heard, and it was music to my ears, because it was my name falling from her lips as she came. Seconds later, I was following her there, charging into a fantastic climax that was better than any other.

Because it was with her.

The girl that I'd fallen in love with.

My American girl.

* * *

We ordered a pizza later that night. The best part? She actually ate it. Well, she ate two slices.

"I can have this because we're going to work it off," she said.

"You have no idea how happy it makes me that you're not freaking out about food because of us," I said, gesturing from her to me.

She flashed me a smile. "Me too. I was so sure I wouldn't be able to handle it all. But I'm thrilled to say I have no desire to barf because of falling for you," she said, bumping her shoulder against mine.

"Ah, I've never been so thrilled at not making a woman toss her cookies."

"I have a way with words, don't I?" she said, wiggling her eyebrows.

"You are blunt and it's adorable."

"Besides, as long as we keep working out like this, I don't think I'm going to have to worry about food one bit," she said.

A few minutes later, we christened her couch, and our second time was even better than our first as she climbed over me, riding me with a kind of wildness that made me lose my mind with pleasure.

Eventually, we returned to her bed where we tried several positions, laughing at the ones that didn't work so well, then not laughing at the ones that did.

Hell, we were both twenty-one. We had loads of energy. We had endless stamina. We had raging hormones, and we took advantage of all those points in our favor.

<u>Jess</u>

I stretched my arms over my head after my fourth orgasm of the night. It wasn't likely to be my last. William was insatiable, and that was fine with me. Sex with him rocked. It was so good it made me even more determined to help him find a job. I wasn't ready to give up this, or him.

"Hey, what time is your meeting tomorrow morning?"

"Nine."

"I have to meet Riley at eleven. Should we have coffee in between our meetings?" I asked, and I wasn't the slightest bit nervous about presuming we'd want to see each other as much as we could. I knew he wanted the same thing.

"You can't get enough of me," he said, grabbing my hip and pulling me close. "Now that you've had me, you're powerless to resist me."

"Well, duh," I said, rolling my eyes. "You're my Hot British Guy."

"The answer then is yes. On one condition."

"And that is?"

"You have to meet my brother. He's in town for work for the day, so we're getting together for brunch."

"I would love to meet him," I said, amazed at how quickly we were falling into being a couple, especially when our clock was ticking. In less than two months, he might be gone, and the thought was a tight knot in my chest that I wanted to eradicate. For now, I turned my focus elsewhere, tapping the clock on my nightstand that blared ten-thirty p.m. "The night is young. I'm going to expect several more rounds, William."

He saluted me. "Yes, ma'am. More sex coming your way, shortly." His gaze returned to the clock again. "Are those your flash cards next to the clock?"

Reaching for the stack of index cards, I nodded. "Yup. I practice before bed." I handed him the cards. "Try me."

"That's about twenty feet tall," he said as he held the huge mass of cards.

"A list to D list celebs," I said, and patted the cards. "C'mon. Quiz me. I can name everyone on here. I even added publicists the other night. They're on the top. Learned my lesson that I need to be able to recognize their faces."

He picked up the first card, and displayed the picture for me.

"Cassidy James," I said in less than a second. "She handles press for the cast of *Restless Roommates,* as well as for the actress Peach Winship from that LGO show *Powder* on drug dealers."

"Impressive," he said as he verified on the back, then showed me another one.

"Trivoli Lipton. He reps most of the *Stay-at-Home Moms with Sharp Claws* shows."

"Indeed he does," William said as he read the back of the card.

He showed me another index card. "Lacey Cordona. Does PR for the *Smith Street Blues* series."

Then Keats' photo.

I laughed. "I think we both know who he reps."

"Yep. He reps jackasses," William said and I smiled at his remark.

He brandished a photo of another publicist, a smarmy-looking guy with a mane of wavy gray hair.

"That's Trevor Highsmith. British, as a matter of fact. Runs some big shop and reps a ton of writers and directors. I'm not positive but from a few stories I read, I think he might be Avery Brock's publicist."

William flipped the card around and looked at Trevor's photo. He furrowed his brow, as his expression shifted from amused to serious. "Are you sure?"

"Pretty sure. Why?"

William scratched his chin and studied the card. "He looks a bit like someone I know. But I'm not sure."

"Or maybe you just felt an instant kinship?" I offered. "Countryman and all."

"Right. That must be it," he said, then flashed a quick grin that didn't seem quite natural. He tucked the publicist cards in the middle of the stack, and returned them to the nightstand. "Let's talk about something besides publicists. Tell me more about your non-celebrity photography."

We spent the next few hours talking, and then exploring each other's bodies once again. There was no question it was the best night of my life.

SUNDAY
Weather: 70 degrees, Sunny

CHAPTER TWENTY

<u>Jess</u>

William left my apartment shortly after the sun rose to shower and prep at his place for his meeting. Swatting away my temptation to sleep for another glorious hour, I forced myself out of bed so I could spend the morning studying before I saw him. After tackling biochemistry, I was ready to tackle William, so I showered, dressed and rode over to the promenade, arriving five minutes early.

After I locked my scooter, I checked my phone and found a new text message from William.

Crap. My meeting is running late. Can you give me 30 min?

Like I was going to say no.

Besides, my good mood from falling in love had me walking on cloud nine, so I replied with a *yes*, then made my way to the nearest bookstore to see which shots my colleagues and competitors had landed in magazines last week. When I finished my perusal, I headed to the coffee shop, passing the brunch crowd at Rosanna's Hideout on the way. I scanned the tables on the deck in case I spotted a familiar face, and could whip off a few quick shots for J.P. to cheer him up. He was still sorely depressed over the wedding fiasco. I unzipped my backpack to reach for my camera, when I saw someone I knew.

Avery Brock.

With his publicist.

The smarmy-looking guy with the mane of wavy gray hair.

Avery was wearing shades, drinking a cup of coffee, and looking exceedingly irritated.

His publicist was drinking tea.

He was seated next to an older guy with a bald spot that was shiny in the morning sun.

There was a fourth person at the table, and that person wasn't drinking anything. That person was talking animatedly. That person was the person who'd made love to me less than twelve hours ago.

I blinked several times, trying to wish the tableau away. But every time, the players remained the same and so had the played—*me*. Because William fucking Harrigan was working for Avery fucking Brock.

All along. Throughout all our efforts. During the stakeout. As I passed him information. He was working for the scumbag, two-timing, cheating director and he never told me.

I burned.

No wonder William seemed fake when I showed him Trevor's flash card last night—the bastard knew him. Because the bastard was on his payroll, passing my intel onto the philandering toad.

Fire licked my insides, coating me in righteous anger. If William would lie about that, how on earth could I trust him about anything?

Every nerve ending in me snapped, every muscle in my body tightened, and every survival instinct from living in this town of liars and actors and fakers kicked in. Walking away was not an option. He needed to know I'd seen him. I left the camera safe and sound at the bottom of my backpack, and marched to the tables on the deck, claiming my post by the railing. This was our spectator sport in L.A. and it was one anyone could play—the spotted-someone-on-the-street game.

"Oh my god, William, is that you?" I said in my best over-the-top blond and bubbly California girl impression.

The guy I'd foolishly fallen in love with glanced at me, blinked twice, and swallowed hard. Like a deer in the headlights, he looked the same as when I marched up to him in Manhattan Beach and busted him for following me.

"I haven't seen you in, like, forever," I said, dragging out the last word. "How are you? How's school? How's your dog? You remember me, right? Claire Tinsley."

"Hi, Claire," he said in a strained voice.

"I have to tell you this story about a dog I was training. You gentlemen don't mind, do you?"

Avery said nothing. He crossed his arms, and slinked down further in the chair. The publicist affixed a fake smile that he probably flashed twenty-five times a day on his phony face. The guy with the bald spot grumbled *go ahead.*

"So I had this celebrity client—I can't say who he is, but I'm sure you understand, William, how important it is to not reveal who you work for," I said, giving him a sharp look as I went for the jugular with the reminder that he'd once said he could never tell me who his client was. "But his dog was being so naughty. His dog was literally humping all the lady dogs in the neighborhood."

The publicist cocked his head to the side. He seemed curious to hear my story now. William kept his face stony.

"And my client wanted to know how everyone else in the neighborhood kept taking all these pictures of his dog. How on earth could all the neighbors get shots of his pervy dog? As if it were the neighbors' fault that his dog was so randy. Can you believe that?" I said with an exaggerated huff. "I had to explain to him that the reason his dog kept getting caught on camera," I said, shifting my gaze to Avery Brock, "Was that his dog was doing bad things." I let out a quick, fake laugh. "If he were a good boy, he'd never have to worry about getting caught with his pants down."

Then I waved toodle-loo and walked off down the promenade.

"Jess."

William called out to me thirty seconds later when I'd reached the corner of the street. I didn't turn around. I kept walking, seething inside. I would not give him the satisfaction. He had long legs though, so he caught up to me, and placed a hand on my shoulder. "Jess," he said again. I shrugged off his hand, and turned to him. I took off my shades so he could see I wasn't crying. There was no room for tears.

"You were working for Avery Brock all along," I said pointing my finger sharply at him. "Your client was Avery Brock and you pretended you didn't know it. I told you everything and it went to that guy who you claimed was a dick, who you claimed was giving your countrymen a bad name." My voice rose and wobbled.

"I didn't know it, Jess, I swear," he said, pressing his palms together as if he were praying. "I had literally no idea until last night when you showed me the flash cards and I recognized Trevor because he's the client. But Trevor never told me he was having me do intel on behalf of Avery. I never would have done any of that for Avery."

"You told me last night you were done with the job. One more meeting and you were done with the job. I guess you're not done with the job, are you? Because you're sitting there feeding him information. *From me,*" I said, now poking myself in the chest.

"Jess, it's not what you think."

"If there was ever a tired, old movie line, it's that one," I said with a scoff.

"Listen to me, please. I don't want to have anything to do with him. You have to believe me."

I flashed back to Nick Ballast's reaction when I tried to apologize to him on Friday morning. I could learn a thing or two from actors. They ran this town. They knew what to do. I had to be more like them. I took out my imaginary bow for my make-believe violin and pretended to play it.

Then I put my fake instrument away. "Actually, I don't have to believe you. Because there's this thing called honesty, William. I might be a control freak, I might be skeptical, I might be neurotic. But I never lied to you. Never," I said, biting out that last word. "I never lied about a thing. And you have lied about *so many* things," I said, and my voice started shaking. Fighting back, I reined in the tears that were threatening to flood my eyes. "And you always have an excuse or a reason why it's okay. But it's not. Especially because I *was* in love with you."

He exhaled heavily, his faced looked pinched. "*Was?*"

I was about to repeat myself when William's eyes danced away from me. "Oh bloody hell," he muttered, then waved listlessly. "Hi Matthew."

From behind me, I heard footsteps, and I spun around, nearly smacking into William's ridiculously good-looking older brother. He had the same dark hair, the same chiseled cheekbones, the same fantastic smile; the only difference was Matthew had blue eyes.

"You must be Jess," he said to me with a big grin, then offered a hand to shake. He had no clue we'd been arguing. "I've been looking forward to meeting you. I couldn't be more thrilled that this troublemaker has somehow convinced you he's a good guy."

William cringed, his jaw falling open. He shook his head at his brother, and made a slicing motion at his throat.

"What?" Matthew said, looking at William, then me, then back again. "Shit, did I say something wrong?"

I jumped in. "I assure you, it was nothing *you* said, and while I'd truly love to chat, my brunch meeting was just moved up. Sorry I have to duck out," I said, then I walked off without saying goodbye to William.

William

Matthew apologized profusely. Endlessly.

"I'm so sorry. I had no idea I was going to say the absolute wrong thing. I feel terrible," my brother said once more.

I shook my head, giving him utter absolution because everything was my fault. "Trust me. It's not you. It's me. It's all the things I didn't say. Or should have said at different times," I said, shoving a hand through my hair, then gesturing in the direction of the girl whose silhouette was fading in the distance. Like last night. Like when I saw the flash card. When I realized who Trevor Highsmith was—that's when I should have said something.

"I should go after her," I said, and in a nanosecond, Matthew's palm was flat on my chest.

"No," he said crisply.

"No? Why?"

"Because when a woman walks away that pissed, you shouldn't follow her. She needs breathing space, and she *only* needs to see you again when you have a big, fat, fucking apology properly planned. Send her a text, tell her you're sorry and you love her, and then give her some room."

I narrowed my eyes at him. "I suppose that means you pissed off Jane at some point?"

He nodded several times. "I did. And take it from the voice of experience, the next thing we need to do is sit

364 / LAUREN BLAKELY

down, have a cup and plan that proper apology. Assuming you still feel the same about her?"

I rolled my eyes. "Seriously? Do you have to ask?"

He held up his hands in surrender.

"Hey kid, what the hell?"

James' gruff, aggressive voice landed like wet concrete on my ears. Then I felt his clammy paw on my shoulder. "You don't just walk out when we're talking to a client. You get back in there and finish the hell up. That's how we do it in America," he said, digging his fingers into me.

Shrugging him off in one quick move, I swiveled around. For months, I'd been scratching and clawing at his door, hanging onto the frayed ends of his broken promises. Because I was desperate. Now, I was done. I let go of that tattered rope, and let myself freefall, damn the consequences.

"Actually, James," I began, my tone even and measured. "I don't have to do anything of the sort. I don't have to talk to your client, or to Avery Brock, because I quit," I said and the words tasted like a victory prize. Even if I'd have nothing to show at the end of the day, being the first to leave was a vindication, and it was one I wanted more of. "Because that's how we do it in America. When someone strings us along, and toys with our future, and plays games, we don't have to take it. Thank you for all you've done, and no thanks to the letter of recommendation."

He huffed and puffed, fumes wafting out of his nostrils. "You can't do that."

I nodded and smiled at him. "Oh, I can, and I did, and I'm not done. Watch this," I said, then marched up to Avery Brock, parking my elbows on the railing, and exhaling a *tsk tsk tsk*. "Avery, let me make this really simple for you," I said to the two-timing bastard. "Your publicist hired a security firm to find out why the paparazzi keeps getting so many pictures of you with your pants down. The answer is precisely what my friend Claire Tinsley said, but allow me to spell it out even more directly for you. You've been caught on camera because you're an ass. Because you cheat on your wife. Because you're doing something wrong. Here's the way not to get caught–*don't cheat*. Easy as pie. Good luck in your directorial endeavors, and may these latest foibles be a reminder to keep your dick in your pants."

A hand clamped down on my shoulder and jerked me away, possibly dislodging a shoulder blade in the process, though I couldn't be entirely certain. James' coffee-scented breath painted my cheek as he growled in my ear, "Leave the client alone, and get the hell out of here."

"No, Uncle James. You leave my brother the hell alone," Matthew said, interjecting as he grabbed me and steered me away from the bastard.

CHAPTER TWENTY-ONE

<u>Jess</u>

I did my best to pretend I wasn't in the foulest of moods. My effort was aided by the staff at the restaurant because I was treated like royalty when I gave the maitre d' the name of the party, Ms. McDoodle, as Riley had instructed me. He escorted me to the best table in the restaurant and offered juice, tea, espresso, coconut water, or ginger soda, calorie-free of course, all compliments of the restaurant. I opted for a coffee.

A few minutes later, Riley arrived with Sparky McDoodle in her arms. Though the place was stuffed with other familiar faces, a noticeable buzz filled the air when Riley walked in and it wasn't simply because the restaurant had skirted all health code rules by allowing entry to a dog. She was such a rising star; no one could take their eyes off her. Riley waved to me, then flashed a big smile to a well-dressed man in a crisp white shirt and a yellow tie at a nearby table. He was seated next to a gorgeous

STARS IN THEIR EYES / 367

redhead, who looked like she could be an actress, but since she was actually enjoying her food, I knew she wasn't. Riley held up her index finger to me, the sign she'd be right over, then stopped to give the man a quick hug. Next, she threw her arms around the woman. After the three of them chatted for a few seconds, Riley joined me.

"That was my new lawyer, Clay, and his wife, Julia. I hired him when I started my own production company. He's the best–he's all no-nonsense and works like hell to get me everything I could want in a deal," Riley said, breezily, as she sat down. Sparky McDoodle stayed in her lap, but thumped his tail at me.

"Look! He remembers that you saved his life," she said, beaming at her little pet as she stroked him between the ears. Unable to resist joining in the Sparky love, I reached over and scratched him on the chin.

"It is so good to see you," Riley said. "How are you, Jess?"

"Great," I said, but I don't think I was very convincing because Riley pushed her red sunglasses on top of her thick brown hair and asked me pointedly. "Really? You don't sound great. You sound like you're acting."

I managed a small laugh. "I guess I'm not a good actress."

"It's okay. I like it when people don't act. What's wrong?"

"I kind of had a crummy morning," I admitted, then reined in the truth, as I waved a hand in the air to dismiss the too-honest remark. "But don't worry about it. How are you? How was the wedding?"

"Amazing," she said, emphasizing every syllable. "It was so fun, and so silly, and I just got back from Vegas two hours ago, but it was exactly what my sister wanted. Only family, and we had a blast, and went to see one of those really cheesy over-the-top cabarets with showgirls and feathers, and we played poker, and she took off for Tahiti with Bradley this morning." She clapped her hand over her mouth. Then when she removed her hand, she whispered, "Oh, I'm not supposed to say that. Pretend you don't know she's in Tahiti."

I placed my fingers on my head as if they were brain suckers removing the information. "Gone. Removed. I totally forgot."

She laughed, and then we both ordered very little food, and after the waiter left, Riley leaned forward and said, "I wish I could do that to totally forget the script to *The Weekenders*. It starts shooting in a week, and like I told you it's a wretched mess. The run-through Friday was a disaster," she said, picking up the thread of our phone chat about the movie.

"The script's really that bad?"

"It's awful. The director changed everything from the original. He doesn't have a clue what he's doing," Riley said, and she didn't sound fond of Avery, nor did she seem as if she were talking about a man she was canoodling with on the side.

"What's he like?" I asked carefully because I was treading on unfamiliar ground. I wasn't entirely sure of my own motives for asking—angling for info, or having a casual conversation with my dining companion.

"He's a total dick," she said, the disdain thick in her voice, and shocking me.

She seemed so into him the other night.

Seemed.

And that's when I started putting two and two together. Known for his speedy exits, Avery must have already dumped Riley, and now she was ticked at him because she'd been the one spurned. Glancing furtively from side to side, as if she were scanning for spies, she leaned even closer, and whispered. "He broke my best friend's heart."

Or maybe not. Because the plot was thickening, and now I didn't question my own motives because they were simple–I was damn curious for curiosity's sake.

"Who's that?"

"Andy Blue," she mouthed, referring to Andromeda Blue, one of the other young actresses on Avery's list of prior conquests.

"Was she in love with him or something?"

"Completely."

As I opened my mouth to ask how on earth Riley could be fooling around with him when he'd broken her best friend's heart, I stopped myself before I said a word–I couldn't let on that I knew Riley was involved with him. That information wasn't public knowledge, so I said nothing.

"And because of that, I would so love to take him down," she added.

I laughed once, because that desire—to take someone down—seemed to be going around. "You want to get him off the picture?" I joked, returning the conversation to *The Weekenders*.

But she didn't laugh. She seemed intensely serious as she nodded several times. "He has a no-cheating clause. If he's caught cheating again, the studio boots him."

"I've never heard of a studio doing that."

"The studio didn't do it," she said, continuing in her I'm-sharing-a-secret-whisper. "His wife did. She made sure it was in his contract. But enough about this sordid business. Tell me more about you."

The cogs in my brain were already turning, and I re-wound to the day I first learned from Keats about the Avery-Riley pairing. My initial instinct had been that Riley was too smart to get involved with her director. Had my instinct been right after all? Because something else was going on behind the scenes. The real story was playing out while no one thought anyone was watching. And the real story was something else entirely—it was subterfuge, it was revenge on behalf of the best friend, it was every-one-has-an-agenda.

But her agenda right now was of the getting-to-know-you kind.

"Where do you go to school?" Riley continued, and she sounded truly interested in me. Even though I'd vowed not to be seduced by actors again, the fact was she was good. Whether she was playing or not, I wanted to tell her the truth. Because I wasn't an actor. I wasn't a player. I was no good at pretending, and I didn't want to fake my way through this meal with Riley any longer.

Besides, I had nothing to lose. And if I'd learned any-thing from my week with William it was that any relationship—even one that promised to be as brief as this moment in time with Riley—ought to be based on honesty.

"I'm pre-med at the University of Los Angeles. I graduate in two months, and then I'm going to med school, and I pay my way through school by taking pictures of celebrities," I said in as business-like a tone as I could manage.

As if I hadn't just dropped the worst bombshell possible into a celebrity's lap. *Hello, you're having lunch with a paparazzo! Sucker!*

Riley's eyes widened, and she clutched Sparky McDoodle to her chest. His ears perked up, and he looked sharply at me too, as if he were admonishing me.

"You do?" she asked, raising an eyebrow.

"Yeah, I do," I said matter of factly. "That's why I was there that day in Manhattan Beach. I was there to take your picture at the bridesmaid fitting. Or fake bridesmaid fitting, I should say. Only I never got the picture because of what happened with Sparky McDoodle. And I also tried to crash your sister's wedding yesterday, only I wound up crashing the fake wedding down in Ojai Ranch and I got some great photos of all the actors hired as stand-ins for guests, and even the actress they hired for you," I said and I leaned back in my chair, feeling in control as I unspooled the very true story of my life.

She listened with her mouth agape as I told the tale of the moment when her sister's doppelganger walked down the aisle. Her big brown eyes widened to planet-size, and she motioned with her fingers for me to tell her more. Oh, did I ever have more to tell. I had the goods, and I went for broke, laying it all out. "But I have real pictures of you too, because Jenner Davies hired me through his publicist's younger brother to take pictures of you and Avery making out outside the smog facility in Burbank the other night, and Jenner used them to bribe Avery to get Nick's role in *The Weekenders*. But supposedly, and I have no idea if this is true because it came from a guy who pretended to like me but was really playing me, Nick wanted off the movie to go do a TV show, so both Nick and Jenner were in on the blackmail scheme. Oh, there's one more thing. I got your right side when I took the pictures."

There it was. The whole damn story.

Riley's mouth turned into a giant O. She didn't speak. She sat there in shock that might have morphed into admiration, because soon she was grinning. "You got my right side?" she said, as amazed as if I had just told her I'd stolen a Van Gogh and fenced it for millions.

I nodded.

"Do you have them still? The pictures?"

"I do. I may even have them on my phone. Want to see them?"

"Yes," she said, and I found it odd that she wasn't walking away, or throwing a fit, or tossing ice cold water on me. But that could still come. Even so, I reached into my back pocket for my phone. I'd put it on silent, and I had missed a few calls, but I didn't look at the missed call list. Quickly locating one of the shots, I held my phone out to show her, careful to keep a tight grip on it.

She shook her head in appreciation. "That is a great picture," she declared, tapping a finger on the screen. "And do you know what this means?"

"What does it mean?" I asked, figuring this would be the moment when she went full actress on me, drama queen and all. Tablecloth yanked, drink tossed in my face, the works.

Instead, she raised one eyebrow, then rested her chin in her hands, the most delighted look spreading across her face. "It means I don't have to get together with that toad again to take him down. I don't have to kiss him again. I was going to let it slip to the media that we were hooking up tonight. I didn't say anything the first night because I didn't know how it would go. But I was going to drop a hint to the press before tonight, so that the girl who took the shots of my sister's wedding could get pictures of him and me. Then, I could get him off the movie because of his no-cheating clause. But I don't have to now," she said, with wide eyes, and a massive smile, as if I've just presented her with the greatest gift in the world. Then she turned serious. "That is, if you'll let me leak these photos."

My head spun, and my jaw dropped. Talk about a turn of events. Even as the shock coursed through my veins, my natural skepticism quickly returned. "But aren't you annoyed that I'm a paparazzo?"

"Let's see," Riley said, lifting her perfectly manicured hands and counting off on each finger as she spoke. "You snapped pictures of my good side when I had to face-lock with that scum. You never once asked for details of my sister's wedding when we were on the phone and you easily could have used me for information. And the first time we sat down and talked for more than two minutes, you told me exactly who you were and why. Not to mention the most important thing. You saved my dog's life. In case it's not clear, this dog," she said, stopping to pet the pampered pooch again, "is the love of my life, and you made sure he's still in my life. So, no. I'm not annoyed. In fact, I'm dying to hear more."

William

A little later, we were drinking tea, like proper English men on a Sunday morning, and hatching a plan to get the girl back.

"What does she love? I mean, besides the second most handsome Harrigan brother?" Matthew asked as he leaned back in his chair, crossed his legs, and took a drink of his English Breakfast tea.

"Movies. She's completely besotted with Hollywood."

Matthew dipped his hand into the back pocket of his jeans, and grabbed a small notebook. "Let's be scientific and write this down," he said, then opened it to a random page and jotted down in his blocky handwriting *films*.

"Dogs," I added, thinking of Jennifer and the pet therapy work Jess did with her at the hospital. I quickly told Matthew about her volunteer gig.

"She's a keeper. Seriously. Smart, kind, hot, loves dogs, and somehow she can tolerate you," Matthew said, then flashed me a quick grin. "See, I can mock you now since it's only you and me."

"Mock away. But if this doesn't work, I reserve the right to knock you one on the chin."

"Okay, what else?" he asked, flipping to another page. Then he pointed to a few names written on the opposite page in the notebook. "I don't want to write on the backside of that page. That's the name and number of the publicist I'm meeting who set up the interview with the band I'm here to see."

I snapped my fingers. "Publicists!"

"Publicists?"

"That's another thing she loves."

"Publicists?" he repeated, incredulous.

"Let me explain," I said, and rewound to the flash cards that started this whole fiasco.

When I was finished, Matthew eyed his notebook knowingly, then waved it in front of me. "I have the answer."

CHAPTER TWENTY-TWO

<u>Jess</u>

As our food arrived, I told her everything, like she'd asked for. I shared the story of how I became a celebrity photographer, how I worked the pedicure patrol and shopping beats regularly, how we'd gotten the tip about her and Miles last week, and how that shot had led Keats to call me for his phony photo agency. I told her about William as well, and how he turned out to be working for Avery Brock.

"Miles is such a sweetie," she said, twirling a strand of her hair.

"Are you going out with him?"

"Oh no," she said, shaking her head. "Miles and I are just friends. I would never have kissed Avery, even though I was faking it, if I was with someone. And now, you and I are going to take Avery down, right?" Riley said, as if the two of us were now in cahoots in the ultimate heist.

"Sure," I said with a weirdly happy shrug. I wasn't happy about William. But I was happy–in some way–to talk to Riley and tell her the whole truth. "He deserves it."

Riley twirled a strand of her hair. "You know, Jess. I've been looking for a great story for my production company."

"Yeah?"

"This is a great story. This would make a great movie."

"You think so?" I asked as I took a sip of my water, eyeing her over the top of the glass.

She narrowed her eyes, held out her hands as if she were framing a shot. "I can see it now. *My Life as a Teen Paparazzo.*"

"Not a bad title. Even though I'm twenty-one."

"I know. But in the film we'll make you eighteen. I'm serious. I want to buy your story. For my production company."

"Really?" I said with a scoff. I didn't believe her, because this simply wasn't believable. Not in my world where my *tuition due* dreams had been foiled by a sea of extras under a rented tent.

But the next thing I knew, Riley was waving to her lawyer across the restaurant.

"Give me one second," she said, then scurried over to his table, Sparky McDoodle snug in her arms, and chatted briefly with him. Then, he and his wife stood up, left their napkins on their chairs, and joined us at our table. In a heartbeat, a waiter appeared with chairs for them. It was good to be Hollywood royalty.

Riley introduced me to her lawyer and his wife, and I shook hands with both of them, then waited to see what was up her sleeve.

"Clay, do you and your fabulous wife have two seconds to hear a pitch for my production company?" Riley asked.

"Of course," he said, in a deep, gravelly voice, and if he weren't a lawyer, he'd make a hell of a voice-over actor. Come to think of it, he'd be pretty damn fine on camera too, since he had the tall, dark and handsome look down pat. His wife, all curves and confident beauty, was a perfect match.

"Lay it on us," she chimed in, and he gripped her hand, and smiled briefly at her. I felt a momentary pang of missing–these two seemed like such a team, and I had felt that with William. But I had to brush away the thoughts of him.

Riley began by holding up her hands and spreading them slowly, the universal sign language in Hollywood signaling the start of a pitch. *My Life as a Teen Paparazzo.* Celebrity photographer and senior in high school–we'll call her Tess in the script–becomes involved in a plot to take down a director who can't keep his hands to himself. Everyone has an agenda and everyone is trying to give someone else the screw, except for our fearless heroine who's simply trying to pay for medical school. Along the way she has to team up with a hotshot young private eye to try to crash the wedding of the century, but in the end he's working for the director. She wonders if she can ever trust him again?"

She held out her hands in a what-more-could-I-want gesture. "What do you think?" she asked, directing her question to Clay. "Should I do it for McDoodles Productions?"

"Riley, you should work on the projects that make you happy," he said, keeping his eyes fixed on his client the whole time. "That's my best advice to you as a person. As your lawyer, it sounds like the kind of project that you would love, which means, it sounds like you could turn it into a big hit."

"I'd go see that movie, and I'm not just saying that because my husband's client is behind it," his wife said.

"What do you think?" Riley asked, and I wasn't sure who she was speaking to at first. Then I noticed she was looking down. At her lap. Asking her dog. "Do you think it's a good idea?" She lowered her ear to the dog, pretending to listen to him. When she raised her head, she said, "Sparky McDoodle agrees, so it's settled. Clay, can you draw up a deal memo tomorrow and get it to my friend Jess? It's her life story, and I'm buying the rights, and I'm playing her."

Riley tossed around some figures, and they all sounded marvelous to me, but then again, numbers in the high five-figures with dollar signs attached to them had a way of sounding marvelous to me. Even so, I wasn't going to fall in love with the possibility of a big payday again. I didn't know if Riley meant any of this. I didn't know if I'd ever hear from her again. I'd believe it when and if it happened, because I've seen enough of this town to know that a deal isn't done until it's signed, sealed and delivered, and even then the terms could change.

I couldn't let myself get wrapped up in the prospect of winning the lottery, when the lottery could just as easily go bust. I'd saved enough already for a few classes, as Anaka had said, and if I had to keep taking pictures of pedicures and parking tickets to pay for another year and then another, I'd do that. If I had to find a loan, then I'd go that route. I knew who I was, and I knew who I would be. I wasn't the star, I wasn't an actor, I was simply a paparazzo who wanted to be a doctor, and who had to pay her own way through Hollywood. That was fine by me.

"I'll get you the deal memo in the morning," Clay said as his wife stroked the little dog's tan chin. He lifted his tiny snout closer to her hand, savoring the attention.

"Is Sparky McDoodle going to play himself?" Julia asked, and it was endearing how everyone treated the dog as if he were a vital cog in the Riley machinery, because, of course, he was. Sparky McDoodle made this actress tick. He was her one true thing; the creature in her life whose reactions she could trust completely, I suspected.

Riley shook her head and covered the dog's ears. "I want him to grow up and have a normal life. I don't want him to feel the pressure of show biz. There's only one thing though," Riley said to me and I figured this would be the moment when she told me it was all a joke. That once again, I'd been played. "We need a happy ending," she said to me.

I furrowed my brow. "What do you mean? The actress and the photog take down the director. That's the happy ending," I said as if it were obvious. Because, well, wasn't it?

"No," Riley said, as if she had a secret up her sleeve. "That's the ending of a girl-power buddy flick. This movie is going to be a romantic comedy mystery with a twisty, turny plot. It's going to be about the clever photog and the gorgeous private eye, and how they fall for each other while trying to crash a celebrity wedding. We need a happy ending with the guy."

"But there is no happy ending with the guy," I said in a firm voice. After all, William was working for the bad guy. How could there be a happy ending?

Riley sighed. "Jess, call me crazy. But I just have a feeling this guy really was doing what he said he was doing this morning. I don't know why. But I believe it in my heart. I believe this is the part where the girl thinks the boy screwed her over, but he really didn't, so she needs to make up with him."

Julia nodded, flashing a gorgeous smile. "That's your happy ending." Then she shifted closer to me, and dropped her hand on top of mine. "And listen, sometimes men just do dumbass things. They don't think. Or if they do, they think they're doing something for your best interests. And in the end, you give him a chance to explain and then you forgive him. So long as he's the real deal," she said, and the last few words were directed to her husband, who looked at her with such a combination of adoration and lust that I'd never seen before.

Except...maybe...when William looked at me?

I weighed my options as I replayed the last seven days with William. On the one hand, I could conclude that every moment had been a smooth and well-orchestrated ruse. Or I could go with my gut. When I was with him I didn't feel all work and no play. I felt carefree and light-hearted. I felt wanted and desired. I felt fun and happy. And I felt all those things without spiraling back into my bad habits. William was ice cream and French fries without the guilt. He was something I'd denied myself for years. Something I wanted again.

And just like that, the movie montage began, reel after reel of our times together playing before my eyes. Our first kiss when I surprised him on the boardwalk. His text that night: *How do I move that maybe to a yes?* The things he said to me in Italian when we made out on his motor-cycle. The kiss outside the hospital, the Busy Bee Eatery when I fed him a pineapple, the dinner he made me and how it was exactly what I wanted to eat. Then the couch, oh the couch, the things we did on the couch. The roller-coaster, and after the rollercoaster, and then yesterday at my apartment. My insides melted from the memories, and if I let myself linger on yesterday–yesterday evening to be precise–I was going to start squirming in this chair and then rocket on out of this restaurant on lust alone.

And love. Because damn it. I *was* in love with him. Present tense. Future tense. All tenses. In every single way. And I hoped to hell he had a reasonable explana-tion. Somewhere, inside, I knew he did. Because I trusted myself and I wouldn't have felt the way I did for him if he were a jerk. I had to give him the benefit of the doubt, and give him a chance to explain.

I could believe everyone in Hollywood was a bastard. Or I could believe that only some people in Hollywood were, and that the rest were just people. Besides, the one thing I knew to be a cold hard fact of the movies and of life was this—when someone gives you a chance for a happy ending, you don't leave the audience hanging. You give them what they want, and what the audience wants often has a funny way of being exactly what you want too.

"I bet he's been trying to call you and explain," Riley said softly.

"Maybe he has," I said in a small voice, hoping she was right as I took out my phone again and scrolled through my text messages.

HBG: I'm sorry. Please let me explain, but I also want to say I was never playing you. I'm not working for James or Avery anymore, and I told them both exactly what I think of them. And I'm not just falling in love with you. I'm madly in love with you. Let's be mad together. Can we get to the part in the script where we make up?

I didn't even try to contain the wild smile curving up my lips.

"I told you so," Riley said as if she'd just won a bet. "He said it was all a misunderstanding, right?"

"Sort of," I said, then lifted my face from the phone. The three of them were all grinning knowingly, and even though I rarely let people in, even though I kept a distance most of the time, I was with kindred spirits. Movie lovers. Lovers of a happy ending. I sensed it from spending the tiniest bit of time with Julia and Clay, and I knew it innately from my moments with Riley. Setting my phone aside, I laced my fingers together. "I think I need to do that thing at the end of the movies where they run to the airport, stop the plane, clear up the misunder-standing kind of thing."

"Yes, you do," Riley said, and she and her lawyer and his wife waved me off.

CHAPTER TWENTY-THREE

<u>William</u>

My phone stared at me from the center of the table as Matthew paid the bill. The screen seemed dreadfully naked without her name popping up in reply to my text. I had a sinking feeling Jess was masterful at the silent treatment. Not because she was cold or cruel; but because she was focused and determined, and if she wanted to keep me out of her life for good, she'd do so. That same steeliness that drove her to excel in school and work surely was going to bite me in the ass, because it would give her the fuel to blow me off. For good.

But she was right–I should have told her Trevor was the client when I saw his face on the flash cards. I simply hadn't known who Trevor was repping. Perhaps he'd told James, and James knew he was sending me hunting for intel for Avery Brock, but then James had a way of never disclosing the details, so I'd never known I was fishing for Avery.

Matthew pushed back in his chair. "I should hit the road and head over to my interview. Remind me now, I drive on the left side of the road here, correct?" he said, teasing.

"You've been in this country for ten years," I said. "Right side, man. Right side."

"And I have the pleasure of living in New York City, which means I rarely have to drive."

"Why don't you just try the left side then and see how well that works out for you," I suggested as we weaved through the tables on our way out of the restaurant where coffee had turned into eggs, potatoes and pancakes. Matthew was a lot like me–we liked our food, and we liked to exercise and work it off.

Outside the restaurant, he dropped his shades over his eyes, and I did the same. It was a typical Los Angeles day, sunny and 70 degrees without a cloud in the sky. A pang of longing scratched through my veins; I would miss this town.

"I really need to find a job," I said, stating the obvious.

Matthew clapped me on the back. "There's time, Will. We've got two months. Do you have any more interviews lined up?"

"I'm going to reconnect with a few of the employment agencies this week," I said.

"We'll keep talking. We'll keep brainstorming, and we'll figure something out," he said, then gave me a brief brotherly hug. "For now, you are a man on a mission. Get your woman back. I expect a full report tonight on how successful our plan was."

I arched an eyebrow. "Full report? If we're successful, I'll be too busy for that."

He shook his head, laughing. "Let me amend that. All I want is a modified report that you won her heart. The rest of the details, please keep to yourself."

Then he said goodbye, and I walked the two blocks to my bike, strapped on a helmet and revved the engine. Just as I was about to take off, I felt a buzzing in my back pocket. A flicker of hope ignited in me. *Please let it be her.*

When I saw her name flashing on my screen, that flicker turned into a full flame. "Hey," I said when I answered.

"Hi. Are you at home?"

"No, but I'm on my way. Why?"

"Can I meet you there in an hour and twenty-five minutes?" she asked, but her voice gave nothing away. Even so, the fact that she wanted to meet in person gave me hope that I was out of the doghouse.

"That's a rather precise time," I said with a laugh.

Rewarded with a small chuckle in response, my heart lightened more. I'd won her over in the first place with laughter; I wanted to keep her with it, and everything else too. "Yes. Timing matters," she said, then added in a softer voice. "I'll see you soon, William."

It was the way she said my name as she hung up that thrilled me the most. She said it like I was the only one who knew that softer side of her. With the wind at my back, I pulled onto the road, then darted in between cars on the way to my apartment. Time was ticking, and I had to finish a project for her. After a quick stop at the office supply store, I reached my building and dashed up the steps to my apartment, bumping into John on the landing for the second floor. His fist was raised in a knock on my door.

Rubbing my eyes as if the sight shocked me, I said, "Is it you, John? Or your twin brother since you've never been known to request entry to my humble abode. You usually just enter."

He raised the plastic shopping bag he was holding. "And to think, I was about to replenish the milk I drank. I think I'll keep it now."

"Did you bring me cereal too? It goes well with milk," I said, as I unlocked the door and let him in. As the door fell shut, I swiped the bag from him, said thanks, and tucked the milk carton neatly on the shelf in the fridge.

"Funny how that slipped my mind" he said, scratching his chin. "But I'm happy to check your cupboards and finish off whatever cereal you have."

"Let's take a raincheck on that. I need to do something right now before Jess comes over."

He wiggled an eyebrow. "Be sure to leave a sock on the door. It's the only sure-fire way to guarantee I won't enter unannounced."

I shook my head and laughed. "Good to know that socks, not locks, are where you draw the line at breaking and entering."

"It's not breaking in when you don't lock it. Anyway, you up for volleyball tomorrow?"

"Would love to. But I need to get some stuff done first. Classes and the job hunt, you know."

"Good luck, man," he said and knocked his fist against mine before he left.

Then I emptied the contents of the bag from the office supply store and set to work.

Jess

The toothpick revealed that nirvana had been achieved. There was nothing on it, so I grabbed an oven mitt, then removed the pan and placed it on a cooling rack.

"Smells divine," Anaka said, wafting the sweet scent of the creation into her nostrils.

"I'd give you some...but then I'd have to work you overtime as a screenwriter and make you come up with another suitable gift."

"I'd be more than willing to be used for those skills. But, for now, tell me more about last night while we wait for this to cool," she said, tugging me away from the kitchen and to the couch.

"Speaking of last night, we had a nice time on the couch," I said, patting the cushion.

She grabbed my arm and yanked me up, then pulled me over to the table. "There better be a new couch delivered here by tomorrow," she said, wagging her finger at me.

"Duly noted."

"Now. Details. I want them."

As I shared bits and pieces of last night, my skin grew warm all over. But it wasn't from the memories—oh so potent—of our physical connection. It was from telling the story of what he said, and the way he said it, and how we talked to each other. Like friends. Sure, I kissed him the first day I met him, and I kissed him so many times after that. But we became friends. And then we became more. Telling the story of how we said we were falling in love, was like experiencing it all over again, and telling it reminded me too to trust the guy I was in love with. I'd trusted him with my heart, and I had to trust he had his reasons.

Whatever they were, the bottom line remained the same. No matter what, no matter how, I was going to find a way for him to stay.

CHAPTER TWENTY-FOUR

<u>William</u>

Exactly one hour and twenty-five minutes after her call, I heard the most beautiful sound in the world. A knock on my door. For the briefest of moments, it occurred to me that John might be popping back over. But when I opened the door, it was Jess. She was wearing a short skirt and she was holding a cake.

It smelled delicious.

"I can bake," she said, sounding like the girl I fell for. Confident. Brazen. Certain of herself.

"I see. Or rather, I smell. Smells good."

"It's chocolate cake."

"I like chocolate cake."

"I know. You told me the day I met you. And you told me again the day you asked me to go to the wedding," she said, still standing in my door. Looking hot and edible and *here*. I quickly reached behind her and shut the door. Then I locked it, since that was classier than putting a sock on it and would serve the same purpose.

"And you told me too I was like cake, which I knew was high praise from you," I said, keeping my hands at my sides. My fingers itched to touch her, but I hadn't been given permission again yet.

"It *was*," she said, emphasizing that verb as she kept her eyes locked on me. "And it still *is*. And this cake is my way of saying I'm sorry I walked off this morning. You don't have to explain because I'm choosing to trust that you aren't the type of guy who would ever knowingly work for Avery Brock. And you're not the type of guy who would ever willfully deceive me. I'm choosing to believe you're still the same guy I fell in love with," she said, and my heart damn nearly soared out of my chest.

"I am. I am that guy. I swear," I said, never looking away from her. Never wanting to lose touch with those beautiful blue eyes, so pure and true. "I should have said something when I saw Trevor's picture, but I wanted to focus on you, and us. Being with you was so damn amazing that I didn't want to ruin it by bringing those pigs into our night together. But you have to believe me—James never told me that Avery was the client. All I knew was we were working for Trevor's shop and that was all."

"I know," she said softly. "I believe you."

Her words were the sweetest song playing just for me. They were my catnip.

"When I sat down to the meeting this morning, I was still working out how to extract myself from Avery. Because I don't want to work for someone like that. Or for

James. And I told them both off this morning. You would have loved it, actually."

"What did you say?" she asked, her natural curiosity plain as day in the sparkle in her eyes.

I shared every single detail of the moment by the railing and she nearly squealed in delight. "That is perfect," she said. "I wish I'd been there to see it."

"Me too. But you're here now and that's all that matters."

"Well," she began, eyeing the cake pan in her hands. "There is something else that matters. This cake."

"Was it hard for you to make it?" I asked gently. "Did it tempt you?"

"Yes, and no. It was hard, but I managed it. Because I wanted to do it for you. Want to take off the tinfoil?"

"Yes." I peeled it back to discover a chocolate cake that looked absolutely mouth-watering. The best part was the writing on it. In orange lettering across the frosting, she'd written the word *Stay*. Then under it was a full sentence: *You are the top of my to-do list for the next two months.*

"I don't know if it's dirty or romantic, or both, but I'll take any and all from you. Let me put this cake down so I can kiss you," I said, taking the pan from her outstretched arms and setting it on the table. When I returned to her, she had the sweetest and sexiest look on her face.

"It was both," she said. "And it's a promise that I'll do everything I can to help you stay. When I set my mind on a goal, I'm really good at staying focused on it. You and your job hunt are going to be at the top of my to-do list."

Unable to resist touching her any longer, I threaded my fingers through her hair, loving the feel of it against my skin. "Being on your to-do list in any form is about the best thing I could ever ask for," I said.

"Can this be the part where the hero and heroine kiss and make up?"

I answered her with my lips, kissing her softly as she returned to me. Taking my time, I let the kiss linger as I sucked gently on her lower lip, thrilling at the small gasp that escaped her lips. I covered her mouth with mine, sliding my tongue against hers, and the taste of her was divine. Like sunshine and music, and so damn delicious that I didn't want to go slow anymore.

The kiss changed gears, picking up speed in a heartbeat, as I kissed her more deeply, crushing her to my chest, where she belonged, where I wanted her, and where I needed her. Jess had arrived in my life unexpectedly a mere seven days ago, but she was everything I could ever want–smart, funny, gorgeous, determined and daring as hell. Soon, her hands were in my hair, and she was pulling me even closer, her mouth fusing with mine as we kissed furiously. As if it had been too long since we touched each other. And for us, it had. We made up for the morning and the early afternoon apart with a kiss that made my mind foggy. My body was on high alert, and I was hungry for more of her. For all of her.

The kiss went on and on, and it could have lasted the whole afternoon for all I knew. I lost track of everything but the feel of her, the way she responded, the sweet little murmurs she made as we collided, mouths, lips, teeth and tongue coming together.

Eventually, we came up for air, lips bruised from another epic kiss.

"It's never been like this before," she said, her voice breathy, her cheeks rosy.

"The way we kiss?"

"Yes," she said, her fingers brushing against my neck. "No one has ever kissed me the way you do, William."

There it was. My name on her lips, melting me again for her. "Good. I can't stand the thought of anyone else ever kissing you," I said running my index finger across her lower lip. "And by the way, I'm still madly in love with you. And I just wanted to say that."

"Wait. Last night it was falling in love. Now it's been bumped up to madly in love?" she raised an eyebrow playfully.

"Can you fault me for falling this fast? I think you're amazing, so you only have yourself to blame for how quickly it happened. And now, I have something for you."

"For me?"

I rolled my eyes. "I'm madly in love with a girl who loves romantic comedies. You think I'm going to let you be the only one with a gift?"

A smile tugged up the corners of her lips as I grabbed the gift I'd left on the table. "I hope you'll forgive me for not wrapping it, but here it is," I said, handing her a stack of flash cards.

Her eyes sparkled with curiosity and wonder as she considered the first card. A photo of an auburn-haired woman wearing cat's eye glasses.

"Jasmine Spoonville," she said as she ran her finger over the photo I'd printed out, then she flipped the card, reading aloud the details. "Publicist for Dr. Jade. The rising hip-hop star." She slid it under the pile, moving onto the next one. "Chase Henry." The bleached-blond publicist with plugs in both ears flashed his teeth at Jess. "Reps Protracted Envy. I love their music. I read about their new album in *On the Surface* last week. L.A.'s hottest band. This is like a treasure chest," she said as she held the stack tight against her chest.

I nodded. "I noticed you didn't have publicist cards for rock stars. Or even take photos of rock stars very often. And a ton of musicians are in L.A., and my brother gave me intel on them. I thought this could be a way to expand your repertoire. I know it won't make up for the loss of the wedding shot, but it's a start, right?"

"It's a huge start," she said, throwing her arms around my neck, the cards still in her hands. "I never even thought about focusing on rock stars. Beyond the obvious ones. But this is incredible, and I love it. And you."

"Excellent. Now go put those cards down because I have other plans for you."

Jess

His plans involved hiking my skirt up to my hips and scooting me onto the kitchen table. One of his legs came between mine, and he used it to spread me open. Then he moved closer, tugging off my shirt, and feathering his hands across the bare skin of my shoulders, arms, and then my waist. Mapping my body, like an intrepid explorer, eagerly discovering new lands, he roamed his hands up the soft skin of my belly and around to my back. I trembled from his touch, letting my head fall back as he found the clasp of my bra, unhooked it, and dropped it into a chair. Then he cupped my breasts and moaned appreciatively.

"If you ever can't find me, it's because I got lost touching your breasts," he said, as he ran his thumbs under, over, all around.

I laughed. "I think I'd know where to find you, if that's where you were."

"I could spend all day here," he said, lowering his head to my chest to plant kisses all across my flesh.

My laugh turned into a needy groan as he teased me with his tongue, then nipped me with his teeth. His soft hair brushed against my skin, a sweet reminder of all the ways he could touch me, all the sensations he brought to my body. I slid one hand to the back of his head, holding him against me. He flicked his tongue across me, continuing his slow, sensual torture. Heat spread like wildfire in my veins, and I ached with desire for him.

I couldn't take a slow tease right now. In the grand scheme of time, it hadn't been long since he'd made love to me. The blink of an eye, the tick of the second hand on the clock, but in the narrow span of my life, it felt like ages since I'd had him. And I desperately wanted him inside me. Wanted to be filled up by him. Wanted to feel his hard length slide inside of me, where I was hot and ready for him.

Now.

I opened my eyes, and gently tugged him up.

"I can't wait," I said. "Don't make me wait. Don't tor-ture me right now."

"Torture will come another time," he said, reaching into his pocket for a condom as I pulled off his shirt, and trailed my fingers across the firm planes of his chest and down to his perfectly chiseled abdomen. I unzipped his jeans, and pushed them to his knees as he rolled on the condom. Then, he was rubbing against me as I spread my legs wider. He entered me slowly, my breath catching from the delicious feel of him exactly where I wanted him.

He whispered something in Italian, and I shook my head. "No. No more keeping me in the dark. I want to know what you said."

He started to sink into me, whispering hotly in my ear. "I want you so badly. I love being inside you. I love feel-ing you come on me."

My skin sizzled. I arched into him as he took his time entering me. My body was a neon sign begging for him, as the most thrilling sensations flooded me from his dirty words. "I want you to teach me how to say that. I want to know naughty Italian too so I can say dirty things to you," I said, wriggling closer, trying to bring him deeper. Bring him all the way in.

"I will teach you," he said in a sexy growl as he buried himself in me.

Then we didn't need any more words, and I didn't think I could form them anyway.

He lowered his mouth to mine. As he brushed his lips against me, he started thrusting. Deep, hard, fast. The way I needed it right now, his kisses driving me as wild as the sheer bliss of him inside me did. He held my hips firmly in his hands, rocking into me, all while his soft, sweet lips claimed mine in yet another endlessly perfect kiss.

Kissing him was heaven. Making love to him was better than that; it was another land, bathed only in bliss, as I came apart in his arms.

Forget all the stars with their million dollar movies, their mansions, their fancy cars.

I was the luckiest girl in Hollywood.

* * *

Later that afternoon, we found ourselves in his bed. With his laptop. Cruising Craigslist, and all the job boards we could find, and coming up with plans for him.

We were a team again, and that's how we worked best.

ONE WEEK LATER
Weather: 70 degrees, Sunny

CHAPTER TWENTY-FIVE

<u>Jess</u>

I tapped open the article in *Hollywood Breakdown*, the premiere magazine for all of the insider Hollywood news. But not the kind I documented. There were no nail salon shots or latte-sipping images. This magazine was for the power brokers, and it covered the deals inked by agents, lawyers, producers, and the money men and women who poured cash into the creations that audiences longed to see. A thrill rushed down my spine as I read the news report.

Oscar-nommed teen star Riley Belle signed the first project under her production company McDoodles. Titled My Life as a Teen Paparazzo, *the film tells the story of a young paparazzo who teams up with a teen private eye and becomes embroiled in a blackmail plot to sabotage an irrevocably bad film. "It's a romantic-comedy mystery and I'm delighted to bring this original story to the screen," Belle said in a statement. The script will be penned by first-time screenwriter Anaka Griffin, daughter of Griffin Studios head Graham Griffin. He was not involved in the deal. In other news, Avery Brock has been replaced as director of The Weekenders. Chelsea Knox has been nabbed to helm the film which has suffered script problems for years. Knox said she'll be returning to the original script. "The Weekenders was a classic hit of the last generation and I'm delighted to reintroduce it to the new generation with its original script intact, with one small change. The character played by Riley Belle will eat vegetarian sushi rather than raw fish sushi during her lunch in detention." As a result of the script change, the cast has been whittled down to the original five members of weekend detention. Jenner Davies has been cut from the film.*

Then, I headed to class, and crossed my fingers that the employment agency on tap for today would be suitably impressed with William's language skills. I knew I was, in so many ways.

TWO MONTHS LATER
Weather: 70 degrees, Sunny

CHAPTER TWENTY-SIX

<u>William</u>

She winced when she saw the open suitcases in my apartment.

"I hate them," she said as she sank down heavily on the couch, tossing her mortarboard on the floor, next to mine. Cruel reminders that we'd crossed such a major milestone together, but *together* was ending in two days. We'd both graduated five days ago. Matthew and Jane and my parents had attended. After the ceremony we all had dinner with Jess, her parents and her brother and his wife, toasting and celebrating a day I'd been dreading. Graduation was the end of something all right. The end of college. The end of my student visa. The end of us.

True to her word, Jess had been a masterful project manager, overseeing Action Item Number One on her To-Do-List: Get William a Job. I'd had plenty of nibbles, loads of close chances, and so many opportunities in my hands. After Riley had mentioned wanting to expand her next slate of productions globally like other shops were doing, Jess had tracked down a part-time opening at a studio that was importing its TV series to Asia. I'd worked part-time four nights a week teaching basic Japanese to a group of their executives, and the HR manager had loved my work. But, the gig was temporary. The executives only needed basic skills, and the studio wasn't committing to full-time employment. Then, the agency that had snubbed me for not having graduated yet called, desperate for help when a translator went on medical leave for knee surgery. But her knee healed in four weeks, and that was the end of my job there.

I'd come up short, and even though I wanted to rail against the system, the fact was this was how the system worked. Finding a permanent job for a non-citizen was phenomenally difficult. You had to have the most unique skills. I had them; but there were simply no openings.

"I hate the suitcases too," I echoed. "Let's stop looking at them. Maybe if we don't see them, I don't have to go," I said, wishing we could delay the inevitable by ignoring it. Pulling her up from the couch, I led her to my bedroom where I stripped her naked and she did the same for me. I joined her under the covers, tasting the salty streak of her tears as I kissed her while making love to her.

It wouldn't be our last time. I was leaving on Monday, two days from now, and surely there would be many more times. The problem was, I fell deeper in love with her every second I spent with her, and that was going to make Monday suck even harder. The last two months with her had been the best of my life. Not that I had gobs and gobs of years to compare it to, but even at twenty-one, I *knew* a love like this came around once in a blue moon.

Jess

Lying on my side in his bed, I ran my hand down his waist, over his hips, along his thigh. I was memorizing him for later, even though he was imprinted on me. Even without him here, I could close my eyes and picture every muscle and line in his hard body. But in forty-eight hours, memories would be all I had left of him.

We had agreed that it made no sense to continue this long-distance. With med school starting in September, I wasn't going to be in a position to fly to England and visit him on weekends. Nor did I have the kind of spare cash lying around to fund that sort of travel. The money from selling my life story to Riley had covered a full two and a half years of medical school, and that's where every single cent went.

"I'll miss you every day," I said, my voice etched with sadness I didn't even try to mask. I was sad; I was ridiculously sad. I wasn't going to hide it. "Some day, when you're old and married to some fabulous English woman, I hope you'll still look back on me fondly as the girl you fell in love with your last year of college in America."

He pressed a finger to my lips, shushing me. "You will be more than that. And I haven't given up hope. Maybe I'll land a job in London, and I'll request a transfer here in a few months, and we'll be together again."

I shot him a look as if to say *don't be silly.* "That only happens in the movies."

"But you believe in the movies, don't you?" he said, insistent in the possibility that there might be another *us* someday. He was always the dreamer; I was always more practical. I was science; he was words. The statistical probability of *us* working out was slim to none.

"Sure," I said, but my answer sounded noncommittal even to me.

"You never know what fate has in store," he said, then whispered something to me in Italian.

This time I knew what it meant, because he'd taught me. He'd taught me all the things he said when we were making love. His words this time were both beautiful and sexy, and they filled me with joy and sorrow as he told me how much he loved me, more than he's ever loved anyone, more than he ever will, and how he'll miss every inch of me inside and out.

Always.

* * *

Later that night, as I lay awake in his bed, staring out the window, searching for something that wasn't destined to come true, I was blinded with a possibility. Out of nowhere, like a comet tearing through the sky, blasting a message just for me, I knew the answer. I had it with me all along. It had never been far away from me. It had always been a part of me.

I sat up straight, my heart skittering wildly in my chest. I alone had the power to make him stay.

CHAPTER TWENTY-SEVEN

<u>Jess</u>

All through lunch at my parents' house the next day, I could barely concentrate.

Kat and Bryan were here for a farewell meal. They'd stayed in the area after the graduation ceremony, heading to Santa Barbara for a vacation, and they were on their way back to New York tomorrow morning. My mom chatted about why she thought they should find out the genders of the babies at Kat's ultrasound next week. Kat nodded and smiled, then said that she wanted to be surprised at their birth. I hardly listened, because I had only one thing on my mind.

The persistent drumbeat of possibility.

My mom attempted a new angle, suggesting Kat have the ultrasound technician email the genders to *her*, and that way Kat would still be surprised, but my mom could still shop for the babies.

Bryan laughed, and clasped his hand over his wife's. "Mom, I think it's Kat's decision in the end."

I had to get away from all this talk of babies, and couples, and the future, because it was clouding my judgement. I had to make this choice free of all the noise, so I pushed back and said, "Excuse me for a minute."

I slipped away from the table, and headed for the back yard, Jennifer close by my side. I slid the glass door shut behind me, and sank down onto a plastic chair on the deck. Jennifer rested her snout on my leg, and I pet her.

The memory of Riley asking her dog for advice flashed before me. Maybe Jennifer had answers.

As I stroked the big dog's nose, I tried Riley's tactic. "Should I do it, Jennifer? I can be the reason he stays. He's never asked me to do this. We've never even talked about it. But are we ready to take that step?"

Jennifer lifted her snout and tilted her head. She revealed no answers.

A creaking sound filled my ears. Kat had opened the door and was sliding it shut behind her.

"Hey Jess," she said, taking the seat next to me on the deck. "You seemed out of sorts at lunch. Are you okay?"

"No," I said, not bothering to fake it.

"What's wrong? Is it William leaving?"

"Yes," I said because they all knew the clock was ticking.

"And you're missing him like crazy."

"I am," I said, staring off into the small yard, and the wood fence at the edge. I couldn't look at her. I couldn't look at anyone. I needed to find the answer myself. "And I want him to stay."

She shifted her chair, moving closer to me, forcing me to look at her. "So are you going to do it?"

I furrowed my brows. "Do what?"

"Ask him to marry you so he can stay."

My heart nearly stopped and my eyes widened. "Did you hear me talking to the dog?" I asked in a hushed voice.

She shook her head. "No. But it doesn't take a genius to see that you're sad, nor does it take much to figure out that you're trying to make a hard decision."

"But if it's a hard decision, doesn't that mean it's the wrong decision, Kat? I'm only twenty-one. I'm going to med school. Should I really get married now? Do I marry him just so he can stay? Assuming he'd even say yes?"

She smiled sweetly at me. "That's a lot of questions, and I don't have the answers to any except for the last one, and I suspect you know the answer to it as well."

"It just seems wrong to marry him just so he can stay."

"Then don't do it."

"But I can't stand the thought of him leaving. And I have the power to make him stay. All I have to do is go down to the courthouse with him and we say I do, and voilà. Instant citizen."

"So do it."

I scoffed. "You're not helpful," I said with a small pout.

"Because marriage isn't an easy decision when it's complicated by factors beyond love. If love was the only reason, then it would be an easy choice."

I slinked down in the chair, sighing heavily. "But if it was meant to be, why did it not even occur to me until last night that I could even do this? I literally never even thought about it or considered it until last night. Then it hit me like that," I said, snapping my fingers. "Why did it never even enter the realm of possibility until last night?"

Kat quirked up her lips, a knowing twinkle in her pretty brown eyes. "Maybe it occurred to you because you were finally ready to consider it. Maybe you never thought about it because it was never something you would do. Maybe the idea came to you because it's what you want?"

"But am I even ready to be married?" I asked, my voice starting to break.

"All I know, Jess, is that love comes around when you least expect it. It has a way of wreaking havoc on your life and your plans and challenging you in ways you never saw coming. But when you meet the person you want to spend the rest of your life with, you'll often upend all your plans." Then her chair legs scratched across the deck. "I need to pee. These babies," she said, patting her belly. She dropped a kiss to my forehead and whispered, "Listen to your heart. The heart knows what's right for you."

She walked inside, leaving me alone with my dog, and my racing thoughts. I closed my eyes and raised my face to the sun, letting the last two months wash over me until it was time to head to the hospital for my volunteer shift.

I leashed up Jennifer and visited the children's ward for the next hour, the visit reminding me that nothing in life was easy.

But one thing *was* easy. Texting William and asking him to meet me here when my shift ended.

* * *

Helen peppered me with questions as she walked with me down the hall and to the emergency room exit. "Are they going to let you on the set of *My Life As a Teen Paparazzo* when they start shooting?"

I laughed. "Why? You want a report on all the hot young actors?"

"Duh," she said, rolling her eyes.

"Anaka just finished the first rewrite last week so we're still a ways off."

"Promise me one thing," she said, tucking the papers she was carrying under her elbow.

"Sure."

"You'll snap some photos just for me of the guys."

"Of course, Helen."

"Thank God. I could use a little eye candy in my life. I've been up to my ears in HR paperwork these days."

"Less time to read the gossip rags?" I asked, as Jennifer trotted by my side.

"It's killing me," she said in mock desperation. Then she lowered her voice to a whisper. "There's your hottie, and I swear he gets better looking by the day."

I scanned the lobby up ahead, my eyes landing on William as he walked through the door. He did get better looking every day, and my eyes would surely miss looking at his fabulous face. I raised my hand to wave, but then, as fast as a whip, William turned his gaze away from me. As we rounded the corner, the lobby coming into full view, I saw a man crumpled in a chair, bent over at the waist, clutching his belly.

The black-haired man seemed to be wincing, his face screwed up in pain. A nurse was kneeling by his side, her palm resting on his knee, as she shook her head. "I'm sorry, I don't understand you." The nurse spotted Helen and called out. "Helen, where's our Chinese translator? I think that's the language he's speaking."

"She quit the other day. I haven't found a new one yet. Do you know how hard it is to find someone who knows the language well enough to work in a hospital in Los Angeles?"

The nurse shook her head, shooting the man a rueful look.

Time stopped as I tried to speak, as the bubble of hope inside of me turned into a geyser. I opened my mouth, but before I could say anything, I heard words. Words I didn't know at all. Words that made no earthly sense to me. Spoken with just a sliver of a British accent.

The sun ignited in my chest. A supernova streaked across the sky.

You never know what fate has in store.

William asked more questions as he kneeled next to the man, who looked up with so much pain in his eyes, but some kind of relief too. Finally, someone understood him. Someone could speak for his pain. The man answered, and William nodded, then asked a few more questions, then nodded again.

Feet planted wide, Helen stood in place, her jaw agape. The nurse stared, dumbstruck. Jennifer wagged her tail. And William alone had the answers they needed. He patted the man gently on the knee, rose and turned to the ER nurse.

"He said he's had stomach pains on his right side for five days now. They're not going away; they're only intensifying. He was told last week by urgent care that he had a stomach virus, but it's worsened," William explained, and I wanted to jump up and down.

"It's not a stomach virus," I said quickly, answering like I was on a game show. "He has a ruptured appendix."

The nurse's eyes lit up and she shot me a look that said she was impressed. "That's exactly what I was going to say. Let's take him back to see a doctor about a possible emergency appendectomy."

The nurse took two steps toward the patient, then stopped and spoke to Helen. "Wait. What if we need more help translating?"

"Can you work right now?" Helen said to William.

"Yes. I can. Absolutely," he said, as the nurse offered her elbow to the man and helped him up.

"He speaks Japanese, Spanish and Italian too," I said, practically bouncing on my toes.

Helen emitted a low whistle of appreciation. "Damn, girl. He's a keeper."

"I know."

"And a keeper for me too. William, any chance you can work tomorrow, the rest of the week and into the foreseeable future?"

A wild grin erupted on his face. "Yes."

"Then consider yourself hired."

"That's it?" he asked carefully. "You're hiring me full-time? I don't need an interview?"

"I've never had a more convincing job interview in my life," Helen said.

"You know I'm on a student visa and I'd have to transfer it to a work visa if you can sponsor me for it?"

She waved a hand as if to say *no big deal.* "Been there. Done that. Nothing I can't handle. I'll get moving on all the paperwork right now."

Some things in life were easy, if they were meant to be. Maybe William had run into such trouble with work because this was the job he was meant to have.

I turned to him. "You're staying," I said, and I was ready to jump into his arms, hug him and smother him in kisses. But there was no time for that because he was clocking in.

"I'm staying," he said, and I'd never seen him look happier in all our days together.

"And to think, I was just about to ask you to marry me so you could stay."

His gray eyes sparkled so brightly they seemed silver. "You were?"

I nodded. "I was."

"I'd have said yes so I could see you every day."

"Good. Now get to work. I'm going to find some musicians to snap photos of now. I'll see you after work," I said.

"I'll see you after work," he echoed, then followed the nurse and the patient into the job that he alone could do.

SIX MONTHS LATER
Weather: 70 degrees, Sunny

CHAPTER TWENTY-EIGHT

<u>Jess</u>

I married him anyway six months later. Sometimes you just know when it's right. Besides, when you meet the person you want to spend the rest of your life with, you'd be stupid to let a little thing like an ocean, or a passport, or a nationality stand between you.

We said *I do* at the L.A County Courthouse. We said it because we wanted to. Not because we had to. But because we were ready.

I wore a white sundress and carried a bouquet of daisies. He wore slacks, a white button-down and the cufflinks I'd given him. The ceremony lasted all of two minutes, and then the justice of the peace pronounced us husband and wife. We signed the marriage certificate, and then we walked out of the courthouse into another perfect day. The sun was dropping in the sky, tipping near the horizon. We were living together now. Anaka had moved into her own place, and William was working hard at the hospital. Medical school was insane, and we didn't see each other much, but we made the most of our time together. We had time together. That was the best part of all.

"You made me an American," he said, holding my hand as we walked down the street.

"You made me happy," I said, squeezing his hand in emphasis, as I smiled at him.

"You've done the same for me."

"There's only one thing we haven't figured out yet, William," I said, as we headed to his motorcycle a few blocks away.

"What's that?"

"Since I'm giving you the thing you want most, I'm going to insist you take my name now that I've made you a citizen."

He laughed. "But that's where you're wrong, Jess. You're what I want most in the world."

"Then you're mine forever, Mr. William Leighton."

"Mrs. Jess Harrigan," he fired back at me.

"We can keep this up for a long time."

"Like, say, forever?"

"Yes, forever," I said, looking at him and loving the playful glint in his eyes.

"Sounds good to me," he said, then stopped walking and pulled me in close. "And now I'm going to kiss my bride."

As the sun began to set, we kissed on the Los Angeles street for a long, long time. When we pulled apart, he smiled that boyish smile I adored. "So what happens next?" he asked.

"I think this is where they roll the credits."

"And after the credits?"

"Nobody knows what happens then," I said.

"We should find out."

"Actually, I think I know what happens."

"What happens?"

"They live happily ever after and eat ice cream."

"Then hop on my bike, wrap your arms around me and let's go to the ice cream shack."

When we arrived at the beach, I ordered chocolate with a chocolate shell, and took a big bite. It tasted delicious. So good in fact that I shared it with my husband.

Three Days Later
Weather: 70 degrees, Sunny

EPILOGUE

<u>Matthew</u>

I laced my fingers together and dove for the ball, managing to send it flying across the net where it slammed in front of the sand at William's feet.

"Damn!" he shouted as I pumped a fist, having landed the winning point. "How the hell did you manage that?"

I shrugged playfully. "You're not the only in the family who has volleyball skills."

"You live in New York. You're not supposed to play beach sports," William said, as he walked around from his side of the net to extend a hand.

"Will, when are you going to remember that I can't let you beat me at everything. You were the first to marry. The least I could do was beat you at volleyball."

He clapped me on the back. "Yeah, who would have thought that would happen. But I'm looking forward to your wedding."

"You didn't even invite me to yours," I said in mock sadness, as we returned to the rest of our families at the picnic tables near the barbecue along the beach. Jess' brother Bryan was relaxing at the table, drinking a beer and holding one of his baby girls. His wife Kat, rocked the other. The girls were tiny; just one month old, and the happy couple had named the identical twins Chloe and Cara.

"You're not going to be first to that too, are you?" I asked, nodding at the babies.

William's eyes widened in fear, and he held up his hands in surrender. "That's not happening to Jess and me for a long time. You can absolutely feel free to be the first brother to produce an heir."

I laughed. "Yes. An heir to the great Harrigan family fortune," I joked as we walked through the sand, the warm sun casting perfect golden rays.

Jane and I were in California for William and Jess' *after wedding party*. Those sneaky kids had gone off and gotten married at the courthouse, and he'd beaten me to the altar. Not that it was a true race, of course. It was just funny, in that odd, twisting way that life often has, that my younger brother — younger by nine years — had been first to say *I do*.

I'd be saying those words soon enough though since Jane and I were engaged. I walked up to her, wrapped my arms around her waist and kissed her softly on the neck, her curly brown hair brushing against my cheek.

"I'm thinking about another time when we were in California," I whispered to her. "Can you think of which one?"

She furrowed her brow, as if she were remembering. "The Grammys?" she asked. "Two years ago? Has it really been that long?"

I nodded. "That's when it all started. I knew you were hot for me that night."

She laughed. "I'd been hot for you since before that night."

I turned her around and pulled her in for a kiss, as my mind slipped back to the night when it all began with her...

The End

To read about how Jane and Matthew met and fell in love, please check out FAR TOO TEMPTING, available now across all retailers.

Check out my contemporary romance novels!

The New York Times and USA Today
Bestselling Seductive Nights series including
Night After Night, After This Night,
and *One More Night*

Caught Up In Us, a New York Times and
USA Today Bestseller! (Kat and Bryan's romance!)

Pretending He's Mine, a Barnes & Noble and
iBooks Bestseller! (Reeve & Sutton's romance)

Trophy Husband, a New York Times and
USA Today Bestseller! (Chris & McKenna's romance)

Playing With Her Heart, a
USA Today bestseller! (Davis and Jill's romance)

Far Too Tempting, an Amazon
romance bestseller! (Matthew and Jane's romance)

My USA Today bestselling
No Regrets series that includes

The Thrill of It
(Meet Harley and Trey)

and its sequel

Every Second With You

My New York Times and USA Today
Bestselling Fighting Fire series that includes

Burn For Me,
(Smith and Jamie's romance!)

and *Melt for Him*
(Megan and Becker's romance!)

ACKNOWLEDGEMENTS

Thank you so much to my readers. You rock my world. You keep me going. You are the reason I write. Thank you for making my dreams come true.

Thank you to Violet Duke, who brainstormed with me until we found the key. Thank you to early readers Tanya and Kim, who helped shape the fine details. Kara and Dawn scoured each line. Michelle Wolfson had her hands in this from the start and has believed in it in all its shapes and forms. Jennifer from Jen's Book Reviews was my Los Angeles quality control and I am so grateful for that.

Sarah Hansen makes the most amazing covers. Helen Williams devises beautiful graphics. Jesse turns raw files into pretty books.

Kelly Simmons is responsible for my sanity. (Ha, good luck with that, KP!) Kelley keeps the ship running. My amazing book friends from Cara to Kim to Hetty to Yvette to Gretchen to Nelle to Megan to many many more are passionate voices for books!

I must give a thank you to US Magazine. I love that damn publication. With a passion. It provides lightness and fun in my days. And I love movies, deeply and truly. And I have always wanted to write a story that didn't take itself too seriously, while at the same time being true and authentic to the characters. I hope STARS IN THEIR EYES is just that.

Of course, I must thank my dogs, my daily companions. Violet and Flipper are part of my family, and Flipper McDoodle is the inspiration for Riley's true love.

Last, but first, thank you to my family - to my parents, my in-laws, my husband and my children for dealing with the madness and the magic of every day.

CONTACT

I love hearing from readers! You can find me on Twitter at LaurenBlakely3, or Facebook at LaurenBlakelyBooks, or online at LaurenBlakely.com. You can also email me at laurenblakelybooks@gmail.com.

OCT 0 3 2017

CPSIA information can be obtained
at www.ICGtesting.com
Printed in the USA
LVOW13s1733290817
546821LV00006B/744/P

9 781497 342279